EVERYMAN'S LIBRARY

853

FICTION

Everyman, I will go with thee, and be thy guide,
In thy most need to go by thy side

HENRY FIELDING, born at Sharpham Park near Glastonbury, in 1707. Studied law at Leyden; became financially connected with the stage in London; failed, took to law again, and was called to the Bar in 1740. Travelled to Lisbon in 1754 for reasons of health, and died there on 8th October.

HENRY FIELDING

AMELIA

IN TWO VOLUMES · VOLUME TWO

INTRODUCTION BY
GEORGE SAINTSBURY

LONDON J. M. DENT & SONS LTD
NEW YORK E. P. DUTTON & CO INC

CONTENTS

BOOK VII

BOOK VIII

BOOK IX

BOOK X

BOOK XI

BOOK XII

BOOK VII

CHAPTER I

A very short chapter, and consequently requiring no preface.

MRS. BENNET having fastened the door, and both the ladies having taken their places, she once or twice offered to speak, when passion stopped her utterance; and, after a minute's silence, she burst into a flood of tears. Upon which Amelia, expressing the utmost tenderness for her, as well by her look as by her accent, cried, "What can be the reason, dear madam, of all this emotion?" "O Mrs. Booth!" answered she, "I find I have undertaken what I am not able to perform. You would not wonder at my emotion if you knew you had an adulteress and a murderer now standing before you."

Amelia turned pale as death at these words, which Mrs. Bennet observing, collected all the force she was able, and, a little composing her countenance, cried, "I see, madam, I have terrified you with such dreadful words; but I hope you will not think me guilty of these crimes in the blackest degree." "Guilty!" cried Amelia. "O Heavens!" "I believe, indeed, your candour," continued Mrs. Bennet, "will be readier to acquit me than I am to acquit myself. Indiscretion, at least, the highest, most unpardonable indiscretion, I shall always lay to my own charge: and, when I reflect on the fatal consequences, I can never, never forgive myself." Here she again began to lament in so bitter a manner, that Amelia endeavoured, as much as she could (for she was herself greatly shocked), to soothe and comfort her; telling her that, if indiscretion was her highest crime, the unhappy consequences made her rather an unfortunate than a guilty person; and concluded by saying—"Indeed, madam, you have raised my curiosity to the highest pitch, and I beg you will proceed with your story."

Mrs. Bennet then seemed a second time going to begin her relation, when she cried out, "I would, if possible, tire you with no more of my unfortunate life than just with that part which leads to a catastrophe in which I think you may yourself be interested; but I protest I am at a loss where to begin."

"Begin wherever you please, dear madam," cries Amelia; "but I beg you will consider my impatience." "I do consider it," answered Mrs. Bennet; "and therefore would begin with that part of my story which leads directly to what concerns yourself; for how, indeed, should my life produce anything worthy your notice?" "Do not say so, madam," cries Amelia; "I assure you I have long suspected there were some very remarkable incidents in your life, and have only wanted an opportunity to impart to you my desire of hearing them: I beg, therefore, you would make no more apologies." "I will not, madam," cries Mrs. Bennet, "and yet I would avoid anything trivial; though, indeed, in stories of distress, especially where love is concerned, many little incidents may appear trivial to those who have never felt the passion, which, to delicate minds, are the most interesting part of the whole." "Nay, but, dear madam," cries Amelia, "this is all preface."

"Well, madam," answered Mrs. Bennet, "I will consider your impatience." She then rallied all her spirits in the best manner she could, and began as is written in the next chapter.

And here possibly the reader will blame Mrs. Bennet for taking her story so far back, and relating so much of her life in which Amelia had no concern; but, in truth, she was desirous of inculcating a good opinion of herself, from recounting those transactions where her conduct was unexceptionable, before she came to the more dangerous and suspicious part of her character. This I really suppose to have been her intention; for to sacrifice the time and patience of Amelia at such a season to the mere love of talking of herself would have been as unpardonable in her as the bearing it was in Amelia a proof of the most perfect good breeding.

CHAPTER II

The beginning of Mrs. Bennet's history.

"I was the younger of two daughters of a clergyman in Essex; of one in whose praise if I should indulge my fond heart in speaking, I think my invention could not outgo the reality. He was indeed well worthy of the cloth he wore; and that, I think, is the highest character a man can obtain.

"During the first part of my life, even till I reached my sixteenth year, I can recollect nothing to relate to you. All was one long serene day, in looking back upon which, as when we cast our eyes on a calm sea, no object arises to my view. All appears one scene of happiness and tranquillity.

"On the day, then, when I became sixteen years old, must I begin my history; for on that day I first tasted the bitterness of sorrow.

"My father, besides those prescribed by our religion, kept five festivals every year. These were on his wedding-day, and on the birthday of each of his little family; on these occasions he used to invite two or three neighbours to his house, and to indulge himself, as he said, in great excess; for so he called drinking a pint of very small punch; and, indeed, it might appear excess to one who on other days rarely tasted any liquor stronger than small beer.

"Upon my unfortunate birthday, then, when we were all in a high degree of mirth, my mother having left the room after dinner, and staying away pretty long, my father sent me to see for her. I went according to his orders; but, though I searched the whole house, and called after her without-doors, I could neither see nor hear her. I was a little alarmed at this (though far from suspecting any great mischief had befallen her), and ran back to acquaint my father, who answered coolly (for he was a man of the calmest temper), 'Very well, my dear, I suppose she is not gone far, and will be here immediately.' Half an hour or more passed after this, when, she not returning, my father himself expressed some surprise at her stay; declaring it must be some matter of importance which could detain her at that time from her company. His surprise now increased every minute, and he began to grow uneasy, and to show sufficient symptoms in his countenance of what he felt within. He then despatched the servant-maid to inquire after her mistress in the parish, but waited not her return; for she was scarce gone out of doors before he begged leave of his guests to go himself on the same errand. The company now all broke up, and attended my father, all endeavouring to give him hopes that no mischief had happened. They searched the whole parish, but in vain; they could neither see my mother, nor hear any news of her. My father returned home in a state little short of distraction. His friends in vain attempted to administer either advice or comfort; he threw himself on the floor in the most bitter agonies of despair.

"Whilst he lay in this condition, my sister and myself lying by him, all equally, I believe, and completely miserable, our old servant-maid came into the room, and cried out, her mind misgave her that she knew where her mistress was. Upon these words, my father sprung from the floor, and asked her eagerly, where? But oh! Mrs. Booth, how can I describe the particulars of a scene to you, the remembrance of which chills my blood with horror, and which the agonies of my mind, when it passed, made all a scene of confusion! The fact then in short was this: my mother, who was a most indulgent mistress to one servant, which was all we kept, was unwilling, I suppose, to disturb her at her dinner, and therefore went herself to fill her tea-kettle at a well, into which, stretching herself too far, as we imagine, the water then being very low, she fell with the tea-kettle in her hand. The missing this gave the poor old wretch the first hint of her suspicion, which, upon examination, was found to be too well grounded.

"What we all suffered on this occasion may more easily be felt than described." "It may indeed," answered Amelia, "and I am so sensible of it, that, unless you have a mind to see me faint before your face, I beg you will order me something; a glass of water, if you please." Mrs. Bennet immediately complied with her friend's request; a glass of water was brought, and some hartshorn drops infused into it; which Amelia having drank off, declared she found herself much better; and then Mrs. Bennet proceeded thus:

"I will not dwell on a scene which I see hath already so much affected your tender heart, and which is as disagreeable to me to relate as it can be to you to hear. I will therefore only mention to you the behaviour of my father on this occasion, which was indeed becoming a philospher and a Christian divine. On the day after my mother's funeral he sent for my sister and myself into his room, where, after many caresses and every demonstration of fatherly tenderness as well in silence as in words, he began to exhort us to bear with patience the great calamity that had befallen us; saying, 'That as every human accident, how terrible soever, must happen to us by divine permission at least, a due sense of our duty to our great Creator must teach us an absolute submission to his will. Not only religion, but common sense, must teach us this; for oh! my dear children,' cries he, 'how vain is all resistance, all repining! could tears wash back again my angel from the grave, I should drain all the juices of my body through my eyes; but oh, could we fill up that cursed well with our tears, how fruitless would be all our sorrow!'—I think I repeat you his very words; for the impression they made on me is never to be obliterated. He then proceeded to comfort us with the chearful thought that the loss was entirely our own, and that my mother was greatly a gainer by the accident which we lamented. 'I have a wife,' cries he, 'my children, and you have a mother, now amongst the heavenly choir; how selfish therefore is all our grief! how cruel to her are all our wishes!' In this manner he talked to us near half an hour, though I must frankly own to you his arguments had not the immediate good effect on us which they deserved, for we retired from him very little the better for his exhortations; however, they became every day more and more forcible upon our recollection; indeed, they were greatly strengthened by his example; for in this, as in all other instances, he practised the doctrines which he taught. From this day he never mentioned my mother more, and soon after recovered his usual chearfulness in public; though I have reason to think he paid many a bitter sigh in private to that remembrance which neither philosophy nor Christianity could expunge.

"My father's advice, enforced by his example, together with the kindness of some of our friends, assisted by that ablest of all the mental physicians, Time, in a few months pretty well restored my tranquillity, when fortune made a second attack on my quiet. My sister, whom I dearly loved, and who as warmly returned my affection, had fallen into an ill state of health some time before the fatal accident which I have related. She was indeed at that time so much better, that we had great hopes of her perfect recovery; but the disorders of her mind on that dreadful occasion so affected her body, that she presently relapsed to her former declining state, and thence grew continually worse and worse, till, after a decay of near seven months, she followed my poor mother to the grave.

"I will not tire you, dear madam, with repetitions of grief; I will only mention two observations which have occurred to me from reflections on the two losses I have mentioned. The first is, that a mind once violently hurt grows, as it were, callous to any future impressions of grief, and is never capable of feeling the same pangs a second time. The other observation is, that the arrows of fortune, as well as all others, derive their force from the velocity with which they are discharged; for, when they approach you by slow and perceptible degrees, they have but very little power to do you mischief.

"The truth of these observations I experienced, not only in my own heart, but in the behaviour of my father, whose philosophy seemed to gain a complete triumph over this latter calamity.

"Our family was now reduced to two, and my father grew extremely fond of me, as if he had now conferred an entire stock of affection on me, that had before been divided. His words, indeed, testified no less, for he daily called me his only darling, his whole comfort, his all. He committed the whole charge of his house to my care, and gave me the name of his little housekeeper, an appellation of which I was then as proud as any minister of state can be of his titles. But, though I was very industrious in the discharge of my occupation, I did not, however, neglect my studies, in which I had made so great a proficiency, that I was become a pretty good mistress of the Latin language, and had made some progress in the Greek. I believe, madam, I have formerly acquainted you, that learning was the chief estate I inherited of my father, in which he had instructed me from my earliest youth.

"The kindness of this good man had at length wiped off the remembrance of all losses; and I during two years led a life of great tranquillity, I think I might almost say of perfect happiness.

"I was now in the nineteenth year of my age, when my father's good fortune removed us from the county of Essex into Hampshire, where a living was conferred on him by one of his old schoolfellows, of twice the value of what he was before possessed of.

"His predecessor in this new living had died in very indifferent circumstances, and had left behind him a widow with two small children. My father, therefore, who, with great economy, had a most generous soul, bought the whole furniture of the parsonage-house at a very high price; some of it, indeed, he would have wanted; for, though our little habitation in Essex was most completely furnished, yet it bore no proportion to the largeness of that house in which he was now to dwell.

"His motive, however, to the purchase was, I am convinced, solely generosity; which appeared sufficiently by the price he gave, and may be further enforced by the kindness he showed the widow in another instance; for he assigned her an apartment for the use of herself and her little family, which, he told her, she was welcome to enjoy as long as it suited her conveniency.

"As this widow was very young, and generally thought to be tolerably pretty, though I own she had a cast with her eyes which I never liked, my father, you may suppose, acted from a less noble principle than I have hinted; but I must in justice acquit him, for these kind offers were made her before ever he had seen her face; and I have the greatest reason to think that, for a long time after he had seen her, he beheld her with much indifference.

"This act of my father's gave me, when I first heard it, great satisfaction; for I may at least, with the modesty of the ancient philosophers, call myself a lover of generosity, but when I became acquainted with the widow I was still more delighted with what my father had done; for though I could not agree with those who thought her a consummate beauty, I must allow that she was very fully possessed of the power of making herself agreeable; and this power she exerted with so much success, with such indefatigable industry to oblige, that within three months I became in the highest manner pleased with my new acquaintance, and had contracted the most sincere friendship for her.

"But, if I was so pleased with the widow, my father was by this time enamoured of her. She had, indeed, by the most artful conduct in the world, so insinuated herself into his favour, so entirely infatuated him, that he never showed the least marks of chearfulness in her absence, and could, in truth, scarce bear that she should be out of his sight.

"She had managed this matter so well (O, she is the most artful of women!) that my father's heart was gone before I ever suspected it was in danger. The discovery you may easily believe, madam, was not pleasing. The name of a mother-in-law sounded dreadful in my ears; nor could I bear the thought of parting again with a share in those dear affections, of which I had purchased the whole by the loss of a beloved mother and sister.

"In the first hurry and disorder of my mind on this occasion I committed a crime of the highest kind against all the laws of prudence and discretion. I took the young lady herself very roundly to task, treated her designs on my father as little better than a design to commit a theft, and in my passion, I believe, said she might be ashamed to think of marrying a man old enough to be her grandfather; for so in reality he almost was.

"The lady on this occasion acted finely the part of a hypocrite. She affected to be highly affronted at my unjust suspicions, as she called them; and proceeded to such asseverations of her innocence, that she almost brought me to discredit the evidence of my own eyes and ears.

"My father, however, acted much more honestly, for he fell the next day into a more violent passion with me than I had ever seen him in before, and asked me whether I intended to return his paternal fondness by assuming the right of controlling his inclinations? with more of the like kind, which fully convinced me what had passed between him and the lady, and how little I had injured her in my suspicions.

"Hitherto, I frankly own, my aversion to this match had

been principally on my own account; for I had no ill opinion of the woman, though I thought neither her circumstances nor my father's age promised any kind of felicity from such a union; but now I learnt some particulars, which, had not our quarrel become public in the parish, I should perhaps have never known. In short, I was informed that this gentle obliging creature, as she had at first appeared to me, had the spirit of a tigress, and was by many believed to have broken the heart of her first husband.

"The truth of this matter being confirmed to me upon examination, I resolved not to suppress it. On this occasion fortune seemed to favour me, by giving me a speedy opportunity of seeing my father alone and in good humour. He now first began to open his intended marriage, telling me that he had formerly had some religious objections to bigamy, but he had very fully considered the matter, and had satisfied himself of its legality. He then faithfully promised me that no second marriage should in the least impair his affection for me; and concluded with the highest eulogiums on the goodness of the widow, protesting that it was her virtues and not her person with which he was enamoured.

"I now fell upon my knees before him, and bathing his hand in my tears, which flowed very plentifully from my eyes, acquainted him with all I had heard, and was so very imprudent, I might almost say so cruel, to disclose the author of my information.

"My father heard me without any indication of passion, and answered coldly, that if there was any proof of such facts he should decline any further thought of this match: 'But, child,' said he, 'though I am far from suspecting the truth of what you tell me, as far as regards your knowledge, yet you know the inclination of the world to slander.' However, before we parted he promised to make a proper inquiry into what I had told him. But I ask your pardon, dear madam, I am running minutely into those particulars of my life in which you have not the least concern."

Amelia stopped her friend short in her apology; and though, perhaps, she thought her impertinent enough, yet (such was her good breeding) she gave her many assurances of a curiosity to know every incident of her life which she could remember; after which Mrs. Bennet proceeded as in the next chapter.

CHAPTER III

Continuation of Mrs. Bennet's story.

"I THINK, madam," said Mrs. Bennet, "I told you my father promised me to inquire further into the affair, but he had hardly time to keep his word; for we separated pretty late in the evening, and early the next morning he was married to the widow.

"But, though he gave no credit to my information, I had sufficient reason to think he did not forget it, by the resentment which he soon discovered to both the persons whom I had named as my informers.

"Nor was it long before I had good cause to believe that my father's new wife was perfectly well acquainted with the good opinion I had of her, not only from her usage of me, but from certain hints which she threw forth with an air of triumph. One day, particularly, I remember she said to my father, upon his mentioning his age, 'O, my dear! I hope you have many years yet to live! unless, indeed, I should be so cruel as to break your heart.' She spoke these words looking me full in the face, and accompanied them with a sneer in which the highest malice was visible, under a thin covering of affected pleasantry.

"I will not entertain you, madam, with anything so common as the cruel usage of a stepmother; nor of what affected me much more, the unkind behaviour of a father under such an influence. It shall suffice only to tell you that I had the mortification to perceive the gradual and daily decrease of my father's affection. His smiles were converted into frowns; the tender appellations of child and dear were exchanged for plain Molly, that girl, that creature, and sometimes much harder names. I was at first turned all at once into a cypher, and at last seemed to be considered as a nuisance in the family.

"Thus altered was the man of whom I gave you such a character at the entrance on my story; but, alas! he no longer acted from his own excellent disposition, but was in everything governed and directed by my mother-in-law. In fact, whenever there is great disparity of years between husband and wife, the younger is, I believe, always possessed of absolute power over the elder; for superstition itself is a less firm support of absolute power than dotage.

"But though his wife was so entirely mistress of my father's will that she could make him use me ill, she could not so perfectly subdue his understanding as to prevent him from being conscious of such ill-usage; and from this consciousness, he began inveterately to hate me. Of this hatred he gave me numberless instances, and I protest to you I know not any other reason for it than what I have assigned; and the cause, as experience hath convinced me, is adequate to the effect.

"While I was in this wretched situation, my father's unkindness having almost broken my heart, he came one day into my room with more anger in his countenance than I had ever seen, and, after bitterly upbraiding me with my undutiful behaviour both to himself and his worthy consort, he bid me pack up my alls, and immediately prepare to quit his house; at the same time gave me a letter, and told me that would acquaint me where I might find a home; adding that he doubted not but I expected, and had indeed solicited, the invitation; and left me with a declaration that he would have no spies in his family.

"The letter, I found on opening it, was from my father's own sister; but before I mention the contents I will give you a short sketch of her character, as it was somewhat particular. Her personal charms were not great; for she was very tall, very thin, and very homely. Of the defect of her beauty she was, perhaps, sensible; her vanity, therefore, retreated into her mind, where there is no looking-glass, and consequently where we can flatter ourselves with discovering almost whatever beauties we please. This is an encouraging circumstance; and yet I have observed, dear Mrs. Booth, that few women ever seek these comforts from within till they are driven to it by despair of finding any food for their vanity from without. Indeed, I believe the first wish of our whole sex is to be handsome."

Here both the ladies fixed their eyes on the glass, and both smiled.

"My aunt, however," continued Mrs. Bennet, "from

despair of gaining any appplause this way, had applied herself entirely to the contemplation of her understanding, and had improved this to such a pitch, that at the age of fifty, at which she was now arrived, she had contracted a hearty contempt for much the greater part of both sexes; for the women, as being idiots, and for the men, as the admirers of idiots. That word, and fool, were almost constantly in her mouth, and were bestowed with great liberality among all her acquaintance.

"This lady had spent one day only at my father's house in near two years; it was about a month before his second marriage. At her departure she took occasion to whisper me her opinion of the widow, whom she called a pretty idiot, and wondered how her brother could bear such company under his roof; for neither she nor I had at that time any suspicion of what afterwards happened.

"The letter which my father had just received, and which was the first she had sent him since his marriage, was of such a nature that I should be unjust if I blamed him for being offended; fool and idiot were both plentifully bestowed in it as well on himself as on his wife. But what, perhaps, had principally offended him was that part which related to me; for, after much panegyric on my understanding, and saying he was unworthy of such a daughter, she considered his match not only as the highest indiscretion as it related to himself, but as a downright act of injustice to me. One expression in it I shall never forget. 'You have placed,' said she, 'a woman above your daughter, who, in understanding, the only valuable gift of nature, is the lowest in the whole class of pretty idiots.' After much more of this kind, it concluded with inviting me to her house.

"I can truly say that when I read the letter I entirely forgave my father's suspicion that I had made some complaints to my aunt of his behaviour; for, though I was indeed innocent, there was surely colour enough to suspect the contrary.

"Though I had never been greatly attached to my aunt, nor indeed had she formerly given me any reason for such an attachment, yet I was well enough pleased with her present invitation. To say the truth, I led so wretched a life where I then was, that it was impossible not to be a gainer by any exchange.

"I could not, however, bear the thoughts of leaving my father with an impression on his mind against me which I did not deserve. I endeavoured, therefore, to remove all his suspicion of my having complained to my aunt by the most earnest asservations of my innocence; but they were all to no purpose. All my tears, all my vows, and all my entreaties were fruitless. My new mother, indeed, appeared to be my advocate; but she acted her part very poorly, and, far from counterfeiting any desire of succeeding in my suit, she could not conceal the excessive joy which she felt on the occasion.

"Well, madam, the next day I departed for my aunt's, where, after a long journey of forty miles, I arrived, without having once broke my fast on the road; for grief is as capable as food of filling the stomach, and I had too much of the former to admit any of the latter. The fatigue of my journey, and the agitation of my mind, joined to my fasting, so overpowered my spirits, that when I was taken from my horse I immediately fainted away in the arms of the man who helped me from my saddle. My aunt expressed great astonishment at seeing me in this condition, with my eyes almost swollen out of my head with tears; but my father's letter, which I delivered her soon after I came to myself, pretty well, I believe, cured her surprise. She often smiled with a mixture of contempt and anger while she was reading it; and, having pronounced her brother to be a fool, she turned to me, and, with as much affability as possible (for she is no great mistress of affability), said, 'Don't be uneasy, dear Molly, for you are come to the house of a friend—of one who hath sense enough to discern the author of all the mischief: depend upon it, child, I will, ere long, make some people ashamed of their folly.' This kind reception gave me some comfort, my aunt assuring me that she would convince him how unjustly he had accused me of having made any complaints to her. A paper war was now begun between these two, which not only fixed an irreconcileable hatred between them, but confirmed my father's displeasure against me; and, in the end, I believe, did me no service with my aunt; for I was considered by both as the cause of their dissension, though, in fact, my stepmother, who very well knew the affection my aunt had for her, had long since done her business with my father; and as for my aunt's affection towards him, it had been abating several years, from an apprehension that he did not pay sufficient deference to her understanding.

"I had lived about half a year with my aunt when I heard of my stepmother's being delivered of a boy, and the great joy my father expressed on that occasion; but, poor man, he lived not long enough to enjoy his happiness; for within a month afterwards I had the melancholy news of his death.

"Notwithstanding all the disobligations I had lately received from him, I was sincerely afflicted at my loss of him. All his kindness to me in my infancy, all his kindness to me while I was growing up, recurred to my memory, raised a thousand tender, melancholy ideas, and totally obliterated all thoughts of his latter behaviour, for which I made also every allowance and every excuse in my power.

"But what may perhaps appear more extraordinary, my aunt began soon to speak of him with concern. She said he had some understanding formerly, though his passion for that vile woman had, in a great measure, obscured it; and one day, when she was in an ill-humour with me, she had the cruelty to throw out a hint that she had never quarrelled with her brother if it had not been on my account.

"My father, during his life, had allowed my aunt very handsomely for my board; for generosity was too deeply riveted in his nature to be plucked out by all the power of his wife. So far, however, she prevailed, that, though he died possessed of upwards of £2000, he left me no more than £100, which, as he expressed in his will, was to set me up in some business, if I had the grace to take to any.

"Hitherto my aunt had in general treated me with some degree of affection; but her behaviour began now to be changed. She soon took an opportunity of giving me to understand that her fortune was insufficient to keep me; and, as I could not live on the interest of my own, it was high time for me to consider about going into the world. She added, that her brother having mentioned my setting up in some business in his will was very foolish; that I had been bred to nothing; and, besides, that the sum was too trifling to set me up in any way of reputation; she desired me therefore to think of immediately going into service.

"This advice was perhaps right enough; and I told her I was very ready to do as she directed me, but I was at that time in an ill state of health; I desired her therefore to let me stay with her till my legacy, which was not to be paid till a year after my father's death, was due; and I then promised to satisfy her for my board, to which she readily consented.

"And now, madam," said Mrs. Bennet, sighing, "I am going to open to you those matters which lead directly to that great catastrophe of my life which hath occasioned my giving you this trouble, and of trying your patience in this manner."

Amelia, notwithstanding her impatience, made a very civil answer to this; and then Mrs. Bennet proceeded to relate what is written in the next chapter.

CHAPTER IV

Further continuation.

"THE curate of the parish where my aunt dwelt was a young fellow of about four and twenty. He had been left an orphan in his infancy, and entirely unprovided for, when an uncle had the goodness to take care of his education, both at school and at the university. As the young gentleman was intended for the church, his uncle, though he had two daughters of his own, and no very large fortune, purchased for him the next presentation of a living of near £200 a year. The incumbent, at the time of the purchase, was under the age of sixty, and in apparent good health; notwithstanding which, he died soon after the bargain, and long before the nephew was capable of orders; so that the uncle was obliged to give the living to a clergyman, to hold it till the young man came of proper age.

"The young gentleman had not attained his proper age of taking orders when he had the misfortune to lose his uncle and only friend, who, thinking he had sufficiently provided for his nephew by the purchase of the living, considered him no further in his will, but divided all the fortune of which he died possessed between his two daughters; recommending it to them, however, on his deathbed, to assist their cousin with money sufficient to keep him at the university till he should be capable of ordination.

"But, as no appointment of this kind was in the will, the young ladies, who received about £2000 each, thought proper to disregard the last words of their father; for, besides that both of them were extremely tenacious of their money, they were great enemies to their cousin, on account of their father's kindness to him; and thought proper to let him know that they thought he had robbed them of too much already.

"The poor young fellow was now greatly distressed; for he had yet above a year to stay at the university, without any visible means of sustaining himself there.

"In this distress, however, he met with a friend, who had the good nature to lend him the sum of twenty pounds, for which he only accepted his bond for forty, and which was to be paid within a year after his being possessed of his living; that is, within a year after his becoming qualified to hold it.

"With this small sum thus hardly obtained the poor gentleman made a shift to struggle with all difficulties till he became of due age to take upon himself the character of a deacon. He then repaired to that clergyman to whom his uncle had given the living upon the conditions above mentioned, to procure a title to ordination; but this, to his great surprise and mortification, was absolutely refused him.

"The immediate disappointment did not hurt him so much as the conclusion he drew from it; for he could have but little hopes that the man who could have the cruelty to refuse him a title would vouchsafe afterwards to deliver up to him a living of so considerable a value; nor was it long before this worthy incumbent told him plainly that he valued his uncle's favours at too high a rate to part with them to any one; nay, he pretended scruples of conscience, and said that, if he had made any slight promises, which he did not now well remember, they were wicked and void; that he looked upon himself as married to his parish, and he could no more give it up than he could give up his wife without sin.

"The poor young fellow was now obliged to seek farther for a title, which, at length, he obtained from the rector of the parish where my aunt lived.

"He had not long been settled in the curacy before an intimate acquaintance grew between him and my aunt; for she was a great admirer of the clergy, and used frequently to say they were the only conversible creatures in the country.

"The first time she was in this gentleman's company was at a neighbour's christening, where she stood godmother. Here she displayed her whole little stock of knowledge, in order to captivate Mr. Bennet (I suppose, madam, you already guess that to have been his name), and before they parted gave him a very strong invitation to her house.

"Not a word passed at this christening between Mr. Bennet and myself, but our eyes were not unemployed. Here, madam, I first felt a pleasing kind of confusion, which I know not how to describe. I felt a kind of uneasiness, yet did not wish to be without it. I longed to be alone, yet dreaded the hour of parting. I could not keep my eyes off from the object which caused my confusion, and which

I was at once afraid of and enamoured with. But why do I attempt to describe my situation to one who must, I am sure, have felt the same?"

Amelia smiled, and Mrs. Bennet went on thus: "O, Mrs. Booth! had you seen the person of whom I am now speaking, you would not condemn the suddenness of my love. Nay, indeed, I had seen him there before, though this was the first time I had ever heard the music of his voice. Oh! it was the sweetest that was ever heard.

"Mr. Bennet came to visit my aunt the very next day. She imputed this respectful haste to the powerful charms of her understanding, and resolved to lose no opportunity in improving the opinion which she imagined he had conceived of her. She became by this desire quite ridiculous, and ran into absurdities and a galimatias scarce credible.

"Mr. Bennet, as I afterwards found, saw her in the same light with myself; but, as he was a very sensible and well-bred man, he so well concealed his opinion from us both, that I was almost angry, and she was pleased even to raptures, declaring herself charmed with his understanding, though, indeed, he had said very little; but I believe he heard himself into her good opinion, while he gazed himself into love.

"The two first visits which Mr. Bennet made to my aunt, though I was in the room all the time, I never spoke a word; but on the third, on some argument which arose between them, Mr. Bennet referred himself to me. I took his side of the question, as indeed I must to have done justice, and repeated two or three words of Latin. My aunt reddened at this, and expressed great disdain of my opinion, declaring she was astonished that a man of Mr. Bennet's understanding could appeal to the judgment of a silly girl. 'Is she,' said my aunt, bridling herself, 'fit to decide between us?' Mr. Bennet spoke very favourable of what I had said; upon which my aunt burst almost into a rage, treated me with downright scurrility, called me conceited fool, abused my poor father for having taught me Latin, which, she said, had made me a downright coxcomb, and made me prefer myself to those who were a hundred times my superiors in knowledge. She then fell foul on the learned languages, declared they were totally useless, and concluded that she had read all that was worth reading, though, she thanked heaven, she understood no language but her own.

"Before the end of this visit Mr. Bennet reconciled himself very well to my aunt, which, indeed, was no difficult task for him to accomplish; but from that hour she conceived a hatred and rancour towards me which I could never appease.

"My aunt had, from my first coming into her house, expressed great dislike to my learning. In plain truth, she envied me that advantage. This envy I had long ago discovered, and had taken great pains to smother it, carefully avoiding ever to mention a Latin word in her presence, and always submitting to her authority; for indeed I despised her ignorance too much to dispute with her. By these means I had pretty well succeeded, and we lived tolerably together; but the affront paid to her understanding by Mr. Bennet in my favour was an injury never to be forgiven to me. She took me severely to task that very evening, and reminded me of going to service in such earnest terms as almost amounted to literally turning me out of doors; advising me, in the most insulting manner, to keep my Latin to myself, which she said was useless to any one, but ridiculous when pretended to by a servant.

"The next visit Mr. Bennet made at our house I was not suffered to be present. This was much the shortest of all his visits; and when he went away he left my aunt in a worse humour than ever I had seen her. The whole was discharged on me in the usual manner, by upbraiding me with my learning, conceit, and poverty; reminding me of obligations, and insisting on my going immediately to service. With all this I was greatly pleased, as it assured me that Mr. Bennet had said something to her in my favour; and I would have purchased a kind expression of his at almost any price.

"I should scarce, however, have been so sanguine as to draw this conclusion, had I not received some hints that I had not unhappily placed my affections on a man who made me no return; for, though he had scarce addressed a dozen sentences to me (for, indeed, he had no opportunity), yet his eyes had revealed certain secrets to mine with which I was not displeased.

"I remained, however, in a state of anxiety near a month; sometimes pleasing myself with thinking Mr. Bennet's heart was in the same situation with my own; sometimes doubting that my wishes had flattered and deceived me, and not in the least questioning that my aunt was my rival; for I thought

CHAPTER V

The story of Mrs. Bennet continued.

"I SCARCE know where I left off—Oh! I was, I think, telling you that I esteemed my aunt as my rival; and it is not easy to conceive a greater degree of detestation than I had for her; and what may, perhaps, appear strange, as she daily grew more and more civil to me, my hatred increased with her civility; for I imputed it all to her triumph over me, and to her having secured, beyond all apprehension, the heart I longed for.

"How was I surprised when, one day, with as much good-humour as she was mistress of (for her countenance was not very pleasing), she asked me how I liked Mr. Bennet? The question, you will believe, madam, threw me into great confusion, which she plainly perceived, and, without waiting for my answer, told me she was very well satisfied, for that it did not require her discernment to read my thoughts in my countenance. 'Well, child,' she said, 'I have suspected this a great while, and I believe it will please you to know that I yesterday made the same discovery in your lover.' This, I confess to you, was more than I could well bear, and I begged her to say no more to me at that time on that subject. 'Nay, child,' answered she, 'I must tell you all, or I should not act a friendly part. Mr. Bennet, I am convinced, hath a passion for you; but it is a passion which, I think, you should not encourage. For, to be plain with you, I fear he is in love with your person only. Now this is a love, child, which cannot produce that rational happiness which a woman of sense ought to expect.' In short, she ran on with a great deal of stuff about rational happiness, and women of sense, and concluded with assuring me that, after the strictest scrutiny, she could not find that Mr. Bennet had an adequate opinion of my understanding; upon which she vouchsafed to make me many compliments, but mixed with several sarcasms concerning my learning.

"I hope, madam, however," said she to Amelia, "you have

not so bad an opinion of my capacity as to imagine me dull enough to be offended with Mr. Bennet's sentiments, for which I presently knew so well to account. I was, indeed, charmed with his ingenuity, who had discovered, perhaps, the only way of reconciling my aunt to those inclinations which I now assured myself he had for me.

"I was not long left to support my hopes by my sagacity. He soon found an opportunity of declaring his passion. He did this in so forcible though gentle a manner, with such a profusion of fervency and tenderness at once, that his love, like a torrent, bore everything before it; and I am almost ashamed to own to you how very soon he prevailed upon me to—to—in short, to be an honest woman, and to confess to him the plain truth.

"When we were upon a good footing together he gave me a long relation of what had passed at several interviews with my aunt, at which I had not been present. He said he had discovered that, as she valued herself chiefly on her understanding, so she was extremely jealous of mine, and hated me on account of my learning. That, as he had loved me passionately from his first seeing me, and had thought of nothing from that time but of throwing himself at my feet, he saw no way so open to propitiate my aunt as that which he had taken by commending my beauty, a perfection to which she had long resigned all claim, at the expense of my understanding, in which he lamented my deficiency to a degree almost of ridicule. This he imputed chiefly to my learning; on this occasion he advanced a sentiment which so pleased my aunt that she thought proper to make it her own; for I heard it afterwards more than once from her own mouth. Learning, he said, had the same effect on the mind that strong liquors have on the constitution; both tending to eradicate all our natural fire and energy. His flattery had made such a dupe of my aunt that she assented, without the least suspicion of his sincerity, to all he said; so sure is vanity to weaken every fortress of the understanding, and to betray us to every attack of the enemy.

"You will believe, madam, that I readily forgave him all he had said, not only from that motive which I have mentioned, but as I was assured he had spoke the reverse of his real sentiments. I was not, however, quite so well pleased with my aunt, who began to treat me as if I was

really an idiot. Her contempt, I own, a little piqued me;
and I could not help often expressing my resentment, when
we were alone together, to Mr. Bennet, who never failed to
gratify me by making her conceit the subject of his wit; a
talent which he possessed in the most extraordinary degree.

"This proved of very fatal consequence; for one day,
while we were enjoying my aunt in a very thick arbour in
the garden, she stole upon us unobserved, and overheard
our whole conversation. I wish, my dear, you understood
Latin, that I might repeat you a sentence in which the rage
of a tigress that hath lost her young is described. No
English poet, as I remember, hath come up to it; nor am I
myself equal to the undertaking. She burst in upon us,
open-mouthed, and after discharging every abusive word
almost, in the only language she understood, on poor Mr.
Bennet, turned us both out of doors, declaring she would
send my rags after me, but would never more permit me to
set my foot within her threshold.

"Consider, dear madam, to what a wretched condition
we were now reduced. I had not yet received the small
legacy left me by my father; nor was Mr. Bennet master
of five pounds in the whole world.

"In this situation, the man I doated on to distraction had
but little difficulty to persuade me to a proposal which, indeed, I thought generous in him to make, as it seemed to
proceed from that tenderness for my reputation to which he
ascribed it; indeed, it could proceed from no motive with
which I should have been displeased. In a word, within
two days we were man and wife.

"Mr. Bennet now declared himself the happiest of men;
and, for my part, I sincerely declared I envied no woman upon
earth. How little, alas! did I then know or suspect the
price I was to pay for all my joys! A match of real love is,
indeed, truly paradise; and such perfect happiness seems to
be the forbidden fruit to mortals, which we are to lament
having tasted during the rest of our lives.

"The first uneasiness which attacked us after our marriage
was on my aunt's account. It was very disagreeable to
live under the nose of so near a relation, who did not acknowledge us, but on the contrary, was ever doing us all the ill
turns in her power, and making a party against us in the
parish, which is always easy enough to do amongst the vulgar

against persons who are their superiors in rank, and, at the same time, their inferiors in fortune. This made Mr. Bennet think of procuring an exchange, in which intention he was soon after confirmed by the arrival of the rector. It was the rector's custom to spend three months every year at his living, for which purpose he reserved an apartment in his parsonage-house, which was full large enough for two such little families as then occupied it. We at first promised ourselves some little convenience from his boarding with us; and Mr. Bennet began to lay aside his thoughts of leaving his curacy, at least for some time. But these golden ideas presently vanished; for, though we both used our utmost endeavours to please him, we soon found the impossibility of succeeding. He was, indeed, to give you his character in a word, the most peevish of mortals. This temper, notwithstanding that he was both a good and a pious man, made his company so insufferable that nothing could compensate it. If his breakfast was not ready to a moment— if a dish of meat was too much or too little done—in short, if anything failed of exactly hitting his taste, he was sure to be out of humour all that day, so that, indeed, he was scarce ever in a good temper a whole day together; for fortune seems to take a delight in thwarting this kind of disposition, to which human life, with its many crosses and accidents, is, in truth, by no means fitted.

"Mr. Bennet was now, by my desire as well as his own, determined to quit the parish; but when he attempted to get an exchange, he found it a matter of more difficulty than he had apprehended; for the rector's temper was so well known among the neighbouring clergy, that none of them could be brought to think of spending three months in a year with him.

"After many fruitless inquiries, Mr. Bennet thought best to remove to London, the great mart of all affairs, ecclesiastical and civil. This project greatly pleased him, and he resolved, without more delay, to take his leave of the rector, which he did in the most friendly manner possible, and preached his farewell sermon; nor was there a dry eye in the church, except among the few, whom my aunt, who remained inexorable, had prevailed upon to hate us without any cause.

"To London we came, and took up our lodging the first night at the inn where the stage-coach set us down: the next morning my husband went out early on his business, and returned with the good news of having heard of a curacy, and of having equipped himself with a lodging in the neighbourhood of a worthy peer, 'who,' said he, 'was my fellow-collegiate; and, what is more, I have a direction to a person who will advance your legacy at a very reasonable rate.'

"This last particular was extremely agreeable to me, for our last guinea was now broached; and the rector had lent my husband ten pounds to pay his debts in the country, for, with all his peevishness, he was a good and a generous man, and had, indeed, so many valuable qualities, that I lamented his temper, after I knew him thoroughly, as much on his account as on my own.

"We now quitted the inn and went to our lodgings, where my husband having placed me in safety, as he said, he went about the business of the legacy with good assurance of success.

"My husband returned elated with his success, the person to whom he applied having undertaken to advance the legacy, which he fulfilled as soon as the proper inquiries could be made, and proper instruments prepared for that purpose.

"This, however, took up so much time, that, as our fund was so very low, we were reduced to some distress, and obliged to live extremely penurious; nor would all do without my taking a most disagreeable way of procuring money by pawning one of my gowns.

"Mr. Bennet was now settled in a curacy in town, greatly to his satisfaction, and our affairs seemed to have a prosperous aspect, when he came home to me one morning in much apparent disorder, looking as pale as death, and begged me by some means or other to get him a dram, for that he was taken with a sudden faintness and lowness of spirits.

"Frighted as I was, I immediately ran down-stairs, and procured some rum of the mistress of the house; the first time, indeed, I ever knew him drink any. When he came to himself he begged me not to be alarmed, for it was no distemper, but something that had vexed him, which had caused his disorder, which he had now perfectly recovered.

"He then told me the whole affair. He had hitherto deferred paying a visit to the lord whom I mentioned to have been formerly his fellow-collegiate, and was now his neighbour, till he could put himself in decent rigging. He had now purchased a new cassock, hat, and wig, and went to pay his respects to his old acquaintance, who had received from him many civilities and assistances in his learning at the university, and had promised to return them fourfold hereafter.

"It was not without some difficulty that Mr. Bennet got into the antechamber. Here he waited, or as the phrase is, cooled his heels, for above an hour before he saw his lordship; nor had he seen him then but by an accident; for my lord was going out when he casually intercepted him in his passage to his chariot. He approached to salute him with some familiarity, though with respect, depending on his former intimacy, when my lord, stepping short, very gravely told him he had not the pleasure of knowing him. How! my lord, said he, can you have so soon forgot your old acquaintance Tom Bennet? O, Mr. Bennet! cries his lordship, with much reserve, is it you? you will pardon my memory. I am glad to see you, Mr. Bennet, but you must excuse me at present, for I am in very great haste. He then broke from him, and without more ceremony, or any further invitation, went directly into his chariot.

"This cold reception from a person for whom my husband had a real friendship, and from whom he had great reason to expect a very warm return of affection, so affected the poor man, that it caused all those symptoms which I have mentioned before.

"Though this incident produced no material consequence, I could not pass it over in silence, as, of all the misfortunes which ever befel him, it affected my husband the most. I need not, however, to a woman of your delicacy, make any comments on a behaviour which, though I believe it is very common, is, nevertheless, cruel and base beyond description, and is diametrically opposite to true honour as well as to goodness.

"To relieve the uneasiness which my husband felt on account of his false friend, I prevailed with him to go every night, almost for a fortnight together, to the play; a diversion of which he was greatly fond, and from which he did not think his being a clergyman excluded him; indeed, it is well if those austere persons who would be inclined to censure him on this head have themselves no greater sins to answer for.

"From this time, during three months, we passed our time very agreeably, a little too agreeably perhaps for our circumstances; for, however innocent diversions may be in other respects, they must be owned to be expensive. When you consider then, madam, that our income from the curacy was less than forty pounds a year, and that, after payment of the debt to the rector, and another to my aunt, with the costs in law which she had occasioned by suing for it, my legacy was reduced to less than seventy pounds, you will not wonder that, in diversions, clothes, and the common expenses of life, we had almost consumed our whole stock.

"The inconsiderate manner in which we had lived for some time will, I doubt not, appear to you to want some excuse; but I have none to make for it. Two things, however, now happened, which occasioned much serious reflection to Mr. Bennet; the one was that I grew near my time; the other, that he now received a letter from Oxford, demanding the debt of forty pounds which I mentioned to you before. The former of these he made a pretence of obtaining a delay for the payment of the latter, promising, in two months, to pay off half the debt, by which means he obtained a forbearance during that time.

"I was now delivered of a son, a matter which should in reality have increased our concern, but, on the contrary, it gave us great pleasure; greater indeed could not have been conceived at the birth of an heir to the most plentiful estate: so entirely thoughtless were we, and so little forecast had we of those many evils and distresses to which we had rendered a human creature, and one so dear to us, liable. The day of a christening is, in all families, I believe, a day of jubilee and rejoicing; and yet, if we consider the interest of that little wretch who is the occasion, how very little reason would the most sanguine persons have for their joy!

"But, though our eyes were too weak to look forward, for the sake of our child, we could not be blinded to those dangers that immediately threatened ourselves. Mr. Bennet, at the expiration of the two months, received a second letter from Oxford, in a very peremptory style, and threatening a suit without any further delay. This alarmed us in the strongest manner; and my husband, to secure his liberty, was advised for a while to shelter himself in the verge of the court.

CHAPTER VI

Further continued.

Mrs. Bennet, returning into the room, made a short apology for her absence, and then proceeded in these words:

"We now left our lodging, and took a second floor in that very house where you now are, to which we were recommended by the woman where we had before lodged, for the mistresses of both houses were acquainted; and, indeed, we had been all at the play together. To this new lodging then (such was our wretched destiny) we immediately repaired, and were received by Mrs. Ellison (how can I bear the sound of that detested name?) with much civility; she took care, however, during the first fortnight of our residence, to wait upon us every Monday morning for her rent; such being, it seems, the custom of this place, which, as it was inhabited chiefly by persons in debt, is not the region of credit.

"My husband, by the singular goodness of the rector, who greatly compassionated his case, was enabled to continue his curacy, though he could only do the duty on Sundays. He was, however, sometimes obliged to furnish a person to officiate at his expense; so that our income was very scanty, and the poor little remainder of the legacy being almost spent, we were reduced to some difficulties, and, what was worse, saw still a prospect of greater before our eyes.

"Under these circumstances, how agreeable to poor Mr. Bennet must have been the behaviour of Mrs. Ellison, who, when he carried her her rent on the usual day, told him, with a benevolent smile, that he needed not to give himself the trouble of such exact punctuality. She added that, if it was at any time inconvenient to him, he might pay her when he pleased. 'To say the truth,' says she, 'I never was so much pleased with any lodgers in my life; I am convinced, Mr. Bennet, you are a very worthy man, and you are a very happy one too; for you have the prettiest wife and the prettiest child I ever saw.' These, dear madam, were the words she was pleased to make use of: and I am sure she behaved to me with such an appearance of friendship and affection, that, as I could not perceive any possible views of interest which she could have in her professions, I easily believed them real.

"There lodged in the same house—O, Mrs. Booth! the blood runs cold to my heart, and should run cold to yours, when I name him—there lodged in the same house a lord—the lord, indeed, whom I have since seen in your company. This lord, Mrs. Ellison told me, had taken a great fancy to my little Charley. Fool that I was, and blinded by my own passion, which made me conceive that an infant, not three months old, could be really the object of affection to any besides a parent, and more especially to a gay young fellow! But, if I was silly in being deceived, how wicked was the wretch who deceived me—who used such art, and employed such pains, such incredible pains, to deceive me! He acted the part of a nurse to my little infant; he danced it, he lulled it, he kissed it; declared it was the very picture of a nephew of his—his favourite sister's child; and said so many kind and fond things of its beauty, that I myself, though, I believe, one of the tenderest and fondest of mothers, scarce carried my own ideas of my little darling's perfection beyond the compliments which he paid it.

"My lord, however, perhaps from modesty, before my face, fell far short of what Mrs. Ellison reported from him. And now, when she found the impression which was made on me by these means, she took every opportunity of insinuating to me his lordship's many virtues, his great goodness to his sister's children in particular; nor did she fail to drop some hints which gave me the most simple and groundless hopes of strange consequences from his fondness to my Charley.

"When, by these means, which, simple as they may appear, were, perhaps, the most artful, my lord had gained something more, I think, than my esteem, he took the surest method to confirm himself in my affection. This was, by professing the highest friendship for my husband; for, as to myself, I do assure you he never showed me more than common respect; and I hope you will believe I should have immediately startled and flown off if he had. Poor I accounted for all the friendship which he expressed for my husband, and all the fondness which he showed to my boy, from the great prettiness of the one and the great merit of the other;

foolishly conceiving that others saw with my eyes and felt with my heart. Little did I dream that my own unfortunate person was the fountain of all this lord's goodness, and was the intended price of it.

"One evening, as I was drinking tea with Mrs. Ellison by my lord's fire (a liberty which she never scrupled taking when he was gone out), my little Charley, now about half a year old, sitting in her lap, my lord—accidentally, no doubt, indeed, I then thought it so—came in. I was confounded, and offered to go; but my lord declared, if he disturbed Mrs. Ellison's company, as he phrased it, he would himself leave the room. When I was thus prevailed on to keep my seat, my lord immediately took my little baby into his lap, and gave it some tea there, not a little at the expense of his embroidery; for he was very richly dressed; indeed, he was as fine a figure as perhaps ever was seen. His behaviour on this occasion gave me many ideas in his favour. I thought he discovered good sense, good nature, condescension, and other good qualities, by the fondness he showed to my child, and the contempt he seemed to express for his finery, which so greatly became him; for I cannot deny but that he was the handsomest and genteelest person in the world, though such considerations advanced him not a step in my favour.

"My husband now returned from church (for this happened on a Sunday), and was, by my lord's particular desire, ushered into the room. My lord received him with the utmost politeness, and with many professions of esteem, which, he said, he had conceived from Mrs. Ellison's representations of his merit. He then proceeded to mention the living which was detained from my husband, of which Mrs. Ellison had likewise informed him; and said, he thought it would be no difficult matter to obtain a restoration of it by the authority of the bishop, who was his particular friend, and to whom he would take an immediate opportunity of mentioning it. This, at last, he determined to do the very next day, when he invited us both to dinner, where we were to be acquainted with his lordship's success.

"My lord now insisted on my husband's staying supper with him, without taking any notice of me; but Mrs. Ellison declared he should not part man and wife, and that she herself would stay with me. The motion was too agreeable to me to be rejected; and, except the little time I retired to put my child to bed, we spent together the most agreeable evening imaginable; nor was it, I believe, easy to decide whether Mr. Bennet or myself were most delighted with his lordship and Mrs. Ellison; but this, I assure you, the generosity of the one, and the extreme civility and kindness of the other, were the subjects of our conversation all the ensuing night, during which we neither of us closed our eyes.

"The next day at dinner my lord acquainted us that he had prevailed with the bishop to write to the clergyman in the country; indeed, he told us that he had engaged the bishop to be very warm in our interest, and had not the least doubt of success. This threw us both into a flow of spirits; and in the afternoon Mr. Bennet, at Mrs. Ellison's request, which was seconded by his lordship, related the history of our lives from our first acquaintance. My lord seemed much affected with some tender scenes, which, as no man could better feel, so none could better describe, than my husband. When he had finished, my lord begged pardon for mentioning an occurrence which gave him such a particular concern, as it had disturbed that delicious state of happiness in which we had lived at our former lodging. 'It would be ungenerous,' said he, 'to rejoice at an accident which, though it brought me fortunately acquainted with two of the most agreeable people in the world, was yet at the expense of your mutual felicity. The circumstance, I mean, is your debt at Oxford; pray, how doth that stand? I am resolved it shall never disturb your happiness hereafter.' At these words the tears burst from my poor husband's eyes; and, in an ecstasy of gratitude, he cried out, 'Your lordship overcomes me with generosity. If you go on in this manner, both my wife's gratitude and mine must be bankrupt.' He then acquainted my lord with the exact state of the case, and received assurances from him that the debt should never trouble him. My husband was again breaking out into the warmest expressions of gratitude, but my lord stopped him short, saying, 'If you have any obligation, it is to my little Charley here, from whose little innocent smiles I have received more than the value of this trifling debt in pleasure.' I forgot to tell you that, when I offered to leave the room after dinner upon my child's account, my lord would not suffer me, but ordered the child to be brought to me. He now took it out of my arms, placed it upon his own knee, and fed it with some fruit from the dessert. In short, it would be more tedious to you than to myself to relate the thousand little tendernesses he showed to the child. He gave it many baubles; amongst the rest was a coral worth at least three pounds; and, when my husband was confined near a fortnight to his chamber with a cold, he visited the child every day (for to this infant's account were all the visits placed), and seldom failed of accompanying his visit with a present to the little thing.

"Here, Mrs. Booth, I cannot help mentioning a doubt which hath often arisen in my mind since I have been enough mistress of myself to reflect on this horrid train which was laid to blow up my innocence. Wicked and barbarous it was to the highest degree without any question; but my doubt is, whether the art or folly of it be the more conspicuous; for, however delicate and refined the art must be allowed to have been, the folly, I think, must upon a fair examination appear no less astonishing: for to lay all considerations of cruelty and crime out of the case, what a foolish bargain doth the man make for himself who purchases so poor a pleasure at so high a price!

"We had lived near three weeks with as much freedom as if we had been all of the same family, when, one afternoon, my lord proposed to my husband to ride down himself to solicit the surrender; for he said the bishop had received an unsatisfactory answer from the parson, and had writ a second letter more pressing, which his lordship now promised us to strengthen by one of his own that my husband was to carry with him. Mr. Bennet agreed to this proposal with great thankfulness, and the next day was appointed for his journey. The distance was near seventy miles.

"My husband set out on his journey, and he had scarce left me before Mrs. Ellison came into my room, and endeavoured to comfort me in his absence; to say the truth, though he was to be from me but a few days, and the purpose of his going was to fix our happiness on a sound foundation for all our future days, I could scarce support my spirits under this first separation. But though I then thought Mrs. Ellison's intentions to be most kind and friendly, yet the means she used were utterly ineffectual, and appeared to me injudicious. Instead of soothing my uneasiness, which is always the first physic to be given to grief, she rallied me upon it, and began to talk in a very unusual style of gaiety, in which she treated conjugal love with much ridicule.

"I gave her to understand that she displeased me by this discourse; but she soon found means to give such a turn to it as made a merit of all she had said. And now, when she had worked me into a good humour—she made a proposal to me which I at first rejected—but at last fatally, too fatally, suffered myself to be over-persuaded. This was to go to a masquerade at Ranelagh, for which my lord had furnished her with tickets."

At these words Amelia turned pale as death, and hastily begged her friend to give her a glass of water, some air, or anything. Mrs. Bennet, having thrown open the window, and procured the water, which prevented Amelia from fainting, looked at her with much tenderness, and cried, "I do not wonder, my dear madam, that you are affected with my mentioning that fatal masquerade; since I firmly believe the same ruin was intended for you at the same place; the apprehension of which occasioned the letter I sent you this morning, and all the trial of your patience which I have made since."

Amelia gave her a tender embrace, with many expressions of the warmest gratitude; assured her she had pretty well recovered her spirits, and begged her to continue her story, which Mrs. Bennet then did. However, as our readers may likewise be glad to recover their spirits also, we shall here put an end to this chapter.

CHAPTER VII

The story further continued.

MRS. BENNET proceeded thus:

"I was at length prevailed on to accompany Mrs. Ellison to the masquerade. Here, I must confess, the pleasantness of the place, the variety of the dresses, and the novelty of the thing, gave me much delight, and raised my fancy to the highest pitch. As I was entirely void of all suspicion, my mind threw off all reserve, and pleasure only filled my thoughts. Innocence, it is true, possessed my heart; but it was innocence unguarded, intoxicated with foolish desires, and liable to every temptation. During the first two hours we had many trifling adventures not worth remembering. At length my lord joined us, and continued with me all the evening; and we danced several dances together.

"I need not, I believe, tell you, madam, how engaging his conversation is. I wish I could with truth say I was not pleased with it; or, at least, that I had a right to be pleased with it. But I will disguise nothing from you. I now began to discover that he had some affection for me, but he had already too firm a footing in my esteem to make the discovery shocking. I will—I will own the truth; I was delighted with perceiving a passion in him, which I was not unwilling to think he had had from the beginning, and to derive his having concealed it so long from his awe of my virtue, and his respect to my understanding. I assure you, madam, at the same time, my intentions were never to exceed the bounds of innocence. I was charmed with the delicacy of his passion; and, in the foolish thoughtless turn of mind in which I then was, I fancied I might give some very distant encouragement to such a passion in such a man with the utmost safety— that I might indulge my vanity and interest at once, without being guilty of the least injury.

"I know Mrs. Booth will condemn all these thoughts, and I condemn them no less myself; for it is now my stedfast opinion that the woman who gives up the least outwork of her virtue doth, in that very moment, betray the citadel.

"About two o'clock we returned home, and found a very handsome collation provided for us. I was asked to partake of it, and I did not, I could not, refuse, I was not, however, entirely void of all suspicion, and I made many resolutions; one of which was, not to drink a drop more than my usual stint. This was, at the utmost, little more than half a pint of small punch.

"I adhered strictly to my quantity; but in the quality I am convinced I was deceived; for before I left the room I found my head giddy. What the villain gave me I know not; but, besides being intoxicated, I perceived effects from it which are not to be described.

"Here, madam, I must draw a curtain over the residue of that fatal night. Let it suffice that it involved me in the most dreadful ruin; a ruin to which I can truly say I never consented, and of which I was scarce conscious when the villanous man avowed it to my face in the morning.

"Thus I have deduced my story to the most horrid period; happy had I been had this been the period of my life, but I was reserved for greater miseries; but before I enter on them I will mention something very remarkable, with which I was now acquainted, and that will show there was nothing of accident which had befallen me, but that all was the effect of a long, regular, premeditated design.

"You may remember, madam, I told you that we were recommended to Mrs. Ellison by the woman at whose house we had before lodged. This woman, it seems, was one of my lord's pimps, and had before introduced me to his lordship's notice.

"You are to know then, madam, that this villain, this lord, now confessed to me that he had first seen me in the gallery at the oratorio, whither I had gone with tickets with which the woman where I first lodged had presented me, and which were, it seems, purchased by my lord. Here I first met the vile betrayer, who was disguised in a rug coat and a patch upon his face."

At these words Amelia cried, "O gracious heavens!" and fell back in her chair. Mrs. Bennet, with proper applications, brought her back to life; and then Amelia acquainted her that she herself had first seen the same person in the same place, and in the same disguise. "O, Mrs. Bennet!" cried she, "how am I indebted to you! what words, what thanks, what actions can demonstrate the gratitude of my sentiments! I look upon you, and always shall look upon you, as my preserver from the brink of a precipice, from which I was falling into the same ruin which you have so generously, so kindly, and so nobly disclosed for my sake."

Here the two ladies compared notes; and it appeared that his lordship's behaviour at the oratorio had been alike to both; that he had made use of the very same word, the very same actions to Amelia, which he had practised over before on poor unfortunate Mrs. Bennet. It may, perhaps, be thought strange that neither of them could afterwards recollect him; but so it was. And, indeed, if we consider the force of disguise, the very short time that either of them was with him at this first interview, and the very little curiosity that must have been supposed in the minds of the ladies, together with the amusement in which they were then engaged, all wonder will, I apprehend, cease. Amelia, how-ever, now declared she remembered his voice and features perfectly well, and was thoroughly satisfied he was the same person. She then accounted for his not having visited in the afternoon, according to his promise, from her declared resolutions to Mrs. Ellison not to see him. She now burst forth into some very satirical invectives against that lady, and declared she had the art, as well as the wickedness, of the devil himself.

Many congratulations now passed from Mrs. Bennet to Amelia, which were returned with the most hearty acknow-ledgments from that lady. But, instead of filling our paper with these, we shall pursue Mrs. Bennet's story, which she resumed as we shall find in the next chapter.

CHAPTER VIII

Further continuation.

"No sooner," said Mrs. Bennet, continuing her story, "was my lord departed, than Mrs. Ellison came to me. She behaved in such a manner, when she became acquainted with what had passed, that, though I was at first satisfied of her guilt, she began to stagger my opinion, and at length prevailed upon me entirely to acquit her. She raved like a mad woman against my lord, swore he should not stay a moment in her house, and that she would never speak to him more. In short, had she been the most innocent woman in the world she could not have spoke nor acted any otherwise, nor could she have vented more wrath and indignation against the betrayer.

"The part of her denunciation of vengeance which concerned my lord's leaving the house she vowed should be executed immediately, but then seeming to recollect herself, she said, 'Consider, my dear child, it is for your sake alone I speak; will not such a proceeding give some suspicion to your husband?' I answered, that I valued not that; that I was resolved to inform my husband of all the moment I saw him; with many expressions of detestation of myself and an indifference for life and for everything else.

"Mrs. Ellison, however, found means to soothe me, and to satisfy me with my own innocence, a point in which, I believe, we are all easily convinced. In short, I was persuaded to acquit both myself and her, to lay the whole guilt upon my lord, and to resolve to conceal it from my husband.

"That whole day I confined myself to my chamber and saw no other person but Mrs. Ellison. I was, indeed, ashamed to look any one in the face. Happily for me, my lord went into the country without attempting to come near me, for I believe his sight would have driven me to madness.

"The next day I told Mrs. Ellison that I was resolved to leave her lodgings the moment my lord came to town; not on her account (for I really inclined to think her innocent), but on my lord's, whose face I was resolved, if possible, never more to behold. She told me I had no reason to quit her house on that score, for that my lord himself had left her lodgings that morning in resentment, she believed, of the abuses which she had cast on him the day before.

"This confirmed me in the opinion of her innocence; nor hath she from that day to this, till my acquaintance with you, madam, done anything to forfeit my opinion. On the contrary, I owe her many good offices; amongst the rest, I have an annuity of one hundred and fifty pounds a year from my lord, which I know was owing to her solicitations, for she is not void of generosity or good-nature; though by what I have lately seen, I am convinced she was the cause of my ruin, and hath endeavoured to lay the same snares for you.

"But to return to my melancholy story. My husband returned at the appointed time; and I met him with an agitation of mind not to be described. Perhaps the fatigue which he had undergone in his journey, and his dissatisfaction at his ill success, prevented his taking notice of what I feared was too visible. All his hopes were entirely frustrated; the clergyman had not received the bishop's letter, and as to my lord's he treated it with derision and contempt. Tired as he was, Mr. Bennet would not sit down till he had inquired for my lord, intending to go and pay his compliments. Poor man! he little suspected that he had deceived him, as I have since known, concerning the bishop; much less did he suspect any other injury. But the lord—the villain was gone out of town, so that he was forced to postpone all his gratitude.

"Mr. Bennet returned to town late on the Saturday night, nevertheless he performed his duty at church the next day, but I rfeused to go with him. This, I think, was the first refusal I was guilty of since our marriage; but I was become so miserable, that his presence, which had been the source of all my happiness, was become my bane. I will not say I hated to see him, but I can say I was ashamed, indeed afraid to look him in the face. I was conscious of I knew not what ——guilt I hope it cannot be called."

"I hope not, nay, I think not," cries Amelia.

"My husband," continued Mrs. Bennet, "perceived my dissatisfaction, and imputed it to his ill-success in the country. I was pleased with this self-delusion, and yet, when I fairly compute the agonies I suffered at his endeavours to comfort me on that head, I paid most severely for it. O, my dear Mrs. Booth! happy is the deceived party between true lovers, and wretched indeed is the author of the deceit!

"In this wretched condition I passed a whole week, the most miserable I think of my whole life, endeavouring to humour my husband's delusion and to conceal my own tortures; but I had reason to fear I could not succeed long, for on the Saturday night I perceived a visible alteration in his behaviour to me. He went to bed in an apparent ill-humour, turned sullenly from me, and if I offered at any endearments he gave me only peevish answers.

"After a restless turbulent night, he rose early on Sunday morning and walked down-stairs. I expected his return to breakfast, but was soon informed by the maid that he was gone forth, and that it was no more than seven o'clock. All this you may believe, madam, alarmed me. I saw plainly he had discovered the fatal secret, though by what means I could not divine. The state of my mind was very little short of madness. Sometimes I thought of running away from my injured husband, and sometimes of putting an end to my life.

"In the midst of such perturbations I spent the day. My husband returned in the evening. O, Heavens! can I describe what followed?—It is impossible! I shall sink under the relation. He entered the room with a face as white as a sheet, his lips trembling and his eyes red as coals of fire starting as it were from his head. 'Molly,' cries he, throwing himself into his chair, 'are you well?' 'Good Heavens!' says I, 'what 's the matter?—Indeed I can't say I am well,' 'No!' says he, starting from his chair, 'false monster, you have betrayed me, destroyed me, you have ruined your husband!' Then looking like a fury, he snatched off a large book from the table, and, with the malice of a madman, threw it at my head and knocked me down backwards. He then caught me up in his arms and kissed me with most extravagant tenderness; then, looking me stedfastly in the face for several moments, the tears gushed in a torrent from his eyes, and with his utmost violence he threw me again on the floor, kicked me, stamped upon me. I believe, indeed, his intent was to kill me, and I believe he thought he had accomplished it.

"I lay on the ground for some minutes, I believe, deprived of my senses. When I recovered myself I found my husband lying by my side on his face, and the blood running from him. It seems, when he thought he had despatched me, he ran his head with all his force against a chest of drawers which stood in the room, and gave himself a dreadful wound in his head.

"I can truly say I felt not the least resentment for the usage I had received; I thought I deserved it all; though, indeed, I little guessed what he had suffered from me. I now used the most earnest entreaties to him to compose himself; and endeavoured, with my feeble arms, to raise him from the ground. At length he broke from me, and, springing from the ground, flung himself into a chair, when, looking wildly at me, he cried—'Go from me, Molly. I beseech you, leave me. I would not kill you.'—He then discovered to me —O Mrs. Booth! can you not guess it?—I was indeed polluted by the villain—I had infected my husband.—O heavens! why do I live to relate anything so horrid—I will not, I cannot yet survive it. I cannot forgive myself. Heaven cannot forgive me!"

Here she became inarticulate with the violence of her grief, and fell presently into such agonies, that the frighted Amelia began to call aloud for some assistance. Upon this a maid-servant came up, who, seeing her mistress in a violent convulsion fit, presently screamed out she was dead. Upon which one of the other sex made his appearance: and who should this be but the honest serjeant? whose countenance soon made it evident that, though a soldier, and a brave one too, he was not the least concerned of all the company on this occasion.

The reader, if he hath been acquainted with scenes of this kind, very well knows that Mrs. Bennet, in the usual time, returned again to the possession of her voice: the first use of which she made was to express her astonishment at the presence of the serjeant, and, with a frantic air, to inquire who he was.

The maid, concluding that her mistress was not yet returned to her senses, answered, "Why, 'tis my master, madam. Heaven preserve your senses, madam!—Lord, sir, my mistress must be very bad not to know you!"

What Atkinson thought at this instant, I will not say;

but certain it is he looked not over-wise. He attempted twice to take hold of Mrs. Bennet's hand, but she withdrew it hastily, and presently after, rising up from her chair, she declared herself pretty well again, and desired Atkinson and the maid to withdraw. Both of whom presently obeyed, the serjeant appearing by his countenance to want comfort almost as much as the lady did to whose assistance he had been summoned.

It is a good maxim to trust a person entirely or not at all; for a secret is often innocently blabbed out by those who know but half of it. Certain it is that the maid's speech communicated a suspicion to the mind of Amelia which the behaviour of the serjeant did not tend to remove: what that is, the sagacious readers may likewise probably suggest to themselves; if not, they must wait our time for disclosing it. We shall now resume the history of Mrs. Bennet, who, after many apologies, proceeded to the matters in the next chapter.

CHAPTER IX

The conclusion of Mrs. Bennet's history.

"WHEN I became sensible," cried Mrs. Bennet, "of the injury I had done my husband, I threw myself at his feet, and embracing his knees, while I bathed them with my tears, I begged a patient hearing, declaring, if he was not satisfied with what I should say, I would become a willing victim of his resentment. I said, and I said truly, that, if I owed my death that instant to his hands, I should have no other terror but of the fatal consequence which it might produce to himself.

"He seemed a little pacified, and bid me say whatever I pleased.

"I then gave him a faithful relation of all that had happened. He heard me with great attention, and at the conclusion cried, with a deep sigh—'O Molly! I believe it all.—You must have been betrayed as you tell me; you could not be guilty of such baseness, such cruelty, such ingratitude.' He then—Oh! it is impossible to describe his behaviour—he expressed such kindness, such tenderness, such concern for the manner in which he had used me—I cannot dwell on this scene—I shall relapse—you must excuse me."

Amelia begged her to omit anything which so affected her; and she proceeded thus:

"My husband, who was more convinced than I was of Mrs. Ellison's guilt, declared he would not sleep that night in her house. He then went out to see for a lodging; he gave me all the money he had, and left me to pay her bill, and put up the clothes, telling me, if I had not money enough, I might leave the clothes as a pledge; but he vowed he could not answer for himself if he saw the face of Mrs. Ellison.

"Words cannot scarce express the behaviour of that artful woman, it was so kind and so generous. She said, she did not blame my husband's resentment, nor could she expect any other, but that he and all the world should censure her —that she hated her house almost as much as we did, and detested her cousin, if possible, more. In fine, she said I might leave my clothes there that evening, but that she would send them to us the next morning; that she scorned the thought of detaining them; and as for the paltry debt, we might pay her whenever we pleased; for, to do her justice, with all her vices, she hath some good in her."

"Some good in her, indeed!" cried Amelia, with great indignation.

"We were scarce settled in our new lodgings," continued Mrs. Bennet, "when my husband began to complain of a pain in his inside. He told me he feared he had done himself some injury in his rage, and burst something within him. As to the odious—I cannot bear the thought, the great skill of his surgeon soon entirely cured him; but his other complaint, instead of yielding to any application, grew still worse and worse, nor ever ended till it brought him to his grave.

"O Mrs. Booth! could I have been certain that I had occasioned this, however innocently I had occasioned it, I could never have survived it; but the surgeon who opened him after his death assured me that he died of what they called a polypus in his heart, and that nothing which had happened on account of me was in the least the occasion of it.

"I have, however, related the affair truly to you. The first complaint I ever heard of the kind was within a day or two after we left Mrs. Ellison's; and this complaint remained till his death, which might induce him perhaps to attribute his death to another cause; but the surgeon, who is a man of the highest eminence, hath always declared the contrary to me, with the most positive certainty; and this opinion hath been my only comfort.

"When my husband died, which was about ten weeks after we quitted Mrs. Ellison's, of whom I had then a different opinion from what I have now, I was left in the most wretched condition imaginable. I believe, madam, she showed you my letter. Indeed, she did everything for me at that time which I could have expected from the best of friends. She supplied me with money from her own pocket, by which means I was preserved from a distress in which I must have otherwise inevitably perished.

"Her kindness to me in this season of distress prevailed on me to return again to her house. Why, indeed, should I have refused an offer so very convenient for me to accept, and which seemed so generous in her to make? Here I lived a very retired life with my little babe, seeing no company but Mrs. Ellison herself for a full quarter of a year. At last Mrs. Ellison brought me a parchment from my lord, in which he had settled upon me, at her instance, as she told me, and as I believe it was, an annuity of one hundred and fifty pounds a year. This was, I think, the very first time she had mentioned his hateful name to me since my return to her house. And she now prevailed upon me, though I assure you not without some difficulty, to suffer him to execute the deed in my presence.

"I will not describe our interview—I am not able to describe it, and I have often wondered how I found spirits to support it. This I will say for him, that, if he was not a real penitent, no man alive could act the part better.

"Beside resentment, I had another motive of my backwardness to agree to such a meeting; and this was—fear. I apprehended, and surely not without reason, that the annuity was rather meant as a bribe than a recompence, and that further designs were laid against my innocence; but in this I found myself happily deceived; for neither then, nor at any time since, have I ever had the least solicitation of that kind. Nor, indeed, have I seen the least occasion to think my lord had any such desires.

"Good heavens! what are these men? what is this appetite which must have novelty and resistance for its provocatives, and which is delighted with us no longer than while we may be considered in the light of enemies?"

"I thank you, madam," cries Amelia, "for relieving me from my fears on your account; I trembled at the consequence of this second acquaintance with such a man, and in such a situation."

"I assure you, madam, I was in no danger," returned Mrs. Bennet; "for, besides that I think I could have pretty well relied on my own resolution, I have heard since, at St. Edmundsbury, from an intimate acquaintance of my lord's, who was an entire stranger to my affairs, that the highest degree of inconstancy is his character; and that few of his numberless mistresses have ever received a second visit from him.

"Well, madam," continued she, "I think I have little

more to trouble you with; unless I should relate to you my long ill state of health, from which I am lately, I thank Heaven, recovered; or unless I should mention to you the most grievous accident that ever befell me, the loss of my poor dear Charley." Here she made a full stop, and the tears ran down into her bosom.

Amelia was silent a few minutes, while she gave the lady time to vent her passion; after which she began to pour forth a vast profusion of acknowledgments for the trouble she had taken in relating her history, but chiefly for the motive which had induced her to it, and for the kind warning which she had given her by the little note which Mrs. Bennet had sent her that morning.

"Yes, madam," cries Mrs. Bennet, "I am convinced, by what I have lately seen, that you are the destined sacrifice to this wicked lord; and that Mrs. Ellison, whom I no longer doubt to have been the instrument of my ruin, intended to betray you in the same manner. The day I met my lord in your apartment I began to entertain some suspicions, and I took Mrs. Ellison very roundly to task upon them; her behaviour, notwithstanding many asseverations to the contrary, convinced me I was right; and I intended, more than once, to speak to you, but could not; till last night the mention of the masquerade determined me to delay it no longer. I therefore sent you that note this morning, and am glad you so luckily discovered the writer, as it hath given me this opportunity of easing my mind, and of honestly showing you how unworthy I am of your friendship, at the same time that I so earnestly desire it."

CHAPTER X

Being the last chapter of the seventh book.

AMELIA did not fail to make proper compliments to Mrs. Bennet on the conclusion of her speech in the last chapter. She told her that, from the first moment of her acquaintance, she had the strongest inclination to her friendship, and that her desires of that kind were much increased by hearing her story. "Indeed, madam," says she, "you are much too severe a judge on yourself; for they must have very little candour, in my opinion, who look upon your case with any severe eye. To me, I assure you, you appear highly the object of compassion; and I shall always esteem you as an innocent and an unfortunate woman."

Amelia would then have taken her leave, but Mrs. Bennet so strongly pressed her to stay to breakfast, that at length she complied; indeed, she had fasted so long, and her gentle spirits had been so agitated with variety of passions, that nature very strongly seconded Mrs. Bennet's motion.

Whilst the maid was preparing the tea-equipage, Amelia, with a little slyness in her countenance, asked Mrs. Bennet if serjeant Atkinson did not lodge in the same house with her? The other reddened so extremely at the question, repeated the serjeant's name with such hesitation, and behaved so awkwardly, that Amelia wanted no further confirmation of her suspicions. She would not, however, declare them abruptly to the other, but began a dissertation on the serjeant's virtues; and, after observing the great concern which he had manifested when Mrs. Bennet was in her fit, concluded with saying she believed the serjeant would make the best husband in the world, for that he had great tenderness of heart and a gentleness of manners not often to be found in any man, and much seldomer in persons of his rank.

"And why not in his rank?" said Mrs. Bennet. "Indeed, Mrs. Booth, we rob the lower order of mankind of their due. I do not deny the force and power of education; but, when we consider how very injudicious is the education of the better sort in general, how little they are instructed in the practice of virtue, we shall not expect to find the heart much improved by it. And even as to the head, how very slightly do we commonly find it improved by what is called a genteel education! I have myself, I think, seen instances of as great goodness, and as great understanding too, among the lower sort of people as among the higher. Let us compare your serjeant, now, with the lord who hath been the subject of conversation; on which side would an impartial judge decide the balance to incline?"

"How monstrous then," cries Amelia, "is the opinion of those who consider our matching ourselves the least below us in degree as a kind of contamination!"

"A most absurd and preposterous sentiment," answered Mrs. Bennet warmly; "how abhorrent from justice, from common sense, and from humanity—but how extremely incongruous with a religion which professes to know no difference of degree, but ranks all mankind on the footing of brethren! Of all kinds of pride, there is none so unchristian as that of station; in reality, there is none so contemptible. Contempt, indeed, may be said to be its own object; for my own part, I know none so despicable as those who despise others."

"I do assure you," said Amelia, "you speak my own sentiments. I give you my word, I should not be ashamed of being the wife of an honest man in any station.—Nor if I had been much higher than I was, should I have thought myself degraded by calling our honest serjeant my husband."

"Since you have made this declaration," cries Mrs. Bennet, "I am sure you will not be offended at a secret I am going to mention to you."

"Indeed, my dear," answered Amelia, smiling, "I wonder rather you have concealed it so long; especially after the many hints I have given you."

"Nay, pardon me, madam," replied the other; "I do not remember any such hints; and, perhaps, you do not even guess what I am going to say. My secret is this; that no woman ever had so sincere, so passionate a lover, as you have had in the serjeant."

"I a lover in the serjeant!—I!" cries Amelia, a little surprised.

"Have patience," answered the other;—"I say, you, my dear. As much surprised as you appear, I tell you no more than the truth; and yet it is a truth you could hardly expect to hear from me, especially with so much good-humour; since I will honestly confess to you—But what need have I to confess what I know you guess already? Tell me now sincerely, don't you guess?"

"I guess, indeed, and hope," said she, "that he is your husband."

"He is, indeed, my husband," cried the other; "and I am most happy in your approbation. In honest truth, you ought to approve my choice; since you was every way the occasion of my making it. What you said of him very greatly recommended him to my opinion; but he endeared himself to me most by what he said of you. In short, I have discovered that he hath always loved you with such a faithful, honest, noble, generous passion, that I was consequently convinced his mind must possess all the ingredients of such a passion; and what are these but true honour, goodness, modesty, bravery, tenderness, and, in a word, every human virtue?—Forgive me, my dear; but I was uneasy till I became myself the object of such a passion."

"And do you really think," said Amelia, smiling, "that I shall forgive you robbing me of such a lover? or, supposing what you banter me with was true, do you really imagine you could change such a passion?"

"No, my dear," answered the other; "I only hope I have changed the object; for be assured, there is no greater vulgar error than that it is impossible for a man who loves one woman ever to love another. On the contrary, it is certain that a man who can love one woman so well at a distance will love another better that is nearer to him. Indeed, I have heard one of the best husbands in the world declare, in the presence of his wife, that he had always loved a princess with adoration. These passions, which reside only in very amorous and very delicate minds, feed only on the delicacies there growing; and leave all the substantial food, and enough of the delicacy too, for the wife."

The tea being now ready, Mrs. Bennet, or, if you please, for the future, Mrs. Atkinson, proposed to call in her husband; but Amelia objected. She said she should be glad to see him any other time, but was then in the utmost hurry, as she had been three hours absent from all she most loved. However, she had scarce drank a dish of tea before she changed her mind; and, saying she would not part man and wife, desired Mr. Atkinson might appear.

The maid answered that her master was not at home; which words she had scarce spoken, when he knocked hastily at the door, and immediately came running into the room, all pale and breathless, and, addressing himself to Amelia, cried out, "I am sorry, my dear lady, to bring you ill news; but Captain Booth"—"What! what!" cries Amelia, dropping the tea-cup from her hand, "is anything the matter with him?"—"Don't be frightened, my dear lady," said the serjeant: "he is in very good health; but a misfortune hath happened."—"Are my children well?" said Amelia.—"O, very well," answered the serjeant. "Pray, madam, don't be frightened; I hope it will signify nothing—he is arrested, but I hope to get him out of their damned hands immediately." "Where is he?" cries Amelia; "I will go to him this instant!" "He begs you will not," answered the serjeant. "I have sent his lawyer to him, and am going back with Mrs. Ellison this moment; but I beg your ladyship for his sake, and for your own sake, not to go." "Mrs. Ellison! what is Mrs. Ellison to do?" cries Amelia: "I must and will go." Mrs. Atkinson then interposed, and begged that she would not hurry her spirits, but compose herself, and go home to her children, whither she would attend her. She comforted her with the thoughts that the captain was in no immediate danger; that she could go to him when she would; and desired her to let the serjeant return with Mrs. Ellison, saying she might be of service, and that there was much wisdom, and no kind of shame, in making use of bad people on certain occasions.

"And who," cries Amelia, a little come to herself, "hath done this barbarous action?"

"One I am ashamed to name," cries the serjeant; "indeed I had always a very different opinion of him: I could not have believed anything but my own ears and eyes; but Dr. Harrison is the man who hath done the deed."

"Dr. Harrison!" cries Amelia. "Well, then, there is an end of all goodness in the world. I will never have a good opinion of any human being more."

The serjeant begged that he might not be detained from

the captain; and that, if Amelia pleased to go home, he would wait upon her. But she did not choose to see Mrs. Ellison at this time; and, after a little consideration, she resolved to stay where she was; and Mrs. Atkinson agreed to go and fetch her children to her, it being not many doors distant.

The serjeant then departed; Amelia, in her confusion, never having once thought of wishing him joy on his marriage.

BOOK VIII

CHAPTER I

Being the first chapter of the eighth book.

THE history must now look a little backwards to those circumstances which led to the catastrophe mentioned at the end of the last book.

When Amelia went out in the morning she left her children to the care of her husband. In this amiable office he had been engaged near an hour, and was at that very time lying along on the floor, and his little things crawling and playing about him, when a most violent knock was heard at the door; and immediately a footman, running upstairs, acquainted him that his lady was taken violently ill, and carried into Mrs. Chenevix's toy-shop.

Booth no sooner heard this account, which was delivered with great appearance of haste and earnestness, than he leaped suddenly from the floor, and, leaving his children, roaring at the news of their mother's illness, in strict charge with his maid, he ran as fast as his legs could carry him to the place; or towards the place rather: for, before he arrived at the shop, a gentleman stopped him full butt, crying, "Captain, whither so fast?"—Booth answered eagerly, "Whoever you are, friend, don't ask me any questions now."—"You must pardon me, captain," answered the gentleman; "but I have a little business with your honour—In short, captain, I have a small warrant here in my pocket against your honour, at the suit of one Dr. Harrison." "You are a bailiff then?" says Booth. "I am an officer, sir," answered the other. "Well, sir, it is in vain to contend," cries Booth; "but let me beg you will permit me only to step to Mrs. Chenevix's—I will attend you, upon my honour, wherever you please; but my wife lies violently ill there." "Oh, for that matter," answered the bailiff, "you may set your heart at ease. Your lady, I hope, is very well; I assure you she is not there. You will excuse me, captain, these are only stratagems of war. *Bolus and virtus, quis in a hostess*

equirit?" "Sir, I honour your learning," cried Booth,
"and could almost kiss you for what you tell me. I assure
you I would forgive you five hundred arrests for such a piece
of news. Well, sir, and whither am I to go with you?"
"O anywhere: where your honour pleases," cries the bailiff.
"Then suppose we go to Brown's coffee-house," said the
prisoner. "No," answered the bailiff, "that will not do;
that's in the verge of the court." "Why then, to the
nearest tavern," said Booth. "No, not to a tavern," cries
the other, "that is not a place of security; and you know,
captain, your honour is a shy cock; I have been after your
honour these three months. Come, sir, you must go to my
house, if you please." "With all my heart," answered
Booth, "if it be anywhere hereabouts." "Oh, it is but a
little way off," replied the bailiff; "it is only in Gray's-inn-
lane, just by almost." He then called a coach, and desired
his prisoner to walk in.

Booth entered the coach without any resistance, which,
had he been inclined to make, he must have plainly perceived would have been ineffectual, as the bailiff appeared
to have several followers at hand, two of whom, beside the
commander in chief, mounted with him into the coach.
As Booth was a sweet-tempered man, as well as somewhat
of a philosopher, he behaved with all the good-humour
imaginable, and indeed, with more than his companions;
who, however, showed him what they call civility, that is,
they neither struck him nor spit in his face.

Notwithstanding the pleasantry which Booth endeavoured
to preserve, he in reality envied every labourer whom he saw
pass by him in his way. The charms of liberty, against his
will, rushed on his mind; and he could not avoid suggesting
to himself how much more happy was the poorest wretch
who, without control, could repair to his homely habitation
and to his family, compared to him, who was thus violently,
and yet lawfully, torn away from the company of his wife
and children. And their condition, especially that of his
Amelia, gave his heart many a severe and bitter pang.

At length he arrived at the bailiff's mansion, and was
ushered into a room in which were several persons. Booth
desired to be alone; upon which the bailiff waited on him
up-stairs into an apartment, the windows of which were well
fortified with iron bars, but the walls had not the least out-

work raised before them; they were, indeed, what is generally called naked; the bricks having been only covered with a thin plaster, which in many places was mouldered away.

The first demand made upon Booth was for coach-hire, which amounted to two shillings, according to the bailiff's account; that being just double the legal fare. He was then asked if he did not choose a bowl of punch? to which he having answered in the negative, the bailiff replied, "Nay, sir, just as you please. I don't ask you to drink, if you don't choose it; but certainly you know the custom; the house is full of prisoners, and I can't afford gentlemen a room to themselves for nothing."

Booth presently took this hint—indeed it was a pretty broad one—and told the bailiff he should not scruple to pay him his price; but in fact he never drank unless at his meals. "As to that, sir," cries the bailiff, "it is just as your honour pleases. I scorn to impose upon any gentleman in misfortunes: I wish you well out of them, for my part. Your honour can take nothing amiss of me; I only does my duty, what I am bound to do; and, as you say you don't care to drink anything, what will you be pleased to have for dinner?"

Booth then complied in bespeaking a dish of meat, and told the bailiff he would drink a bottle with him after dinner. He then desired the favour of pen, ink, and paper, and a messenger; all which were immediately procured him, the bailiff telling him he might send wherever he pleased, and repeating his concern for Booth's misfortunes, and a hearty desire to see the end of them.

The messenger was just dispatched with the letter, when who should arrive but honest Atkinson? A soldier of the guards, belonging to the same company with the serjeant, and who had known Booth at Gibraltar, had seen the arrest, and heard the orders given to the coachman. This fellow, accidentally meeting Atkinson, had acquainted him with the whole affair.

At the appearance of Atkinson, joy immediately overspread the countenance of Booth. The ceremonials which passed between them are unnecessary to be repeated. Atkinson was soon dispatched to the attorney and to Mrs. Ellison, as the reader hath before heard from his own mouth.

Booth now greatly lamented that he had writ to his wife. He thought she might have been acquainted with the affair better by the serjeant. Booth begged him, however, to do everything in his power to comfort her; to assure her that he was in perfect health and good spirits; and to lessen as much as possible the concern which he knew she would have at the reading his letter.

The serjeant, however, as the reader hath seen, brought himself the first account of the arrest. Indeed, the other messenger did not arrive till a full hour afterwards. This was not owing to any slowness of his, but to many previous errands which he was to execute before the delivery of the letter; for, notwithstanding the earnest desire which the bailiff had declared to see Booth out of his troubles, he had ordered the porter, who was his follower, to call upon two or three other bailiffs, and as many attorneys, to try to load his prisoner with as many actions as possible.

Here the reader may be apt to conclude that the bailiff, instead of being a friend, was really an enemy to poor Booth; but, in fact, he was not so. His desire was no more than to accumulate bail-bonds; for the bailiff was reckoned an honest and good sort of man in his way, and had no more malice against the bodies in his custody than a butcher hath to those in his: and as the latter, when he takes his knife in hand, hath no idea but of the joints into which he is to cut the carcase; so the former, when he handles his writ, hath no other design but to cut out the body into as many bail-bonds as possible. As to the life of the animal, or the liberty of the man, they are thoughts which never obtrude themselves on either.

CHAPTER II

Containing an account of Mr. Booth's fellow-sufferers.

BEFORE we return to Amelia we must detain our reader a little longer with Mr. Booth, in the custody of Mr. Bondum the bailiff, who now informed his prisoner that he was welcome to the liberty of the house with the other gentlemen.

Booth asked who those gentlemen were. "One of them sir," says Mr. Bondum, "is a very great writer or author, as they call him; he hath been here these five weeks at the suit of a bookseller for eleven pound odd money; but he expects to be discharged in a day or two, for he hath writ out the debt. He is now writing for five or six booksellers, and he will get you sometimes, when he sits to it, a matter of fifteen shillings a day. For he is a very good pen, they say, but is apt to be idle. Some days he won't write above five hours; but at other times I have know him at it above sixteen." "Ay!" cries Booth; "pray, what are his productions? What does he write?" "Why, sometimes," answered Bondum, "he writes your history books for your numbers, and sometimes your verses, your poems, what do you call them? and then again he writes news for your newspapers." "Ay, indeed! he is a most extraordinary man, truly!—How doth he get his news here?" "Why he makes it, as he doth your parliament speeches for your magazines. He reads them to us sometimes over a bowl of punch. To be sure it is all one as if one was in the parliament-house—it is about liberty and freedom, and about the constitution of England. I say nothing for my part, for I will keep my neck out of a halter; but, faith, he makes it out plainly to me that all matters are not as they should be. I am all for liberty, for my part." "Is that so consistent with your calling?" cries Booth. "I thought, my friend, you had lived by depriving men of their liberty." "That's another matter," cries the bailiff; "that's all according to law, and in the way of business. To be sure, men must be obliged to pay their debts, or else there would be an end of everything." Booth desired the bailiff to give him his opinion on liberty. Upon which, he hesitated a moment, and then cried out, "Oh, 'tis a fine thing, 'tis a very fine thing, and the constitution of England." Booth told him, that by the old constitution of England he had heard that men could not be arrested for debt; to which the bailiff answered, that must have been in very bad times; "because as why," says he, "would it not be the hardest thing in the world if a man could not arrest another for a just and lawful debt? besides, sir, you must be mistaken; for how could that ever be? is not liberty the constitution of England? well, and is not the constitution, as a man may say—whereby the constitution, that is the law and liberty, and all that——"

Booth had a little mercy upon the poor bailiff, when he found him rounding in this manner, and told him he had made the matter very clear. Booth then proceeded to inquire after the other gentlemen, his fellows in affliction; upon which Bondum acquainted him that one of the prisoners was a poor fellow. "He calls himself a gentleman," said Bondum; "but I am sure I never saw anything genteel by him. In a week that he hath been in my house he hath drank only part of one bottle of wine. I intend to carry him to Newgate within a day or two, if he can't find bail, which, I suppose, he will not be able to do; for everybody says he is an undone man. He hath run out all he hath by losses in business, and one way or other; and he hath a wife and seven children. Here was the whole family here the other day, all howling together. I never saw such a beggarly crew; I was almost ashamed to see them in my house. I thought they seemed fitter for Bridewell than any other place. To be sure, I do not reckon him as proper company for such as you, sir; but there is another prisoner in the house that I dare say you will like very much. He is, indeed, very much of a gentleman, and spends his money like one. I have had him only three days, and I am afraid he won't stay much longer. They say, indeed, he is a gamester; but what is that to me or any one, as long as a man appears as a gentleman? I always love to speak by people as I find; and, in my opinion, he is fit company for the greatest lord in the land; for he hath very good clothes, and money enough. He is not here for debt, but upon a judge's warrant for an assault and battery; for the tipstaff locks up here."

The bailiff was thus haranguing when he was interrupted by the arrival of the attorney whom the trusty serjeant had, with the utmost expedition, found out and dispatched to the relief of his distressed friend. But before we proceed any further with the captain we will return to poor Amelia, for whom, considering the situation in which we left her, the good-natured reader may be, perhaps, in no small degree solicitous.

CHAPTER III

Containing some extraordinary behaviour in Mrs. Ellison.

THE serjeant being departed to convey Mrs. Ellison to the captain, his wife went to fetch Amelia's children to their mother.

Amelia's concern for the distresses of her husband was aggravated at the sight of her children. "Good Heavens!" she cried, "what will—what can become of these poor little wretches? why have I produced these little creatures only to give them a share of poverty and misery?" At which words she embraced them eagerly in her arms, and bedewed them both with her tears.

The children's eyes soon overflowed as fast as their mother's, though neither of them knew the cause of her affliction. The little boy, who was the elder and much the sharper of the two, imputed the agonies of his mother to her illness, according to the account brought to his father in his presence.

When Amelia became acquainted with the child's apprehensions, she soon satisfied him that she was in a perfect state of health; at which the little thing expressed great satisfaction, and said he was glad she was well again. Amelia told him she had not been in the least disordered. Upon which the innocent cried out, "La! how can people tell such fibs? a great tall man told my papa you was taken very ill at Mrs. Somebody's shop, and my poor papa presently ran down-stairs: I was afraid he would have broke his neck, to come to you."

"Oh, the villains!" cries Mrs. Atkinson, "what a stratagem was here to take away your husband!"

"Take away!" answered the child—"What! hath anybody taken away papa?—Sure that naughty fibbing man hath not taken away papa?"

Amelia begged Mrs. Atkinson to say something to her children, for that her spirits were overpowered. She then threw herself into a chair, and gave a full vent to a passion almost too strong for her delicate constitution.

The scene that followed, during some minutes, is beyond my power of description; I must beg the readers' hearts to suggest it to themselves. The children hung on their mother, whom they endeavoured in vain to comfort, as Mrs. Atkinson did in vain attempt to pacify them, telling them all would be well, and they would soon see their papa again.

At length, partly by the persuasions of Mrs. Atkinson, partly from consideration of her little ones, and more, perhaps, from the relief which she had acquired by her tears, Amelia became a little composed.

Nothing worth notice passed in this miserable company from this time till the return of Mrs. Ellison from the bailiff's house; and to draw out scenes of wretchedness to too great a length is a task very uneasy to the writer, and for which none but readers of a most gloomy complexion will think themselves ever obliged to his labours.

At length Mrs. Ellison arrived, and entered the room with an air of gaiety rather misbecoming the occasion. When she had seated herself in a chair she told Amelia that the captain was very well and in good spirits, and that he earnestly desired her to keep up hers. "Come, madam," said she, "don't be disconsolate; I hope we shall soon be able to get him out of his troubles. The debts, indeed, amount to more than I expected; however, ways may be found to redeem him. He must own himself guilty of some rashness in going out of the verge, when he knew to what he was liable; but that is now not to be remedied. If he had followed my advice this had not happened; but men will be headstrong."

"I cannot bear this," cries Amelia; "shall I hear that best of creatures blamed for his tenderness to me?"

"Well, I will not blame him," answered Mrs. Ellison; "I am sure I propose nothing but to serve him; and if you will do as much to serve him yourself, he will not be long a prisoner."

"I do!" cries Amelia: "O Heavens! is there a thing upon earth——"

"Yes, there is a thing upon earth," said Mrs. Ellison, "and a very easy thing too; and yet I will venture my life you start when I propose it. And yet, when I consider

that you are a woman of understanding, I know not why
I should think so; for sure you must have too much good
sense to imagine that you can cry your husband out of prison.
If this would have done, I see you have almost cried your
eyes out already. And yet you may do the business by a
much pleasanter way than by crying and bawling."

"What do you mean, madam?" cries Amelia.—"For my
part, I cannot guess your meaning."

"Before I tell you then, madam," answered Mrs. Ellison,
"I must inform you, if you do not already know it, that
the captain is charged with actions to the amount of near
five hundred pounds. I am sure I would willingly be his
bail; but I know my bail would not be taken for that sum.
You must consider, therefore, madam, what chance you have
of redeeming him; unless you choose, as perhaps some wives
would, that he should lie all his life in prison."

At these words Amelia discharged a shower of tears, and
gave every mark of the most frantic grief.

"Why, there now," cries Mrs. Ellison, "while you will
indulge these extravagant passions, how can you be capable
of listening to the voice of reason? I know I am a fool in
concerning myself thus with the affairs of others. I know
the thankless office I undertake; and yet I love you so, my
dear Mrs. Booth, that I cannot bear to see you afflicted, and
I would comfort you if you would suffer me. Let me beg
you to make your mind easy; and within these two days I
will engage to set your husband at liberty.

"Harkee, child; only behave like a woman of spirit this
evening, and keep your appointment, notwithstanding what
hath happened; and I am convinced there is one who hath
the power and the will to serve you."

Mrs. Ellison spoke the latter part of her speech in a whisper
so that Mrs. Atkinson, who was then engaged with the
children, might not hear her; but Amelia answered aloud,
and said, "What appointment would you have me keep this
evening?"

"Nay, nay, if you have forgot," cries Mrs. Ellison, "I
will tell you more another time; but come, will you go
home? my dinner is ready by this time, and you shall dine
with me."

"Talk not to me of dinners," cries Amelia; "my stomach
is too full already."

"Nay, but, dear madam," answered Mrs. Ellison, "let me beseech you to go home with me. I do not care," says she, whispering, "to speak before some folks."

"I have no secret, madam, in the world," replied Amelia aloud, "which I would not communicate to this lady; for I shall always acknowledge the highest obligations to her for the secrets she hath imparted to me."

"Madam," said Mrs. Ellison, "I do not interfere with obligations. I am glad the lady hath obliged you so much; and I wish all people were equally mindful of obligations. I hope I have omitted no opportunity of endeavouring to oblige Mrs. Booth, as well as I have some other folks."

"If by other folks, madam, you mean me," cries Mrs. Atkinson, "I confess I sincerely believe you intended the same obligation to us both; and I have the pleasure to think it is owing to me that this lady is not as much obliged to you as I am."

"I protest, madam, I can hardly guess your meaning," said Mrs. Ellison.—"Do you really intend to affront me, madam?"

"I intend to preserve innocence and virtue, if it be in my power, madam," answered the other. "And sure nothing but the most eager resolution to destroy it could induce you to mention such an appointment at such a time."

"I did not expect this treatment from you, madam," cries Mrs. Ellison; "such ingratitude I could not have believed had it been reported to me by any other."

"Such impudence," answered Mrs. Atkinson, "must exceed, I think, all belief; but, when women once abandon that modesty which is the characteristic of their sex, they seldom set any bounds to their assurance."

"I could not have believed this to have been in human nature," cries Mrs. Ellison. "Is this the woman whom I have fed, have clothed, have supported; who owes to my charity and my intercessions that she is not at this day destitute of all the necessaries of life?"

"I own it all," answered Mrs. Atkinson; "and I add the favour of a masquerade ticket to the number. Could I have thought, madam, that you would before my face have asked another lady to go to the same place with the same man?—but I ask your pardon; I impute rather more assurance to you than you are mistress of.—You have endeavoured to keep the assignation a secret from me; and it was by mere accident only that I discovered it; unless there are some guardian angels that in general protect innocence and virtue; though I may say, I have not always found them so watchful."

"Indeed, madam," said Mrs. Ellison, "you are not worth my answer; nor will I stay a moment longer with such a person.—So, Mrs. Booth, you have your choice, madam, whether you will go with me, or remain in the company of this lady."

"If so, madam," answered Mrs. Booth, "I shall not be long in determining to stay where I am."

Mrs. Ellison then, casting a look of great indignation at both the ladies, made a short speech full of invectives against Mrs. Atkinson, and not without oblique hints of ingratitude against poor Amelia; after which she burst out of the room, and out of the house, and made haste to her own home, in a condition of mind to which fortune without guilt cannot, I believe, reduce any one.

Indeed, how much the superiority of misery is on the side of wickedness may appear to every reader who will compare the present situation of Amelia with that of Mrs. Ellison. Fortune had attacked the former with almost the highest degree of her malice. She was involved in a scene of most exquisite distress, and her husband, her principal comfort, torn violently from her arms; yet her sorrow, however exquisite, was all soft and tender, nor was she without many consolations. Her case, however hard, was not absolutely desperate; for scarce any condition of fortune can be so. Art and industry, chance and friends, have often relieved the most distressed circumstances, and converted them into opulence. In all these she had hopes on this side the grave, and perfect virtue and innocence gave her the strongest assurances on the other. Whereas, in the bosom of Mrs. Ellison, all was storm and tempest; anger, revenge, fear, and pride, like so many raging furies, possessed her mind, and tortured her with disappointment and shame. Loss of reputation, which is generally irreparable, was to be her lot; loss of friends is of this the certain consequence; all on this side the grave appeared dreary and comfortless; and endless misery on the other, closed the gloomy prospect.

Hence, my worthy reader, console thyself, that however few of the other good things of life are thy lot, the best of all things, which is innocence, is always within thy own power; and, though Fortune may make thee often unhappy, she can never make thee completely and irreparably miserable without thy own consent.

CHAPTER IV

Containing, among many matters, the exemplary behaviour of Colonel James.

WHEN Mrs. Ellison was departed, Mrs. Atkinson began to apply all her art to soothe and comfort Amelia, but was presently prevented by her. "I am ashamed, dear madam," said Amelia, "of having indulged my affliction so much at your expense. The suddenness of the occasion is my only excuse; for, had I had time to summon my resolution to my assistance, I hope I am mistress of more patience than you have hitherto seen me exert. I know, madam, in my unwarrantable excesses, I have been guilty of many transgressions. First, against that Divine will and pleasure without whose permission, at least, no human accident can happen; in the next place, madam, if anything can aggravate such a fault, I have transgressed the laws of friendship as well as decency, in throwing upon you some part of the load of my grief; and again, I have sinned against common sense, which should teach me, instead of weakly and heavily lamenting my misfortunes, to rouse all my spirits to remove them. In this light I am shocked at my own folly, and am resolved to leave my children under your care, and go directly to my husband. I may comfort him. I may assist him. I may relieve him. There is nothing now too difficult for me to undertake."

Mrs. Atkinson greatly approved and complimented her friend on all the former part of her speech, except what related to her self, on which she spoke very civilly, and I believe with great truth; but as to her determination of going to her husband she endeavoured to dissuade her, at least she begged her to defer it for the present, and till the serjeant returned home. She then reminded Amelia that it was now past five in the afternoon, and that she had not taken any refreshment but a dish of tea the whole day, and desired she would give her leave to procure her a chick, or anything she liked better, for her dinner.

Amelia thanked her friend, and said she would sit down with her to whatever she pleased; "but if I do not eat," said she, "I would not have you impute it to anything but want of appetite; for I assure you all things are equally indifferent to me. I am more solicitous about these poor little things, who have not been used to fast so long. Heaven knows what may hereafter be their fate!"

Mrs. Atkinson bid her hope the best, and then recommended the children to the care of her maid.

And now arrived a servant from Mrs. James, with an invitation to Captain Booth and to his lady to dine with the colonel the day after the next. This a little perplexed Amelia; but after a short consideration she despatched an answer to Mrs. James, in which she concisely informed her of what had happened.

The honest serjeant, who had been on his legs almost the whole day, now returned, and brought Amelia a short letter from her husband, in which he gave her the most solemn assurances of his health and spirits, and begged her with great earnestness to take care to preserve her own, which if she did, he said, he had no doubt but that they should shortly be happy. He added something of hopes from my lord, with which Mrs. Ellison had amused him, and which served only to destroy the comfort that Amelia received from the rest of his letter.

Whilst Amelia, the serjeant, and his lady, were engaged in a cold collation, for which purpose a cold chicken was procured from the tavern for the ladies, and two pound of cold beef for the serjeant, a violent knocking was heard at the door, and presently afterwards Colonel James entered the room. After proper compliments had passed, the colonel told Amelia that her letter was brought to Mrs. James while they were at table, and that on her showing it him he had immediately rose up, made an apology to his company, and took a chair to her. He spoke to her with great tenderness on the occasion, and desired her to make herself easy; assuring her that he would leave nothing in his power undone to serve her husband. He then gave her an invitation, in his wife's name, to his own house, in the most pressing manner.

Amelia returned him very hearty thanks for all his kind offers, but begged to decline that of an apartment in his house. She said, as she could not leave her children, so neither could she think of bringing such a trouble with her into his family; and, though the colonel gave her many assurances that her children, as well as herself, would be very welcome to Mrs. James, and even betook himself to entreaties, she still persisted obstinately in her refusal.

In real truth, Amelia had taken a vast affection for Mrs. Atkinson, of the comfort of whose company she could not bear to be deprived in her distress, nor to exchange it for that of Mrs. James, to whom she had lately conceived no little dislike.

The colonel, when he found he could not prevail with Amelia to accept his invitation, desisted from any further solicitations. He then took a bank-bill of fifty pounds from his pocket-book, and said, "You will pardon me, dear madam, if I choose to impute your refusal of my house rather to a dislike of my wife, who I will not pretend to be the most agreeable of women (all men," said he, sighing, "have not Captain Booth's fortune), than to any aversion or anger to me. I must insist upon it, therefore, to make your present habitation as easy to you as possible—I hope, madam, you will not deny me this happiness; I beg you will honour me with the acceptance of this trifle." He then put the note into her hand, and declared that the honour of touching it was worth a hundred times that sum.

"I protest, Colonel James," cried Amelia, blushing, "I know not what to do or say, your goodness so greatly confounds me. Can I, who am so well acquainted with the many great obligations Mr. Booth already hath to your generosity, consent that you should add more to a debt we can never pay?"

The colonel stopped her short, protesting that she misplaced the obligation; for, that if to confer the highest happiness was to oblige, he was obliged to her acceptance. "And I do assure you, madam," said he, "if this trifling sum or a much larger can contribute to your ease, I shall consider myself as the happiest man upon earth in being able to supply it, and you, madam, my greatest benefactor in receiving it."

Amelia then put the note in her pocket, and they entered into a conversation in which many civil things were said on both sides; but what was chiefly worth remark was, that Amelia had almost her husband constantly in her mouth, and the colonel never mentioned him: the former seemed desirous to lay all obligations, as much as possible, to the account of her husband; and the latter endeavoured, with the utmost delicacy, to insinuate that her happiness was the main and indeed the only point which he had in view.

Amelia had made no doubt, at the colonel's first appearance, but that he intended to go directly to her husband. When he dropped therefore a hint of his intention to visit him next morning, she appeared visibly shocked at the delay. The colonel, perceiving this, said, "However inconvenient it may be, yet, madam, if it will oblige you, or if you desire it, I will even go to-night." Amelia answered, "My husband will be far from desiring to derive any good from your inconvenience; but, if you put it to me, I must be excused for saying I desire nothing more in the world than to send him so great a comfort as I know he will receive from the presence of such a friend." "Then, to show you, madam," cries the colonel, "that I desire nothing more in the world than to give you pleasure, I will go to him immediately."

Amelia then bethought herself of the serjeant, and told the colonel his old acquaintance Atkinson, whom he had known at Gibraltar, was then in the house, and would conduct him to the place. The serjeant was immediately called in, paid his respects to the colonel, and was acknowledged by him. They both immediately set forward, Amelia to the utmost of her power pressing their departure.

Mrs. Atkinson now returned to Amelia, and was by her acquainted with the colonel's late generosity; for her heart so boiled over with gratitude that she could not conceal the ebullition. Amelia likewise gave her friend a full narrative of the colonel's former behaviour and friendship to her husband, as well abroad as in England; and ended with declaring that she believed him to be the most generous man upon earth.

Mrs. Atkinson agreed with Amelia's conclusion, and said she was glad to hear there was any such man. They then proceeded with the children to the tea-table, where panegyric, and not scandal, was the topic of their conversation; and of this panegyric the colonel was the subject; both the ladies seeming to vie with each other in celebrating the praises of his goodness.

CHAPTER V

Comments upon authors.

HAVING left Amelia in as comfortable a situation as could possibly be expected, her immediate distresses relieved, and her heart filled with great hopes from the friendship of the colonel, we will now return to Booth, who, when the attorney and serjeant had left him, received a visit from that great author of whom honourable mention is made in our second chapter.

Booth, as the reader may be pleased to remember, was a pretty good master of the classics; for his father, though he designed his son for the army, did not think it necessary to breed him up a blockhead. He did not, perhaps, imagine that a competent share of Latin and Greek would make his son either a pedant or a coward. He considered likewise, probably, that the life of a soldier is in general a life of idleness; and might think that the spare hours of an officer in country quarters would be as well employed with a book as in sauntering about the streets, loitering in a coffee-house, sotting in a tavern, or in laying schemes to debauch and ruin a set of harmless ignorant country girls.

As Booth was therefore what might well be called, in this age at least, a man of learning, he began to discourse our author on subjects of literature. "I think, sir," says he, "that Dr. Swift hath been generally allowed, by the critics in this kingdom, to be the greatest master of humour that ever wrote. Indeed, I allow him to have possessed most admirable talents of this kind; and, if Rabelais was his master, I think he proves the truth of the common Greek proverb— that the scholar is often superior to the master. As to Cervantes, I do not think we can make any just comparison; for, though Mr. Pope compliments him with sometimes taking Cervantes' serious air——" "I remember the passage," cries the author;

> "O thou, whatever title please thine ear,
> Dean, Drapier, Bickerstaff, or Gulliver;
> Whether you take Cervantes' serious air,
> Or laugh and shake in Rabelais' easy chair—"

"You are right, sir," said Booth; "but though I should agree that the doctor hath sometimes condescended to imitate Rabelais, I do not remember to have seen in his works the least attempt in the manner of Cervantes. But there is one in his own way, and whom I am convinced he studied above all others—you guess, I believe, I am going to name Lucian. This author, I say, I am convinced, he followed; but I think he followed him at a distance: as, to say the truth, every other writer of this kind hath done in my opinion; for none, I think, hath yet equalled him. I agree, indeed, entirely with Mr. Moyle, in his Discourse on the age of the Philopatris, when he gives him the epithet of the incomparable Lucian; and incomparable, I believe, he will remain as long as the language in which he wrote shall endure. What an inimitable piece of humour is his Cock!" "I remember it very well," cries the author; "his story of a Cock and a Bull is excellent." Booth stared at this, and asked the author what he meant by the Bull? "Nay," answered he, "I don't know very well, upon my soul. It is a long time since I read him. I learnt him all over at school; I have not read him much since. And pray, sir," said he, "how do you like his Pharsalia?" don't you think Mr. Rowe's translation a very fine one?" Booth replied, "I believe we are talking of different authors. The Pharsalia, which Mr. Rowe translated, was written by Lucan; but I have been speaking of Lucian, a Greek writer, and, in my opinion, the greatest in the humorous way that ever the world produced." "Ay!" cries the author, "he was indeed so, a very excellent writer indeed! I fancy a translation of him would sell very well!" "I do not know, indeed," cries Booth. "A good translation of him would be a valuable book. I have seen a wretched one published by Mr. Dryden, but translated by others, who in many places have misunderstood Lucian's meaning, and have nowhere preserved the spirit of the original." "That is great pity," says the author. "Pray, sir, is he well translated in the French?" Booth answered, he could not tell; but that he doubted it very much, having never seen a good version into that language out of the Greek. "To confess the truth, I believe," said he, "the French translators have generally consulted the Latin only; which, in some of the few Greek writers I have read, is intolerably bad. And as the English translators, for the most part, pursue the French, we may easily guess what spirit those copies of bad copies must preserve of the original."

"Egad, you are a shrewd guesser," cries the author. "I am glad the booksellers have not your sagacity. But how should it be otherwise, considering the price they pay by the sheet? The Greek, you will allow, is a hard language; and there are few gentlemen that write who can read it without a good lexicon. Now, sir, if we were to afford time to find out the true meaning of words, a gentleman would not get bread and cheese by his work. If one was to be paid, indeed, as Mr. Pope was for his Homer—Pray, sir, don't you think that the best translation in the world?"

"Indeed, sir," cries Booth, "I think, though it is certainly a noble paraphrase, and of itself a fine poem, yet in some places it is no translation at all. In the very beginning, for instance, he hath not rendered the true force of the author. Homer invokes his muse in the five first lines of the Iliad; and, at the end of the fifth, he gives his reason:

$$\text{Διὸς δ' ἐτελείετο Βουλή.}$$

For all these things," says he, "were brought about by the decree of Jupiter; and, therefore, he supposes their true sources are known only to the deities. Now, the translation takes no more notice of the ΔΕ than if no such word had been there."

"Very possibly," answered the author; "it is a long time since I read the original. Perhaps, then, he followed the translations. I observe, indeed, he talks much in the notes of Madam Dacier and Monsieur Eustathius."

Booth had now received conviction enough of his friend's knowledge of the Greek language; without attempting, therefore, to set him right, he made a sudden transition to the Latin. "Pray, sir," said he, "as you have mentioned Rowe's translation of the Pharsalia, do you remember how he hath rendered that passage in the character of Cato?

"————Venerisque huic maximus usus
Progenies ; urbi Pater est, urbique Maritus.

For I appprehend that passage is generally misunderstood."

"I really do not remember," answered the author. "Pray, sir, what do you take to be the meaning?"

"I apprehend, sir," replied Booth, "that by these words, *Urbi Pater est, urbique Maritus*, Cato is represented as the father and husband to the city of Rome."

"Very true, sir," cries the author; "very fine, indeed.— Not only the father of his country, but the husband too; very noble, truly!"

"Pardon me, sir," cries Booth; "I do not conceive that to have been Lucan's meaning. If you please to observe the context; Lucan, having commended the temperance of Cato in the instances of diet and clothes, proceeds to venereal pleasures; of which, says the poet, his principal use was pro- creation: then he adds, *Urbi Pater est, urbique Maritus;* that he became a father and a husband for the sake only of the city."

"Upon my word that 's true," cries the author; "I did not think of it. It is much finer than the other.—*Urbis Pater est*—what is the other?—ay—*Urbis Maritus.*—It is certainly as you say, sir."

Booth was by this pretty well satisfied of the author's profound learning; however, he was willing to try him a little further. He asked him, therefore, what was his opinion of Lucan in general, and in what class of writers he ranked him?

The author stared a little at this question; and, after some hesitation, answered, "Certainly, sir, I think he is a fine writer and a very great poet."

"I am very much of the same opinion," cries Booth; "but where do you class him—next to what poet do you place him?"

"Let me see," cries the author; "where do I class him? next to whom do I place him?—Ay!—why—why, pray, where do you yourself place him?"

"Why, surely," cries Booth, "if he is not to be placed in the first rank with Homer, and Virgil, and Milton, I think clearly he is at the head of the second, before either Statius or Silius Italicus—though I allow to each of these their merits; but, perhaps, an epic poem was beyond the genius of either. I own, I have often thought, if Statius had ventured no further than Ovid or Claudian, he would have succeeded better; for his Sylvæ are, in my opinion, much better than his Thebaïs."

"I believe I was of the same opinion formerly," said the author.

"And for what reason have you altered it?" cries Booth.

"I have not altered it," answered the author; "but, to tell you the truth, I have not any opinion at all about these matters at present. I do not trouble my head much with poetry; for there is no encouragement to such studies in this age. It is true, indeed, I have now and then wrote a poem or two for the magazines, but I never intend to write any more; for a gentleman is not paid for his time. A sheet is a sheet with the booksellers; and, whether it be in prose or verse, they make no difference; though certainly there is as much difference to a gentleman in the work as there is to a taylor between making a plain and a laced suit. Rhimes are difficult things; they are stubborn things, sir. I have been sometimes longer in tagging a couplet than I have been in writing a speech on the side of the opposition which hath been read with great applause all over the kingdom."

"I am glad you are pleased to confirm that," cries Booth; "for I protest it was an entire secret to me till this day. I was so perfectly ignorant, that I thought the speeches published in the magazines were really made by the members themselves."

"Some of them, and I believe I may, without vanity, say the best," cries the author, "are all the productions of my own pen! but I believe I shall leave it off soon, unless a sheet of speech will fetch more than it does at present. In truth, the romance-writing is the only branch of our business now that is worth following. Goods of that sort have had so much success lately in the market, that a bookseller scarce cares what he bids for them. And it is certainly the easiest work in the world; you may write it almost as fast as you can set pen to paper; and if you interlard it with a little scandal, a little abuse on some living characters of note, you cannot fail of success."

"Upon my word, sir," cries Booth, "you have greatly instructed me. I could not have imagined there had been so much regularity in the trade of writing as you are pleased to mention; by what I can perceive, the pen and ink is likely to become the staple commodity of the kingdom."

"Alas! sir," answered the author, "it is overstocked. The market is overstocked. There is no encouragement to merit, no patrons. I have been these five years soliciting a subscription for my new translation of Ovid's Metamorphoses, with notes explanatory, historical, and critical; and I have scarce collected five hundred names yet."

The mention of this translation a little surprised Booth; not only as the author had just declared his intentions to forsake the tuneful muses; but, for some other reasons which he had collected from his conversation with our author, he little expected to hear of a proposal to translate any of the Latin poets. He proceeded, therefore, to catechise him a little further; and by his answers was fully satisfied that he had the very same acquaintance with Ovid that he had appeared to have with Lucan.

The author then pulled out a bundle of papers containing proposals for his subscription, and receipts; and, addressing himself to Booth, said, "Though the place in which we meet, sir, is an improper place to solicit favours of this kind, yet, perhaps, it may be in your power to serve me if you will charge your pockets with some of these." Booth was just offering an excuse, when the bailiff introduced Colonel James and the serjeant.

The unexpected visit of a beloved friend to a man in affliction, especially in Mr. Booth's situation, is a comfort which can scarce be equalled; not barely from the hopes of relief or redress by his assistance, but as it is an evidence of sincere friendship which scarce admits of any doubt or suspicion. Such an instance doth indeed make a man amends for all ordinary troubles and distresses; and we ought to think ourselves gainers by having had such an opportunity of discovering that we are possessed of one of the most valuable of all human possessions.

Booth was so transported at the sight of the colonel, that he dropped the proposals which the author had put into his hands, and burst forth into the highest professions of gratitude to his friend; who behaved very properly on his side, and said everything which became the mouth of a friend on the occasion.

It is true, indeed, he seemed not moved equally either with Booth or the serjeant, both whose eyes watered at the scene. In truth, the colonel, though a very generous man, had not the least grain of tenderness in his disposition. His mind was formed of those firm materials of which nature formerly hammered out the Stoic, and upon which the sorrows of no man living could make an impression. A man of this temper, who doth not much value danger, will fight for the person he calls his friend, and the man that hath but little value for his money will give it him; but such friendship is never to be absolutely depended on; for, whenever the favourite passion interposes with it, it is sure to subside and vanish into air. Whereas the man whose tender disposition really feels the miseries of another will endeavour to relieve them for his own sake; and, in such a mind, friendship will often get the superiority over every other passion.

But, from whatever motive it sprung, the colonel's behaviour to Booth seemed truly amiable; and so it appeared to the author, who took the first occasion to applaud it in a very florid oration; which the reader, when he recollects that he was a speech-maker by profession, will not be surprised at; nor, perhaps, will be much more surprised that he soon after took an occasion of clapping a proposal into the colonel's hands, holding at the same time a receipt very visible in his own.

The colonel received both, and gave the author a guinea in exchange, which was double the sum mentioned in the receipt; for which the author made a low bow, and very politely took his leave, saying, "I suppose, gentlemen, you may have some private business together; I heartily wish a speedy end to your confinement, and I congratulate you on the possessing so great, so noble, and so generous a friend."

CHAPTER VI

Which inclines rather to satire than panegyric.

THE colonel had the curiosity to ask Booth the name of the gentleman who, in the vulgar language, had struck, or taken him in for a guinea with so much ease and dexterity. Booth answered, he did not know his name; all that he knew of him was, that he was the most impudent and illiterate fellow he had ever seen, and that, by his own account, he was the author of most of the wonderful productions of the age. "Perhaps," said he, "it may look uncharitable in me to blame you for your generosity; but I am convinced the fellow hath not the least merit or capacity, and you have subscribed to the most horrid trash that ever was published."

"I care not a farthing what he publishes," cries the colonel. "Heaven forbid I should be obliged to read half the nonsense I have subscribed to."

"But don't you think," said Booth, "that by such indis-criminate encouragement of authors you do a real mischief to the society? By propagating the subscriptions of such fellows, people are tired out and withhold their contributions to men of real merit; and, at the same time, you are con-tributing to fill the world, not only with nonsense, but with all the scurrility, indecency, and profaneness with which the age abounds, and with which all bad writers supply the defect of genius."

"Pugh!" cries the colonel, "I never consider these matters. Good or bad, it is all one to me; but there's an acquaintance of mine, and a man of great wit too, that thinks the worst the best, as they are the surest to make him laugh."

"I ask pardon, sir," says the serjeant; "but I wish your honour would consider your own affairs a little, for it grows late in the evening."

"The serjeant says true," answered the colonel. "What is it you intend to do?"

"Faith, colonel, I know not what I shall do. My affairs seem so irreparable, that I have been driving them as much as possibly I could from my mind. If I was to suffer alone, I think I could bear them with some philosophy; but when I consider who are to be the sharers in my fortune—the dearest of children, and the best, the worthiest and the noblest of women—— Pardon me, my dear friend, these sensations are above me; they convert me into a woman; they drive me to despair, to madness."

The colonel advised him to command himself, and told him this was not the way to retrieve his fortune. "As to me, my dear Booth," said he, "you know you may command me as far as is really within my power."

Booth answered eagerly, that he was so far from expecting any more favours from the colonel, that he had resolved not to let him know anything of his misfortune. "No, my dear friend," cries he, "I am too much obliged to you already"; and then burst into many fervent expressions of gratitude, till the colonel himself stopped him, and begged him to give an account of the debt or debts for which he was detained in that horrid place.

Booth answered, he could not be very exact, but he feared it was upwards of four hundred pounds.

"It is but three hundred pounds, indeed, sir," cries the serjeant; "if you can raise three hundred pounds, you are a free man this moment."

Booth, who did not apprehend the generous meaning of the serjeant as well as, I believe, the reader will, answered he was mistaken; that he had computed his debts, and they amounted to upwards of four hundred pounds; nay, that the bailiff had shown him writs for above that sum.

"Whether your debts are three or four hundred," cries the colonel, "the present business is to give bail only, and then you will have some time to try your friends: I think you might get a company abroad, and then I would advance the money on the security of half your pay; and, in the meantime, I will be one of your bail with all my heart."

Whilst Booth poured forth his gratitude for all this kindness, the serjeant ran downstairs for the bailiff, and shortly after returned with him into the room.

The bailiff, being informed that the colonel offered to be bail for his prisoner, answered a little surlily, "Well, sir, and who will be the other? you know, I suppose, there must be two; and I must have time to inquire after them."

The colonel replied, "I believe, sir, I am well known to be responsible for a much larger sum than your demand on this gentleman; but, if your forms require two, I suppose the serjeant here will do for the other."

"I don't know the serjeant nor you either, sir," cries Bondum; "and, if you propose yourselves bail for the gentleman, I must have time to inquire after you."

"You need very little time to inquire after me," says the colonel, "for I can send for several of the law, whom I suppose you know, to satisfy you; but consider, it is very late."

"Yes, sir," answered Bondum, "I do consider it is too late for the captain to be bailed to-night."

"What do you mean by too late?" cries the colonel.

"I mean, sir, that I must search the office, and that is now shut up; for, if my lord mayor and the court of aldermen would be bound for him, I would not discharge him till I had searched the office."

"How, sir!" cries the colonel, "hath the law of England no more regard for the liberty of the subject than to suffer such fellows as you to detain a man in custody for debt, when he can give undeniable security?"

"Don't fellow me," said the bailiff; "I am as good a fellow as yourself, I believe, though you have that riband in your hat there."

"Do you know whom you are speaking to?" said the serjeant. "Do you know you are talking to a colonel of the army?"

"What's a colonel of the army to me?" cries the bailiff. "I have had as good as he in my custody before now."

"And a member of parliament?" cries the serjeant.

"Is the gentleman a member of parliament?—Well, and what harm have I said? I am sure I meant no harm; and, if his honour is offended, I ask his pardon; to be sure his honour must know that the sheriff is answerable for all the writs in the office, though they were never so many, and I am answerable to the sheriff. I am sure the captain can't say that I have shown him any manner of incivility since he hath been here.—And I hope, honourable sir," cries he, turning to the colonel, "you don't take anything amiss that I said, or meant by way of disrespect, or any such matter. I did not, indeed, as the gentleman here says, know who I was speaking to; but I did not say anything uncivil as I know of, and I hope no offence."

The colonel was more easily pacified than might have been expected, and told the bailiff that, if it was against the rules of law to discharge Mr. Booth that evening, he must be contented. He then addressed himself to his friend, and began to prescribe comfort and patience to him; saying, he must rest satisfied with his confinement that night; and the next morning he promised to visit him again.

Booth answered, that as for himself, the lying one night in any place was very little worth his regard. "You and I, my dear friend, have both spent our evening in a worse situation than I shall in this house. All my concern is for my poor Amelia, whose sufferings on account of my absence I know, and I feel with unspeakable tenderness. Could I be assured she was tolerably easy, I could be contented in chains or in a dungeon."

"Give yourself no concern on her account," said the colonel; "I will wait on her myself, though I break an engagement for that purpose, and will give her such assurances as I am convinced will make her perfectly easy."

Booth embraced his friend, and, weeping over him, paid his acknowledgment with tears for all his goodness. In words, indeed, he was not able to thank him; for gratitude, joining with his other passions, almost choked him, and stopped his utterance.

After a short scene in which nothing passed worth recounting, the colonel bid his friend good night, and leaving the serjeant with him, made the best of his way back to Amelia.

CHAPTER VII

Worthy a very serious perusal.

THE colonel found Amelia sitting very disconsolate with Mrs. Atkinson. He entered the room with an air of great gaiety, assured Amelia that her husband was perfectly well, and that he hoped the next day he would again be with her.

Amelia was a little comforted at this account, and vented many grateful expressions to the colonel for his unparalleled friendship, as she was pleased to call it. She could not, however, help giving way soon after to a sigh at the thoughts of her husband's bondage, and declared that night would be the longest she had ever known.

"This lady, madam," cries the colonel, "must endeavour to make it shorter. And, if you will give me leave, I will join in the same endeavour." Then, after some more consolatory speeches, the colonel attempted to give a gay turn to the discourse, and said, "I was engaged to have spent this evening disagreeably at Ranelagh, with a set of company I did not like. How vastly am I obliged to you, dear Mrs. Booth, that I pass it so infinitely more to my satisfaction!"

"Indeed, colonel," said Amelia, "I am convinced that to a mind so rightly turned as yours there must be a much sweeter relish in the highest offices of friendship than in any pleasures which the gayest public places can afford."

"Upon my word, madam," said the colonel, "you now do me more than justice. I have, and always had, the utmost indifference for such pleasures. Indeed, I hardly allow them worthy of that name, or, if they are so at all, it is in a very low degree. In my opinion the highest friendship must always lead us to the highest pleasure."

Here Amelia entered into a long dissertation on friendship in which she pointed several times directiy at the colonel as the heroe of her tale.

The colonel highly applauded all her sentiments; and when he could not avoid taking the compliment to himself, he received it with a most respectful bow. He then tried his hand likewise at description, in which he found means to repay all Amelia's panegyric in kind. This, though he did with all possible delicacy, yet a curious observer might have been apt to suspect that it was chiefly on her account that the colonel had avoided the masquerade.

In discourses of this kind they passed the evening, till it was very late, the colonel never offering to stir from his chair before the clock had struck one; when he thought, perhaps, that decency obliged him to take his leave.

As soon as he was gone Mrs. Atkinson said to Mrs. Booth, "I think, madam, you told me this afternoon that the colonel was married?"

Amelia answered, she did so.

"I think likewise, madam," said Mrs. Atkinson, "you was acquainted with the colonel's lady?"

Amelia answered that she had been extremely intimate with her abroad.

"Is she young and handsome?" said Mrs. Atkinson. "In short, pray, was it a match of love or convenience?"

Amelia answered, entirely of love, she believed, on his side; for that the lady had little or no fortune.

"I am very glad to hear it," said Mrs. Atkinson; "for I am sure the colonel is in love with somebody. I think I never saw a more luscious picture of love drawn than that which he was pleased to give us as the portraiture of friendship. I have read, indeed, of Pylades and Orestes, Damon and Pythias, and other great friends of old; nay, I sometimes flatter myself that I am capable of being a friend myself; but as for that fine soft, tender, delicate passion, which he was pleased to describe, I am convinced there must go a he and a she to the composition."

"Upon my word, my dear, you are mistaken," cries Amelia. "If you had known the friendship which hath always subsisted between the colonel and my husband, you would not imagine it possible for any description to exceed it. Nay, I think his behaviour this very day is sufficient to convince you."

"I own what he hath done to-day hath great merit," said Mrs. Atkinson; "and yet, from what he hath said to-night— You will pardon me, dear madam; perhaps I am too quick-sighted in my observations; nay, I am afraid I am even impertinent."

"Fie upon it!" cries Amelia; "how can you talk in that strain? Do you imagine I expect ceremony? Pray speak what you think with the utmost freedom."

"Did he not then," said Mrs. Atkinson, "repeat the words, *the finest woman in the world*, more than once? did he not make use of an expression which might have become the mouth of Oroöndates himself? If I remember, the words were these—that, had he been Alexander the Great, he should have thought it more glory to have wiped off a tear from the bright eyes of Statira than to have conquered fifty worlds."

"Did he say so?" cries Amelia—"I think he did say something like it; but my thoughts were so full of my husband that I took little notice. But what would you infer from what he said? I hope you don't think he is in love with me?"

"I hope he doth not think so himself," answered Mrs. Atkinson; "though, when he mentioned the bright eyes of Statira, he fixed his own eyes on yours with the most languishing air I ever beheld."

Amelia was going to answer, when the serjeant arrived, and then she immediately fell to inquiring after her husband, and received such satisfactory answers to all her many questions concerning him, that she expressed great pleasure. These ideas so possessed her mind, that, without once casting her thoughts on any other matters, she took her leave of the serjeant and his lady, and repaired to bed to her children, in a room which Mrs. Atkinson had provided her in the same house; where we will at present wish her a good night.

CHAPTER VIII

Consisting of grave matters.

WHILE innocence and chearful hope, in spite of the malice of fortune, closed the eyes of the gentle Amelia on her homely bed, and she enjoyed a sweet and profound sleep, the colonel lay restless all night on his down; his mind was affected with a kind of ague fit; sometimes scorched up with flaming desires, and again chilled with the coldest despair.

There is a time, I think, according to one of our poets, *when lust and envy sleep.* This, I suppose, is when they are well gorged with the food they most delight in; but, while either of these are hungry,

> Nor poppy, nor mandragora,
> Nor all the drousy syrups of the East,
> Will ever medicine them to slumber.

The colonel was at present unhappily tormented by both these fiends. His last evening's conversation with Amelia had done his business effectually. The many kind words she had spoken to him, the many kind looks she had given him, as being, she conceived, the friend and preserver of her husband, had made an entire conquest of his heart. Thus the very love which she bore him, as the person to whom her little family were to owe their preservation and happiness, inspired him with thoughts of sinking them all in the lowest abyss of ruin and misery; and, while she smiled with all her sweetness on the supposed friend of her husband, she was converting that friend into his most bitter enemy.

> Friendship, take heed; if woman interfere,
> Be sure the hour of thy destruction 's near.

These are the lines of Vanbrugh; and the sentiment is better than the poetry. To say the truth, as a handsome wife is the cause and cement of many false friendships, she is often too liable to destroy the real ones.

Thus the object of the colonel's lust very plainly appears, but the object of his envy may be more difficult to discover.

Nature and Fortune had seemed to strive with a kind of rivalship which should bestow most on the colonel. The former had given him person, parts, and constitution, in all which he was superior to almost every other man. The latter had given him rank in life, and riches, both in a very eminent degree. Whom then should this happy man envy? Here, lest ambition should mislead the reader to search the palaces of the great, we will direct him at once to Gray's inn lane; where, in a miserable bed, in a miserable room, he will see a miserable broken lieutenant, in a miserable condition, with several heavy debts on his back, and without a penny in his pocket. This, and no other, was the object of the colonel's envy. And why? Because this wretch was possessed of the affections of a poor little lamb, which all the vast flocks that were within the power and reach of the colonel could not prevent that glutton's longing for. And sure this image of the lamb is not improperly adduced on this occasion; for what was the colonel's desire but to lead this poor lamb, as it were, to the slaughter, in order to purchase a feast of a few days by her final destruction, and to tear her away from the arms of one where she was sure of being fondled and caressed all the days of her life.

While the colonel was agitated with these thoughts, his greatest comfort was, that Amelia and Booth were now separated; and his greatest terror was of their coming again together. From wishes, therefore, he began to meditate designs; and so far was he from any intention of procuring the liberty of his friend, that he began to form schemes of prolonging his confinement, till he could procure some means of sending him away far from her; in which case he doubted not but of succeeding in all he desired.

He was forming this plan in his mind when a servant informed him that one serjeant Atkinson desired to speak with his honour. The serjeant was immediately admitted, and acquainted the colonel that, if he pleased to go and become bail for Mr. Booth, another unexceptionable house-keeper would be there to join with him. This person the serjeant had procured that morning, and had, by leave of his wife, given him a bond of indemnification for the purpose.

The colonel did not seem so elated with this news as Atkinson expected. On the contrary, instead of making a direct answer to what Atkinson said, the colonel began thus:

"I think, serjeant, Mr. Booth hath told me that you was foster-brother to his lady. She is really a charming woman, and it is a thousand pities she should ever have been placed in the dreadful situation she is now in. There is nothing so silly as for subaltern officers of the army to marry, unless where they meet with women of very great fortunes indeed. What can be the event of their marrying otherwise, but entailing misery and beggary on their wives and their posterity?"

"Ah! sir," cries the serjeant, "it is too late to think of those matters now. To be sure, my lady might have married one of the top gentlemen in the country; for she is certainly one of the best as well as one of the handsomest women in the kingdom; and, if she had been fairly dealt by, would have had a very great fortune into the bargain. Indeed, she is worthy of the greatest prince in the world; and, if I had been the greatest prince in the world, I should have thought myself happy with such a wife; but she was pleased to like the lieutenant, and certainly there can be no happiness in marriage without liking."

"Lookee, serjeant," said the colonel; "you know very well that I am the lieutenant's friend. I think I have shown myself so."

"Indeed your honour hath," quoth the serjeant, "more than once to my knowledge."

"But I am angry with him for his imprudence, greatly angry with him for his imprudence; and the more so, as it affects a lady of so much worth."

"She is, indeed, a lady of the highest worth," cries the serjeant. "Poor dear lady! I knew her, an't please your honour, from her infancy; and the sweetest-tempered, best-natured lady she is that ever trod on English ground. I have always loved her as if she was my own sister. Nay, she hath very often called me brother; and I have taken it to be a greater honour than if I was to be called a general officer."

"What pity it is," said the colonel, "that this worthy creature should be exposed to so much misery by the thoughtless behaviour of a man who, though I am his friend, I cannot help saying, hath been guilty of imprudence at least! Why could he not live upon his half-pay? What had he to do to run himself into debt in this outrageous manner?"

"I wish, indeed," cries the serjeant, "he had been a little more considerative; but I hope this will be a warning to him."

"How am I sure of that," answered the colonel; "or what reason is there to expect it? extravagance is a vice of which men are not so easily cured. I have thought a great deal of this matter, Mr. serjeant; and, upon the most mature deliberation, I am of opinion that it will be better, both for him and his poor lady, that he should smart a little more."

"Your honour, sir, to be sure is in the right," replied the serjeant; "but yet, sir, if you will pardon me for speaking, I hope you will be pleased to consider my poor lady's case. She suffers, all this while, as much or more than the lieutenant; for I know her so well, that I am certain she will never have a moment's ease till her husband is out of confinement."

"I know women better than you, serjeant," cries the colonel; "they sometimes place their affections on a husband as children do on their nurse; but they are both to be weaned. I know you, serjeant, to be a fellow of sense as well as spirit, or I should not speak so freely to you; but I took a fancy to you a long time ago, and I intend to serve you; but first, I ask you this question—Is your attachment to Mr. Booth or his lady?"

"Certainly, sir," said the serjeant, "I must love my lady best. Not but I have a great affection for the lieutenant too, because I know my lady hath the same; and, indeed, he hath been always very good to me as far as was in his power. A lieutenant, your honour knows, can't do a great deal; but I have always found him my friend upon all occasions."

"You say true," cries the colonel; "a lieutenant can do but little; but I can do much to serve you, and will too. But let me ask you one question: Who was the lady whom I saw last night with Mrs. Booth at her lodgings?"

Here the serjeant blushed, and repeated, "The lady, sir?"

"Ay, a lady, a woman," cries the colonel, "who supped with us last night. She looked rather too much like a gentlewoman for the mistress of a lodging-house."

The serjeant's cheeks glowed at this compliment to his wife; and he was just going to own her when the colonel proceeded: "I think I never saw in my life so ill-looking, sly, demure a b——; I would give something, methinks, to know who she was."

"I don't know, indeed," cries the serjeant, in great confusion; "I know nothing about her."

"I wish you would inquire," said the colonel, "and let me know her name, and likewise what she is: I have a strange curiosity to know, and let me see you again this evening exactly at seven."

"And will not your honour then go to the lieutenant this morning?" said Atkinson.

"It is not in my power," answered the colonel; "I am engaged another way. Besides, there is no haste in this affair. If men will be imprudent they must suffer the consequences. Come to me at seven, and bring me all the particulars you can concerning that ill-looking jade I mentioned to you, for I am resolved to know who she is. And so good-morrow to you, serjeant; be assured I will take an opportunity to do something for you."

Though some readers may, perhaps, think the serjeant not unworthy of the freedom with which the colonel treated him; yet that haughty officer would have been very backward to have condescended to such familiarity with one of his rank had he not proposed some design from it. In truth, he began to conceive hopes of making the serjeant instrumental to his design on Amelia; in other words, to convert him into a pimp; an office in which the colonel had been served by Atkinson's betters, and which, as he knew it was in his power very well to reward him, he had no apprehension that the serjeant would decline—an opinion which the serjeant might have pardoned, though he had never given the least grounds for it, since the colonel borrowed it from the knowledge of his own heart. This dictated to him that he, from a bad motive, was capable of desiring to debauch his friend's wife; and the same heart inspired him to hope that another, from another bad motive, might be guilty of the same breach of friendship in assisting him. Few men, I believe, think better of others than of themselves; nor do they easily allow the existence of any virture of which they perceive no traces in their own minds; for which reason I have observed, that it is extremely difficult to persuade a rogue that you are an honest man; nor would you ever succeed in the attempt by the strongest evidence, was it not for the comfortable conclusion which the rogue draws, that he who proves himself to be honest proves himself to be a fool at the same time.

CHAPTER IX

*A curious chapter, from which a curious reader may draw
sundry observation .*

THE serjeant retired from the colonel in a very dejected
state of mind: in which, however, we must leave him awhile
and return to Amelia; who, as soon as she was up, had despatched Mrs. Atkinson to pay off her former lodgings, and
to bring off all clothes and other movables.

The trusty messenger returned without performing her
errand, for Mrs. Ellison had locked up all her rooms, and was
gone out very early that morning, and the servant knew not
whither she was gone.

The two ladies now sat down to breakfast, together with
Amelia's two children; after which, Amelia declared she
would take a coach and visit her husband. To this motion
Mrs. Atkinson soon agreed, and offered to be her companion.
To say truth, I think it was reasonable enough; and the
great abhorrence which Booth had of seeing his wife in a
bailiff's house was, perhaps, rather too nice and delicate.

When the ladies were both dressed, and just going to send
for their vehicle, a great knocking was heard at the door,
and presently Mrs. James was ushered into the room.

This visit was disagreeable enough to Amelia, as it
detained her from the sight of her husband, for which she
so eagerly longed. However, as she had no doubt but that
the visit would be reasonably short, she resolved to receive
the lady with all the complaisance in her power.

Mrs. James now behaved herself so very unlike the person
that she lately appeared, that it might have surprised any
one who doth not know that besides that of a fine lady,
which is all mere art and mummery, every such woman
hath some real character at the bottom, in which, whenever
nature gets the better of her, she acts. Thus the finest
ladies in the world will sometimes love, and sometimes
scratch, according to their different natural dispositions,

with great fury and violence, though both of these are equally inconsistent with a fine lady's artificial character.

Mrs. James then was at the bottom a very good-natured woman, and the moment she heard of Amelia's misfortune was sincerely grieved at it. She had acquiesced on the very first motion with the colonel's design of inviting her to her house; and this morning at breakfast, when he had acquainted her that Amelia made some difficulty in accepting the offer, very readily undertook to go herself and persuade her friend to accept the invitation.

She now pressed this matter with such earnestness, that Amelia, who was not extremely versed in the art of denying, was hardly able to refuse her importunity; nothing, indeed, but her affection to Mrs. Atkinson could have prevailed on her to refuse; that point, however, she would not give up, and Mrs. James, at last, was contented with a promise that, as soon as their affairs were settled, Amelia, with her husband and family, would make her a visit, and stay some time with her in the country, whither she was soon to retire.

Having obtained this promise, Mrs. James, after many very friendly professions, took her leave, and, stepping into her coach, reassumed the fine lady, and drove away to join her company at an auction.

The moment she was gone, Mrs. Atkinson, who had left the room upon the approach of Mrs. James, returned into it, and was informed by Amelia of all that had passed.

"Pray, madam," said Mrs. Atkinson, "do this colonel and his lady live, as it is called, well together?"

"If you mean to ask," cries Amelia, "whether they are a very fond couple, I must answer that I believe they are not."

"I have been told," says Mrs. Atkinson, "that there have been instances of women who have become bawds to their own husbands, and the husbands pimps for them."

"Fie upon it!" cries Amelia. "I hope there are no such people. Indeed, my dear, this is being a little too censorious."

"Call it what you please," answered Mrs. Atkinson; "it arises from my love to you and my fears for your danger. You know the proverb of a burnt child; and, if such a one hath any good-nature, it will dread the fire on the account of others as well as on its own. And, if I may speak my sentiments freely, I cannot think you will be in safety at this colonel's house."

"I cannot but believe your apprehensions to be sincere," replied Amelia; "and I must think myself obliged to you for them; but I am convinced you are entirely in an error. I look on Colonel James as the most generous and best of men. He was a friend, and an excellent friend too, to my husband, long before I was acquainted with him, and he hath done him a thousand good offices. What do you say of his behaviour yesterday?"

"I wish," cries Mrs. Atkinson, "that this behaviour to-day had been equal. What I am now going to undertake is the most disagreeable office of friendship, but it is a necessary one. I must tell you, therefore, what passed this morning between the colonel and Mr. Atkinson; for, though it will hurt you, you ought, on many accounts, to know it." Here she related the whole, which we have recorded in the preceding chapter, and with which the serjeant had acquainted her while Mrs. James was paying her visit to Amelia. And as the serjeant had painted the matter rather in stronger colours than the colonel, so Mrs. Atkinson again a little improved on the serjeant. Neither of these good people, perhaps, intended to aggravate any circumstance; but such is, I believe, the unavoidable consequence of all reports. Mrs. Atkinson, indeed, may be supposed not to see what related to James in the most favourable light, as the serjeant with more honesty than prudence, had suggested to his wife that the colonel had not the kindest opinion of her, and had called her a sly and demure ——: it is true he omitted ill-looking b——; two words which are, perhaps, superior to the patience of any Job in petticoats that ever lived. He made amends, however, by substituting some other phrases in their stead, not extremely agreeable to a female ear.

It appeared to Amelia, from Mrs. Atkinson's relation, that the colonel had grossly abused Booth to the serjeant, and had absolutely refused to become his bail. Poor Amelia became a pale and motionless statue at this account. At length she cried, "If this be true, I and mine are all, indeed, undone. We have no comfort, no hope, no friend left. I cannot disbelieve you. I know you would not deceive me. Why should you, indeed, deceive me? But what can have caused this alteration since last night? Did I say or do anything to offend him?"

"You said and did rather, I believe, a great deal too

much to please him," answered Mrs. Atkinson. "Besides, he is not in the least offended with you. On the contrary, he said many kind things."

"What can my poor love have done?" said Amelia. "He hath not seen the colonel since last night. Some villain hath set him against my husband; he was once before suspicious of such a person. Some cruel monster hath belied his innocence!"

"Pardon me, dear madam," said Mrs. Atkinson; "I believe the person who hath injured the captain with this friend of his is one of the worthiest and best of creatures—nay, do not be surprised; the person I mean is even your fair self: sure you would not be so dull in any other case; but in this, gratitude, humility, modesty, every virtue, shuts your eyes.

"*Mortales hebetant visus,*

as Virgil says. What in the world can be more consistent than his desire to have you at his own house and to keep your husband confined in another? All that he said and all that he did yesterday, and, what is more convincing to me than both, all that he looked last night, are very consistent with both these designs."

"O Heavens!" cries Amelia, "you chill my blood with horror! the idea freezes me to death; I cannot, must not, will not think it. Nothing but conviction! Heaven forbid I should ever have more conviction! And did he abuse my husband? what? did he abuse a poor, unhappy, distressed creature, oppressed, ruined, torn from his children, torn away from his wretched wife; the honestest, worthiest, noblest, tenderest, fondest, best——" Here she burst into an agony of grief, which exceeds the power of description.

In this situation Mrs. Atkinson was doing her utmost to support her when a most violent knocking was heard at the door, and immediately the serjeant ran hastily into the room, bringing with him a cordial which presently relieved Amelia. What this cordial was, we shall inform the reader in due time. In the meanwhile he must suspend his curiosity; and the gentlemen at White's may lay wagers whether it was Ward's pill or Dr. James's powder.

But before we close this chapter, and return back to the bailiff's house, we must do our best to rescue the character of our heroine from the dulness of apprehension, which several of our quick-sighted readers may lay more heavily to her charge than was done by her friend Mrs. Atkinson.

I must inform, therefore, all such readers, that it is not because innocence is more blind than guilt that the former often overlooks and tumbles into the pit which the latter foresees and avoids. The truth is, that it is almost impossible guilt should miss the discovering of all the snares in its way, as it is constantly prying closely into every corner in order to lay snares for others. Whereas innocence, having no such purpose, walks fearlessly and carelessly through life, and is consequently liable to tread on the gins which cunning hath laid to entrap it. To speak plainly and without allegory or figure, it is not want of sense, but want of suspicion, by which innocence is often betrayed. Again, we often admire the folly of the dupe, when we should transfer our whole surprise to the astonishing guilt of the betrayer. In a word, many an innocent person hath owed his ruin to this circumstance alone, that the degree of villany was such as must have exceeded the faith of every man who was not himself a villain.

CHAPTER X

In which are many profound secrets of philosophy.

BOOTH, having had enough of the author's company the preceding day, chose now another companion. Indeed the author was not very solicitous of a second interview; for, as he could have no hope from Booth's pocket, so he was not likely to receive much increase to his vanity from Booth's conversation; for, low as this wretch was in virtue, sense, learning, birth, and fortune, he was by no means low in his vanity. This passion, indeed, was so high in him, and at the same time so blinded him to his own demerits, that he hated every man who did not either flatter him or give him money. In short, he claimed a strange kind of right, either to cheat all his acquaintance of their praise or to pick their pockets of their pence, in which latter case he himself repaid very liberally with panegyric.

A very little specimen of such a fellow must have satisfied a man of Mr. Booth's temper. He chose, therefore, now to associate himself with that gentleman of whom Bondum had given so shabby a character. In short, Mr. Booth's opinion of the bailiff was such, that he recommended a man most where he least intended it. Nay, the bailiff in the present instance, though he had drawn a malicious conclusion honestly avowed that this was drawn only from the poverty of the person, which is never, I believe, any forcible dis-recommendation to a good mind: but he must have had a very bad mind indeed, who, in Mr. Booth's circumstances, could have disliked or despised another man because that other man was poor.

Some previous conversation having passed between the gentleman and Booth, in which they had both opened their several situations to each other, the former, casting an affectionate look on the latter, expressed great compassion for his circumstances, for which Booth, thanking him, said, "You must have a great deal of compassion, and be a very

good man, in such a terrible situation as you describe yourself, to have any pity to spare for other people."

"My affairs, sir," answered the gentleman, "are very
bad, it is true, and yet there is one circumstance which makes
you appear to me more the object of pity than I am to myself;
and it is this—that you must from your years be a novice
in affliction, whereas I have served a long apprenticeship to
misery, and ought, by this time, to be a pretty good master
of my trade. To say the truth, I believe habit teaches men
to bear the burthens of the mind, as it inures them to
bear heavy burthens on their shoulders. Without use and
experience, the strongest minds and bodies both will stagger
under a weight which habit might render easy and even
contemptible."

"There is great justice," cries Booth, "in the comparison;
and I think I have myself experienced the truth of it; for
I am not that tyro in affliction which you seem to apprehend me. And perhaps it is from the very habit you mention
that I am able to support my present misfortunes a little
like a man."

The gentleman smiled at this, and cried, "Indeed, captain,
you are a young philosopher."

"I think," cries Booth, "I have some pretensions to that
philosophy which is taught by misfortunes, and you seem
to be of opinion, sir, that is one of the best schools of
philosophy."

"I mean no more, sir," said the gentleman, "than that
in the days of our affliction we are inclined to think more
seriously than in those seasons of life when we are engaged
in the hurrying pursuits of business or pleasure, when we have
neither leisure nor inclination to sift and examine things to
the bottom. Now there are two considerations which, from
my having long fixed my thoughts upon them, have greatly
supported me under all my afflictions. The one is the
brevity of life even at its longest duration, which the wisest
of men hath compared to the short dimension of a span.
One of the Roman poets compares it to the duration of a
race; and another, to the much shorter transition of a
wave.

"The second consideration is the uncertainty of it. Short
as its utmost limits are, it is far from being assured of reach-
ing those limits. The next day, the next hour, the next

moment, may be the end of our course. Now of what value is so uncertain, so precarious a station? This consideration, indeed, however lightly it is passed over in our conception, doth, in a great measure, level all fortunes and conditions, and gives no man a right to triumph in the happiest state, or any reason to repine in the most miserable. Would the most worldly men see this in the light in which they examine all other matters, they would soon feel and acknowledge the force of this way of reasoning; for which of them would give any price for an estate from which they were liable to be immediately ejected? or, would they not laugh at him as a madman who accounted himself rich from such an uncertain possession? This is the fountain, sir, from which I have drawn my philosophy. Hence it is that I have learnt to look on all those things which are esteemed the blessings of life, and those which are dreaded as its evils, with such a degree of indifference that, as I should not be elated with possessing the former, so neither am I greatly dejected and depressed by suffering the latter. Is the actor esteemed happier to whose lot it falls to play the principal part than he who plays the lowest? and yet the drama may run twenty nights together, and by consequence may outlast our lives; but, at the best, life is only a little longer drama, and the business of the great stage is consequently a little more serious than that which is performed at the Theatre-royal. But even here, the catastrophes and calamities which are represented are capable of affecting us. The wisest men can deceive themselves into feeling the distresses of a tragedy though they know them to be merely imaginary; and the children will often lament them as realities: what wonder then, if these tragical scenes which I allow to be a little more serious, should a little more affect us? where then is the remedy but in the philosophy I have mentioned, which, when once by a long course of meditation it is reduced to a habit, teaches us to set a just value on everything, and cures at once all eager wishes and abject fears, all violent joy and grief concerning objects which cannot endure long, and may not exist a moment."

"You have expressed yourself extremely well," cries Booth; "and I entirely agree with the justice of your sentiments; but, however true all this may be in theory, I still doubt its efficacy in practice. And the cause of the difference between these two is this: that we reason from our heads, but act from our hearts:

——Video meliora, proboque ;
Deteriora sequor.

Nothing can differ more widely than wise men and fools in their estimation of things; but, as both act from their uppermost passion, they both often act alike. What comfort then can your philosophy give to an avaricious man who is deprived of his riches or to an ambitious man who is stripped of his power? to the fond lover who is torn from his mistress or to the tender husband who is dragged from his wife? Do you really think that any meditations on the shortness of life will soothe them in their afflictions? Is not this very shortness itself one of their afflictions? and if the evil they suffer be a temporary deprivation of what they love, will they not think their fate the harder, and lament the more, that they are to lose any part of an enjoyment to which there is so short and so uncertain a period?"

"I beg leave, sir," said the gentleman, "to distinguish here. By philosophy, I do not mean the bare knowledge of right and wrong, but an energy, a habit, as Aristotle calls it; and this I do firmly believe, with him and with the Stoics, is superior to all the attacks of fortune."

He was proceeding when the bailiff came in, and in a surly tone bad them both good-morrow; after which he asked the philosopher if he was prepared to go to Newgate; for that he must carry him thither that afternoon.

The poor man seemed very much shocked with this news. "I hope," cries he, "you will give a little longer time, if not till the return of the writ. But I beg you particularly not to carry me thither to-day, for I expect my wife and children here in the evening."

"I have nothing to do with wives and children," cried the bailiff; "I never desire to see any wives and children here. I like no such company."

"I intreat you," said the prisoner, "give me another day. I shall take it as a great obligation; and you will disappoint me in the cruellest manner in the world if you refuse me."

"I can't help people's disappointments," cries the bailiff; "I must consider myself and my own family. I know not where I shall be paid the money that 's due already. I can't afford to keep prisoners at my own expense."

"I don't intend it shall be at your expense," cries the philosopher; "my wife is gone to raise money this morning; and I hope to pay you all I owe you at her arrival. But we intend to sup together to-night at your house; and, if you should remove me now, it would be the most barbarous disappointment to us both, and will make me the most miserable man alive."

"Nay, for my part," said the bailiff, "I don't desire to do anything barbarous. I know how to treat gentlemen with civility as well as another. And when people pay as they go, and spend their money like gentlemen, I am sure nobody can accuse me of any incivility since I have been in the office. And if you intend to be merry to-night I am not the man that will prevent it. Though I say it, you may have as good a supper dressed here as at any tavern in town."

"Since Mr. Bondum is so kind, captain," said the philosopher, "I hope for the favour of your company. I assure you, if it ever be my fortune to go abroad into the world, I shall be proud of the honour of your acquaintance."

"Indeed, sir," cries Booth, "it is an honour I shall be very ready to accept; but as for this evening, I cannot help saying I hope to be engaged in another place."

"I promise you, sir," answered the other, "I shall rejoice at your liberty, though I am a loser by it."

"Why as to that matter," cries Bondum with a sneer, "I fancy, captain, you may engage yourself to the gentleman without any fear of breaking your word; for I am very much mistaken if we part to-day."

"Pardon me, my good friend," said Booth, "but I expect my bail every minute."

"Lookee, sir," cries Bondum, "I don't love to see gentlemen in an error. I shall not take the serjeant's bail; and as for the colonel, I have been with him myself this morning (for to be sure I love to do all I can for gentlemen), and he told me he could not possibly be here to-day; besides, why should I mince the matter? there is more stuff in the office."

"What do you mean by stuff?" cries Booth.

"I mean that there is another writ," answered the bailiff, "at the suit of Mrs. Ellison, the gentlewoman that was here yesterday; and the attorney that was with her is concerned against you. Some officers would not tell you all this; but I loves to show civility to gentlemen while they behave themselves as such. And I loves the gentlemen of the army in particular. I had like to have been in the army myself once; but I liked the commission I have better. Come, captain, let not your noble courage be cast down; what say you to a glass of white wine, or a tiff of punch, by way of whet?"

"I have told you, sir, I never drink in the morning," cries Booth a little peevishly.

"No offence I hope, sir," said the bailiff; "I hope I have not treated you with any incivility. I don't ask any gentleman to call for liquor in my house if he doth not choose it; nor I don't desire anybody to stay here longer than they have a mind to. Newgate, to be sure, is the place for all debtors that can't find bail. I knows what civility is, and I scorn to behave myself unbecoming a gentleman: but I'd have you consider that the twenty-four hours appointed by act of parliament are almost out; and so it is time to think of removing. As to bail, I would not have you flatter yourself; for I knows very well there are other things coming against you. Besides, the sum you are already charged with is very large, and I must see you in a place of safety. My house is no prison, though I lock up for a little time in it. Indeed, when gentlemen are gentlemen, and likely to find bail, I don't stand for a day or two; but I have a good nose at a bit of carrion, captain; I have not carried so much carrion to Newgate, without knowing the smell of it."

"I understand not your cant," cries Booth; "but I did not think to have offended you so much by refusing to drink in a morning."

"Offended me, sir!" cries the bailiff. "Who told you so? Do you think, sir, if I want a glass of wine I am under any necessity of asking my prisoners for it? Damn it, sir, I'll show you I scorn your words. I can afford to treat you with a glass of the best wine in England, if you comes to that." He then pulled out a handful of guineas, saying, "There, sir, they are all my own; I owe nobody a shilling. I am no beggar, nor no debtor. I am the king's officer as well as you, and I will spend guinea for guinea as long as you please."

"Harkee, rascal," cries Booth, laying hold of the bailiff's collar. "How dare you treat me with this insolence? doth the law give you any authority to insult me in my mis-

fortunes?" At which words he gave the bailiff a good
shove, and threw him from him.

"Very well, sir," cries the bailiff; "I will swear both an
assault and an attempt to a rescue. If officers are to be
used in this manner, there is an end of all law and justice.
But, though I am not a match for you myself, I have those
below that are." He then ran to the door and called up two
ill-looking fellows, his followers, whom, as soon as they
entered the room, he ordered to seize on Booth, declaring
he would immediately carry him to Newgate; at the same
time pouring out a vast quantity of abuse, below the dignity
of history to record.

Booth desired the two dirty fellows to stand off, and
declared he would make no resistance; at the same time
bidding the bailiff carry him wherever he durst.

"I'll show you what I dare," cries the bailiff; and again
ordered the followers to lay hold of their prisoner, saying,
"He has assaulted me already, and endeavoured a rescue.
I shan't trust such a fellow to walk at liberty. A gentleman, indeed! ay, ay, Newgate is the properest place for such
gentry; as arrant carrion as ever was carried thither."

The fellows then both laid violent hands on Booth, and
the bailiff stepped to the door to order a coach; when, on a
sudden, the whole scene was changed in an instant; for now
the serjeant came running out of breath into the room; and,
seeing his friend the captain roughly handled by two ill-
looking fellows, without asking any questions stepped briskly
up to his assistance, and instantly gave one of the assailants
so violent a salute with his fist, that he directly measured his
length on the floor.

Booth, having by this means his right arm at liberty, was
unwilling to be idle, or entirely to owe his rescue from both
the ruffians to the serjeant; he therefore imitated the example
which his friend had set him, and with a lusty blow levelled
the other follower with his companion on the ground.

The bailiff roared out, "A rescue, a rescue!" to which the
serjeant answered there was no rescue intended. "The
captain," said he, "wants no rescue. Here are some friends
coming who will deliver him in a better manner."

The bailiff swore heartily he would carry him to Newgate
in spite of all the friends in the world.

"You carry him to Newgate!" cried the serjeant, with the

highest indignation. "Offer but to lay your hands on him, and I will knock your teeth down your ugly jaws." Then, turning to Booth, he cried, "They will be all here within a minute, sir; we had much ado to keep my lady from coming herself; but she is at home in good health, longing to see your honour; and I hope you will be with her within this half-hour."

And now three gentlemen entered the room; these were an attorney, the person whom the serjeant had procured in the morning to be his bail with Colonel James, and lastly Doctor Harrison himself.

The bailiff no sooner saw the attorney, with whom he was well acquainted (for the others he knew not), than he began, as the phrase is, to pull in his horns, and ordered the two followers, who were now got again on their legs, to walk downstairs.

"So, captain," says the doctor, "when last we parted, I believe we neither of us expected to meet in such a place as this."

"Indeed, doctor," cries Booth, "I did not expect to have been sent hither by the gentleman who did me that favour."

"How so, sir?" said the doctor; "you was sent hither by some person, I suppose, to whom you was indebted. This is the usual place, I apprehend, for creditors to send their debtors to. But you ought to be more surprised that the gentleman who sent you hither is come to release you. Mr. Murphy, you will perform all the necessary ceremonials."

The attorney then asked the bailiff with how many actions Booth was charged, and was informed there were five besides the doctor's, which was much the heaviest of all. Proper bonds were presently provided, and the doctor and the serjeant's friend signed them; the bailiff, at the instance of the attorney, making no objection to the bail.

Booth, we may be assured, made a handsome speech to the doctor for such extraordinary friendship, with which, however, we do not think proper to trouble the reader; and now everything being ended, and the company ready to depart, the bailiff stepped up to Booth, and told him he hoped he would remember civility-money.

"I believe," cries Booth, "you mean incivility-money; if there are any fees due for rudeness, I must own you have a very just claim."

"I am sure, sir," cries the bailiff, "I have treated your honour with all the respect in the world; no man, I am sure, can charge me with using a gentleman rudely. I knows what belongs to a gentleman better; but you can't deny that two of my men have been knocked down; and I doubt not but, as you are a gentleman, you will give them something to drink."

Booth was about to answer with some passion, when the attorney interfered, and whispered in his ear that it was usual to make a compliment to the officer, and that he had better comply with the custom.

"If the fellow had treated me civilly," answered Booth, "I should have had no objection to comply with a bad custom in his favour; but I am resolved I will never reward a man for using me ill; and I will not agree to give him a single farthing."

"'Tis very well, sir," said the bailiff; "I am rightly served for my good-nature; but, if it had been to do again, I would have taken care you should not have been bailed this day."

Doctor Harrison, to whom Booth referred the cause, after giving him a succinct account of what had passed, declared the captain to be in the right. He said it was a most horrid imposition that such fellows were ever suffered to prey on the necessitous; but that the example would be much worse to reward them where they had behaved themselves ill. "And I think," says he, "the bailiff is worthy of great rebuke for what he hath just now said; in which I hope he hath boasted of more power than is in him. We do, indeed, with great justice and propriety value ourselves on our freedom if the liberty of the subject depends on the pleasure of such fellows as these!"

"It is not so neither altogether," cries the lawyer; "but custom hath established a present or fee to them at the delivery of a prisoner, which they call civility-money, and expect as in a manner their due, though in reality they have no right."

"But will any man," cries Doctor Harrison, "after what the captain hath told us, say that the bailiff hath behaved himself as he ought; and, if he had, is he to be rewarded for not acting in an unchristian and inhuman manner? it is pity that, instead of a custom of feeing them out of the pockets of the poor and wretched, when they do not behave themselves ill, there was not both a law and a practice to punish them severely when they do. In the present case, I am so far from agreeing to give the bailiff a shilling, that, if there be any method of punishing him for his rudeness, I shall be heartily glad to see it put in execution; for there are none whose conduct should be so strictly watched as that of these necessary evils in the society, as their office concerns for the most part those poor creatures who cannot do themselves justice, and as they are generally the worst of men who undertake it."

The bailiff then quitted the room, muttering that he should know better what to do another time; and shortly after, Booth and his friends left the house; but, as they were going out, the author took Doctor Harrison aside, and slipped a receipt into his hand, which the doctor returned, saying, he never subscribed when he neither knew the work nor the author; but that, if he would call at his lodgings, he would be very willing to give all the encouragement to merit which was in his power.

The author took down the doctor's name and direction, and made him as many bows as he would have done had he carried off the half-guinea for which he had been fishing.

Mr. Booth then took his leave of the philosopher, and departed with the rest of his friends.

BOOK IX

CHAPTER I

In which the history looks backwards.

BEFORE we proceed farther with our history it may be proper to look back a little, in order to account for the late conduct of Doctor Harrison; which, however inconsistent it may have hitherto appeared, when examined to the bottom will be found, I apprehend, to be truly congruous with all the rules of the most perfect prudence as well as with the most consummate goodness.

We have already partly seen in what light Booth had been represented to the doctor abroad. Indeed, the accounts which were sent of the captain, as well by the curate as by a gentleman of the neighbourhood, were much grosser and more to his disadvantage than the doctor was pleased to set them forth in his letter to the person accused. What sense he had of Booth's conduct was, however, manifest by that letter. Nevertheless, he resolved to suspend his final judgment till his return; and, though he censured him, would not absolutely condemn him without ocular demonstration.

The doctor, on his return to his parish, found all the accusations which had been transmitted to him confirmed by many witnesses, of which the curate's wife, who had been formerly a friend to Amelia, and still preserved the outward appearance of friendship, was the strongest. She introduced all with—"I am sorry to say it; and it is friendship which bids me speak; and it is for their good it should be told you." After which beginnings she never concluded a single speech without some horrid slander and bitter invective.

Besides the malicious turn which was given to these affairs in the country, which were owing a good deal to misfortune, and some little perhaps to imprudence, the whole neighbourhood rung with several gross and scandalous lies, which were merely the inventions of his enemies, and of which the scene was laid in London since his absence.

Poisoned with all this malice, the doctor came to town;

and, learning where Booth lodged, went to make him a visit. Indeed, it was the doctor, and no other, who had been at his lodgings that evening when Booth and Amelia were walking in the Park, and concerning which the reader may be pleased to remember so many strange and odd conjectures.

Here the doctor saw the little gold watch and all those fine trinkets with which the noble lord had presented the children, and which, from the answers given him by the poor ignorant, innocent girl, he could have no doubt had been purchased within a few days by Amelia.

This account tallied so well with the ideas he had imbibed of Booth's extravagance in the country, that he firmly believed both the husband and wife to be the vainest, silliest, and most unjust people alive. It was, indeed, almost incredible that two rational beings should be guilty of such absurdity; but, monstrous and absurd as it was, ocular demonstration appeared to be the evidence against them.

The doctor departed from their lodgings enraged at this supposed discovery, and, unhappily for Booth, was engaged to supper that very evening with the country gentleman of whom Booth had rented a farm. As the poor captain happened to be the subject of conversation, and occasioned their comparing notes, the account which the doctor gave of what he had seen that evening so incensed the gentleman, to whom Booth was likewise a debtor, that he vowed he would take a writ out against him the next morning, and have his body alive or dead; and the doctor was at last persuaded to do the same. Mr. Murphy was thereupon immediately sent for; and the doctor in his presence repeated again what he had seen at his lodgings as the foundation of his suing him, which the attorney, as we have before seen, had blabbed to Atkinson.

But no sooner did the doctor hear that Booth was arrested than the wretched condition of his wife and family began to affect his mind. The children, who were to be utterly undone with their father, were entirely innocent; and as for Amelia herself, though he thought he had most convincing proofs of very blameable levity, yet his former friendship and affection to her were busy to invent every excuse, till, by very heavily loading the husband, they lightened the suspicion against the wife.

In this temper of mind he resolved to pay Amelia a second

visit, and was on his way to Mrs. Ellison when the serjeant met him and made himself known to him. The doctor took his old servant into a coffee-house, where he received from him such an account of Booth and his family, that he desired the serjeant to show him presently to Amelia; and this was the cordial which we mentioned at the end of the ninth chapter of the preceding book.

The doctor became soon satisfied concerning the trinkets which had given him so much uneasiness, and which had brought so much mischief on the head of poor Booth. Amelia likewise gave the doctor some satisfaction as to what he had heard of her husband's behaviour in the country; and assured him, upon her honour, that Booth could so well answer every complaint against his conduct, that she had no doubt but that a man of the doctor's justice and candour would entirely acquit him, and would consider him as an innocent unfortunate man, who was the object of a good man's compassion, not of his anger or resentment.

This worthy clergyman, who was not desirous of finding proofs to condemn the captain or to justify his own vindictive proceedings, but, on the contrary, rejoiced heartily in every piece of evidence which tended to clear up the character of his friend, gave a ready ear to all which Amelia said. To this, indeed, he was induced by the love he always had for that lady, by the good opinion he entertained of her, as well as by pity for her present condition, than which nothing appeared more miserable; for he found her in the highest agonies of grief and despair, with her two little children crying over their wretched mother. These are, indeed, to a well-disposed mind, the most tragical sights that human nature can furnish, and afford a juster motive to grief and tears in the beholder than it would be to see all the heroes who have ever infested the earth hanged all together in a string.

The doctor felt this sight as he ought. He immediately endeavoured to comfort the afflicted; in which he so well succeeded, that he restored to Amelia sufficient spirits to give him the satisfaction we have mentioned: after which he declared he would go and release her husband, which he accordingly did in the manner we have above related.

CHAPTER II

In which the history goes forward.

WE now return to that period of our history to which we had brought it at the end of our last book.

Booth and his friends arrived from the bailiff's, at the serjeant's lodgings, where Booth immediately ran upstairs to his Amelia; between whom I shall not attempt to describe the meeting. Nothing certainly was ever more tender or more joyful. This, however, I will observe, that a very few of these exquisite moments, of which the best minds only are capable, do in reality over-balance the longest enjoyments which can ever fall to the lot of the worst.

Whilst Booth and his wife were feasting their souls with the most delicious mutual endearments, the doctor was fallen to play with the two little children below-stairs. While he was thus engaged the little boy did somewhat amiss; upon which the doctor said, "If you do so any more I will take your papa away from you again."—"Again! sir," said the child; "why, was it you then that took away my papa before?" "Suppose it was," said the doctor; "would not you forgive me?" "Yes," cries the child, "I would forgive you; because a Christian must forgive everybody; but I should hate you as long as I live."

The doctor was so pleased with the boy's answer, that he caught him in his arms and kissed him; at which time Booth and his wife returned. The doctor asked which of them was their son's instructor in his religion; Booth answered that he must confess Amelia had all the merit of that kind. "I should have rather thought he had learnt of his father," cries the doctor; "for he seems a good soldier-like Christian, and professes to hate his enemies with a very good grace."

"How, Billy!" cries Amelia. "I am sure I did not teach you so."

"I did not say I would hate my enemies, madam," cries the boy; "I only said I would hate papa's enemies. Sure, mamma, there is no harm in that; nay, I am sure there is no harm in it, for I have heard you say the same thing a thousand times."

The doctor smiled on the child, and, chucking him under the chin, told him he must hate nobody; and now Mrs. Atkinson, who had provided a dinner for them all, desired them to walk up and partake of it.

And now it was that Booth was first made acquainted with the serjeant's marriage, as was Dr. Harrison; both of whom greatly felicitated him upon it.

Mrs. Atkinson, who was, perhaps, a little more confounded than she would have been had she married a colonel, said, "If I have done wrong, Mrs. Booth is to answer for it, for she made the match; indeed, Mr. Atkinson, you are greatly obliged to the character which this lady gives of you." "I hope he will deserve it," said the doctor; "and, if the army hath not corrupted a good boy, I believe I may answer for him."

While our little company were enjoying that happiness which never fails to attend conversation where all present are pleased with each other, a visitant arrived who was, perhaps, not very welcome to any of them. This was no other than Colonel James, who, entering the room with much gaiety, went directly up to Booth, embraced him, and expressed great satisfaction at finding him there; he then made an apology for not attending him in the morning, which he said had been impossible; and that he had, with the utmost difficulty, put off some business of great consequence in order to serve him this afternoon; "but I am glad on your account," cried he to Booth, "that my presence was not necessary."

Booth himself was extremely satisfied with this declaration, and failed not to return him as many thanks as he would have deserved had he performed his promise; but the two ladies were not quite so well satisfied. As for the serjeant, he had slipped out of the room when the colonel entered, not entirely out of that bashfulness which we have remarked him to be tainted with, but indeed, from what had passed in the morning, he hated the sight of the colonel as well on the account of his wife as on that of his friend.

The doctor, on the contrary, on what he had formerly heard from both Amelia and her husband of the colonel's generosity and friendship, had built so good an opinion of him, that he was very much pleased with seeing him, and took the opportunity of telling him so. "Colonel," said the doctor, "I have not the happiness of being known to you; but I have long been desirous of an acquaintance with a gentleman in whose commendation I have heard so much from some present." The colonel made a proper answer to this compliment, and they soon entered into a familiar conversation together; for the doctor was not difficult of access; indeed, he held the strange reserve which is usually practised in this nation between people who are in any degree strangers to each other to be very unbecoming the Christian character.

The two ladies soon left the room; and the remainder of the visit, which was not very long, passed in discourse on various common subjects, not worth recording. In the conclusion, the colonel invited Booth and his lady, and the doctor, to dine with him the next day.

To give Colonel James his due commendation, he had shown a great command of himself and great presence of mind on this occasion; for, to speak the plain truth, the visit was intended to Amelia, alone; nor did he expect or perhaps desire, anything less than to find the captain at home. The great joy which he suddenly conveyed into his countenance at the unexpected sight of his friend is to be attributed to that noble art which is taught in those excellent schools called the several courts of Europe. By this, men are enabled to dress out their countenances as much at their own pleasure as they do their bodies, and to put on friendship with as much ease as they can a laced coat.

When the colonel and doctor were gone, Booth acquainted Amelia with the invitation he had received. She was so struck with the news, and betrayed such visible marks of confusion and uneasiness, that they could not have escaped Booth's observation had suspicion given him the least hint to remark; but this, indeed, is the great optic-glass helping us to discern plainly almost all that passes in the minds of others, without some use of which nothing is more purblind than human nature.

Amelia, having recovered from her first perturbation, answered, "My dear, I will dine with you wherever you please to lay your commands on me." "I am obliged to you, my dear soul," cries Booth; "your obedience shall be very easy, for my command will be that you shall always follow your own inclinations." "My inclinations," answered she, "would, I am afraid, be too unreasonable a confinement to you; for they would always lead me to be with you and your children, with at most a single friend or two now and then." "O my dear!" replied he, "large companies give us a greater relish for our own society when we return to it; and we shall be extremely merry, for Doctor Harrison dines with us." "I hope you will, my dear," cries she; "but I own I should have been better pleased to have enjoyed a few days with yourself and the children, with no other person but Mrs. Atkinson, from whom I have conceived a violent affection, and who would have given us but little interruption. However, if you have promised, I must undergo the penance." "Nay, child," cried he, "I am sure I would have refused, could I have guessed it had been in the least disagreeable to you; though I know your objection." "Objection!" cries Amelia eagerly; "I have no objection." "Nay, nay," said he, "come, be honest, I know your objection, though you are unwilling to own it." "Good Heavens!" cried Amelia, frightened, "what do you mean? what objection?" "Why," answered he, "to the company of Mrs. James; and I must confess she hath not behaved to you lately as you might have expected; but you ought to pass all that by for the sake of her husband, to whom we have both so many obligations, who is the worthiest, honestest, and most generous fellow in the universe, and the best friend to me that ever man had."

Amelia, who had far other suspicions, and began to fear that her husband had discovered them, was highly pleased when she saw him taking a wrong scent. She gave, therefore, a little in to the deceit, and acknowledged the truth of what he had mentioned; but said that the pleasure she should have in complying with his desires would highly recompense any dissatisfaction which might arise on any other account; and shortly after ended the conversation on this subject with her cheerfully promising to fulfil his promise.

In reality, poor Amelia had now a most unpleasant task to undertake; for she thought it absolutely necessary to conceal from her husband the opinion she had conceived of the colonel. For, as she knew the characters, as well of her husband as of his friend, or rather enemy (both being often

CHAPTER III

A conversation between Dr. Harrison and others.

THE next day Booth and his lady, with the doctor, met at
Colonel James's, where Colonel Bath likewise made one of
the company.

Nothing very remarkable passed at dinner, or till the ladies
withdrew. During this time, however, the behaviour of
Colonel James was such as gave some uneasiness to Amelia,
who well understood his meaning, though the particulars
were too refined and subtle to be observed by any other
present.

When the ladies were gone, which was as soon as Amelia
could prevail on Mrs. James to depart, Colonel Bath, who
had been pretty brisk with champagne at dinner, soon began
to display his magnanimity. "My brother tells me, young
gentleman," said he to Booth, "that you have been used very
ill lately by some rascals, and I have no doubt but you will
do yourself justice."

Booth answered that he did not know what he meant.
"Since I must mention it then," cries the colonel, "I hear
you have been arrested; and I think you know what satisfaction is to be required by a man of honour."

"I beg, sir," says the doctor, "no more may be mentioned
of that matter. I am convinced no satisfaction will be
required of the captain till he is able to give it."

"I do not understand what you mean by able," cries
the colonel. To which the doctor answered, "that it was
of too tender a nature to speak more of."

"Give me your hand, doctor," cries the colonel; "I see
you are a man of honour, though you wear a gown. It is,
as you say, a matter of a tender nature. Nothing, indeed,
is so tender as a man's honour. Curse my liver, if any man—
I mean, that is, if any gentleman, was to arrest me, I would
as surely cut his throat as——"

"How, sir!" said the doctor, "would you compensate

one breach of the law by a much greater, and pay your debts
by committing murder?"

"Why do you mention law between gentlemen?" says
the colonel. "A man of honour wears his law by his side;
and can the resentment of an affront make a gentleman
guilty of murder? and what greater affront can one man cast
upon another than by arresting him? I am convinced that
he who would put up an arrest would put up a slap in the
face."

Here the colonel looked extremely fierce, and the divine
stared with astonishment at this doctrine; when Booth,
who well knew the impossibility of opposing the colonel's
humour with success, began to play with it; and, having
first conveyed a private wink to the doctor, he said there
might be cases undoubtedly where such an affront ought to
be resented; but that there were others where any resentment was impracticable: "As, for instance," said he, "where
the man is arrested by a woman."

"I could not be supposed to mean that case," cried the
colonel; "and you are convinced I did not mean it."

"To put an end to this discourse at once, sir," said the
doctor, "I was the plaintiff at whose suit this gentleman was
arrested."

"Was you so, sir?" cries the colonel; "then I have no
more to say. Women and the clergy are upon the same
footing. The long-robed gentry are exempted from the
laws of honour."

"I do not thank you for that exemption, sir," cries the
doctor; "and, if honour and fighting are, as they seem to
be, synonymous words with you, I believe there are some
clergymen, who in defence of their religion, or their country,
or their friend, the only justifiable causes of fighting, except
bare self-defence, would fight as bravely as yourself, colonel!
and that without being paid for it."

"Sir, you are privileged," says the colonel, with great
dignity; "and you have my leave to say what you please.
I respect your order, and you cannot offend me."

"I will not offend you, colonel," cries the doctor; "and
our order is very much obliged to you, since you profess so
much respect to us, and pay none to our Master."

"What Master, sir?" said the colonel.

"That Master," answered the doctor, "who hath expressly

forbidden all that cutting of throats to which you discover so much inclination."

"Oh! your servant, sir," said the colonel; "I see what you are driving at; but you shall not persuade me to think that religion forces me to be a coward."

"I detest and despise the name as much as you can," cries the doctor; "but you have a wrong idea of the word, colonel. What were all the Greeks and Romans? were these cowards? and yet, did you ever hear of this butchery, which we call duelling, among them?"

"Yes, indeed, have I," cries the colonel. "What else is all Mr. Pope's Homer full of but duels? Did not what's his name, one of the Agamemnons, fight with that paltry rascal Paris? and Diomede with what d'ye call him there? and Hector with I forget his name, he that was Achilles's bosom-friend; and afterwards with Achilles himself? Nay, and in Dryden's *Virgil*, is there anything almost besides fighting?"

"You are a man of learning, colonel," cried the doctor; "but——"

"I thank you for that compliment," said the colonel. —"No, sir, I do not pretend to learning; but I have some little reading, and I am not ashamed to own it."

"But are you sure, colonel," cries the doctor, "that you have not made a small mistake? for I am apt to believe both Mr. Pope and Mr. Dryden (though I cannot say I ever read a word of either of them) speak of wars between nations, and not of private duels; for of the latter I do not remember one single instance in all the Greek and Roman story. In short, it is a modern custom, introduced by barbarous nations since the times of Christianity; though it is a direct and audacious defiance of the Christian law, and is consequently much more sinful in us than it would have been in the heathens."

"Drink about, doctor," cries the colonel; "and let us call a new cause; for I perceive we shall never agree on this. You are a Churchman, and I don't expect you to speak your mind."

"We are both of the same Church, I hope," cries the doctor.

"I am of the Church of England, sir," answered the colonel, "and will fight for it to the last drop of my blood."

"It is very generous in you colonel," cries the doctor,

"to fight so zealously for a religion by which you are to be damned."

"It is well for you, doctor," cries the colonel, "that you wear a gown; for, by all the dignity of a man, if any other person had said the words you have just uttered, I would have made him eat them; ay, d—n me, and my sword into the bargain."

Booth began to be apprehensive that this dispute might grow too warm; in which case he feared that the colonel's honour, together with the champagne, might hurry him so far as to forget the respect due, and which he professed to pay, to the sacerdotal robe. Booth therefore interposed between the disputants, and said that the colonel had very rightly proposed to call a new subject; for that it was impossible to reconcile accepting a challenge with the Christian religion, or refusing it with the modern notion of honour. "And you must allow it, doctor," said he, "to be a very hard injunction for a man to become infamous; and more especially for a soldier, who is to lose his bread into the bargain."

"Ay, sir," says the colonel, with an air of triumph, "what say you to that?"

"Why, I say," cries the doctor, "that it is much harder to be damned on the other side."

"That may be," said the colonel; "but damn me, if I would take an affront of any man breathing, for all that. And yet I believe myself to be as good a Christain as wears a head. My maxim is, never to give an affront, nor ever to take one; and I say that it is the maxim of a good Christian and no man shall ever persuade me to the contrary."

"Well, sir," said the doctor, "since that is your resolution, I hope no man will ever give you an affront."

"I am obliged to you for your hope, doctor," cries the colonel, with a sneer; "and he that doth will be obliged to you for lending him your gown; for, by the dignity of a man, nothing out of petticoats, I believe, dares affront me."

Colonel James had not hitherto joined in the discourse, In truth, his thoughts had been otherwise employed; nor is it very difficult for the reader to guess what had been the subject of them. Being waked, however, from his reverie, and having heard the two or three last speeches, he turned to his brother, and asked him, why he would introduce

such a topic of conversation before a gentleman of Doctor
Harrison's character?

"Brother," cried Bath, "I own it was wrong, and I ask
the doctor's pardon: I know not how it happened to arise;
for you know, brother, I am not used to talk of these matters.
They are generally poltroons that do. I think I need not
be beholden to my tongue to declare I am none. I have
shown myself in a line of battle. I believe there is no man
will deny that; I believe I may say no man dares deny that
I have done my duty."

The colonel was thus proceeding to prove that his prowess
was neither the subject of his discourse nor the object of
his vanity, when a servant entered and summoned the
company to tea with the ladies; a summons which Colonel
James instantly obeyed, and was followed by all the rest.

But as the tea-table conversation, though extremely
delightful to those who are engaged in it, may probably
appear somewhat dull to the reader, we will here put an
end to the chapter.

CHAPTER IV

A dialogue between Booth and Amelia.

THE next morning early, Booth went by appointment and waited on Colonel James; whence he returned to Amelia in that kind of disposition which the great master of human passions would describe in Andromache, when he tells us she cried and smiled at the same instant.

Amelia plainly perceived the discomposure of his mind, in which the opposite affections of joy and grief were struggling for the superiority, and begged to know the occasion; upon which Booth spoke as follows:

"My dear," said he, "I had no intention to conceal from you what hath passed this morning between me and the colonel, who hath oppressed me, if I may use that expression, with obligations. Sure never man had such a friend; for never was there so noble, so generous a heart—I cannot help this ebullition of gratitude, I really cannot." Here he paused a moment, and wiped his eyes, and then proceeded: "You know, my dear, how gloomy the prospect was yesterday before our eyes, how inevitable ruin stared me in the face; and the dreadful idea of having entailed beggary on my Amelia and her posterity racked my mind; for though, by the goodness of the doctor, I had regained my liberty, the debt yet remained; and, if that worthy man had a design of forgiving me his share, this must have been my utmost hope, and the condition in which I must still have found myself need not to be expatiated on. In what light, then, shall I see, in what words shall I relate the colonel's kindness? O my dear Amelia! he hath removed the whole gloom at once, hath driven all despair out of my mind, and hath filled it with the most sanguine, and, at the same time, the most reasonable hopes of making a comfortable provision for yourself and my dear children. In the first place, then, he will advance me a sum of money to pay off all my debts; and this on a bond to be repaid only when I shall become colonel of a regiment, and not before. In the next place, he is gone this very morning to ask a company for me, which is now vacant in the West Indies; and, as he intends to push this with all his interest, neither he nor I have any doubt of his success. Now, my dear, comes the thirdly which, though perhaps it ought to give me the greatest joy, such is, I own, the weakness of my nature, it rends my very heartstrings asunder. I cannot mention it, for I know it will give you equal pain; though I know, on all proper occasions, you can exert a manly resolution. You will not, I am convinced, oppose it, whatever you must suffer in complying. O my dear Amelia! I must suffer likewise; yet I have resolved to bear it. You know not what my poor heart hath suffered since he made the proposal. It is love for you alone which could persuade me to submit to it. Consider our situation; consider that of our children; reflect but on those poor babes, whose future happiness is at stake, and it must arm your resolution. It is your interest and theirs that reconciled me to a proposal which, when the colonel first made it, struck me with the utmost horror; he hath, indeed, from these motives, persuaded me into a resolution which I thought impossible for any one to have persuaded me into. O my dear Amelia! let me entreat you to give me up to the good of your children, as I have promised the colonel to give you up to their interest and your own. If you refuse these terms we are still undone, for he insists absolutely upon them. Think, then, my love, however hard they may be, necessity compels us to submit to them. I know in what light a woman, who loves like you, must consider such a proposal; and yet how many instances have you of women who, from the same motives, have submitted to the same!"

"What can you mean, Mr. Booth?" cries Amelia, trembling.

"Need I explain my meaning to you more?" answered Booth.—"Did I not say I must give up my Amelia?"

"Give me up!" said she.

"For a time only, I mean," answered he: "for a short time perhaps. The colonel himself will take care it shall not be long—for I know his heart; I shall scarce have more joy in receiving you back than he will have in restoring you to my arms. In the meantime, he will not only be a father to my children, but a husband to you."

"A husband to me!" said Amelia.

"Yes, my dear; a kind, a fond, a tender, an affectionate husband. If I had not the most certain assurances of this, doth my Amelia think I could be prevailed on to leave her? No, my Amelia, he is the only man on earth who could have prevailed on me; but I know his house, his purse, his protection, will be all at your command. And as for any dislike you have conceived to his wife, let not that be any objection; for I am convinced he will not suffer her to insult you; besides, she is extremely well bred, and, how much soever she may hate you in her heart, she will at least treat you with civility.

"Nay, the invitation is not his, but hers; and I am convinced they will both behave to you with the greatest friendship; his I am sure, will be sincere, as to the wife of a friend entrusted to his care; and hers will, from good-breeding, have not only the appearances but the effects of the truest friendship."

"I understand you, my dear, at last," said she (indeed she had rambled into very strange conceits from some parts of his discourse); "and I will give you my resolution in a word: I will do the duty of a wife, and that is, to attend her husband wherever he goes."

Booth attempted to reason with her, but all to no purpose. She gave, indeed, a quiet hearing to all he said, and even to those parts which most displeased her ears; I mean those in which he exaggerated the great goodness and disinterested generosity of his friend; but her resolution remained inflexible, and resisted the force of all his arguments with a steadiness of opposition, which it would have been almost excusable in him to have construed into stubbornness.

The doctor arrived in the midst of the dispute; and, having heard the merits of the cause on both sides, delivered his opinion in the following words.

"I have always thought it, my dear children, a matter of the utmost nicety to interfere in any differences between husband and wife; but, since you both desire me with such earnestness to give you my sentiments on the present contest between you, I will give you my thoughts as well as I am able. In the first place then, can anything be more reasonable than for a wife to desire to attend her husband? It is, as my favourite child observes, no more than a desire to do her duty; and I make no doubt but that is one great reason of her insisting on it. And how can you yourself oppose it? Can love be its own enemy? or can a husband who is fond of his wife, content himself almost on any account with a long absence from her?"

"You speak like an angel, my dear Doctor Harrison," answered Amelia: "I am sure, if he loved as tenderly as I do, he could on no account submit to it."

"Pardon me, child," cries the doctor; "there are some reasons which would not only justify his leaving you, but which must force him, if he hath any real love for you, joined with common sense, to make that election. If it was necessary, for instance, either to your good or to the good of your children, he would not deserve the name of a man, I am sure not that of a husband, if he hesitated a moment. Nay, in that case, I am convinced you yourself would be an advocate for what you now oppose. I fancy therefore I mistook him when I apprehended he said that the colonel made his leaving you behind as the condition of getting him the commission; for I know my dear child hath too much goodness, and too much sense, and too much resolution, to prefer any temporary indulgence of her own passions to the solid advantages of her whole family."

"There, my dear!" cries Booth; "I knew what opinion the doctor would be of. Nay, I am certain there is not a wise man in the kingdom who would say otherwise."

"Don't abuse me, young gentleman," said the doctor, "with appellations I don't deserve."

"I abuse you, my dear doctor!" cries Booth.

"Yes, my dear sir," answered the doctor; "you insinuated slily that I was wise, which, as the world understands the phrase, I should be ashamed of; and my comfort is that no one can accuse me justly of it. I have just given an instance of the contrary by throwing away my advice."

"I hope, sir," cries Booth, "that will not be the case."

"Yes, sir," answered the doctor. "I know it will be the case in the present instance, for either you will not go at all, or my little turtle here will go with you."

"You are in the right, doctor," cries Amelia.

"I am sorry for it," said the doctor, "for then I assure you you are in the wrong."

"Indeed," cries Amelia, "if you knew all my reasons you would say they were very strong ones."

"Very probably," cries the doctor. "The knowledge that they are in the wrong is a very strong reason to some women to continue so."

"Nay, doctor," cries Amelia, "you shall never persuade me of that. I will not believe that any human being ever did an action merely because they knew it to be wrong."

" I am obliged to you, my dear child," said the doctor, "for declaring your resolution of not being persuaded. Your husband would never call me a wise man again if, after that declaration, I should attempt to persuade you."

"Well, I must be content," cries Amelia, "to let you think as you please."

"That is very gracious, indeed," said the doctor. "Surely, in a country where the Church suffers others to think as they please, it would be very hard if they had not themselves the same liberty. And yet, as unreasonable as the power of controlling men's thoughts is represented, I will show you how you shall control mine whenever you desire it."

"How, pray?" cries Amelia. "I should greatly esteem that power."

"Why, whenever you act like a wise woman," cries the doctor, "you will force me to think you so: and, whenever you are pleased to act as you do now, I shall be obliged, whether I will or no, to think as I do now."

"Nay, dear doctor," cries Booth, "I am convinced my Amelia will never do anything to forfeit your good opinion. Consider but the cruel hardship of what she is to undergo, and you will make allowances for the difficulty she makes in complying. To say the truth, when I examine my own heart, I have more obligations to her than appear at first sight; for, by obliging me to find arguments to persuade her, she hath assisted me in conquering myself. Indeed, if she had shown more resolution, I should have shown less."

"So you think it necessary, then," said the doctor, "that there should be one fool at least in every married couple. A mighty resolution, truly! and well worth your valuing yourself upon, to part with your wife for a few months in order to make the fortune of her and your children; when you are to leave her, too, in the care and protection of a friend that gives credit to the old stories of friendship, and doth an honour to human nature. What, in the name of goodness! do either of you think that you have made an union to endure for ever? How will either of you bear that separation which must, some time or other, and perhaps very soon, be the lot of one of you? Have you forgot that you are both mortal? As for Christianity, I see you have resigned all pretensions to it; for I make no doubt but that you have so set your hearts on the happiness you enjoy here together, that neither of you ever think a word of hereafter."

Amelia now burst into tears; upon which Booth begged the doctor to proceed no farther. Indeed, he would not have wanted the caution; for, however blunt he appeared in his discourse, he had a tenderness of heart which is rarely found among men; for which I know no other reason than that true goodness is rarely found among them; for I am firmly persuaded that the latter never possessed any human mind in any degree, without being attended by as large a portion of the former.

Thus ended the conversation on this subject; what followed is not worth relating, till the doctor carried off Booth with him to take a walk in the Park.

CHAPTER V

*A conversation between Amelia and Doctor Harrison,
with the result.*

AMELIA, being left alone, began to consider seriously of
her condition; she saw it would be very difficult to resist
the importunities of her husband, backed by the authority
of the doctor, especially as she well knew how unreasonable
her declarations must appear to every one who was ignorant
of her real motives to persevere in it. On the other hand,
she was fully determined, whatever might be the consequence, to adhere firmly to her resolution of not accepting
the colonel's invitation.

When she had turned the matter every way in her mind,
and vexed and tormented herself with much uneasy reflection upon it, a thought at last occurred to her which
immediately brought her some comfort. This was, to make
a confidant of the doctor, and to impart to him the whole
truth. This method, indeed, appeared to her now to be so
adviseable, that she wondered she had not hit upon it sooner;
but it is the nature of despair to blind us to all the means of
safety, however easy and apparent they may be.

Having fixed her purpose in her mind, she wrote a short
note to the doctor, in which she acquainted him that she
had something of great moment to impart to him, which
must be an entire secret from her husband, and begged that
she might have an opportunity of communicating it as soon
as possible.

Doctor Harrison received the letter that afternoon, and
immediately complied with Amelia's request in visiting her.
He found her drinking tea with her husband and Mrs.
Atkinson, and sat down and joined the company.

Soon after the removal of the tea-table Mrs. Atkinson
left the room. The doctor then, turning to Booth, said,
"I hope, captain, you have a true sense of the obedience
due to the Church, though our clergy do not often exact it.

However, it is proper to exercise our power sometimes, in order to remind the laity of their duty. I must tell you, therefore, that I have some private business with your wife; and I expect your immediate absence."

"Upon my word, doctor," answered Booth, "no Popish confessor, I firmly believe, ever pronounced his will and pleasure with more gravity and dignity; none therefore was ever more immediately obeyed than you shall be." Booth then quitted the room, and desired the doctor to recall him when his business with the lady was over.

Doctor Harrison promised he would; and then turning to Amelia he said, "Thus far, madam, I have obeyed your commands, and am now ready to receive the important secret which you mention in your note." Amelia now informed her friend of all she knew, all she had seen and heard, and all that she suspected, of the colonel. The good man seemed greatly shocked at the relation, and remained in a silent astonishment. Upon which Amelia said, "Is villany so rare a thing, sir, that it should so much surprise you?" "No, child," cries he; "but I am shocked at seeing it so artfully disguised under the appearance of so much virtue; and, to confess the truth, I believe my own vanity is a little hurt in having been so grossly imposed upon. Indeed, I had a very high regard for this man; for, besides the great character given him by your husband, and the many facts I have heard so much redounding to his honour, he hath the fairest and most promising appearance I ever yet beheld. A good face, they say, is a letter of recommendation. O Nature, Nature! why art thou so dishonest as ever to send men with these false recommendations into the world?"

"Indeed, my dear sir, I begin to grow entirely sick of it," cries Amelia; "for sure all mankind almost are villains in their hearts."

"Fie, child!" cries the doctor. "Do not make a conclusion so much to the dishonour of the great Creator. The nature of man is far from being in itself evil; it abounds with benevolence, charity, and pity, coveting praise and honour, and shunning shame and disgrace. Bad education, bad habits, and bad customs, debauch our nature, and drive it headlong as it were into vice. The governors of the world, and I am afraid the priesthood, are answerable for the

badness of it. Instead of discouraging wickedness to the
utmost of their power, both are too apt to connive at it. In
the great sin of adultery, for instance; hath the government
provided any law to punish it? or doth the priest take any
care to correct it? On the contrary, is the most notorious
practice of it any detriment to a man's fortune or to his
reputation in the world? doth it exclude him from any
preferment in the State, I had almost said in the Church?
is it any blot in his escutcheon? any bar to his honour? is
he not to be found every day in the assemblies of women of
the highest quality? in the closets of the greatest men, and
even at the tables of bishops? What wonder then if the
community in general treat this monstrous crime as a matter
of jest, and that men give way to the temptations of a
violent appetite, when the indulgence of it is protected by
law and countenanced by custom? I am convinced there
are good stamina in the nature of this very man; for he hath
done acts of friendship and generosity to your husband
before he could have any evil design on your chastity; and
in a Christian society, which I no more esteem this nation
to be than I do any part of Turkey, I doubt not but this
very colonel would have made a worthy and valuable
member."

"Indeed, my dear sir," cries Amelia, "you are the wisest
as well as best man in the world——"

"Not a word of my wisdom," cries the doctor. "I have
not a grain—I am not the least versed in the Chrematistic [1]
art, as an old friend of mine calls it. I know not how to get
a shilling, nor how to keep it in my pocket if I had it."

"But you understand human nature to the bottom,"
answered Amelia; "and your mind is the treasury of all
ancient and modern learning."

"You are a little flatterer," cries the doctor; "but I
dislike you not for it. And, to show you I don't, I will
return your flattery, and tell you you have acted with great
prudence in concealing this affair from your husband; but
you have drawn me into a scrape; for I have promised to
dine with this fellow again to-morrow, and you have made
it impossible for me to keep my word."

"Nay, but, dear sir," cries Amelia, "for Heaven's sake
take care! If you show any kind of disrespect to the colonel,

[1] The art of getting wealth is so called by Aristotle in his Politics.

my husband may be led into some suspicion—especially after our conference."

"Fear nothing, child. I will give him no hint; and, that I may be certain of not doing it, I will stay away. You do not think, I hope, that I will join in a cheerful conversation with such a man; that I will so far betray my character as to give any countenance to such flagitious proceedings. Besides, my promise was only conditional; and I do not know whether I could otherwise have kept it; for I expect an old friend every day who comes to town twenty miles on foot to see me, whom I shall not part with on any account; for, as he is very poor, he may imagine I treat him with disrespect."

"Well, sir," cries Amelia, "I must admire you and love you for your goodness."

"Must you love me?" cries the doctor. "I could cure you now in a minute if I pleased."

"Indeed, I defy you, sir," said Amelia.

"If I could but persuade you," answered he, "that I thought you not handsome, away would vanish all ideas of goodness in an instant. Confess honestly, would they not?"

"Perhaps I might blame the goodness of your eyes," replied Amelia; "and that is perhaps an honester confession than you expected. But do, pray, sir, be serious, and give me your advice what to do. Consider the difficult game I have to play; for I am sure, after what I have told you, you would not even suffer me to remain under the roof of this colonel."

"No, indeed, would I not," said the doctor, "whilst I have a house of my own to entertain you."

"But how to dissuade my husband," continued she, "without giving him any suspicion of the real cause, the consequences of his guessing at which I tremble to think upon."

"I will consult my pillow upon it," said the doctor; "and in the morning you shall see me again. In the meantime be comforted, and compose the perturbations of your mind."

"Well, sir," said she, "I put my whole trust in you."

"I am sorry to hear it," cries the doctor. "Your innocence may give you a very confident trust in a much more powerful assistance. However, I will do all I can to serve you: and now, if you please, we will call back your husband; for, upon my word, he hath shown a good catholic patience. And where is the honest serjeant and his wife? I am pleased with the behaviour of you both to that worthy fellow, in opposition to the custom of the world; which, instead of being formed on the precepts of our religion to consider each other as brethren, teaches us to regard those who are a degree below us, either in rank or fortune, as a species of beings of an inferior order in the creation."

The captain now returned into the room, as did the serjeant and Mrs. Atkinson; and the two couple, with the doctor, spent the evening together in great mirth and festivity; for the doctor was one of the best companions in the world, and a vein of cheerfulness, good humour, and pleasantry, ran through his conversation, with which it was impossible to resist being pleased.

CHAPTER VI

*Containing as surprising an accident as is perhaps
recorded in history.*

BOOTH had acquainted the serjeant with the great goodness
of Colonel James, and with the cheerful prospects which he
entertained from it. This Atkinson, behind the curtain,
communicated to his wife. The conclusion which she drew
from it need scarce be hinted to the reader. She made,
indeed, no scruple of plainly and bluntly telling her husband
that the colonel had a most manifest intention to attack the
chastity of Amelia.

This thought gave the poor serjeant great uneasiness,
and, after having kept him long awake, tormented him in
his sleep with a most horrid dream, in which he imagined
that he saw the colonel standing by the bedside of Amelia,
with a naked sword in his hand, and threatening to stab her
instantly unless she complied with his desires. Upon this
the serjeant started up in his bed, and, catching his wife by
the throat, cried out, "D—n you, put up your sword this
instant, and leave the room, or by Heaven I'll drive mine
to your heart's blood!"

This rough treatment immediately roused Mrs. Atkinson
from her sleep, who no sooner perceived the position of her
husband, and felt his hand grasping her throat, than she
gave a violent shriek and presently fell into a fit.

Atkinson now waked likewise, and soon became sensible
of the violent agitations of his wife. He immediately leapt
out of bed, and running for a bottle of water, began to sprinkle
her very plentifully; but all to no purpose: she neither
spoke nor gave any symptoms of recovery. Atkinson then
began to roar aloud; upon which Booth, who lay under
him, jumped from his bed, and ran up with the lighted
candle in his hand. The serjeant had no sooner taken the
candle than he ran with it to the bedside. Here he beheld
a sight which almost deprived him of his senses. The bed
appeared to be all over blood, and his wife weltering in the

midst of it. Upon this the serjeant, almost in a frenzy, cried out, "O Heavens! I have killed my wife. I have stabbed her! I have stabbed her!" "What can be the meaning of all this?" said Booth. "O sir!" cries the serjeant, "I dreamt I was rescuing your lady from the hands of Colonel James, and I have killed my poor wife."—Here he threw himself upon the bed by her, caught her in his arms, and behaved like one frantic with despair.

By this time Amelia had thrown on a wrapping-gown, and was come up into the room, where the serjeant and his wife were lying on the bed and Booth standing like a motionless statue by the bed-side. Amelia had some difficulty to conquer the effects of her own surprise on this occasion; for a more ghastly and horrible sight than the bed presented could not be conceived.

Amelia sent Booth to call up the maid of the house, in order to lend her assistance; but before his return Mrs. Atkinson began to come to herself; and soon after, to the inexpressible joy of the serjeant, it was discovered she had no wound. Indeed, the delicate nose of Amelia soon made that discovery, which the grosser smell of the serjeant, and perhaps his fright, had prevented him from making; for now it appeared that the red liquor with which the bed was stained, though it may, perhaps, sometimes run through the veins of a fine lady, was not what is properly called blood, but was, indeed, no other than cherry-brandy, a bottle of which Mrs. Atkinson always kept in her room to be ready for immediate use, and to which she used to apply for comfort in all her afflictions. This the poor serjeant, in his extreme hurry, had mistaken for a bottle of water. Matters were now soon accommodated, and no other mischief appeared to be done, unless to the bed-clothes. Amelia and Booth returned back to their room, and Mrs. Atkinson rose from her bed in order to equip it with a pair of clean sheets.

And thus this adventure would have ended without producing any kind of consequence, had not the words which the serjeant uttered in his frenzy made some slight impression on Booth; so much, at least, as to awaken his curiosity; so that in the morning when he arose he sent for the serjeant, and desired to hear the particulars of this dream, since Amelia was concerned in it.

AMELIA

The serjeant at first seemed unwilling to comply, and endeavoured to make excuses. This, perhaps, increased Booth's curiosity, and he said, "Nay, I am resolved to hear it. Why, you simpleton, do you imagine me weak enough to be affected by a dream, however terrible it may be?"

"Nay, sir," cries the serjeant, "as for that matter, dreams have sometimes fallen out to be true. One of my own, I know, did so, concerning your honour; for, when you courted my young lady, I dreamt you was married to her; and yet it was at a time when neither I myself, nor any of the country, thought you would ever obtain her. But Heaven forbid this dream should ever come to pass!"

"Why, what was this dream?" cries Booth. "I insist on knowing."

"To be sure, sir," cries the serjeant, "I must not refuse you; but I hope you will never think any more of it. Why then, sir, I dreamt that your honour was gone to the West Indies, and had left my lady in the care of Colonel James; and last night I dreamt the colonel came to my lady's bedside, offering to ravish her, and with a drawn sword in his hand, threatening to stab her that moment unless she would comply with his desires. How I came to be by I know not; but I dreamt I rushed upon him, caught him by the throat, and swore I would put him to death unless he instantly left the room. Here I waked, and this was my dream. I never paid any regard to a dream in my life—but, indeed, I never dreamt anything so very plain as this. It appeared downright reality. I am sure I have left the marks of my fingers in my wife's throat. I would not have taken a hundred pounds to have used her so."

"Faith," cries Booth, "it was an odd dream, and not so easily accounted for as that you had formerly of my marriage; for, as Shakespear says, 'dreams denote a foregone conclusion.' Now it is impossible you should ever have thought of any such matter as this."

"However, sir," cries the serjeant, "it is in your honour's power to prevent any possibility of this dream's coming to pass, by not leaving my lady to the care of the colonel; if you must go from her, certainly there are other places where she may be with great safety; and, since my wife tells me that my lady is so very unwilling, whatever reasons she may have, I hope your honour will oblige her."

"Now I recollect it," cries Booth, "Mrs. Atkinson hath once or twice dropped some disrespectful words of the colonel. He hath done something to disoblige her."

"He hath indeed, sir," replied the serjeant: "he hath said that of her which she doth not deserve, and for which, if he had not been my superior officer, I would have cut both his ears off. Nay, for that matter, he can speak ill of other people besides her."

"Do you know, Atkinson," cries Booth, very gravely, "that you are talking of the dearest friend I have?"

"To be honest then," answered the serjeant, "I do not think so. If I did, I should love him much better than I do."

"I must and will have this explained," cries Booth. "I have too good an opinion of you, Atkinson, to think you would drop such things as you have without some reason—and I will know it."

"I am sorry I have dropped a word," cries Atkinson. "I am sure I did not intend it; and your honour hath drawn it from me unawares."

"Indeed, Atkinson," cries Booth, "you have made me very uneasy, and I must be satisfied."

"Then, sir," said the serjeant, "you shall give me your word of honour, or I will be cut into ten thousand pieces before I will mention another syllable."

"What shall I promise?" said Booth.

"That you will not resent anything I shall lay to the colonel," answered Atkinson.

"Resent!—Well, I give you my honour," said Booth.

The serjeant made him bind himself over and over again, and then related to him the scene which formerly passed between the colonel and himself, as far as concerned Booth himself; but concealed all that more immediately related to Amelia.

"Atkinson," cries Booth, "I cannot be angry with you, for I know you love me, and I have many obligations to you; but you have done wrong in censuring the colonel for what he said of me. I deserve all that he said, and his censures proceeded from his friendship."

"But it was not so kind, sir," said Atkinson, "to say such things to me who am but a serjeant, and at such a time too."

"I will hear no more," cries Booth. "Be assured you

are the only man I would forgive on this occasion; and I forgive you only on condition you never speak a word more of this nature. This silly dream hath intoxicated you."

"I have done, sir," cries the serjeant. "I know my distance, and whom I am to obey; but I have one favour to beg of your honour, never to mention a word of what I have said to my lady; for I know she never would forgive me; I know she never would, by what my wife hath told me. Besides, you need not mention it, sir, to my lady, for she knows it all already, and a great deal more."

Booth presently parted from the serjeant, having desired him to close his lips on this occasion, and repaired to his wife, to whom he related the serjeant's dream.

Amelia turned as white as snow, and fell into so violent a trembling that Booth plainly perceived her emotion, and immediately partook of it himself. "Sure, my dear," said he, staring wildly, "there is more in this than I know. A silly dream could not so discompose you. I beg you, I intreat you to tell me—hath ever Colonel James——"

At the very mention of the colonel's name Amelia fell on her knees, and begged her husband not to frighten her.

"What do I say, my dear love," cried Booth, "that can frighten you?"

"Nothing, my dear," said she; "but my spirits are so discomposed with the dreadful scene I saw last night, that a dream, which at another time I should have laughed at, hath shocked me. Do but promise me that you will not leave me behind you, and I am easy."

"You may be so," cries Booth, "for I will never deny you anything. But make me easy too. I must know if you have seen anything in Colonel James to displease you."

"Why should you suspect it?" cries Amelia.

"You torment me to death," cries Booth. "By Heavens! I will know the truth. Hath he ever said or done anything which you dislike?"

"How, my dear," said Amelia, "can you imagine I should dislike a man who is so much your friend? Think of all the obligations you have to him, and then you may easily resolve yourself. Do you think, because I refuse to stay behind you in his house, that I have any objection to him? No, my dear, had he done a thousand times more than he hath— was he an angel instead of a man, I would not quit my

Billy. There's the sore, my dear—there's the misery, to be left by you."

Booth embraced her with the most passionate raptures, and, looking on her with inexpressible tenderness, cried, "Upon my soul, I am not worthy of you: I am a fool, and yet you cannot blame me. If the stupid miser hoards, with such care, his worthless treasure—if he watches it with such anxiety—if every apprehension of another's sharing the least part fills his soul with such agonies—O Amelia! what must be my condition, what terrors must I feel, while I am watching over a jewel of such real, such inestimable worth!"

"I can, with great truth, return the compliment," cries Amelia. "I have my treasure too; and am so much a miser, that no force shall ever tear me from it."

"I am ashamed of my folly," cries Booth; "and yet it is all from extreme tenderness. Nay, you yourself are the occasion. Why will you ever attempt to keep a secret from me? Do you think I should have resented to my friend his just censure of my conduct?"

"What censure, my dear love?" cries Amelia.

"Nay, the serjeant hath told me all," cries Booth—"nay, and that he hath told it to you. Poor soul! thou couldst not endure to hear me accused, though never so justly, and by so good a friend. Indeed, my dear, I have discovered the cause of that resentment to the colonel which you could not hide from me. I love you, I adore you for it; indeed, I could not forgive a slighting word on you. But, why do I compare things so unlike?—what the colonel said of me was just and true; every reflection on my Amelia must be false and villainous."

The discernment of Amelia was extremely quick, and she now perceived what had happened, and how much her husband knew of the truth. She resolved therefore to humour him, and fell severely on Colonel James for what he had said to the serjeant, which Booth endeavoured all he could to soften; and thus ended this affair, which had brought Booth to the very brink of a discovery which must have given him the highest torment, if it had not produced any of those tragical effects which Amelia apprehended.

CHAPTER VII

*In which the author appears to be master of that profound
learning called the knowledge of the town.*

MRS. JAMES now came to pay a morning's visit to Amelia.
She entered the room with her usual gaiety, and after a slight
preface, addressing herself to Booth, said she had been
quarrelling with her husband on his account. "I know
not," said she, "what he means by thinking of sending you
the Lord knows whither. I have insisted on his asking
something for you nearer home; and it would be the hardest
thing in the world if he should not obtain it. Are we
resolved never to encourage merit; but to throw away all
our preferments on those who do not deserve them? What
a set of contemptible wretches do we see strutting about the
town in scarlet!"

Booth made a very low bow, and modestly spoke in
disparagement of himself. To which she answered, "Indeed,
Mr. Booth, you have merit; I have heard it from my brother,
who is a judge of those matters, and I am sure cannot be
suspected of flattery. He is your friend as well as myself,
and we will never let Mr. James rest till he hath got you a
commission in England."

Booth bowed again, and was offering to speak, but she
interrupted him, saying, "I will have no thanks, nor no
fine speeches; if I can do you any service I shall think I am
paying the debt of friendship to my dear Mrs. Booth."

Amelia, who had long since forgot the dislike she had
taken to Mrs. James at her first seeing her in town, had
attributed it to the right cause, and had begun to resume
her former friendship for her, expressed very warm sentiments of gratitude on this occasion. She told Mrs. James
she should be eternally obliged to her if she could succeed
in her kind endeavours; for that the thoughts of parting
again with her husband had given her the utmost concern.
"Indeed," added she, "I cannot help saying he hath some
merit in the service, for he hath received two dreadful

wounds in it, one of which very greatly endangered his life; and I am convinced, if his pretensions were backed with any interest, he would not fail of success."

"They shall be backed with interest," cries Mrs. James, "if my husband hath any. He hath no favour to ask for himself, nor for any other friend that I know of; and, indeed, to grant a man his just due, ought hardly to be thought a favour. Resume your old gaiety, therefore, my dear Emily. Lord! I remember the time when you was much the gayer creature of the two. But you make an arrant mope of your-self by confining yourself at home—one never meets you anywhere. Come, you shall go with me to the Lady Betty Castleton's."

"Indeed, you must excuse me, my dear," answered Amelia, "I do not know Lady Betty."

"Not know Lady Betty! how, is that possible?—but no matter, I will introduce you. She keeps a morning rout; hardly a rout, indeed; a little bit of a drum—only four or five tables. Come, take your capuchine; you positively shall go. Booth, you shall go with us too. Though you are with your wife, another woman will keep you in countenance."

"La! child," cries Amelia, "how you rattle!"

"I am in spirits," answered Mrs. James, "this morning; for I won four rubbers together last night; and betted the things, and won almost every bet. I am in luck, and we will contrive to be partners—Come."

"Nay, child, you shall not refuse Mrs. James," said Booth.

"I have scarce seen my children to-day," answered Amelia. "Besides, I mortally detest cards."

"Detest cards!" cries Mrs. James. "How can you be so stupid? I would not live a day without them—nay, indeed, I do not believe I should be able to exist. Is there so delightful a sight in the world as the four honours in one's own hand, unless it be three natural aces at bragg?—And you really hate cards?"

"Upon reflection," cries Amelia, "I have sometimes had great pleasure in them—in seeing my children build houses with them. My little boy is so dexterous that he will some-times build up the whole pack."

"Indeed, Booth," cries Mrs. James, "this good woman of yours is strangely altered since I knew her first; but she will always be a good creature."

"Upon my word, my dear," cries Amelia, "you are altered too very greatly; but I doubt not to live to see you alter again, when you come to have as many children as I have."

"Children!" cries Mrs. James; "you make me shudder. How can you envy me the only circumstance which makes matrimony comfortable?"

"Indeed, my dear," said Amelia, "you injure me; for I envy no woman's happiness in marriage." At these words such looks passed between Booth and his wife as, to a sensible bystander, would have made all the airs of Mrs. James appear in the highest degree contemptible, and would have rendered herself the object of compassion. Nor could that lady avoid looking a little silly on the occasion.

Amelia now, at the earnest desire of her husband, accoutred herself to attend her friend; but first she insisted on visiting her children, to whom she gave several hearty kisses, and then, recommending them to the care of Mrs. Atkinson, she and her husband accompanied Mrs. James to the rout; where few of my fine readers will be displeased to make part of the company.

The two ladies and Booth then entered an apartment beset with card-tables, like the rooms at Bath and Tunbridge. Mrs. James immediately introduced her friends to Lady Betty, who received them very civilly, and presently engaged Booth and Mrs. James in a party at whist; for, as to Amelia, she so much declined playing, that as the party could be filled without her, she was permitted to sit by.

And now, who should make his appearance but the noble peer of whom so much honourable mention hath already been made in this history? He walked directly up to Amelia, and addressed her with as perfect a confidence as if he had not been in the least conscious of having in any manner displeased her; though the reader will hardly suppose that Mrs. Ellison had kept anything a secret from him.

Amelia was not, however, so forgetful. She made him a very distant courtesy, would scarce vouchsafe an answer to anything he said, and took the first opportunity of shifting her chair and retiring from him.

Her behaviour, indeed, was such that the peer plainly perceived that he should get no advantage by pursuing her any further at present. Instead, therefore, of attempting to follow her, he turned on his heel and addressed his discourse to another lady, though he could not avoid often casting his eyes towards Amelia as long as she remained in the room.

Fortune, which seems to have been generally no great friend to Mr. Booth, gave him no extraordinary marks of her favour at play. He lost two full rubbers, which cost him five guineas; after which, Amelia, who was uneasy at his lordship's presence, begged him in a whisper to return home; with which request he directly complied.

Nothing, I think, remarkable happened to Booth, unless the renewal of his acquaintance with an officer whom he had known abroad, and who made one of his party at the whist-table.

The name of this gentleman, with whom the reader will hereafter be better acquainted, was Trent. He had formerly been in the same regiment with Booth, and there was some intimacy between them. Captain Trent expressed great delight in meeting his brother officer, and both mutually promised to visit each other.

The scene which had passed the preceding night and that morning had so confused Amelia's thoughts, that, in the hurry in which she was carried off by Mrs. James, she had entirely forgot her appointment with Dr. Harrison. When she was informed at her return home that the doctor had been to wait upon her, and had expressed some anger at her being gone out, she became greatly uneasy, and begged of her husband to go to the doctor's lodgings and make her apology.

But lest the reader should be as angry with the doctor as he had declared himself with Amelia, we think proper to explain the matter. Nothing then was farther from the doctor's mind than the conception of any anger towards Amelia. On the contrary, when the girl answered him that her mistress was not at home, the doctor said with great good humour, "How! not at home! then tell your mistress she is a giddy vagabond, and I will come to see her no more till she sends for me." This the poor girl, from misunderstanding one word, and half forgetting the rest, had construed into great passion, several very bad words, and a declaration that he would never see Amelia any more.

CHAPTER VIII

In which two strangers make their appearance.

BOOTH went to the doctor's lodgings, and found him engaged with his country friend and his son, a young gentleman who was lately in orders; both whom the doctor had left, to keep his appointment with Amelia.

After what we mentioned at the end of the last chapter, we need take little notice of the apology made by Booth, or the doctor's reception of it, which was in his peculiar manner. "Your wife," said he, "is a vain hussy to think herself worth my anger; but tell her I have the vanity myself to think I cannot be angry without a better cause. And yet tell her I intend to punish her for her levity; for, if you go abroad, I have determined to take her down with me into the country, and make her do penance there till you return."

"Dear sir," said Booth, "I know not how to thank you if you are in earnest."

"I assure you then I am in earnest," cries the doctor; "but you need not thank me, however, since you know not how."

"But would not that, sir," said Booth, "be showing a slight to the colonel's invitation? and you know I have so many obligations to him."

"Don't tell me of the colonel," cries the doctor; "the Church is to be first served. Besides, sir, I have priority of right, even to you yourself. You stole my little lamb from me; for I was her first love."

"Well, sir," cries Booth, "if I should be so unhappy to leave her to any one, she must herself determine; and, I believe, it will not be difficult to guess where her choice will fall; for of all men, next to her husband, I believe, none can contend with Dr. Harrison in her favour."

"Since you say so," cries the doctor, "fetch her hither to dinner with us; for I am at least so good a Christian to love those that love me—I will show you my daughter, my old friend, for I am really proud of her—and you may bring my grand-children with you if you please."

Booth made some compliments, and then went on his errand. As soon as he was gone the old gentleman said to the doctor, "Pray, my good friend, what daughter is this of yours? I never so much as heard that you was married."

"And what then," cries the doctor; "did you ever hear that a pope was married? and yet some of them have had sons and daughters, I believe; but, however, this young gentleman will absolve me without obliging me to penance."

"I have not yet that power," answered the young clergyman; "for I am only in deacon's orders."

"Are you not?" cries the doctor; "why then I will absolve myself. You are to know then, my good friend, that this young lady was the daughter of a neighbour of mine, who is since dead, and whose sins I hope are forgiven; for she had too much to answer for on her child's account. Her father was my intimate acquaintance and friend; a worthier man, indeed, I believe never lived. He died suddenly when his children were infants; and, perhaps, to the suddenness of his death it was owing that he did not recommend any care of them to me. However, I, in some measure, took that charge upon me; and particularly of her whom I call my daughter. Indeed, as she grew up she discovered so many good qualities that she wanted not the remembrance of her father's merit to recommend her. I do her no more than justice when I say she is one of the best creatures I ever knew. She hath a sweetness of temper, a generosity of spirit, an openness of heart—in a word, she hath a true Christian disposition. I may call her an Israelite indeed, in whom there is no guile."

"I wish you joy of your daughter," cries the old gentleman; "for to a man of your disposition, to find out an adequate object of your benevolence, is, I acknowledge, to find a treasure."

"It is, indeed, a happiness," cries the doctor.

"The greatest difficulty," added the gentleman, "which persons of your turn of mind meet with, is in finding proper objects of their goodness; for nothing sure can be more irksome to a generous mind, than to discover that it hath thrown away all its good offices on a soil that bears no other fruit than ingratitude."

"I remember," cries the doctor, "Phocylides saith,

Μὴ κακὸν εὖ ἔρξῃς σπείρειν ἴσον ἐστ ενὶ πόντῳ.[1]

But he speaks more like a philosopher than a Christian. I am more pleased with a French writer, one of the best, indeed, that I ever read, who blames men for lamenting the ill return which is so often made to the best offices.[2] A true Christian can never be disappointed if he doth not receive his reward in this world; the labourer might as well complain that he is not paid his hire in the middle of the day."

"I own, indeed," said the gentleman, "if we see it in that light——"

"And in what light should we see it?" answered the doctor. "Are we like Agrippa, only almost Christians? or, is Christianity a matter of bare theory, and not a rule for our practice?"

"Practical, undoubtedly; undoubtedly practical," cries the gentleman. "Your example might indeed have convinced me long ago that we ought to do good to every one."

"Pardon me, father," cries the young divine, "that is rather a heathenish than a Christian doctrine. Homer, I remember, introduces in his Iliad one Axylus, of whom he says—

—— Φίλος δ' ἦν ἀνθρώποισι·
Πάντας γὰρ φιλέεσκεν.[3]

But Plato, who, of all the heathens, came nearest to the Christian philosophy, condemned this as impious doctrine; so Eustathius tells us, folio 474."

"I know he doth," cries the doctor, "and so Barnes tells us, in his note upon the place; but if you remember the rest of the quotation as well as you do that from Eustathius, you might have added the observation which Mr. Dryden makes in favour of this passage, that he found not in all the Latin authors, so admirable an instance of extensive humanity. You might have likewise remembered the noble sentiment with which Mr. Barnes ends his note, the sense of which is taken from the fifth chapter of Matthew:

—— ὃς καὶ φάος ἠελίοιο
Μίγδ' ἀγαθοῖσι κακοῖσί τ' ἐπ' ἀνδράσιν ἐξανατέλλει.

---

[1] To do a kindness to a bad man is like sowing your seed in the sea.
[2] D'Esprit.
[3] He was a friend to mankind, for he loved them all.

"It seems, therefore, as if this character rather became a Christian than a heathen, for Homer could not have transcribed it from any of his deities. Whom is it, therefore, we imitate by such extensive benevolence?"

"What a prodigious memory you have!" cries the old gentleman: "indeed, son, you must not contend with the doctor in these matters."

"I shall not give my opinion hastily," cries the son. "I know, again, what Mr. Poole, in his annotations, says on that verse of St. Matthew—That it is only to *heap coals of fire upon their heads*. How are we to understand, pray, the text immediately preceding?—*Love your enemies, bless them that curse you, do good to them that hate you.*"

"You know, I suppose, young gentleman," said the doctor, "how these words are generally understood. The commentator you mention, I think, tells us that love is not here to be taken in the strict sense, so as to signify the complacency of the heart; you may hate your enemies as God's enemies, and seek due revenge of them for his honour; and, for your own sakes too, you may seek moderate satisfaction of them; but then you are to love them with a love consistent with these things; that is to say, in plainer words, you are to love them and hate them, and bless and curse, and do them good and mischief."

"Excellent! admirable!" said the old gentleman; "you have a most inimitable turn to ridicule."

"I do not approve ridicule," said the son, "on such subjects."

"Nor I neither," cries the doctor; "I will give you my opinion, therefore, very seriously. The two verses taken together, contain a very positive precept, delivered in the plainest words, and yet illustrated by the clearest instance in the conduct of the Supreme Being; and lastly, the practice of this precept is most nobly enforced by the reward annexed —*that ye may be the children*, and so forth. No man who understands what it is to love, and to bless, and to do good, can mistake the meaning. But if they required any comment, the Scripture itself affords enough. *If thine enemy hunger, feed him ; if he thirst, give him drink; not rendering evil for evil, or railing for railing, but contrariwise, blessing.* They do not, indeed, want the comments of men, who, when they cannot bend their mind to the obedience of

Scripture, are desirous to wrest Scripture to a compliance
with their own inclinations."

"Most nobly and justly observed," cries the old gentleman. "Indeed, my good friend, you have explained the
text with the utmost perspicuity."

"But if this be the meaning," cries the son, "there must
be an end of all law and justice, for I do not see how any man
can prosecute his enemy in a court of justice."

"Pardon me, sir," cries the doctor. "Indeed, as an enemy
merely, and from a spirit of revenge, he cannot, and he
ought not to prosecute him; but as an offender against the
laws of his country he may, and it is his duty so to do. Is
there any spirit of revenge in the magistrates or officers of
justice when they punish criminals? Why do such, ordinarily
I mean, concern themselves in inflicting punishments, but
because it is their duty? and why may not a private man
deliver an offender into the hands of justice, from the same
laudable motive? Revenge, indeed, of all kinds is strictly
prohibited; wherefore, as we are not to execute it with our
own hands, so neither are we to make use of the law as the
instrument of private malice, and to worry each other with
inveteracy and rancour. And where is the great difficulty
in obeying this wise, this generous, this noble precept? If
revenge be, as a certain divine, not greatly to his honour,
calls it, the most luscious morsel the devil ever dropped into
the mouth of a sinner, it must be allowed at least to cost us
often extremely dear. It is a dainty, if indeed it be one,
which we come at with great inquietude, with great difficulty, and with great danger. However pleasant it may be
to the palate while we are feeding on it, it is sure to leave a
bitter relish behind it; and so far, indeed, it may be called
a luscious morsel, that the most greedy appetites are soon
glutted, and the most eager longing for it is soon turned into
loathing and repentance. I allow there is something tempt-
ing in its outward appearance, but it is like the beautiful
colour of some poisons, from which, however they may
attract our eyes, a regard to our own welfare commands us
to abstain. And this is an abstinence to which wisdom
alone, without any Divine command, hath been often found
adequate, with instances of which the Greek and Latin authors
everywhere abound. May not a Christian, therefore, be
well ashamed of making a stumbling-block of a precept,

which is not only consistent with his worldly interest, but to which so noble an incentive is proposed?"

The old gentleman fell into raptures at this speech, and, after making many compliments to the doctor upon it, he turned to his son, and told him he had an opportunity now of learning more in one day than he had learnt at the university in a twelvemonth.

The son replied, that he allowed the doctrine to be extremely good in general, and that he agreed with the greater part; "but I must make a distinction," said he. However, he was interrupted from his distinction at present, for now Booth returned with Amelia and the children.

CHAPTER IX

A scene of modern wit and humour.

IN the afternoon the old gentleman proposed a walk to
Vauxhall, a place of which, he said, he had heard much,
but had never seen it.

The doctor readily agreed to his friend's proposal, and soon
after ordered two coaches to be sent for to carry the whole
company. But when the servant was gone for them Booth
acquainted the doctor that it was yet too early. "Is it so?"
said the doctor; "why, then, I will carry you first to one
of the greatest and highest entertainments in the world."

The children pricked up their ears at this, nor did any of
the company guess what he meant; and Amelia asked what
entertainment he could carry them to at that time of day?

"Suppose," says the doctor, "I should carry you to
court."

"At five o'clock in the afternoon!" cries Booth.

"Ay, suppose I should have interest enough to introduce
you into the presence."

"You are jesting, dear sir," cries Amelia.

"Indeed, I am serious," answered the doctor. "I will
introduce you into that presence, compared to whom the
greatest emperor on the earth is many millions of degrees
meaner than the most contemptible reptile is to him. What
entertainment can there be to a rational being equal to this?
Was not the taste of mankind most wretchedly depraved,
where would the vain man find an honour, or where would
the love of pleasure propose so adequate an object as divine
worship? with what ecstasy must the contemplation of being
admitted to such a presence fill the mind! The pitiful
courts of princes are open to few, and to those only at particular seasons; but from this glorious and gracious presence
we are none of us, and at no time excluded."

The doctor was proceeding thus when the servant returned,
saying the coaches were ready; and the whole company

with the greatest alacrity attended the doctor to St. James's church.

When the service was ended, and they were again got into their coaches, Amelia returned the doctor many thanks for the light in which he had placed divine worship, assuring him that she had never before had so much transport in her devotion as at this time, and saying she believed she should be the better for this notion he had given her as long as she lived.

The coaches being come to the water-side, they all alighted, and, getting into one boat, proceeded to Vauxhall.

The extreme beauty and elegance of this place is well known to almost every one of my readers; and happy is it for me that it is so, since to give an adequate idea of it would exceed my power of description. To delineate the particular beauties of these gardens would, indeed, require as much pains, and as much paper, too, as to rehearse all the good actions of their master, whose life proves the truth of an observation which I have read in some ethic writer, that a truly elegant taste is generally accompanied with an excellency of heart; or, in other words, that true virtue is, indeed, nothing else but true taste.

Here our company diverted themselves with walking an hour or two before the music began. Of all the seven, Booth alone had ever been here before; so that, to all the rest, the place, with its other charms, had that of novelty. When the music played, Amelia, who stood next to the doctor, said to him in a whisper, "I hope I am not guilty of profaneness; but, in pursuance of that cheerful chain of thoughts with which you have inspired me this afternoon, I was just now lost in a reverie, and fancied myself in those blissful mansions which we hope to enjoy hereafter. The delicious sweetness of the place, the enchanting charms of the music, and the satisfaction which appears in every one's countenance, carried my soul almost to heaven in its ideas. I could not have, indeed, imagined there had been anything like this in this world."

The doctor smiled, and said, "You see, dear madam, there may be pleasures of which you could conceive no idea till you actually enjoyed them."

And now the little boy, who had long withstood the attractions of several cheesecakes that passed to and fro,

could contain no longer, but asked his mother to give him one,
saying, "I am sure my sister would be glad of another,
though she is ashamed to ask." The doctor, overhearing
the child, proposed that they should all retire to some place
where they might sit down and refresh themselves; which
they accordingly did. Amelia now missed her husband;
but, as she had three men in her company, and one of them
was the doctor, she concluded herself and her children to
be safe, and doubted not but that Booth would soon find
her out.

They now sat down, and the doctor very gallantly desired
Amelia to call for what she liked. Upon which the children
were supplied with cakes, and some ham and chicken were
provided for the rest of the company; with which while they
were regaling themselves with the highest satisfaction,
two young fellows walking arm-in-arm, came up, and when
they came opposite to Amelia they stood still, staring Amelia
full in the face, and one of them cried aloud to the other,
"D—n me, my lord, if she is not an angel!"—My lord stood
still, staring likewise at her, without speaking a word; when
two others of the same gang came up, and one of them
cried, "Come along, Jack, I have seen her before; but she is
too well manned already. Three —— are enough for one
woman, or the devil is in it!"

"D—n me," says he that spoke first, and whom they
called Jack, "I will have a brush at her if she belonged to
the whole convocation." And so saying, he went up to the
young clergyman, and cried, "Doctor, sit up a little, if you
please, and don't take up more room in a bed than belongs
to you." At which words he gave the young man a push,
and seated himself down directly over against Amelia, and,
leaning both his elbows on the table, he fixed his eyes on her
in a manner with which modesty can neither look nor bear
to be looked at.

Amelia seemed greatly shocked at this treatment; upon
which the doctor removed her within him, and then, facing
the gentleman, asked him what he meant by this rude
behaviour?—Upon which my lord stepped up and said,
"Don't be impertinent, old gentleman. Do you think such
fellows as you are to keep, d—n me, such fine wenches, d—n
me, to yourselves, d—n me?"

"No, no," cries Jack, "the old gentleman is more

reasonable. Here's the fellow that eats up the tithe-pig. Don't you see how his mouth waters at her? Where's your slabbering bib?" For, though the gentleman had rightly guessed he was a clergyman, yet he had not any of those insignia on with which it would have been improper to have appeared there.

"Such boys as you," cries the young clergyman, "ought to be well whipped at school, instead of being suffered to become nuisances in society."

"Boys, sir!" says Jack; "I believe I am as good a man as yourself, Mr. ——, and as good a scholar too. *Bos fur sus quotque sacerdos*. Tell me what's next. D—n me, I'll hold you fifty pounds you don't tell me what's next."

"You have him, Jack," cries my lord. "It is over with him, d—n me! he can't strike another blow."

"If I had you in a proper place," cries the clergyman, "you should find I would strike a blow, and a pretty hard one too."

"There," cries my lord, "there is the meekness of the clergyman—there spoke the wolf in sheep's clothing. D—n me, how big he looks! You must be civil to him, faith! or else he will burst with pride."

"Ay, ay," cries Jack, "let the clergy alone for pride; there's not a lord in the kingdom now hath half the pride of that fellow."

"Pray, sir," cries the doctor, turning to the other, "are you a lord?"

"Yes, Mr. ——," cries he, "I have that honour, indeed."

"And I suppose you have pride too," said the doctor.

"I hope I have, sir," answered he, "at your service."

"If such a one as you, sir," cries the doctor, "who are not only a scandal to the title you bear as a lord, but even as a man, can pretend to pride, why will you not allow it to a clergyman? I suppose, sir, by your dress, you are in the army? and, by the ribbon in your hat, you seem to be proud of that too. How much greater and more honourable is the service in which that gentleman is enlisted than yours! Why then should you object to the pride of the clergy, since the lowest of the function is in reality every way so much your superior?"

"Tida Tidu Tidum," cries my lord.

"However, gentlemen," cries the doctor, "if you have the

least pretension to that name, I beg you will put an end to your frolic; since you see it gives so much uneasiness to the lady. Nay, I entreat you for your own sakes, for there is one coming who will talk to you in a very different style from ours."

"One coming!" cries my lord; "what care I who is coming?"

"I suppose it is the devil," cries Jack; "for here are two of his livery servants already."

"Let the devil come as soon as he will," cries my lord; "d—n me if I have not a kiss!"

Amelia now fell a trembling; and her children, perceiving her fright, both hung on her, and began to cry; when Booth and Captain Trent both came up.

Booth, seeing his wife disordered, asked eagerly what was the matter? At the same time the lord and his companion, seeing Captain Trent, whom they well knew, said both together, "What, doth this company belong to you?" When the doctor, with great presence of mind, as he was apprehensive of some fatal consequence if Booth should know what had passed, said, "So, Mr. Booth, I am glad you are returned; your poor lady here began to be frighted out of her wits. But now you have him again," said he to Amelia, "I hope you will be easy."

Amelia, frightened as she was, presently took the hint, and greatly chid her husband for leaving her. But the little boy was not so quick-sighted, and cried, "Indeed, papa, those naughty men there have frightened my mamma out of her wits."

"How!" cries Booth, a little moved; "frightened! Hath any one frightened you, my dear?"

"No, my love," answered she, "nothing. I know not what the child means. Everything is well now I see you safe."

Trent had been all the while talking aside with the young sparks; and now, addressing himself to Booth, said, "Here hath been some little mistake; I believe my lord mistook Mrs. Booth for some other lady."

"It is impossible," cries my lord, "to know every one. I am sure, if I had known the lady to be a woman of fashion, and an acquaintance of Captain Trent, I should have said nothing disagreeable to her; but, if I have, I ask her pardon, and the company's."

"I am in the dark," cries Booth. "Pray what is all this matter?"

"Nothing of any consequence," cries the doctor, "nor worth your inquiring into. You hear it was a mistake of the person, and I really believe his lordship that all proceeded from his not knowing to whom the lady belonged."

"Come, come," says Trent, "there is nothing in the matter, I assure you. I will tell you the whole another time."

"Very well; since you say so," cries Booth, "I am contented." So ended the affair, and the two sparks made their *congé* and sneaked off.

"Now they are gone," said the young gentleman, "I must say I never saw two worse-bred jackanapes, nor fellows that deserved to be kicked more. If I had had them in another place I would have taught them a little more respect to the Church."

"You took rather a better way," answered the doctor, "to teach them that respect."

Booth now desired his friend Trent to sit down with them, and proposed to call for a fresh bottle of wine; but Amelia's spirits were too much disconcerted to give her any prospect of pleasure that evening. She therefore laid hold of the pretence of her children, for whom she said the hour was already too late; with which the doctor agreed. So they paid their reckoning and departed, leaving to the two rakes the triumph of having totally dissipated the mirth of this little innocent company, who were before enjoying complete satisfaction.

CHAPTER X

A curious conversation between the doctor, the young clergyman, and the young clergyman's father.

THE next morning, when the doctor and his two friends were at breakfast, the young clergyman, in whose mind the injurious treatment he had received the evening before was very deeply impressed, renewed the conversation on that subject.

"It is a scandal," said he, "to the government, that they do not preserve more respect to the clergy, by punishing all rudeness to them with the utmost severity. It was very justly observed of you, sir," said he to the doctor, "that the lowest clergyman in England is in real dignity superior to the highest nobleman. What then can be so shocking as to see that gown, which ought to entitle us to the veneration of all we meet, treated with contempt and ridicule? Are we not, in fact, ambassadors from heaven to the world? and do they not, therefore, in denying us our due respect, deny it in reality to Him that sent us?"

"If that be the case," says the doctor, "it behoves them to look to themselves; for He who sent us is able to exact most severe vengeance for the ill treatment of His ministers."

"Very true, sir," cries the young one; "and I heartily hope He will; but those punishments are at too great a distance to infuse terror into wicked minds. The government ought to interfere with its immediate censures. Fines and imprisonments and corporal punishments operate more forcibly on the human mind than all the fears of damnation."

"Do you think so?" cries the doctor; "then I am afraid men are very little in earnest in those fears."

"Most justly observed," says the old gentleman. "Indeed I am afraid that is too much the case."

"In that," said the son, "the government is to blame. Are not books of infidelity, treating our holy religion as a mere imposture, nay, somtimes as a mere jest, published daily, and spread abroad amongst the people with perfect impunity?"

"You are certainly in the right," says the doctor; "there is a most blameable remissness with regard to these matters; but the whole blame doth not lie there; some little share of the fault is, I am afraid, to be imputed to the clergy themselves."

"Indeed, sir," cries the young one, "I did not expect that charge from a gentleman of your cloth. Do the clergy give any encouragement to such books? Do they not, on the contrary, cry loudly out against the suffering them? This is the invidious aspersion of the laity; and I did not expect to hear it confirmed by one of our own cloth."

"Be not too impatient, young gentleman," said the doctor. "I do not absolutely confirm the charge of the laity; it is much too general and too severe; but even the laity themselves do not attack them in that part to which you have applied your defence. They are not supposed such fools as to attack that religion to which they owe their temporal welfare. They are not taxed with giving any other support to infidelity than what it draws from the ill example of their lives; I mean of the lives of some of them. Here too the laity carry their censures too far; for there are very few or none of the clergy whose lives, if compared with those of the laity, can be called profligate; but such, indeed, is the perfect purity of our religion, such is the innocence and virtue which it exacts to entitle us to its glorious rewards and to screen us from its dreadful punishments, that he must be a very good man indeed who lives up to it. Thus then these persons argue. This man is educated in a perfect knowledge of religion, is learned in its laws, and is by his profession, obliged, in a manner, to have them always before his eyes. The rewards which it promises to the obedience of these laws are so great, and the punishments threatened on disobedience so dreadful, that it is impossible but all men must fearfully fly from the one, and as eagerly pursue the other. If, therefore, such a person lives in direct opposition to, and in a constant breach of, these laws, the inference is obvious. There is a pleasant story in Matthew Paris, which I will tell you as well as I can remember it. Two young gentlemen, I think they were priests, agreed together that whosoever died first should return and acquaint his friend with the secrets of the other world. One of them died soon after, and fulfilled his promise. The whole relation he gave is not very material; but, among other things, he produced one of his hands, which Satan had made use of to write upon, as the moderns do on a card, and had sent his compliments to the priests for the number of souls which the wicked examples of their lives daily sent to hell. This story is the more remarkable as it was written by a priest, and a great favourer of his order."

"Excellent!" cried the old gentleman; "what a memory you have."

"But, sir," cries the young one, "a clergyman is a man as well as another; and, if such perfect purity be expected——"

"I do not expect it," cries the doctor; "and I hope it will not be expected of us. The Scripture itself gives us this hope, where the best of us are said to fall twenty times a-day. But sure we may not allow the practice of any of those grosser crimes which contaminate the whole mind. We may expect an obedience to the ten commandments, and an abstinence from such notorious vices as, in the first place, avarice, which, indeed, can hardly subsist without the breach of more commandments than one. Indeed, it would be excessive candour to imagine that a man who so visibly sets his whole heart, not only on this world, but on one of the most worthless things in it (for so is money, without regard to its uses), should be, at the same time, laying up his treasure in heaven. Ambition is a second vice of this sort: we are told we cannot serve God and Mammon. I might have applied this to avarice; but I chose rather to mention it here. When we see a man sneaking about in courts and levees, and doing the dirty work of great men, from the hopes of preferment, can we believe that a fellow whom we see to have so many hard task-masters upon earth ever thinks of his Master which is in heaven? Must he not himself think, if ever he reflects at all, that so glorious a Master will disdain and disown a servant who is the dutiful tool of a court-favourite, and employed either as the pimp of his pleasure, or sometimes, perhaps, made a dirty channel to assist in the conveyance of that corruption which is clogging up and destroying the very vitals of his country?

"The last vice which I shall mention is pride. There is not in the universe a more ridiculous nor a more contemptible animal than a proud clergyman; a turkey-cock or a jackdaw are objects of veneration when compared with him. I don't mean, by pride, that noble dignity of mind to which goodness can only administer an adequate object, which delights in the testimony of its own conscience, and could not, without the highest agonies, bear its condemnation. By pride I mean that saucy passion which exults in every little eventual pre-eminence over other men: such are the ordinary gifts of nature, and the paltry presents of fortune, wit, knowledge, birth, strength, beauty, riches, titles, and rank. That passion which is ever aspiring, like a silly child, to look over the heads of all about them; which, while it servilely adheres to the great, flies from the poor, as if afraid of contamination; devouring greedily every murmur of applause and every look of admiration; pleased and elated with all kinds of respect; and hurt and inflamed with the contempt of the lowest and most despicable of fools, even with such as treated you last night disrespectfully at Vauxhall. Can such a mind as this be fixed on things above? Can such a man reflect that he hath the ineffable honour to be employed in the immediate service of his great Creator? or can he please himself with the heart-warming hope that his ways are acceptable in the sight of that glorious, that incomprehensible Being?"

"Hear, child, hear," cries the old gentleman; "hear, and improve your understanding. Indeed, my good friend, no one retires from you without carrying away some good instructions with him. Learn of the doctor, Tom, and you will be the better man as long as you live."

"Undoubtedly, sir," answered Tom, "the doctor hath spoken a great deal of excellent truth; and, without a compliment to him, I was always a great admirer of his sermons, particularly of their oratory. But,

Nec tamen hoc tribuens dederim quoque cætera.

I cannot agree that a clergyman is obliged to put up with an affront any more than another man, and more especially when it is paid to the order."

"I am very sorry, young gentleman," cries the doctor, "that you should be ever liable to be affronted as a clergyman; and I do assure you, if I had known your disposition formerly, the order should never have been affronted through you."

The old gentleman now began to check his son for his opposition to the doctor, when a servant delivered the latter a note from Amelia, which he read immediately to himself, and it contained the following words:

My DEAR SIR,—Something hath happened since I saw you which gives me great uneasiness, and I beg the favour of seeing you as soon as possible to advise with you upon it.

I am

Your most obliged and dutiful daughter,

AMELIA BOOTH.

The doctor's answer was, that he would wait on the lady directly; and then, turning to his friend, he asked him if he would not take a walk in the Park before dinner. "I must go," says he, "to the lady who was with us last night; for I am afraid, by her letter, some bad accident hath happened to her. Come, young gentleman, I spoke a little too hastily to you just now; but I ask your pardon. Some allowance must be made to the warmth of your blood. I hope we shall, in time, both think alike."

The old gentleman made his friend another compliment; and the young one declared he hoped he should always think, and act too, with the dignity becoming his cloth. After which the doctor took his leave for a while, and went to Amelia's lodgings.

As soon as he was gone the old gentleman fell very severly on his son. "Tom," says he, "how can you be such a fool to undo, by your perverseness, all that I have been doing? Why will you not learn to study mankind with the attention which I have employed to that purpose? Do you think, if I had affronted this obstinate old fellow as you do, I should ever have engaged his friendship?"

"I cannot help it, sir," said Tom: "I have not studied six years at the university to give up my sentiments to every one. It is true, indeed, he put together a set of sounding words; but, in the main, I never heard any one talk more foolishly."

"What of that?" cries the father; "I never told you he was a wise man, nor did I ever think him so. If he had any understanding, he would have been a bishop long ago, to my certain knowledge. But, indeed, he hath been always a fool in private life; for I question whether he is worth £100 in the world, more than his annual income. He hath given away above half his fortune to the Lord knows who. I believe I have had above £200 of him, first and last; and would you lose such a milch-cow as this for want of a few compliments? Indeed, Tom, thou art as great a simpleton as himself. How do you expect to rise in the Church if you cannot temporize, and give in to the opinions of your superiors?"

"I don't know, sir," cries Tom, "what you mean by my superiors. In one sense, I own, a doctor of divinity is superior to a bachelor of arts, and so far I am ready to allow his superiority; but I understand Greek and Hebrew as well as he, and will maintain my opinion against him, or any other in the schools."

"Tom," cries the old gentleman, "till thou gettest the better of thy conceit, I shall never have any hopes of thee. If thou art wise, thou wilt think every man thy superior of whom thou canst get anything; at least thou wilt persuade him that thou thinkest so, and that is sufficient. Tom, Tom, thou hast no policy in thee."

"What have I been learning these seven years," answered he, "in the university? However, father, I can account for your opinion. It is the common failing of old men to attribute all wisdom to themselves. Nestor did it long ago: but, if you will inquire my character at college, I fancy you will not think I want to go to school again."

The father and son then went to take their walk, during which the former repeated many good lessons of policy to his son, not greatly perhaps to his edification. In truth, if the old gentleman's fondness had not in a great measure blinded him to the imperfections of his son, he would have soon perceived that he was sowing all his instructions in a soil so choked with self-conceit that it was utterly impossible they should ever bear any fruit.

CHAPTER I

To which we will prefix no preface.

THE doctor found Amelia alone, for Booth was gone to walk with his new-revived acquaintance, Captain Trent, who seemed so pleased with the renewal of his intercourse with his old brother-officer, that he had been almost continually with him from the time of their meeting at the drum.

Amelia acquainted the doctor with the purport of her message, as follows: "I ask your pardon, my dear sir, for troubling you so often with my affairs; but I know your extreme readiness, as well as ability, to assist any one with your advice. The fact is, that my husband hath been presented by Colonel James with two tickets for a masquerade, which is to be in a day or two, and he insists so strongly on my going with him, that I really do not know how to refuse without giving him some reason; and I am not able to invent any other than the true one, which you would not, I am sure, advise me to communicate to him. Indeed I had a most narrow escape the other day; for I was almost drawn in inadvertently by a very strange accident, to acquaint him with the whole matter." She then related the serjeant's dream, with all the consequences that attended it.

The doctor considered a little with himself, and then said, "I am really, child, puzzled as well as you about this matter. I would by no means have you to go to the masquerade; I do not like the diversion itself, as I have heard it described to me; not that I am such a prude to suspect every woman who goes there of any evil intentions; but it is a pleasure of too loose and disorderly a kind for the recreation of a sober mind. Indeed, you have still a stronger and more particular objection. I will try myself to reason him out of it."

"Indeed it is impossible," answered she; "and therefore I would not set you about it. I never saw him more set on anything. There is a party, as they call it, made on the occasion; and he tells me my refusal will disappoint all."

"I really do not know what to advise you," cries the doctor; "I have told you I do not approve of these diversions:

but yet, as your husband is so very desirous, I cannot think there will be any harm in going with him. However, I will consider of it, and do all in my power for you."

Here Mrs. Atkinson came in, and the discourse on this subject ceased; but soon after Amelia renewed it, saying there was no occasion to keep anything a secret from her friend. They then fell to debating on the subject, but could not come to any resolution. But Mrs. Atkinson, who was in an unusual flow of spirits, cried out, "Fear nothing, my dear Amelia, two women will surely be too hard for one man. I think, doctor, it exceeds Virgil:

> *Una dolo divûm si fœmina victa duorum est."*

"Very well repeated, indeed!" cried the doctor. "Do you understand all Virgil as well as you seem to do that line?"

"I hope I do, sir," said she, "and Horace too; or else my father threw away his time to very little purpose in teaching me."

"I ask your pardon, madam," cries the doctor. "I own it was an impertinent question."

"Not at all, sir," says she; "and if you are one of those who imagine women incapable of learning, I shall not be offended at it. I know the common opinion; but

> *Interdum vulgus rectum videt, est ubi peccat."*

"If I was to profess such an opinion, madam," said the doctor, "Madam Dacier and yourself would bear testimony against me. The utmost indeed that I should venture would be to question the utility of learning in a young lady's education."

"I own," said Mrs. Atkinson, "as the world is constituted, it cannot be as serviceable to her fortune as it will be to that of a man; but you will allow, doctor, that learning may afford a woman, at least, a reasonable and an innocent entertainment."

"But I will suppose," cried the doctor, "it may have its inconveniences. As, for instance, if a learned lady should meet with an unlearned husband, might she not be apt to despise him?"

"I think not," cries Mrs. Atkinson—"and, if I may be allowed the instance, I think I have shown, myself, that women who have learning themselves can be contented without that qualification in a man."

"To be sure," cries the doctor, "there may be other qualifications which may have their weight in the balance. But let us take the other side of the question, and suppose the learned of both sexes to meet in the matrimonial union, may it not afford one excellent subject of disputation, which is the most learned?"

"Not at all," cries Mrs. Atkinson; "for, if they had both learning and good sense, they would soon see on which side the superiority lay."

"But if the learned man," said the doctor, "should be a little unreasonable in his opinion, are you sure that the learned woman would preserve her duty to her husband, and submit?"

"But why," cries Mrs. Atkinson, "must we necessarily suppose that a learned man would be unreasonable?"

"Nay, madam," said the doctor, "I am not your husband; and you shall not hinder me from supposing what I please. Surely it is not such a paradox to conceive that a man of learning should be unreasonable. Are there no unreasonable opinions in very learned authors, even among the critics themselves? For instance, what can be a more strange, and indeed unreasonable opinion, than to prefer the Metamorphoses of Ovid to the Æneid of Virgil?"

"It would be indeed so strange," cries the lady, "that you shall not persuade me it was ever the opinion of any man."

"Perhaps not," cries the doctor; "and I believe you and I should not differ in our judgments of any person who maintained such an opinion—What a taste must he have!"

"A most contemptible one indeed," cries Mrs. Atkinson.

"I am satisfied," cries the doctor. "And in the words of your own Horace, *Verbum non amplius addam*."

"But how provoking is this," cries Mrs. Atkinson, "to draw one in such a manner! I protest I was so warm in the defence of my favourite Virgil, that I was not aware of your design; but all your triumph depends on a supposition that one should be so unfortunate as to meet with the silliest fellow in the world."

"Not in the least," cries the doctor. "Doctor Bentley was not such a person; and yet he would have quarrelled, I am convinced, with any wife in the world, in behalf of one of his corrections. I don't suppose he would have given up his *Ingentia Fata* to an angel."

"But do you think," said she, "if I had loved him, I would have contended with him?"

"Perhaps you might sometimes," said the doctor, "be of these sentiments; but you remember your own Virgil— *Varium et mutabile semper fæmina.*"

"Nay, Amelia," said Mrs. Atkinson, "you are now concerned as well as I am; for he hath now abused the whole sex, and quoted the severest thing that ever was said against us, though I allow it is one of the finest."

"With all my heart, my dear," cries Amelia. "I have the advantage of you, however, for I don't understand him."

"Nor doth she understand much better than yourself," cries the doctor; "or she would not admire nonsense, even though in Virgil."

"Pardon me, sir," said she.

"And pardon me, madam," cries the doctor, with a feigned seriousness; "I say, a boy in the fourth form at Eton would be whipped, or would deserve to be whipped at least, who made the neuter gender agree with the feminine. You have heard, however, that Virgil left his Æneid incorrect; and, perhaps, had he lived to correct it, we should not have seen the faults we now see in it."

"Why, it is very true as you say, doctor," cries Mrs. Atkinson; "there seems to be a false concord. I protest I never thought of it before."

"And yet this is the Virgil," answered the doctor, "that you are so fond of, who hath made you all of the neuter gender; or, as we say in English, he hath made mere animals of you; for, if we translate it thus,

   Woman is a various and changeable animal,

there will be no fault, I believe, unless in point of civility to the ladies."

Mrs. Atkinson had just time to tell the doctor he was a provoking creature, before the arrival of Booth and his friend put an end to that learned discourse, in which neither of the parties had greatly recommended themselves to each other; the doctor's opinion of the lady being not at all heightened by her progress in the classics, and she, on the other hand, having conceived a great dislike in her heart towards the doctor, which would have raged, perhaps, with no less fury from the consideration that he had been her husband.

CHAPTER II

What happened at the masquerade.

FROM this time to the day of the masquerade nothing happened of consequence enough to have a place in this history.

On that day Colonel James came to Booth's about nine in the evening, where he stayed for Mrs. James, who did not come till near eleven. The four masques then set out together in several chairs, and all proceeded to the Haymarket.

When they arrived at the Opera-house the colonel and Mrs. James presently left them; nor did Booth and his lady remain long together, but were soon divided from each other by different masques.

A domino soon accosted the lady, and had her away to the upper end of the farthest room on the right hand, where both the masques sat down; nor was it long before the he domino began to make very fervent love to the she. It would, perhaps, be tedious to the reader to run through the whole process, which was not indeed in the most romantic style. The lover seemed to consider his mistress as a mere woman of this world, and seemed rather to apply to her avarice and ambition than to her softer passions.

As he was not so careful to conceal his true voice as the lady was, she soon discovered that this lover of her's was no other than her old friend the peer, and presently a thought suggested itself to her of making an advantage of this accident. She gave him therefore an intimation that she knew him, and expressed some astonishment at his having found her out. "I suspect," says she, "my lord, that you have a friend in the woman where I now lodge, as well as you had in Mrs. Ellison." My lord protested the contrary. To which she answered, "Nay, my lord, do not defend her so earnestly till you are sure I should have been angry with her."

At these words, which were accompanied with a very bewitching softness, my lord flew into raptures rather too strong for the place he was in. These the lady gently checked, and begged him to take care they were not observed; for that her husband, for aught she knew, was then in the room.

Colonel James now came up, and said, "So, madam, I have the good fortune to find you again; I have been extremely miserable since I lost you." The lady answered in her masquerade voice that she did not know him. "I am Colonel James," said he, in a whisper. "Indeed, sir," answered she, "you are mistaken; I have no acquaintance with any Colonel James." "Madam," answered he, in a whisper likewise, "I am positive I am not mistaken, you are certainly Mrs. Booth." "Indeed, sir," said she, "you are very impertinent, and I beg you will leave me." My lord then interposed, and, speaking in his own voice, assured the colonel that the lady was a woman of quality, and that they were engaged in a conversation together; upon which the colonel asked the lady's pardon; for, as there was nothing remarkable in her dress, he really believed he had been mistaken.

He then went again a hunting through the rooms, and soon after found Booth walking without his mask between two ladies, one of whom was in a blue domino, and the other in the dress of a shepherdess. "Will," cries the colonel, "do you know what is become of our wives; for I have seen neither of them since we have been in the room?" Booth answered, "That he supposed they were both together, and they should find them by and by." "What!" cries the lady in the blue domino, "are you both come upon duty then with your wives? as for yours, Mr. Alderman," said she to the colonel, "I make no question but she is got into much better company than her husband's." "How can you be so cruel, madam?" said the shepherdess; "you will make him beat his wife by and by, for he is a military man I assure you." "In the trained bands, I presume," cries the domino, "for he is plainly dated from the city." "I own, indeed," cries the other, "the gentleman smells strongly of Thames-street, and, if I may venture to guess, of the honourable calling of a tailor."

"Why, what the devil hast thou picked up here?" cries James.

"Upon my soul, I don't know," answered Booth; "I wish you would take one of them at least."

"What say you, madam?" cries the domino, "will you go with the colonel? I assure you, you have mistaken your man, for he is no less a person than the great Colonel James himself."

"No wonder, then, that Mr. Booth gives him his choice of us; it is the proper office of a caterer, in which capacity Mr. Booth hath, I am told, the honour to serve the noble colonel."

"Much good may it do you with your ladies!" said James; "I will go in pursuit of better game." At which words he walked off.

"You are a true sportsman," cries the shepherdess; "for your only pleasure, I believe, lies in the pursuit."

"Do you know the gentleman, madam?" cries the domino.

"Who doth not know him?" answered the shepherdess.

"What is his character?" cries the domino; "for though I have jested with him, I only know him by sight."

"I know nothing very particular in his character," cries the shepherdess. "He gets every handsome woman he can, and so they do all."

"I suppose then he is not married?" said the domino.

"Oh, yes! and married for love too," answered the other; "but he hath loved away all his love for her long ago, and now, he says, she makes as fine an object of hatred. I think, if the fellow ever appears to have any wit, it is when he abuses his wife; and, luckily for him, that is his favourite topic. I don't know the poor wretch, but, as he describes her, it is a miserable animal."

"I know her very well," cries the other; "and I am much mistaken if she is not even with him; but hang him! what is become of Booth?"

At this instant a great noise arose near that part where the two ladies were. This was occasioned by a large assembly of young fellows whom they call bucks, who were got together, and were enjoying, as the phrase is, a letter, which one of them had found in the room.

Curiosity hath its votaries among all ranks of people; whenever therefore an object of this appears it is as sure of attracting a crowd in the assemblies of the polite as in those of their inferiors.

When this crowd was gathered together, one of the bucks, at the desire of his companions, as well as of all present, performed the part of a public orator, and read out the following letter, which we shall give the reader, together with the comments of the orator himself, and of all his audience.

The orator then, being mounted on a bench, began as follows:

"Here beginneth the first chapter of—— Saint—— Pox on 't, Jack, what is the saint's name? I have forgot."

"Timothy, you blockhead," answered another; "—— Timothy."

"Well, then," cries the orator, "of Saint Timothy.

"'Sir,—I am very sorry to have any occasion of writing on the following subject in a country that is honoured with the name of Christian; much more am I convinced to address myself to a man whose many advantages, derived both from nature and fortune, should demand the highest return of gratitude to the great Giver of all those good things. Is not such a man guilty of the highest ingratitude to that most beneficent Being, by a direct and avowed disobedience of his most positive laws and commands?

"'I need not tell you that adultery is forbid in the laws of the decalogue; nor need I, I hope, mention that it is expressly forbid in the New Testament.'

"You see, therefore," said the orator, "what the law is, and therefore none of you will be able to plead ignorance when you come to the Old Bailey in the other world. But here goes again:

"'If it had not been so expressly forbidden in Scripture, still the law of nature would have yielded light enough for us to have discovered the great horror and atrociousness of this crime.

"'And accordingly we find that nations, where the Sun of righteousness hath yet never shined, have punished the adulterer with the most exemplary pains and penalties; not only the polite heathens, but the most barbarous nations, have concurred in these; in many places the most severe and shameful corporal punishments, and in some, and those not a few, death itself hath been inflicted on this crime.

"'And sure in a human sense there is scarce any guilt which deserves to be more severely punished. It includes in it almost every injury and every mischief which one man can do to, or can bring on, another. It is robbing him of his property——'

"Mind that, ladies," said the orator; "you are all the property of your husbands.——'And of that property which, if he is a good man, he values above all others. It is poisoning that fountain whence he hath a right to derive the sweetest and most innocent pleasure, the most cordial comfort, the most solid friendship, and most faithful assistance in all his affairs, wants, and distresses. It is the destruction of his peace of mind, and even of his reputation. The ruin of both wife and husband, and sometimes of the whole family, are the probable consequence of this fatal injury. Domestic happiness is the end of almost all our pursuits, and the common reward of all our pains. When men find themselves for ever barred from this delightful fruition, they are lost to all industry, and grow careless of all their worldly affairs. Thus they become bad subjects, bad relations, bad friends, and bad men. Hatred and revenge are the wretched passions which boil in their minds. Despair and madness very commonly ensue, and murder and suicide often close the dreadful scene.'

"Thus, gentlemen and ladies, you see the scene is closed. So here ends the first act—and thus begins the second:

"'I have here attempted to lay before you a picture of this vice, the horror of which no colours of mine can exaggerate. But what pencil can delineate the horrors of that punishment which the Scripture denounces against it?

"'And for what will you subject yourself to this punishment? or for what reward will you inflict all this misery on another? I will add, on your friend? for the possession of a woman; for the pleasure of a moment? But, if neither virtue nor religion can restrain your inordinate appetites, are there not many women as handsome as your friend's wife, whom, though not with innocence, you may possess with a much less degree of guilt? What motive then can thus hurry you on to the destruction of yourself and your friend? doth the peculiar rankness of the guilt add any zest to the sin? doth it enhance the pleasure as much as we may be assured it will the punishment?

"'But if you can be so lost to all sense of fear, and of shame, and of goodness, as not to be debarred by the evil which you are to bring on yourself, by the extreme baseness of the action, nor by the ruin in which you are to involve others, let me still urge the difficulty, I may say, the impossibility of the success. You are attacking a fortress on a rock; a chastity so strongly defended, as well by a happy natural disposition of mind as by the strongest principles of religion and virtue, implanted by education and nourished and improved by habit, that the woman must be invincible even without that firm and constant affection of her husband which would guard a much looser and worse-disposed heart. What therefore are you attempting but to introduce distrust, and perhaps disunion, between an innocent and a happy couple, in which too you cannot succeed without bringing, I am convinced, certain destruction on your own head?

"'Desist, therefore, let me advise you, from this enormous crime; retreat from the vain attempt of climbing a precipice which it is impossible you should ever ascend, where you must probably soon fall into utter perdition, and can have no other hope but of dragging down your best friend into perdition with you.

"'I can think of but one argument more, and that, indeed, a very bad one; you throw away that time in an impossible attempt, which might, in other places, crown your sinful endeavours with success.'

"And so ends the dismal ditty."

"D—n me," cries one, "did ever mortal hear such d—ned stuff?"

"Upon my soul," said another, "I like the last argument well enough. There is some sense in that; for d—n me if I had not rather go to D—g—ss at any time than follow a virtuous b—— for a fortnight."

"Tom," says one of them, "let us set the ditty to music; let us subscribe to have it set by Handel; it will make an excellent oratorio."

"D—n me, Jack," says another, "we'll have it set to a psalm-tune, and we'll sing it next Sunday at St. James's church, and I'll bear a bob, d—n me."

"Fie upon it! gentlemen, fie upon it!" said a friar, who came up; "do you think there is any wit and humour in this ribaldry; or, if there were, would it make any atonement for abusing religion and virtue?"

"Heyday!" cries one, "this is a friar in good earnest."

"Whatever I am," said the friar, "I hope at least you are what you appear to be. Heaven forbid, for the sake of our posterity, that you should be gentlemen."

"Jack," cries one, "let us toss the friar in a blanket."

"Me in a blanket?" said the friar: "by the dignity of man, I will twist the neck of every one of you as sure as ever the neck of a dunghill-cock was twisted." At which words he pulled off his mask, and the tremendous majesty of Colonel Bath appeared, from which the bucks fled away as fast as the Trojans heretofore from the face of Achilles. The colonel did not think it worth while to pursue any other of them except him who had the letter in his hand, which the colonel desired to see, and the other delivered, saying it was very much at his service.

The colonel being possessed of the letter, retired as privately as he could, in order to give it a careful perusal; for, badly as it had been read by the orator, there were some passages in it which had pleased the colonel. He had just gone through it when Booth passed by him; upon which the colonel called to him, and, delivering him the letter, bid him put it in his pocket and read it at his leisure. He made many encomiums upon it, and told Booth it would be of service to him, and was proper for all young men to read.

Booth had not yet seen his wife; but, as he concluded she was safe with Mrs. James, he was not uneasy. He had been prevented searching further after her by the lady in the blue domino, who had joined him again. Booth had now made these discoveries: that the lady was pretty well acquainted with him, that she was a woman of fashion, and that she had a particular regard for him. But, though he was a gay man, he was in reality so fond of his Amelia, that he thought of no other woman; wherefore, though not absolutely a Joseph, as we have already seen, yet could he not be guilty of premeditated inconstancy. He was indeed so very cold and insensible to the hints which were given him, that the lady began to complain of his dullness. When the shepherdess again came up and heard this accusation against him, she confirmed it, saying, "I do assure you, madam, he is the dullest fellow in the world. Indeed, I should almost take you for his wife, by finding you a second time with him; for I do assure you the gentleman very seldom keeps any other company." "Are you so well acquainted with him, madam?" said the domino. "I have had that honour longer than your ladyship, I believe," answered the shepherdess. "Possibly you may, madam," cries the domino; "but I wish you would not interrupt us at present, for we have some business together." "I believe, madam," answered the shepherdess, "my business with the gentleman is altogether as important as yours; and therefore your ladyship may withdraw if you please." "My dear ladies," cries Booth, "I beg you will not quarrel about me." "Not at all," answered the domino; "since you are so indifferent, I resign my pretensions with all my heart. If you had not been the dullest fellow upon earth, I am convinced you must have discovered me." She then went off, muttering to herself that she was satisfied the shepherdess was some wretched creature whom nobody knew.

The shepherdess overheard the sarcasm, and answered it by asking Booth what contemptible wretch he had picked up? "Indeed, madam," said he, "you know as much of her as I do; she is a masquerade acquaintance like yourself." "Like me!" repeated she. "Do you think if this had been our first acquaintance I should have wasted so much time with you as I have? for your part, indeed, I believe a woman will get very little advantage by her having been formerly intimate with you." "I do not know, madam," said Booth, "that I deserve that character any more than I know the person that now gives it me." "And you have the assurance then," said she, in her own voice, "to affect not to remember me?" "I think," cries Booth, "I have heard that voice before; but, upon my soul, I do not recollect it." "Do you recollect," said she, "no woman that you have used with the highest barbarity—I will not say ingratitude?" "No, upon my honour," answered Booth. "Mention not honour," said she, "thou wretch! for, hardened as thou art, I could show thee a face that, in spite of thy consummate impudence, would confound thee with shame and horror. Dost thou not yet know me?" "I do, madam, indeed," answered Booth, "and I confess that of all women in the world you have the most reason for what you said."

Here a long dialogue ensued between the gentleman and the lady, whom, I suppose, I need not mention to have been Miss Matthews; but, as it consisted chiefly of violent upbraidings on her side, and excuses on his, I despair of making it entertaining to the reader, and shall therefore return to the colonel, who, having searched all the rooms with the utmost diligence, without finding the woman he

looked for, began to suspect that he had before fixed on
the right person, and that Amelia had denied herself to him,
being pleased with her paramour, whom he had discovered
to be the noble peer.

He resolved, therefore, as he could have no sport himself,
to spoil that of others; accordingly he found out Booth,
and asked him again what was become of both their wives;
for that he had searched all over the rooms, and could find
neither of them.

Booth was now a little alarmed at this account, and,
parting with Miss Matthews, went along with the colonel in
search of his wife. As for Miss Matthews, he had at length
pacified her with a promise to make her a visit; which
promise she extorted from him, swearing bitterly, in the most
solemn manner, unless he made it to her, she would expose
both him and herself at the masquerade.

As he knew the violence of the lady's passions, and to
what heights they were capable of rising, he was obliged to
come in to these terms: for he had, I am convinced, no fear
upon earth equal to that of Amelia's knowing what it was
in the power of Miss Matthews to communicate to her, and
which to conceal from her, he had already undergone so
much uneasiness.

The colonel led Booth directly to the place where he had
seen the peer and Amelia (such he was now well convinced
she was) sitting together. Booth no sooner saw her than he
said to the colonel, "Sure that is my wife in conversation
with that masque?" "I took her for your lady myself,"
said the colonel; "but I found I was mistaken. Hark ye,
that is my Lord ——, and I have seen that very lady with
him all this night."

This conversation passed at a little distance, and out of the
hearing of the supposed Amelia; when Booth, looking stedfastly at the lady, declared with an oath that he was positive
the colonel was in the right. She then beckoned to him with
her fan; upon which he went directly to her, and she asked
him to go home, which he very readily consented to. The
peer then walked off: the colonel went in pursuit of his wife,
or some other woman; and Booth and his lady returned in
two chairs to their lodgings.

CHAPTER III

Consequences of the masquerade, not uncommon nor surprising.

THE lady, getting first out of her chair, ran hastily up into the nursery to the children; for such was Amelia's constant method at her return home, at whatever hour. Booth then walked into the dining-room, where he had not been long before Amelia came down to him, and, with a most cheerful countenance, said, "My dear, I fancy we have neither of us supped; shall I go down and see whether there is any cold meat in the house?"

"For yourself, if you please," answered Booth; "but I shall eat nothing."

"How, my dear!" said Amelia; "I hope you have not lost your appetite at the masquerade!" for supper was a meal at which he generally eat very heartily.

"I know not well what I have lost," said Booth; "I find myself disordered.—My head aches. I know not what is the matter with me."

"Indeed, my dear, you frighten me," said Amelia; "you look, indeed, disordered. I wish the masquerade had been far enough before you had gone thither."

"Would to Heaven it had!" cried Booth; "but that is over now. But pray, Amelia, answer me one question— Who was that gentleman with you when I came up to you?"

"The gentleman! my dear," said Amelia; "what gentleman?"

"The gentleman—the nobleman—when I came up; sure I speak plain."

"Upon my word, my dear, I don't understand you," answered she; "I did not know one person at the masquerade."

"How!" said he; "what! spend the whole evening with a masque without knowing him?"

"Why, my dear," said she, "you know we were not together."

"I know we were not," said he, "but what is that to the

purpose? Sure you answer me strangely. I know we were
not together; and therefore I ask you whom you were with?"

"Nay, but, my dear," said she, "can I tell people in
masques?"

"I say again, madam," said he, "would you converse
two hours or more with a masque whom you did not know?"

"Indeed, child," says she, "I know nothing of the methods
of a masquerade; for I never was at one in my life."

"I wish to Heaven you had not been at this!" cries
Booth. "Nay, you will wish so yourself if you tell me
truth.—What have I said? do I—can I suspect you of
not speaking truth? Since you are ignorant then I will
inform you: the man you have conversed with was no other
than Lord ——."

"And is that the reason," said she, "you wish I had not
been there?"

"And is not that reason," answered he, "sufficient? Is
he not the last man upon earth with whom I would have
you converse?"

"So you really wish then that I had not been at the
masquerade?"

"I do," cried he, "from my soul."

"So may I ever be able," cried she, "to indulge you in
every wish as in this.—I was not there."

"Do not trifle, Amelia," cried he; "you would not jest
with me if you knew the situation of my mind."

"Indeed I do not jest with you," said she. "Upon my
honour I was not there. Forgive me this first deceit I ever
practised, and indeed it shall be the last; for I have paid
severely for this by the uneasiness it hath given me." She
then revealed to him the whole secret, which was thus:

I think it hath been already mentioned in some part of
this history that Amelia and Mrs. Atkinson were exactly of
the same make and stature, and that there was likewise a
very near resemblance between their voices. When Mrs.
Atkinson, therefore, found that Amelia was so extremely
averse to the masquerade, she proposed to go thither in her
stead, and to pass upon Booth for his own wife.

This was afterwards very easily executed; for, when they
left Booth's lodgings, Amelia, who went last to her chair,
ran back to fetch her masque, as she pretended, which she
had purposely left behind. She then whipped off her domino,

and threw it over Mrs. Atkinson, who stood ready to receive it, and ran immediately downstairs, and, stepping into Amelia's chair, proceeded with the rest to the masquerade.

As her stature exactly suited that of Amelia, she had very little difficulty to carry on the imposition; for, besides the natural resemblance of their voices, and the opportunity of speaking in a feigned one, she had scarce an intercourse of six words with Booth during the whole time; for the moment they got into the crowd she took the first opportunity of slipping from him. And he, as the reader may remember, being seized by other women, and concluding his wife to be safe with Mrs. James, was very well satisfied, till the colonel set him upon the search, as we have seen before.

Mrs. Atkinson, the moment she came home, ran upstairs to the nursery, where she found Amelia, and told her in haste that she might very easily carry on the deceit with her husband; for that she might tell him what she pleased to invent, as they had not been a minute together during the whole evening.

Booth was no sooner satisfied that his wife had not been from home that evening than he fell into raptures with her, gave her a thousand tender caresses, blamed his own judgment, acknowledged the goodness of hers, and vowed never to oppose her will more in any one instance during his life.

Mrs. Atkinson, who was still in the nursery with her masquerade dress, was then summoned down-stairs, and, when Booth saw her and heard her speak in her mimic tone, he declared he was not surprised at his having been imposed upon, for that, if they were both in the same disguise, he should scarce be able to discover the difference between them.

They then sat down to half an hour's chearful conversation, after which they retired all in the most perfect good humour.

CHAPTER IV

Consequences of the masquerade.

WHEN Booth rose in the morning he found in his pocket that letter which had been delivered to him by Colonel Bath, which, had not chance brought to his remembrance, he might possibly have never recollected.

He had now, however, the curiosity to open the letter, and beginning to read it, the matter of it drew him on till he perused the whole; for, notwithstanding the contempt cast upon it by those learned critics the bucks, neither the subject nor the manner in which it was treated was altogether contemptible.

But there was still another motive which induced Booth to read the whole letter, and this was, that he presently thought he knew the hand. He did, indeed, immediately conclude it was Doctor Harrison; for the doctor wrote a very remarkable one, and this letter contained all the particularities of the doctor's character.

He had just finished a second reading of this letter when the doctor himself entered the room. The good man was impatient to know the success of Amelia's stratagem, for he bore towards her all that love which esteem can create in a good mind, without the assistance of those selfish considerations from which the love of wives and children may be ordinarily deduced. The latter of which, Nature, by very subtle and refined reasoning, suggests to us to be part of our dear selves; and the former, as long as they remain the objects of our liking, that same Nature is furnished with very plain and fertile arguments to recommend to our affections. But to raise that affection in the human breast which the doctor had for Amelia, Nature is forced to use a kind of logic which is no more understood by a bad man than Sir Isaac Newton's doctrine of colours is by one born blind. And yet in reality if contains nothing more abstruse than this, that an injury is the object of anger, danger of fear, and praise of vanity;

for in the same simple manner it may be asserted that goodness is the object of love.

The doctor inquired immediately for his child (for so he often called Amelia); Booth answered that he had left her asleep, for that she had had but a restless night. "I hope she is not disordered by the masquerade," cries the doctor. Booth answered he believed she would be very well when she waked. "I fancy," said he, "her gentle spirits were a little too much fluttered last night; that is all."

"I hope, then," said the doctor, "you will never more insist on her going to such places, but know your own happiness in having a wife that hath the discretion to avoid those places; which, though perhaps they may not be as some represent them, such brothels of vice and debauchery as would impeach the character of every virtuous woman who was seen at them, are certainly, however, scenes of riot, disorder, and intemperance, very improper to be frequented by a chaste and sober Christian matron."

Booth declared that he was very sensible of his error, and that, so far from soliciting his wife to go to another masquerade, he did not intend ever to go thither any more himself.

The doctor highly approved the resolution; and then Booth said, "And I thank you, my dear friend, as well as my wife's discretion, that she was not at the masquerade last night." He then related to the doctor the discovery of the plot; and the good man was greatly pleased with the success of the stratagem, and that Booth took it in such good part.

"But, sir," says Booth, "I had a letter given me by a noble colonel there, which is written in a hand so very like yours, that I could almost swear to it. Nor is the style, as far as I can guess, unlike your own. Here it is, sir. Do you own the letter, doctor, or do you not?"

The doctor took the letter, and, having looked at it a moment, said, "And did the colonel himself give you this letter?"

"The colonel himself," answered Booth.

"Why then," cries the doctor, "he is surely the most impudent fellow that the world ever produced. What! did he deliver it with an air of triumph?"

"He delivered it me with air enough," cries Booth, "after his own manner, and bid me read it for my edification. To say the truth, I am a little surprised that he should single me out of all mankind to deliver the letter to; I do not think I deserve the character of such a husband. It is well I am not so very forward to take an affront as some folks."

"I am glad to see you are not," said the doctor; "and your behaviour in this affair becomes both the man of sense and the Christian; for it would be surely the greatest folly, as well as the most daring impiety, to risk your own life for the impertinence of a fool. As long as you are assured of the virtue of your own wife, it is wisdom in you to despise the efforts of such a wretch. Not, indeed, that your wife accuses him of any downright attack, though she hath observed enough in his behaviour to give offence to her delicacy."

"You astonish me, doctor," said Booth. "What can you mean? my wife dislike his behaviour! hath the colonel ever offended her?"

"I do not say he hath ever offended her by any open declarations; nor hath he done anything which, according to the most romantic notion of honour, you can or ought to resent; but there is something extremely nice in the chastity of a truly virtuous woman."

"And hath my wife really complained of anything of that kind in the colonel?"

"Look ye, young gentleman," cries the doctor; "I will have no quarrelling or challenging; I find I have made some mistake, and therefore I insist upon it by all the rights of friendship, that you give me your word of honour you will not quarrel with the colonel on this account."

"I do, with all my heart," said Booth; "for, if I did not know your character, I should absolutely think you was jesting with me. I do not think you have mistaken my wife, but I am sure she hath mistaken the colonel, and hath misconstrued some over-strained point of gallantry, something of the Quixote kind, into a design against her chastity; but I have that opinion of the colonel, that I hope you will not be offended when I declare I know not which of you two I should be the sooner jealous of."

"I would by no means have you jealous of any one," cries the doctor; "for I think my child's virtue may be firmly relied on; but I am convinced she would not have said what she did to me without a cause; nor should I, without such a conviction, have written that letter to the colonel, as I own to you I did. However, nothing I say hath yet passed which, even in the opinion of false honour, you are at liberty to resent; but as to declining any great intimacy, if you will take my advice, I think that would be prudent."

"You will pardon me, my dearest friend," said Booth, "but I have really such an opinion of the colonel that I would pawn my life upon his honour; and as for women, I do not believe he ever had an attachment to any."

"Be it so," said the doctor; "I have only two things to insist on. The first is, that, if ever you change your opinion, this letter may not be the subject of any quarrelling or fighting: the other is, that you never mention a word of this to your wife. By the latter I shall see whether you can keep a secret; and, if it is no otherwise material, it will be a wholesome exercise to your mind; for the practice of any virtue is a kind of mental exercise, and serves to maintain the health and vigour of the soul."

"I faithfully promise both," cries Booth. And now the breakfast entered the room, as did soon after Amelia and Mrs. Atkinson.

The conversation ran chiefly on the masquerade; and Mrs. Atkinson gave an account of several adventures there; but whether she told the whole truth with regard to herself I will not determine, for, certain it is, she never once mentioned the name of the noble peer. Amongst the rest, she said there was a young fellow that had preached a sermon there upon a stool, in praise of adultery, she believed; for she could not get near enough to hear the particulars.

During that transaction Booth had been engaged with the blue domino in another room, so that he knew nothing of it; so that what Mrs. Atkinson had now said only brought to his mind the doctor's letter to Colonel Bath, for to him he supposed it was written; and the idea of the colonel being a lover to Amelia struck him in so ridiculous a light, that it threw him into a violent fit of laughter.

The doctor, who, from the natural jealousy of an author, imputed the agitation of Booth's muscles to his own sermon or letter on that subject, was a little offended, and said gravely, "I should be glad to know the reason of this immoderate mirth. Is adultery a matter of jest in your opinion?"

"Far otherwise," answered Booth. "But how is it possible to refrain from laughter at the idea of a fellow preaching a sermon in favour of it at such a place?"

"I am very sorry," cries the doctor, "to find the age is grown to so scandalous a degree of licentiousness, that we have thrown off not only virtue, but decency. How abandoned must be the manners of any nation where such insults upon religion and morality can be committed with impunity! No man is fonder of true wit and humour than myself; but to profane sacred things with jest and scoffing is a sure sign of a weak and a wicked mind. It is the very vice which Homer attacks in the odious character of Thersites. The ladies must excuse my repeating the passage to you, as I know you have Greek enough to understand it:

> Ὃς ῥ' ἔπεα φρεσὶν ᾗσιν ἄκοσμά τε, πολλά τε ᾔδη.
> Μὰψ, ἀτὰρ οὐ κατὰ κόσμον ἐριζέμεναι βασιλεῦσιν,
> Ἀλλ' ὅ, τι οἱ εἴσαιτο γελοίϊον Ἀργείοισιν
> Ἔμμεναι.[1]

And immediately adds,

> ——αἴσχιστος δὲ ἀνὴρ ὑπὸ Ἴλιον ἦλθε.[2]

"Horace, again, describes such a rascal:

> —— Solutos
> Qui captat risus dominum famamque dicacis,[3]

and says of him,

> Hic niger est, hunc tu, Romane, caveto."[4]

"O charming Homer!" said Mrs. Atkinson, "how much above all other writers!"

"I ask your pardon, madam," said the doctor; "I forgot you was a scholar; but, indeed, I did not know you understood Greek as well as Latin."

"I do not pretend," said she, "to be a critic in the Greek;

---

[1] Thus paraphrased by Mr. Pope:
> Awed by no shame, by no respect controll'd,
> In scandal busy, in reproaches bold,
> With witty malice, studious to defame,
> Scorn all his joy, and laughter all his aim.

[2] He was the greatest scoundrel in the whole army.

[3] Who trivial bursts of laughter strives to raise,
And courts of prating petulance the praise.—FRANCIS.

[4] This man is black; do thou, O Roman! shun this man.

but I think I am able to read a little of Homer, at least with the help of looking now and then into the Latin."

"Pray, madam," said the doctor, "how do you like this passage in the speech of Hector to Andromache:

> ──Εἰς οἶκον ἰοῦσα τὰ σαυτῆς ἔργα κόμιζε,
> Ἱστόν τ᾽ ἠλακάτην τε, καὶ ἀμφιπόλοισι κέλευε
> Εργον ἐποίχεσθαι?[1]

"Or how do you like the character of Hippodamia, who, by being the prettiest girl and best workwoman of her age, got one of the best husbands in all Troy?—I think, indeed, Homer enumerates her discretion with her other qualifications; but I do not remember he gives us one character of a woman of learning.—Don't you conceive this to be a great omission in that charming poet? However, Juvenal makes you amends, for he talks very abundantly of the learning of the Roman ladies in his time."

"You are a provoking man, doctor," said Mrs. Atkinson; "where is the harm in a woman's having learning as well as a man?"

"Let me ask you another question," said the doctor. "Where is the harm in a man's being a fine performer with a needle as well as a woman? And yet, answer me honestly; would you greatly choose to marry a man with a thimble upon his finger? Would you in earnest think a needle became the hand of your husband as well as a halberd?"

"As to war, I am with you," said she. "Homer himself, I well remember, makes Hector tell his wife that warlike works—what is the Greek word—Pollemy—something—belonged to men only; and I readily agree to it. I hate a masculine woman, an Amazon, as much as you can do; but what is there masculine in learning?"

"Nothing so masculine, take my word for it. As for your Pollemy, I look upon it to be the true characteristic of a devil. So Homer everywhere characterizes Mars."

"Indeed, my dear," cries the serjeant, "you had better not dispute with the doctor; for, upon my word, he will be too hard for you."

"Nay, I beg *you* will not interfere," cries Mrs. Atkinson; "I am sure *you* can be no judge in these matters."

[1] Go home and mind your own business. Follow your spinning, and keep your maids to their work.

At which the doctor and Booth burst into a loud laugh; and Amelia, though fearful of giving her friend offence, could not forbear a gentle smile.

"You may laugh, gentleman, if you please," said Mrs. Atkinson; "but I thank Heaven I have married a man who is not jealous of my understanding. I should have been the most miserable woman upon earth with a starched pedant who was possessed of that nonsensical opinion that the difference of sexes causes any difference in the mind. Why don't you honestly avow the Turkish notion that women have no souls? for you say the same thing in effect."

"Indeed, my dear," cries the serjeant, greatly concerned to see his wife so angry, "you have mistaken the doctor."

"I beg, my dear," cried she, "*you* will say nothing upon these subjects—I hope *you* at least do not despise my understanding."

"I assure you, I do not," said the serjeant; "and I hope you will never despise mine; for a man may have some understanding, I hope, without learning."

Mrs. Atkinson reddened extremely at these words; and the doctor, fearing he had gone too far, began to soften matters, in which Amelia assisted him. By these means, the storm rising in Mrs. Atkinson before was in some measure laid, at least suspended from bursting at present; but it fell afterwards upon the poor serjeant's head in a torrent, who had learned perhaps one maxim from his trade, that a cannon-ball always does mischief in proportion to the resistance it meets with, and that nothing so effectually deadens its force as a woolpack. The serjeant therefore bore all with patience; and the idea of a woolpack, perhaps, bringing that of a feather-bed into his head, he at last not only quieted his wife, but she cried out with great sincereity, "Well, my dear, I will say one thing for you, that I believe from my soul, though you have no learning, you have the best understanding of any man upon earth; and I must own I think the latter far the more profitable of the two."

Far different was the idea she entertained of the doctor, whom, from this day, she considered as a conceited pedant; nor could all Amelia's endeavours ever alter her sentiments.

The doctor now took his leave of Booth and his wife for a week, he intending to set out within an hour or two with his old friend, with whom our readers were a little acquainted at the latter end of the ninth book, and of whom, perhaps, they did not then conceive the most favourable opinion.

Nay, I am aware that the esteem which some readers before had for the doctor may be here lessened; since he may appear to have been too easy a dupe to the gross flattery of the old gentleman. If there be any such critics, we are heartily sorry, as well for them as for the doctor; but it is our business to discharge the part of a faithful historian, and to describe human nature as it is, not as we would wish it to be.

CHAPTER V

In which Colonel Bath appears in great glory.

THAT afternoon, as Booth was walking in the Park, he met
with Colonel Bath, who presently asked him for the letter
which he had given him the night before; upon which Booth
immediately returned it.

"Don't you think," cries Bath, "it is writ with great
dignity of expression and emphasis of—of—of judgment?"

"I am surprised, though," cries Booth, "that any one
should write such a letter to you, colonel."

"To me!" said Bath. "What do you mean, sir? I hope
you don't imagine any man durst write such a letter to
me? d—n me, if I knew a man who thought me capable of
debauching my friend's wife, I would—d—n me."

"I believe, indeed, sir," cries Booth, "that no man living
dares put his name to such a letter; but you see it is
anonymous."

"I don't know what you mean by ominous," cries the
colonel; "but, blast my reputation, if I had received such a
letter, if I would not have searched the world to have found
the writer. D—n me, I would have gone to the East Indies
to have pulled off his nose."

"He would, indeed, have deserved it," cries Booth. "But
pray, sir, how came you by it?"

"I took it," said the colonel, "from a set of idle young
rascals, one of whom was reading it out aloud upon a stool,
while the rest were attempting to make a jest, not only of
the letter, but of all decency, virtue, and religion. A set
of fellows that you must have seen or heard of about the
town, that are, d—n me, a disgrace to the dignity of manhood; puppies that mistake noise and impudence, rudeness
and profaneness, for wit. If the drummers of my company
had not more understanding than twenty such fellows, I'd
have them both whipped out of the regiment."

"So, then, you do not know the person to whom it was
writ?" said Booth.

"Lieutenant," cries the colonel, "your question deserves no answer. I ought to take time to consider whether I ought not to resent the supposition. Do you think, sir, I am acquainted with a rascal?"

"I do not suppose, colonel," cries Booth, "that you would willingly cultivate an intimacy with such a person; but a man must have good luck who hath any acquaintance if there are not some rascals among them."

"I am not offended with you, child," says the colonel. "I know you did not intend to offend me."

"No man, I believe, dares intend it," said Booth.

"I believe so too," said the colonel; "d—n me, I know it. But you know, child, how tender I am on this subject. If I had been ever married myself, I should have cleft the man's skull who had dared look wantonly at my wife."

"It is certainly the most cruel of all injuries," said Booth. "How finely doth Shakespeare express it in his *Othello*!

But there, where I had treasured up my soul."

"That Shakespeare," cries the colonel, "was a fine fellow. He was a very pretty poet indeed. Was it not Shakespeare that wrote the play about Hotspur? You must remember these lines. I got them almost by heart at the playhouse; for I never missed that play whenever it was acted, if I was in town:

By Heav'n it was an easy leap,
To pluck bright honour into the full moon,
Or drive into the bottomless deep.

And—and—faith, I have almost forgot them; but I know it is something about saving your honour from drowning— O! it is very fine! I say, d—n me, the man that writ those lines was the greatest poet the world ever produced. There is dignity of expression and emphasis of thinking, d—n me."

Booth assented to the colonel's criticism, and then cried, "I wish, colonel, you would be so kind to give me that letter." The colonel answered, if he had any particular use for it he would give it him with all his heart, and presently delivered it; and soon afterwards they parted.

Several passages now struck all at once upon Booth's mind, which gave him great uneasiness. He became confident now that he had mistaken one colonel for another;

and, though he could not account for the letter's getting into those hands from whom Bath had taken it (indeed James had dropped it out of his pocket), yet a thousand circumstances left him no room to doubt the identity of the person, who was a man much more liable to raise the suspicion of a husband than honest Bath, who would at any time have rather fought with a man than lain with a woman.

The whole behaviour of Amelia now rushed upon his memory. Her resolution not to take up her residence at the colonel's house, her backwardness even to dine there, her unwillingness to go to the masquerade, many of her unguarded expressions, and some where she had been more guarded, all joined together to raise such an idea in Mr. Booth, that he had almost taken a resolution to go and cut the colonel to pieces in his own house. Cooler thoughts, however, suggested themselves to him in time. He recollected the promise he had so solemnly made to the doctor. He considered, moreover, that he was yet in the dark as to the extent of the colonel's guilt. Having nothing, therefore, to fear from it, he contented himself to postpone a resentment which he nevertheless resolved to take of the colonel hereafter, if he found he was in any degree a delinquent.

The first step he determined to take was, on the first opportunity, to relate to Colonel James the means by which he became possessed of the letter, and to read it to him; on which occasion, he thought he should easily discern by the behaviour of the colonel whether he had been suspected either by Amelia or the doctor without a cause; but as for his wife, he fully resolved not to reveal the secret to her till the doctor's return.

While Booth was deeply engaged by himself in these meditations, Captain Trent came up to him, and familiarly slapped him on the shoulder.

They were soon joined by a third gentleman, and presently afterwards by a fourth, both acquaintances of Mr. Trent; and all having walked twice the length of the Mall together, it being now past nine in the evening, Trent proposed going to the tavern, to which the strangers immediately consented; and Booth himself, after some resistance, was at length persuaded to comply.

To the King's Arms then they went, where the bottle went briskly round till after eleven; at which time Trent proposed a game at cards, to which proposal likewise Booth's consent was obtained, though not without much difficulty; for, though he had naturally some inclination to gaming, and had formerly a little indulged it, yet he had entirely left it off for many years.

Booth and his friend were partners, and had at first some success; but Fortune, according to her usual conduct, soon shifted about, and persecuted Booth with such malice, that in about two hours he was stripped of all the gold in his pocket, which amounted to twelve guineas, being more than half the cash which he was at that time worth.

How easy it is for a man who is at all tainted with the itch of gaming to leave off play in such a situation, especially when he is likewise heated with liquor, I leave to the gamester to determine. Certain it is that Booth had no inclination to desist; but, on the contrary, was so eagerly bent on playing on, that he called his friend out of the room, and asked him for ten pieces, which he promised punctually to pay the next morning.

Trent chid him for using so much formality on the occasion. "You know," said he, "dear Booth, you may have what money you please of me. Here is a twenty-pound note at your service; and, if you want five times the sum, it is at your service. We will never let these fellows go away with our money in this manner; for we have so much the advantage, that if the knowing ones were here they would lay odds of our side."

But if this was really Mr. Trent's opinion, he was very much mistaken; for the other two honourable gentlemen were not only great masters of the game, and somewhat soberer than poor Booth, having, with all the art in their power, evaded the bottle, but they had, moreover, another small advantage over their adversaries, both of them, by means of some certain private signs, previously agreed upon between them, being always acquainted with the principal cards in each other's hands. It cannot be wondered, therefore, that Fortune was on their side; for, however she may be reported to favour fools, she never, I believe, shows them any countenance when they engage in play with knaves.

The more Booth lost, the deeper he made his bets; the consequence of which was, that about two in the morning, besides the loss of his own money, he was fifty pounds indebted to Trent: a sum, indeed, which he would not have borrowed, had not the other, like a very generous friend, pushed it upon him.

Trent's pockets became at last dry by means of these loans. His own loss, indeed, was trifling; for the stakes of the games were no higher than crowns, and betting (as it is called) was that to which Booth owed his ruin. The gentlemen, therefore, pretty well knowing Booth's circumstances, and being kindly unwilling to win more of a man than he was worth, declined playing any longer, nor did Booth once ask them to persist, for he was ashamed of the debt which he had already contracted to Trent, and very far from desiring to increase it.

The company then separated. The two victors and Trent went off in their chairs to their several houses near Grosvenor-square, and poor Booth, in a melancholy mood, walked home to his lodgings. He was, indeed, in such a fit of despair, that it more than once came into his head to put an end to his miserable being.

But before we introduce him to Amelia we must do her the justice to relate the manner in which she spent this unhappy evening. It was about seven when Booth left her to walk in the park; from this time till past eight she was employed with her children, in playing with them, in giving them their supper, and in putting them to bed.

When these offices were performed she employed herself another hour in cooking up a little supper for her husband, this being, as we have already observed, his favourite meal, as indeed it was her's; and, in a most pleasant and delightful manner, they generally passed their time at this season, though their fare was very seldom of the sumptuous kind.

It now grew dark, and her hashed mutton was ready for the table, but no Booth appeared. Having waited therefore for him a full hour, she gave him over for that evening; nor was she much alarmed at his absence, as she knew he was in a night or two to be at the tavern with some brother-officers; she concluded therefore that they had met in the park, and had agreed to spend this evening together.

At ten then she sat down to supper by herself, for Mrs. Atkinson was then abroad. And here we cannot help relating a little incident, however trivial it may appear to some. Having sat some time alone, reflecting on their distressed situation, her spirits grew very low; and she was once or twice going to ring the bell to send her maid for half-a-pint of white wine, but checked her inclination in order to save the little sum of sixpence, which she did the more resolutely as she had before refused to gratify her children with tarts for their supper from the same motive. And this self-denial she was very probably practising to save sixpence, while her husband was paying a debt of several guineas incurred by the ace of trumps being in the hands of his adversary.

Instead therefore of this cordial she took up one of the excellent Farquhar's comedies, and read it half through; when, the clock striking twelve, she retired to bed, leaving the maid to sit up for her master. She would, indeed, have much more willingly sat up herself, but the delicacy of her own mind assured her that Booth would not thank her for the compliment. This is, indeed, a method which some wives take of upbraiding their husbands for staying abroad till too late an hour, and of engaging them, through tenderness and good nature, never to enjoy the company of their friends too long when they must do this at the expense of their wives' rest.

To bed then she went, but not to sleep. Thrice indeed she told the dismal clock, and as often heard the more dismal watchman, till her miserable husband found his way home, and stole silently like a thief to bed to her; at which time, pretending then first to awake, she threw her snowy arms around him; though, perhaps, the more witty property of snow, according to Addison, that is to say its coldness, rather belonged to the poor captain.

CHAPTER VI

Read, gamester, and observe.

Booth could not so well disguise the agitations of his mind from Amelia, but that she perceived sufficient symptoms to assure her that some misfortune had befallen him. This made her in her turn so uneasy that Booth took notice of it, and after breakfast said, "Sure, my dear Emily, something hath fallen out to vex you."

Amelia, looking tenderly at him, answered, "Indeed, my dear, you are in the right; I am indeed extremely vexed." "For Heaven's sake," said he, "what is it?" "Nay, my love," cried she, "that you must answer yourself. What ever it is which hath given you all that disturbance that you in vaine ndeavour to conceal from me, this it is which causes all my affliction."

"You guess truly, my sweet," replied Booth; "I am indeed afflicted, and I will not, nay I cannot, conceal the truth from you. I have undone myself, Amelia."

"What have you done, child?" said she, in some consternation; "pray, tell me."

"I have lost my money at play," answered he.

"Pugh!" said she, recovering herself—"what signifies the trifle you had in your pocket? Resolve never to play again, and let it give you no further vexation; I warrant you, we will contrive some method to repair such a loss."

"Thou heavenly angel! thou comfort of my soul!" cried Booth, tenderly embracing her; then starting a little from her arms, and looking with eager fondness in her eyes, he said, "Let me survey thee; art thou really human, or art thou not rather an angel in a human form? Oh, no," cried he, flying again into her arms, "thou art my dearest woman, my best, my beloved wife!"

Amelia, having returned all his caresses with equal kindness, told him she had near eleven guineas in her purse, and asked how much she should fetch him. "I would not advise you, Billy, to carry too much in your pocket, for fear it should be a temptation to you to return to gaming, in order to retrieve your past losses. Let me beg you, on all accounts, never to think more, if possible, on the trifle you have lost, any more than if you had never possessed it."

Booth promised her faithfully he never would, and refused to take any of the money. He then hesitated a moment, and cried—"You say, my dear, you have eleven guineas; you have a diamond ring, likewise, which was your grandmother's—I believe that is worth twenty pounds; and your own and the child's watch are worth as much more."

"I believe they would sell for as much," cried Amelia; "for a pawnbroker of Mrs. Atkinson's acquaintance offered to lend me thirty-five pounds upon them when you was in your last distress. But why are you computing their value now?"

"I was only considering," answered he, "how much we could raise in any case of exigency."

"I have computed it myself," said she; "and I believe all we have in the world, besides our bare necessary apparel, would produce about sixty pounds: and suppose, my dear," said she, "while we have that little sum, we should think of employing it some way or other, to procure some small subsistence for ourselves and our family. As for your dependence on the colonel's friendship, it is all vain, I am afraid, and fallacious. Nor do I see any hopes you have from any other quarter, of providing for yourself again in the army. And though the sum which is now in our power is very small, yet we may possibly contrive with it to put ourselves into some mean way of livelihood. I have a heart, my Billy, which is capable of undergoing anything for your sake; and I hope my hands are as able to work as those which have been more inured to it. But think, my dear, think what must be our wretched condition, when the very little we now have is all mouldered away, as it will soon be in this town."

When poor Booth heard this, and reflected that the time which Amelia foresaw was already arrived (for that he had already lost every farthing they were worth), it touched him to the quick; he turned pale, gnashed his teeth, and cried out, "Damnation! this is too much to bear."

Amelia was thrown into the utmost consternation by this

behaviour; and, with great terror in her countenance, cried out, "Good Heavens! my dear love, what is the reason of this agony?"

"Ask me no questions," cried he, "unless you would drive me to madness."

"My Billy! my love!" said she, "what can be the meaning of this?—I beg you will deal openly with me, and tell me all your griefs."

"Have you dealt fairly with me, Amelia?" said he.

"Yes, surely," said she; "Heaven is my witness how fairly."

"Nay, do not call Heaven," cried he, "to witness a falsehood. You have not dealt openly with me, Amelia. You have concealed secrets from me; secrets which I ought to have known, and which, if I had known, it had been better for us both."

"You astonish me as much as you shock me," cried she. "What falsehood, what treachery have I been guilty of?"

"You tell me," said he, "that I can have no reliance on James; why did not you tell me so before?"

"I call Heaven again," said she, "to witness; nay, I appeal to yourself for the truth of it; I have often told you so. I have told you I disliked the man, notwithstanding the many favours he had done you. I desired you not to have too absolute a reliance upon him. I own I had once an extreme good opinion of him, but I changed it, and I acquainted you that I had so——"

"But not," cries he, "with the reasons why you had changed it."

"I was really afraid, my dear," said she, "of going too far. I knew the obligations you had to him; and if I sus-suspected that he acted rather from vanity than true friendship——"

"Vanity!" cries he; "take care, Amelia: you know his motive to be much worse than vanity—a motive which, if he had piled obligations on me till they had reached the skies, would tumble all down to hell. It is vain to conceal it longer—I know all—your confidant hath told me all."

"Nay, then," cries she, "on my knees I entreat you to be pacified, and hear me out. It was, my dear, for you, my dread of your jealous honour, and the fatal consequences."

"Is not Amelia, then," cried he, "equally jealous of my honour? Would she, from a weak tenderness for my person, go privately about to betray, to undermine the most invaluable treasure of my soul? Would she have me pointed at as the credulous dupe, the easy fool, the tame, the kind cuckold, of a rascal with whom I conversed as a friend?"

"Indeed you injure me," said Amelia. "Heaven forbid I should have the trial! but I think I could sacrifice all I hold most dear to preserve your honour. I think I have shown I can. But I will—when you are cool, I will—satisfy you I have done nothing you ought to blame."

"I am cool then," cries he; "I will with the greatest coolness hear you.—But do not think, Amelia, I have the least jealousy, the least suspicion, the least doubt of your honour. It is your want of confidence in me alone which I blame."

"When you are calm," cried she, "I will speak, and not before."

He assured her he was calm; and then she said,

"You have justified my conduct by your present passion, in concealing from you my suspicions; for they were no more; nay, it is possible they were unjust; for since the doctor, in betraying the secret to you, hath so far falsified my opinion of him, why may I not be as well deceived in my opinion of the colonel, since it was only formed on some particulars in his behaviour which I disliked? for, upon my honour, he never spoke a word to me, nor hath been ever guilty of any direct action, which I could blame." She then went on, and related most of the circumstances which she had mentioned to the doctor, omitting one or two of the strongest, and giving such a turn to the rest, that, if Booth had not had some of Othello's blood in him, his wife would have almost appeared a prude in his eyes. Even he, however, was pretty well pacified by this narrative, and said he was glad to find a possibility of the colonel's innocence; but that he greatly commended the prudence of his wife, and only wished she would for the future make him her only confidant.

Amelia, upon that, expressed some bitterness against the doctor for breaking his trust; when Booth, in his excuse, related all the circumstances of the letter, and plainly convinced her that the secret had dropped by mere accident from the mouth of the doctor.

Thus the husband and wife became again reconciled, and poor Amelia generously forgave a passion of which the sagacious reader is better acquainted with the real cause than was that unhappy lady.

CHAPTER VII

In which Booth receives a visit from Captain Trent.

WHEN Booth grew perfectly cool, and began to reflect that
he had broken his word to the doctor, in having made the
discovery to his wife which we have seen in the last chapter,
that thought gave him great uneasiness; and now, to comfort
him, Captain Trent came to make him a visit.

This was, indeed, almost the last man in the world whose
company he wished for; for he was the only man he was
ashamed to see, for a reason well known to gamesters;
among whom, the most dishonourable of all things is not to
pay a debt, contracted at the gaming-table, the next day,
or the next time at least that you see the party.

Booth made no doubt but that Trent was come on purpose
to receive this debt; the latter had been therefore scarce a
minute in the room before Booth began, in an awkward
manner, to apolgise; but Trent immediately stopped his
mouth, and said, "I do not want the money, Mr. Booth,
and you may pay it me whenever you are able; and, if you
are never able, I assure you I will never ask you for it."

This generosity raised such a tempest of gratitude in
Booth (if I may be allowed the expression), that the tears
burst from his eyes, and it was some time before he could
find any utterance for those sentiments with which his
mind overflowed; but, when he began to express his thankfulness, Trent immediately stopped him, and gave a sudden turn
to their discourse.

Mrs. Trent had been to visit Mrs. Booth on the masquerade
evening, which visit Mrs. Booth had not yet returned.
Indeed, this was only the second day since she had received
it. Trent therefore now told his friend that he should take
it extremely kind if he and his lady would waive all ceremony,
and sup at their house the next evening. Booth hesitated a
moment, but presently said, "I am pretty certain my wife
is not engaged, and I will undertake for her. I am sure she

will not refuse anything Mr. Trent can ask." And soon after Trent took Booth with him to walk in the Park.

There were few greater lovers of a bottle than Trent; he soon proposed therefore to adjourn to the King's Arms tavern, where Booth, though much against his inclination, accompanied him. But Trent was very importunate, and Booth did not think himself at liberty to refuse such a request to a man from whom he had so lately received such obligations.

When they came to the tavern, however, Booth recollected the omission he had been guilty of the night before. He wrote a short note therefore to his wife, acquainting her that he should not come home to supper; but comforted her with a faithful promise that he would on no account engage himself in gaming.

The first bottle passed in ordinary conversation; but, when they had tapped the second, Booth, on some hints which Trent gave him, very fairly laid open to him his whole circumstances, and declared he almost despaired of mending them. "My chief relief," said he, "was in the interest of Colonel James; but I have given up those hopes."

"And very wisely too," said Trent. "I say nothing of the colonel's good will. Very likely he may be your sincere friend; but I do not believe he hath the interest he pretends to. He hath had too many favours in his own family to ask any more yet a while. But I am mistaken if you have not a much more powerful friend than the colonel; one who is both able and willing to serve you. I dined at his table within these two days, and I never heard kinder nor warmer expressions from the mouth of man than he made use of towards you. I make no doubt you know whom I mean."

"Upon my honour I do not," answered Booth; "nor did I guess that I had such a friend in the world as you mention."

"I am glad then," cries Trent, "that I have the pleasure of informing you of it." He then named the noble peer who hath been already so often mentioned in this history.

Booth turned pale and started at his name. "I forgive you my dear Trent," cries Booth, "for mentioning his name to me, as you are a stranger to what hath passed between us."

"Nay, I know nothing that hath passed between you," answered Trent. "I am sure, if there is any quarrel between you of two days' standing, all is forgiven on his part."

"D—n his forgiveness!" said Booth. "Perhaps I ought to blush at what I have forgiven."

"You surprise me!" cries Trent. "Pray what can be the matter?"

"Indeed, my dear Trent," cries Booth, very gravely, "he would have injured me in the tenderest part. I know not how to tell it you; but he would have dishonoured me with my wife."

"Sure, you are not in earnest!" answered Trent; "but, if you are, you will pardon me for thinking that impossible."

"Indeed," cries Booth, "I have so good an opinion of my wife as to believe it impossible for him to succeed; but that he should intend me the favour you will not, I believe, think an impossibility."

"Faith! not in the least," said Trent. "Mrs. Booth is a very fine woman; and, if I had the honour to be her husband, I should not be angry with any man for liking her."

"But you would be angry," said Booth, "with a man, who should make use of stratagems and contrivances to seduce her virtue; especially if he did this under the colour of entertaining the highest friendship for yourself."

"Not at all," cries Trent. "It is human nature."

"Perhaps it is," cries Booth; "but it is human nature depraved, stripped of all its worth, and loveliness, and dignity, and degraded down to a level with the vilest brutes."

"Look ye, Booth," cries Trent, "I would not be misunderstood. I think, when I am talking to you, I talk to a man of sense and to an inhabitant of this country, not to one who dwells in a land of saints. If you have really such an opinion as you express of this noble lord, you have the finest opportunity of making a complete fool and bubble of him that any man can desire, and of making your own fortune at the same time. I do not say that your suspicions are groundless; for, of all men upon earth I know, my lord is the greatest bubble to women, though I believe he hath had very few. And this I am confident of, that he hath not the least jealousy of these suspicions. Now, therefore, if you will act the part of a wise man, I will undertake that you shall make your fortune without the least injury to the chastity of Mrs. Booth."

"I do not understand you, sir," said Booth.

"Nay," cries Trent, "if you will not understand me, I

have done. I meant only your service; and I thought I had known you better."

Booth begged him to explain himself. "If you can," said he, "show me any way to improve such circumstances as I have opened to you, you may depend on it I shall readily embrace it, and own my obligations to you."

"That is spoken like a man," cries Trent. "Why, what is it more than this? Carry your suspicions in your own bosom. Let Mrs. Booth, in whose virtue I am sure you may be justly confident, go to the public places; there let her treat my lord with common civility only; I am sure he will bite. And thus, without suffering him to gain his purpose, you will gain yours. I know several who have succeeded with him in this manner."

"I am very sorry, sir," cries Booth, "that you are acquainted with any such rascals. I do assure you, rather than I would act such a part, I would submit to the hardest sentence that fortune could pronounce against me."

"Do as you please, sir," said Trent; "I have only ventured to advise you as a friend. But do you not think your nicety is a little over-scrupulous?"

"You will excuse me, sir," said Booth; "but I think no man can be too scrupulous in points which concern his honour."

"I know many men of very nice honour," answered Trent, "who have gone much farther; and no man, I am sure, had ever a better excuse for it than yourself. You will forgive me, Booth, since what I speak proceeds from my love to you; nay, indeed, by mentioning your affairs to me, which I am heartily sorry for, you have given me a right to speak. You know best what friends you have to depend upon; but, if you have no other pretensions than your merit, I can assure you you would fail, if it was possible you could have ten times more merit than you have. And, if you love your wife, as I am convinced you do, what must be your condition in seeing her want the necessaries of life?"

"I know my condition is very hard," cries Booth; "but I have one comfort in it, which I will never part with, and that is innocence. As to the mere necessaries of life, however, it is pretty difficult to deprive us of them; this I am sure of, no one can want them long."

"Upon my word, sir," cries Trent, "I did not know you had been so great a philosopher. But, believe me, these matters look much less terrible at a distance than when they are actually present. You will then find, I am afraid, that honour hath no more skill in cookery than Shakspere tells us it hath in surgery. D—n me if I don't wish his lordship loved my wife as well as he doth yours, I promise you I would trust her virtue; and, if he should get the better of it, I should have people of fashion enough to keep me in countenance."

Their second bottle being now almost out, Booth, without making any answer, called for a bill. Trent pressed very much the drinking another bottle, but Booth absolutely refused, and presently afterwards they parted, not extremely well satisfied with each other. They appeared, indeed, one to the other, in disadvantageous lights of a very different kind. Trent concluded Booth to be a very silly fellow, and Booth began to suspect that Trent was very little better than a scoundrel.

CHAPTER VIII

Contains a letter and other matters.

WE will now return to Amelia; to whom, immediately upon
her husband's departure to walk with Mr. Trent, a porter
brought the following letter, which she immediately opened
and read:

MADAM,—The quick despatch which I have given to your
first commands will I hope assure you of the diligence with which
I shall always obey every command that you are pleased to
honour me with.   I have, indeed, in this trifling affair, acted
as if my life itself had been at stake; nay, I know not but it may
be so; for this insignificant matter, you was pleased to tell me,
would oblige the charming person in whose power is not only
my happiness, but, as I am well persauded, my life too.   Let
me reap therefore some little advantage in your eyes, as you
have in mine, from this trifling occasion; for, if anything could
add to the charms of which you are mistress, it would be perhaps
that amiable zeal with which you maintain the cause of your
friend.   I hope, indeed, she will be my friend and advocate with
the most lovely of her sex, as I think she hath reason, and as you
was pleased to insinuate she had been.   Let me beseech you,
madam, let not that dear heart, whose tenderness is so inclined
to compassionate the miseries of others, be hardened only against
the sufferings which itself occasions.   Let not that man alone
have reason to think you cruel, who, of all others, would do the
most to procure your kindness.   How often have I lived over
in my reflections, in my dreams, those two short minutes we
were together!   But, alas! how faint are these mimicries of the
imagination!   What would I not give to purchase the reality
of such another blessing!   This, madam, is in your power to
bestow on the man who hath no wish, no will, no fortune, no
heart, no life, but what are at your disposal.   Grant me only
the favour to be at lady ——'s assembly.   You can have nothing
to fear from indulging me with a moment's sight, a moment's
conversation; I will ask no more.   I know your delicacy, and
had rather die than offend it.   Could I have seen you sometimes, I believe the fear of offending you would have kept my
love for ever buried in my own bosom; but, to be totally excluded
even from the sight of what my soul doats on is what I cannot
bear.   It is that alone which hath extorted the fatal secret from
me.   Let that obtain your forgiveness for me.   I need not sign

this letter otherwise than with that impression of my heart
which I hope it bears; and, to conclude it in any form, no language
hath words of devotion strong enough to tell you with what
truth, what anguish, what zeal, what adoration I love you."

Amelia had just strength to hold out to the end, when her
trembling grew so violent that she dropped the letter, and had
probably dropped herself, had not Mrs. Atkinson come timely
in to support her.

"Good Heavens!" cries Mrs. Atkinson, "what is the
matter with you, madam?"

"I know not what is the matter," cries Amelia; "but I
have received a letter at last from that infamous colonel."

"You will take my opinion again then, I hope, madam,"
cries Mrs. Atkinson. "But don't be so affected; the letter
cannot eat you or run away with you. Here it lies, I see;
will you give me leave to read it?"

"Read it with all my heart," cries Amelia; "and give me
your advice how to act, for I am almost distracted."

"Heydey!" says Mrs. Atkinson, "here is a piece of parchment too—what is that?" In truth, this parchment had
dropped from the letter when Amelia first opened it; but her
attention was so fixed by the contents of the letter itself
that she had never read the other. Mrs. Atkinson had now
opened the parchment first; and, after a moment's perusal,
the fire flashed from her eyes, and the blood flushed into her
cheeks, and she cried out, in a rapture, "It is a commission
for my husband! upon my soul, it is a commission for my
husband:" and, at the same time, began to jump about the
room in a kind of frantic fit of joy.

"What can be the meaning of all this?" cries Amelia,
under the highest degree of astonishment.

"Do not I tell you, my dear madam," cries she, "that it
is a commission for my husband? and can you wonder at
my being overjoyed at what I know will make him so happy?
And now it is all out. The letter is not from the colonel,
but from that noble lord of whom I have told you so much.
But, indeed, madam, I have some pardons to ask of you.
However, I know your goodness, and I will tell you all.

"You are to know then, madam, that I had not been in
the Opera-house six minutes before a masque came up, and,
taking me by the hand, led me aside. I gave the masque
my hand; and, seeing a lady at that time lay hold on Captain

Booth, I took that opportunity of slipping away from him;
for though, by the help of the squeaking voice, and by
attempting to mimic yours, I had pretty well disguised my
own, I was still afraid, if I had much conversation with your
husband, he would discover me. I walked therefore away
with this masque to the upper end of the farthest room, where
we sat down in a corner together. He presently discovered
to me that he took me for you, and I soon after found out
who he was; indeed, so far from attempting to disguise
himself, he spoke in his own voice and in his own person.
He now began to make very violent love to me, but it was
rather in the style of a great man of the present age than of
an Arcadian swain. In short, he laid his whole fortune at
my feet, and bade me make whatever terms I pleased, either
for myself or for others. By others, I suppose he meant your
husband. This, however, put a thought into my head of
turning the present occasion to advantage. I told him there
were two kinds of persons, the fallaciousness of whose
promises had become proverbial in the world. These were
lovers, and great men. What reliance, then, could I have
on the promise of one who united in himself both those
characters? That I had seen a melancholy instance, in a
very worthy woman of my acquaintance (meaning myself,
madam), of his want of generosity. I said I knew the obligations that he had to this woman, and the injuries he had done
her, all which I was convinced she forgave, for that she had
said the handsomest things in the world of him to me. He
answered that he thought he had not been deficient in
generosity to this lady (for I explained to him whom I meant);
but that indeed, if she had spoke well of him to me (meaning
yourself, madam), he would not fail to reward her for such an
obligation. I then told him she had married a very deserv-
ing man, who had served long in the army abroad as a
private man, and who was a serjeant in the guards; that I
knew it was so very easy for him to get him a commission,
that I should not think he had any honour or goodness in
the world if he neglected it. I declared this step must be
a preliminary to any good opinion he must ever hope for
of mine. I then professed the greatest friendship to that
lady (in which I am convinced you will think me serious),
and assured him he would give me one of the highest pleasures
in letting me be the instrument of doing her such a service.

He promised me in a moment to do what you see, madam, he hath since done. And to you I shall always think myself indebted for it."

"I know not how you are indebted to me," cries Amelia. "Indeed, I am very glad of any good fortune that can attend poor Atkinson, but I wish it had been obtained some other way. Good Heavens! what must be the consequence of this? What must this lord think of me for listening to his mention of love? nay, for making any terms with him? for what must he suppose those terms mean? Indeed, Mrs. Atkinson, you carried it a great deal too far. No wonder he had the assurance to write to me in the manner he hath done. It is too plain what he conceives of me, and who knows what he may say to others? You may have blown up my reputation by your behaviour."

"How is that possible?" answered Mrs. Atkinson. "Is it not in my power to clear up all matters? If you will but give me leave to make an appointment in your name I will meet him myself, and declare the whole secret to him."

"I will consent to no such appointment," cries Amelia. "I am heartily sorry I ever consented to practise any deceit. I plainly see the truth of what Dr. Harrison hath often told me, that, if one steps ever so little out of the ways of virtue and innocence, we know not how we may slide, for all the ways of vice are a slippery descent."

"That sentiment," cries Mrs. Atkinson, "is much older than Dr. Harrison. *Omne vitium in proclivi est.*"

"However new or old it is, I find it is true," cries Amelia —"But, pray, tell me all, though I tremble to hear it."

"Indeed, my dear friend," said Mrs. Atkinson, "you are terrified at nothing—indeed, indeed, you are too great a prude."

"I do not know what you mean by prudery," answered Amelia. "I shall never be ashamed of the strictest regard to decency, to reputation, and to that honour in which the dearest of all human creatures hath his share. But, pray, give me the letter, there is an expression in it which alarmed me when I read it. Pray, what doth he mean by his two short minutes, and by purchasing the reality of such another blessing?"

"Indeed, I know not what he means by two minutes," cries Mrs. Atkinson, "unless he calls two hours so; for we were not together much less. And as for any blessing he had, I am a stranger to it. Sure, I hope you have a better opinion of me than to think I granted him the last favour."

"I don't know what favours you granted him, madam," answered Amelia peevishly, "but I am sorry you granted him any in my name."

"Upon my word," cries Mrs. Atkinson, "you use me unkindly, and it is an usage I did not expect at your hands, nor do I know that I have deserved it. I am sure I went to the masquerade with no other view than to oblige you, nor did I say or do anything there which any woman who is not the most confounded prude upon earth would have started at on a much less occasion than what induced me. Well, I declare upon my soul then, that, if I was a man, rather than be married to a woman who makes such a fuss with her virtue, I would wish my wife was without such a troublesome companion."

"Very possibly, madam, these may be your sentiments," cries Amelia, "and I hope they are the sentiments of your husband."

"I desire, madam," cries Mrs. Atkinson, "you would not reflect on my husband. He is a worthy man and as brave a man as yours; yes, madam, and he is now as much a captain."

She spoke those words with so loud a voice, that Atkinson, who was accidentally going up-stairs, heard them; and, being surprised at the angry tone of his wife's voice, he entered the room, and, with a look of much astonishment, begged to know what was the matter.

"The matter, my dear," cries Mrs. Atkinson, "is that I have got a commission for you, and your good old friend here is angry with me for getting it."

"I have not spirits enough," cries Amelia, "to answer you as you deserve; and, if I had, you are below my anger."

"I do not know, Mrs. Booth," answered the other, "whence this great superiority over me is derived; but, if your virtue gives it you, I would have you to know, madam, that I despise a prude as much as you can do a ——."

"Though you have several times," cries Amelia, "insulted me with that word, I scorn to give you any ill language in return. If you deserve any bad appelation, you know it, without my telling it you."

Poor Atkinson, who was more frightened than he had ever been in his life, did all he could to procure peace. He fell upon his knees to his wife, and begged her to compose herself; for indeed she seemed to be in a most furious rage.

While he was in this posture Booth, who had knocked so gently at the door, for fear of disturbing his wife, that he had not been heard in the tempest, came into the room. The moment Amelia saw him, the tears which had been gathering for some time, burst in a torrent from her eyes, which, however, she endeavoured to conceal with her handkerchief. The entry of Booth turned all in an instant into a silent picture, in which the first figure which struck the eyes of the captain was the serjeant on his knees to his wife.

Booth immediately cried, "What's the meaning of this?" but received no answer. He then cast his eyes towards Amelia, and, plainly discerning her condition, he ran to her, and in a very tender phrase begged to know what was the matter. To which she answered, "Nothing, my dear, nothing of any consequence." He replied that he would know, and then turned to Atkinson, and asked the same question.

Atkinson answered, "Upon my honour, sir, I know nothing of it. Something hath passed between madam and my wife; but what it is I know no more than your honour."

"Your wife," said Mrs. Atkinson, "hath used me cruelly ill, Mr. Booth. If you must be satisfied, that is the whole matter."

Booth rapped out a great oath, and cried, "It is impossible; my wife is not capable of using any one ill."

Amelia then cast herself upon her knees to her husband, and cried, "For Heaven's sake do not throw yourself into a passion—some few words have passed—perhaps I may be in the wrong."

"Damnation seize me if I think so!" cries Booth. "And I wish whoever hath drawn these tears from your eyes may pay it with as many drops of their heart's blood."

"You see, madam," cries Mrs. Atkinson, "you have your bully to take your part; so I suppose you will use your triumph."

Amelia made no answer, but still kept hold of Booth, who, in a violent rage, cried out, "My Amelia triumph over such a wretch as thee!—What can lead thy insolence to such presumption! Serjeant, I desire you'll take that monster out of the room, or I cannot answer for myself."

The serjeant was beginning to beg his wife to retire (for he perceived very plainly that she had, as the phrase is, taken a sip too much that evening) when, with a rage little short of madness, she cried out, "And do you tamely see me insulted in such a manner, now that you are a gentleman, and upon a footing with him?"

"It is lucky for us all, perhaps," answered Booth, "that he is not my equal."

"You lie, sirrah," said Mrs. Atkinson; "he is every way your equal; he is as good a gentleman as yourself, and as much an officer. No; I retract what I say; he hath not the spirit of a gentleman, nor of a man neither, or he would not bear to see his wife insulted."

"Let me beg of you, my dear," cries the serjeant, "to go with me and compose yourself."

"Go with thee, thou wretch!" cries she, looking with the utmost disdain upon him; "no, nor ever speak to thee more." At which words she burst out of the room, and the serjeant, without saying a word, followed her.

A very tender and pathetic scene now passed between Booth and his wife, in which, when she was a little composed, she related to him the whole story. For, besides that it was not possible for her otherwise to account for the quarrel which he had seen, Booth was now possessed of the letter that lay on the floor.

Amelia, having emptied her mind to her husband, and obtained his faithful promise that he would not resent the affair to my lord, was pretty well composed, and began to relent a little towards Mrs. Atkinson; but Booth was so highly incensed with her, that he declared he would leave her house the next morning; which they both accordingly did, and immediately accommodated themselves with convenient apartments within a few doors of their friend the doctor.

CHAPTER IX

Containing some things worthy observation.

NOTWITHSTANDING the exchange of his lodgings, Booth did not forget to send an excuse to Mr. Trent, of whose conversation he had taken a full surfeit the preceding evening.

That day in his walks Booth met with an old brother-officer, who had served with him at Gibraltar, and was on half-pay as well as himself. He had not, indeed, had the fortune of being broke with his regiment, as was Booth, but had gone out, as they call it, on half-pay as a lieutenant, a rank to which he had risen in five and thirty years.

This honest gentleman, after some discourse with Booth, desired him to lend him half a crown, which he assured him he would faithfully pay the next day, when he was to receive some money for his sister. The sister was the widow of an officer that had been killed in the sea-service; and she and her brother lived together, on their joint stock, out of which they maintained likewise an old mother and two of the sister's children, the eldest of which was about nine years old. "You must know," said the old lieutenant, "I have been disappointed this morning by an old scoundrel, who wanted fifteen per cent. for advancing my sister's pension; but I have now got an honest fellow who hath promised it me to-morrow at ten per cent."

"And enough too, of all conscience," cries Booth.

"Why, indeed, I think so too," answered the other; "considering it is sure to be paid one time or other. To say the truth, it is a little hard the government doth not pay those pensions better; for my sister's hath been due almost these two years; that is my way of thinking."

Booth answered he was ashamed to refuse him such a sum; but, "Upon my soul," said he, "I have not a single half-penny in my pocket; for I am in a worse condition, if possible, than yourself; for I have lost all my money, and, what is worse, I owe Mr. Trent, whom you remember at Gibraltar, fifty pounds."

"Remember him! yes, d—n him! I remember him very well," cries the old gentleman, "though he will not remember me. He is grown so great now that he will not speak to his old acquaintance; and yet I should be ashamed of myself to be great in such a manner."

"What manner do you mean?" cries Booth, a little eagerly.

"Why, by pimping," answered the other; "he is pimp in ordinary to my Lord ——, who keeps his family; or how the devil he lives else I don't know, for his place is not worth three hundred pounds a year, and he and his wife spend a thousand at least. But she keeps an assembly, which, I believe, if you was to call a bawdy-house, you would not misname it. But d—n me if I had not rather be an honest man, and walk on foot, with holes in my shoes, as I do now, or go without a dinner, as I and all my family will to-day, than ride in a chariot and feast by such means. I am honest Bob Bound, and always will be; that 's my way of thinking; and there 's no man shall call me otherwise; for if he doth, I will knock him down for a lying rascal; that is my way of thinking."

"And a very good way of thinking too," cries Booth. "However, you shall not want a dinner to-day; for if you will go home with me, I will lend you a crown with all my heart."

"Lookee," said the old man, "if it be anywise inconvenient to you I will not have it; for I will never rob another man of his dinner to eat myself—that is my way of thinking."

"Pooh!" said Booth; "never mention such a trifle twice between you and me. Besides, you say you can pay it me to-morrow; and I promise you that will be the same thing."

They then walked together to Booth's lodgings, where Booth, from Amelia's pocket, gave his friend double the little sum he had asked. Upon which the old gentleman shook him heartily by the hand, and repeating his intention of paying him the next day, made the best of his way to a butcher's, whence he carried off a leg of mutton to a family that had lately kept Lent without any religious merit.

When he was gone Amelia asked her husband who that old gentleman was? Booth answered he was one of the scandals of his country; that the Duke of Marlborough had about thirty years before made him an ensign from a private man for very particular merit; and that he had not long since gone out of the army with a broken heart, upon having several boys put over his head. He then gave her an account of his family, which he had heard from the old gentleman in their way to his house, and with which we have already in a concise manner acquainted the reader.

"Good Heavens!" cries Amelia; "what are our great men made of? are they in reality a distinct species from the rest of mankind? are they born without hearts?"

"One would, indeed, sometimes," cries Booth, "be inclined to think so. In truth, they have no perfect idea of those common distresses of mankind which are far removed from their own sphere. Compassion, if thoroughly examined, will, I believe, appear to be the fellow-feeling only of men of the same rank and degree of life for one another, on account of the evils to which they themselves are liable. Our sensations are, I am afraid, very cold towards those who are at a great distance from us, and whose calamities can consequently never reach us."

"I remember," cries Amelia, "a sentiment of Dr. Harrison's, which he told me was in some Latin book; *I am a man myself, and my heart is interested in whatever can befall the rest of mankind.* That is the sentiment of a good man, and whoever thinks otherwise is a bad one."

"I have often told you, my dear Emily," cries Booth "that all men, as well the best as the worst, act alike from the principle of self-love. Where benevolence therefore is the uppermost passion, self-love directs you to gratify it by doing good, and by relieving the distresses of others; for they are then in reality your own. But where ambition, avarice, pride, or any other passion, governs the man and keeps his benevolence down, the miseries of all other men affect him no more than they would a stock or a stone. And thus the man and his statue have often the same degree of feeling or compassion."

"I have often wished, my dear," cries Amelia, "to hear you converse with Dr. Harrison on this subject; for I am sure he would convince you, though I can't, that there are really such things as religion and virtue."

This was not the first hint of this kind which Amelia had given; for she sometimes apprehended from his discourse that he was little better than an atheist: a consideration which did not diminish her affection for him, but gave her great uneasiness. On all such occasions Booth immediately turned the discourse to some other subject; for, though he had in other points a great opinion of his wife's capacity, yet as a divine or a philosopher he did not hold her in a very respectable light, nor did he lay any great stress on her sentiments in such matters. He now, therefore, gave a speedy turn to the conversation, and began to talk of affairs below the dignity of this history.

BOOK XI

CHAPTER I

Containing a very polite scene.

WE will now look back to some personages who, though not the principal characters in this history, have yet made too considerable a figure in it to be abruptly dropped: and these are Colonel James and his lady.

This fond couple never met till dinner the day after the masquerade, when they happened to be alone together in an ante-chamber before the arrival of the rest of the company.

The conversation began with the colonel's saying, "I hope, madam, you got no cold last night at the masquerade." To which the lady answered by much the same kind of question.

They then sat together near five minutes without opening their mouths to each other. At last Mrs. James said, "Pray, sir, who was that masque with you in the dress of a shepherdess? How could you expose yourself by walking with such a trollop in public; for certainly no woman of any figure would appear there in such a dress? You know, Mr. James, I never interfere with your affairs; but I would, methinks, for my own sake, if I was you, preserve a little decency in the face of the world."

"Upon my word," said James, "I do not know whom you mean. A woman in such a dress might speak to me for aught I know. A thousand people speak to me at a masquerade. But, I promise you, I spoke to no woman acquaintance there that I know of. Indeed, I now recollect there was a woman in a dress of a shepherdess; and there was another awkward thing in a blue domino that plagued me a little, but I soon got rid of them."

"And I suppose you do not know the lady in the blue domino neither?"

"Not I, I assure you," said James. "But pray, why do you ask me these questions? it looks so like jealousy."

"Jealousy!" cries she; "I jealous! no, Mr. James, I shall

never be jealous, I promise you, especially of the lady in the blue domino; for, to my knowledge, she despises you of all human race."

"I am heartily glad of it," said James; "for I never saw such a tall awkward monster in my life."

"That is a very cruel way of telling me you knew me."

"You, madam!" said James; "you was in a black domino."

"It is not so unusual a thing, I believe, you yourself know, to change dresses. I own I did it to discover some of your tricks. I did not think you could have distinguished the tall awkward monster so well."

"Upon my soul," said James, "if it was you I did not even suspect it; so you ought not to be offended at what I have said ignorantly."

"Indeed, sir," cries she, "you cannot offend me by anything you can say to my face; no, by my soul, I despise you too much. But I wish, Mr. James, you would not make me the subject of your conversation amongst your wenches. I desire I may not be afraid of meeting them for fear of their insults; that I may not be told by a dirty trollop you make me the subject of your wit amongst them, of which, it seems, I am the favourite topic. Though you have married a tall awkward monster, Mr. James, I think she hath a right to be treated, as your wife, with respect at least: indeed, I shall never require any more; indeed, Mr. James, I never shall. I think a wife hath a title to that."

"Who told you this, madam?" said James.

"Your slut," said she; "your wench, your shepherdess."

"By all that's sacred!" cries James, "I do not know who the shepherdess was."

"By all that's sacred then," says she, "she told me so, and I am convinced she told me truth. But I do not wonder at you denying it; for that is equally consistent with honour as to behave in such a manner to a wife who is a gentle-woman. I hope you will allow me that, sir. Because I had not quite so great a fortune I hope you do not think me beneath you, or that you did me any honour in marrying me. I am come of as good a family as yourself, Mr. James; and if my brother knew how you treated me he would not bear it."

"Do you threaten me with your brother, madam?" said James.

"I will not be ill-treated, sir," answered she.

"Nor I neither, madam," cries he; "and therefore I desire you will prepare to go into the country to-morrow morning."

"Indeed, sir," said she, "I shall not."

"By heavens! madam, but you shall," answered he: "I will have my coach at the door to-morrow morning by seven; and you shall either go into it or be carried."

"I hope, sir, you are not in earnest," said she.

"Indeed, madam," answered he, "but I am in earnest, and resolved; and into the country you go to-morrow."

"But why into the country," said she, "Mr. James? Why will you be so barbarous to deny me the pleasures of the town?"

"Because you interfere with my pleasures," cried James, "which I have told you long ago I would not submit to. It is enough for fond couples to have these scenes together. I thought we had been upon a better footing, and had cared too little for each other to become mutual plagues. I thought you had been satisfied with the full liberty of doing what you pleased."

"So I am; I defy you to say I have ever given you any uneasiness."

"How!" cries he; "have you not just now upbraided me with what you heard at the masquerade?"

"I own," said she, "to be insulted by such a creature to my face stung me to the soul. I must have had no spirit to bear the insults of such an animal. Nay, she spoke of you with equal contempt. Whoever she is, I promise you Mr. Booth is her favourite. But, indeed, she is unworthy any one's regard, for she behaved like an arrant dragoon."

"Hang her!" cries the colonel, "I know nothing of her."

"Well, but, Mr. James, I am sure you will not send me into the country. Indeed I will not go into the country."

"If you was a reasonable woman," cries James, "perhaps I should not desire it. And on one consideration——"

"Come, name your consideration," said she.

"Let me first experience your discernment," said he. "Come, Molly, let me try your judgment. Can you guess at any woman of your acquaintance that I like?"

"Sure," said she, "it cannot be Mrs. Booth!"

"And why not Mrs. Booth?" answered he. "Is she not the finest woman in the world?"

"Very far from it," replied she, "in my opinion."

"Pray what faults," said he, "can you find in her?"

"In the first place," cries Mrs. James, "her eyes are too large; and she hath a look with them that I don't know how to describe; but I know I don't like it. Then her eyebrows are too large; therefore, indeed, she doth all in her power to remedy this with her pincers; for if it was not for those her eyebrows would be preposterous. Then her nose, as well proportioned as it is, has a visible scar on one side. Her neck, likewise, is too protuberant for the genteel size, especially as she laces herself; for no woman, in my opinion, can be genteel who is not entirely flat before. And, lastly, she is both too short and too tall. Well, you may laugh, Mr. James, I know what I mean, though I cannot well express it: I mean that she is too tall for a pretty woman and too short for a fine woman. There is such a thing as a kind of insipid medium—a kind of something that is neither one thing nor another. I know not how to express it more clearly; but when I say such a one is a pretty woman, a pretty thing, a pretty creature, you know very well I mean a little woman; and when I say such a one is a very fine woman, a very fine person of a woman, to be sure I must mean a tall woman. Now a woman that is between both is certainly neither the one nor the other."

"Well, I own," said he, "you have explained yourself with great dexterity; but, with all these imperfections, I cannot help liking her."

"That you need not tell me, Mr. James," answered the lady, "for that I knew before you desired me to invite her to your house. And nevertheless, did not I, like an obedient wife, comply with your desires? did I make any objection to the party you proposed for the masquerade, though I knew very well your motive? what can the best of wives do more? to procure you success is not in my power; and, if I may give you my opinion, I believe you will never succeed with her."

"Is her virtue so very impregnable?" said he, with a sneer.

"Her virtue," answered Mrs. James, "hath the best guard in the world, which is a most violent love for her husband."

"All pretence and affectation," cries the colonel. "It is

impossible she should have so little taste, or indeed so little delicacy, as to like such a fellow."

"Nay, I do not much like him myself," said she. "He is not indeed at all such a sort of man as I should like; but I thought he had been generally allowed to be handsome."

"He handsome!" cries James. "What, with a nose like the proboscis of an elephant, with the shoulders of a porter, and the legs of a chairman? The fellow hath not in the least the look of a gentleman, and one would rather think he had followed the plough than the camp all his life."

"Nay, now I protest," said she, "I think you do him injustice. He is genteel enough in my opinion. It is true, indeed, he is not quite of the most delicate make; but, whatever he is, I am convinced she thinks him the finest man in the world."

"I cannot believe it," answered he peevishly; "but will you invite her to dinner here to-morrow?"

"With all my heart, and as often as you please," answered she. "But I have some favours to ask of you. First, I must hear no more of going out of town till I please."

"Very well," cries he.

"In the next place," said she, "I must have two hundred guineas within these two or three days."

"Well, I agree to that too," answered he.

"And when I do go out of town, I go to Tunbridge—I insist upon that; and from Tunbridge I go to Bath—positively to Bath. And I promise you faithfully I will do all in my power to carry Mrs. Booth with me."

"On that condition," answered he, "I promise you you shall go wherever you please. And, to show you, I will even prevent your wishes by my generosity; as soon as I receive the five thousand pounds which I am going to take up on one of my estates, you shall have two hundred more."

She thanked him with a low curtsy; and he was in such good humour that he offered to kiss her. To the kiss she coldly turned her cheek, and then, flirting her fan, said, "Mr. James, there is one thing I forgot to mention to you—I think you intended to get a commission in some regiment abroad for this young man. Now if you would take my advice, I know this will not oblige his wife; and, besides, I am positive she resolves to go with him. But, if you can provide for him in some regiment at home, I know she will dearly love you for it, and when he is ordered to quarters she will be left behind; and Yorkshire or Scotland, I think, is as good a distance as either of the Indies."

"Well, I will do what I can," answered James; "but I cannot ask anything yet; for I got two places of a hundred a year for two of my footmen, within this fortnight."

At this instant a violent knock at the door signified the arrival of their company, upon which both husband and wife put on their best looks to receive their guests; and, from their behaviour to each other during the rest of the day, a stranger might have concluded he had been in company with the fondest couple in the universe.

CHAPTER II

Matters political.

BEFORE we return to Booth we will relate a scene in which Dr. Harrison was concerned.

This good man, whilst in the country, happened to be in the neighbourhood of a nobleman of his acquaintance, and whom he knew to have very considerable interest with the ministers at that time.

The doctor, who was very well known to this nobleman, took this opportunity of paying him a visit in order to recommend poor Booth to his favour. Nor did he much doubt of his success, the favour he was to ask being a very small one, and to which he thought the service of Booth gave him so just a title.

The doctor's name soon gained him an admission to the presence of this great man, who, indeed, received him with much courtesy and politeness; not so much, perhaps, from any particular regard to the sacred function, nor from any respect to the doctor's personal merit, as from some considerations which the reader will perhaps guess anon. After many ceremonials, and some previous discourse on different subjects, the doctor opened the business, and told the great man that he was come to him to solicit a favour for a young gentleman who had been an officer in the army and was now on half-pay. "All the favour I ask, my lord," said he, "is, that this gentleman may be again admitted *ad eundem.* I am convinced your lordship will do me the justice to think I would not ask for a worthless person; but, indeed, the young man I mean hath very extraordinary merit. He was at the siege of Gibraltar, in which he behaved with distinguished bravery, and was dangerously wounded at two several times in the service of his country. I will add that he is at present in great necessity, and hath a wife and several children, for whom he hath no other means of providing; and, if it will recommend him further to your lordship's favour, his wife, I believe, is one of the best and worthiest of all her sex."

"As to that, my dear doctor," cries the nobleman, "I shall make no doubt. Indeed any service I shall do the gentleman will be upon your account. As to necessity, it is the plea of so many that it is impossible to serve them all. And with regard to the personal merit of these inferior officers I believe I need not tell you that it is very little regarded. But if you recommend him, let the person be what he will, I am convinced it will be done; for I know it is in your power at present to ask for a greater matter than this."

"I depend entirely upon your lordship," answered the doctor.

"Indeed, my worthy friend," replied the lord, "I will not take a merit to myself which will so little belong to me. You are to depend on yourself. It falls out very luckily too at this time, when you have it in your power so greatly to oblige us."

"What, my lord, is in my power?" cries the doctor.

"You certainly know," answered his lordship, "how hard Colonel Trompington is run at your town in the election of a mayor; they tell me it will be a very near thing unless you join us. But we know it is in your power to do the business, and turn the scale. I heard your name mentioned the other day on that account, and I know you may have anything in reason if you will give us your interest."

"Sure, my lord," cries the doctor, "you are not in earnest in asking my interest for the colonel?"

"Indeed I am," answered the peer; "why should you doubt it?"

"For many reasons," answered the doctor. "First, I am an old friend and acquaintance of Mr. Fairfield, as your lordship, I believe, very well knows. The little interest, therefore, that I have, you may be assured, will go in his favour. Indeed, I do not concern myself deeply in these affairs, for I do not think it becomes my cloth so to do. But, as far as I think it decent to interest myself, it will certainly be on the side of Mr. Fairfield. Indeed, I should do so if I was acquainted with both the gentlemen only by reputation; the one being a neighbouring gentleman of a very large estate, a very sober and sensible man, of known probity and attachment to the true interest of his country; the other is a mere stranger, a boy, a soldier of fortune, and, as far as I can discern from the little conversation I have had with him, of a very shallow capacity, and no education."

"No education, my dear friend!" cries the nobleman. "Why, he hath been educated in half the courts of Europe."

"Perhaps so, my lord," answered the doctor; "but I shall always be so great a pedant as to call a man of no learning a man of no education. And, from my own knowledge, I can aver that I am persuaded there is scarce a foot-soldier in the army who is more illiterate than the colonel."

"Why, as to Latin and Greek, you know," replied the lord, "they are not much required in the army."

"It may be so," said the doctor. "Then let such persons keep to their own profession. It is a very low civil capacity indeed for which an illiterate man can be qualified. And, to speak a plain truth, if your lordship is a friend to the colonel, you would do well to advise him to decline an attempt in which I am certain he hath no probability of success."

"Well, sir," said the lord, "if you are resolved against us, I must deal as freely with you, and tell you plainly I cannot serve you in your affair. Nay, it will be the best thing I can do to hold my tongue; for, if I should mention his name with your recommendation after what you have said, he would perhaps never get provided for as long as he lives."

"Is his own merit, then, my lord, no recommendation?" cries the doctor.

"My dear, dear sir," cries the other, "what is the merit of a subaltern officer?"

"Surely, my lord," cries the doctor, "it is the merit which should recommend him to the post of a subaltern officer. And it is a merit which will hereafter qualify him to serve his country in a higher capacity. And I do assure of this young man, that he hath not only a good heart but a good head too. And I have been told by those who are judges that he is, for his age, an excellent officer."

"Very probably!" cries my lord. "And there are abundance with the same merit and the same qualifications who want a morsel of bread for themselves and their families."

"It is an infamous scandal on the nation," cries the doctor; "and I am heartily sorry it can be said even with a colour of truth."

"How can it be otherwise?" says the peer. "Do you think it is possible to provide for all men of merit?"

"Yes, surely do I," said the doctor; "and very easily too."

"How, pray?" cries the lord. "Upon my word, I shall be glad to know."

"Only by not providing for those who have none. The men of merit in any capacity are not, I am afraid, so extremely numerous that we need starve any of them, unless we wickedly suffer a set of worthless fellows to eat their bread."

"This is all mere Utopia," cries his lordship; "the chimerical system of Plato's commonwealth, with which we amused ourselves at the university; politics which are inconsistent with the state of human affairs."

"Sure, my lord," cries the doctor, "we have read of states where such doctrines have been put in practice. What is your lordship's opinion of Rome in the earlier ages of the commonwealth, of Sparta, and even of Athens itself in some periods of its history?"

"Indeed, doctor," cries the lord, "all these notions are obsolete and long since exploded. To apply maxims of government drawn from the Greek and Roman histories to this nation is absurd and impossible. But, if you will have Roman examples, fetch them from those times of the republic that were most like our own. Do you not know, doctor, that this is as corrupt a nation as ever existed under the sun? And would you think of governing such a people by the strict principles of honesty and morality?"

"If it be so corrupt," said the doctor, "I think it is high time to amend it: or else it is easy to foresee that Roman and British liberty will have the same fate; for corruption in the body politic as naturally tends to dissolution as in the natural body."

"I thank you for your simile," cries my lord; "for, in the natural body, I believe, you will allow there is the season of youth, the season of manhood, and the season of old age; and that, when the last of these arrives, it will be an impossible attempt by all the means of art to restore the body again to its youth, or to the vigour of its middle age. The same periods happen to every great kingdom. In its youth it rises by arts and arms to power and prosperity. This it enjoys and flourishes with a while; and then it may be said to be in the vigour of its age, enriched at home with all the emoluments and blessings of peace, and formidable abroad with all the terrors of war. At length this very prosperity introduces corruption, and then comes on its old age. Virtue and learning, art and industry, decay by degrees. The people sink into sloth and luxury and prostitution. It is enervated at home—becomes contemptible abroad; and such indeed is its misery and wretchedness, that it resembles a man in the last decrepit stage of life, who looks with unconcern at his approaching dissolution."

"This is a melancholy picture indeed," cries the doctor; "and, if the latter part of it can be applied to our case, I see nothing but religion, which would have prevented this decrepit state of the constitution, should prevent a man of spirit from hanging himself out of the way of so wretched a contemplation."

"Why so?" said the peer; "why hang myself, doctor? Would it not be wiser, think you, to make the best of your time, and the most you can, in such a nation?"

"And is religion, then, to be really laid out of the question?" cries the doctor.

"If I am to speak my own opinion, sir," answered the peer, "you know I shall answer in the negative. But you are too well acquainted with the world to be told that the conduct of politicians is not formed upon the principles of religion."

"I am very sorry for it," cries the doctor; "but I will talk to them then of honour and honesty; this is a language which I hope they will at least pretend to understand. Now to deny a man the preferment which he merits, and to give it to another man who doth not merit it, is a manifest act of injustice, and is consequently inconsistent with both honour and honesty. Nor is it only an act of injustice to the man himself, but to the public, for whose good principally all public offices are, or ought to be, instituted. Now this good can never be completed nor obtained but by employing all persons according to their capacities. Wherever true merit is liable to be superseded by favour and partiality, and men are entrusted with offices without any regard to capacity or integrity, the affairs of that state will always be in a deplorable situation. Such, as Livy tells us, was the state of Capua a little before its final destruction, and the consequence your lordship well knows. But, my lord, there is another mischief which attends this kind of injustice, and that is, it hath a manifest tendency to destroy all virtue and all ability among the people, by taking away all that

encouragement and incentive which should promote emula-
tion and raise men to aim at excelling in any art, science,
or profession. Nor can anything, my lord, contribute more
to render a nation contemptible among its neighbours;
for what opinion can other countries have of the councils,
or what terror can they conceive of the arms, of such a people?
and it was chiefly owing to the avoiding this error that Oliver
Cromwell carried the reputation of England higher than it
ever was at any other time. I will add only one argument
more, and that is founded on the most narrow and selfish
system of politics; and this is, that such conduct is sure to
create universal discontent and grumbling at home; for
nothing can bring men to rest satisfied, when they see others
preferred to them, but an opinion that they deserved that
elevation; for, as one of the greatest men this country ever
produced observes,

> One worthless man that gains what he pretends
> Disgusts a thousand unpretending friends.

With what heart-burnings then must any nation see themselves obliged to contribute to the support of a set of men
of whose incapacity to serve them they are well apprized,
and who do their country a double diskindness, by being
themselves employed in posts to which they are unequal,
and by keeping others out of those employments for which
they are qualified!"

"And do you really think, doctor," cries the nobleman,
"that any minister could support himself in this country
upon such principles as you recommend? Do you think he
would be able to baffle an opposition unless he should oblige
his friends by conferring places often contrary to his own
inclinations and his own opinion?"

"Yes, really I do," cries the doctor. "Indeed, if a
minister is resolved to make good his confession in the liturgy,
*by leaving undone all those things which he ought to have done,
and by doing all those things which he ought not to have done,*
such a minister, I grant, will be obliged to baffle opposition,
as you are pleased to term it, by these arts; for, as Shakespeare somewhere says,

> Things ill begun strengthen themselves by ill.

But if, on the contrary, he will please to consider the true

interest of his country, and that only in great and national
points; if he will engage his country in neither alliances nor
quarrels but where it is really interested; if he will raise no
money but what is wanted, nor employ any civil or military
officers but what are useful, and place in these employments
men of the highest integrity, and of the greatest abilities;
if he will employ some few of his hours to advance our trade,
and some few more to regulate our domestic government;
if he would do this, my lord, I will answer for it, he shall
either have no opposition to baffle, or he shall baffle it by a
fair appeal to his conduct. Such a minister may, in the
language of the law, put himself on his country when he
pleases, and he shall come off with honour and applause."

"And do you really believe, doctor," cries the peer, "there
ever was such a minister, or ever will be?"

"Why not, my lord?" answered the doctor. "It requires
no very extraordinary parts, nor any extraordinary degree of
virtue. He need practise no great instances of self-denial.
He shall have power, and honour, and riches, and, perhaps,
all in a much greater degree than he can ever acquire by
pursuing a contrary system. He shall have more of each
and much more of safety."

"Pray, doctor," said my lord, "let me ask you one simple
question. Do you really believe any man upon earth was
ever a rogue out of choice?"

"Really, my lord," says the doctor, "I am ashamed to
answer in the affirmative; and yet I am afraid experience
would almost justify me if I should. Perhaps the opinion
of the world may sometimes mislead men to think those
measures necessary which in reality are not so. Or the
truth may be, that a man of good inclinations finds his office
filled with such corruption by the iniquity of his predecessors,
that he may despair of being capable of purging it; and so
sits down contented, as Augeas did with the filth of his stables,
not because he thought them the better, or that such filth
was really necessary to a stable, but that he despaired of
sufficient force to cleanse them."

"I will ask you one question more, and I have done,"
said the nobleman. "Do you imagine that if any minister
was really as good as you would have him, that the people
in general would believe that he was so?"

"Truly, my lord," said the doctor, "I think they may

CHAPTER III

The history of Mr. Trent.

WE will now return to Mr. Booth and his wife. The former had spent his time very uneasily ever since he had discovered what sort of man he was indebted to; but, lest he should forget it, Mr. Trent thought now proper to remind him in the following letter, which he read the next morning after he had put off the appointment.

SIR,—I am sorry the necessity of my affairs obliges me to mention that small sum which I had the honour to lend you the other night at play; and which I shall be much obliged to you if you will let me have some time either to-day or to-morrow. I am sir,

Your most obedient, most humble servant,

GEORGE TRENT.

This letter a little surprised Booth, after the genteel, and indeed, as it appeared, generous behaviour of Trent. But lest it should have the same effect upon the reader, we will now proceed to account for this, as well as for some other phenomena that have appeared in this history, and which, perhaps, we shall be forgiven for not having opened more largely before.

Mr. Trent then was a gentleman possibly of a good family, for it was not certain whence he sprung on the father's side. His mother, who was the only parent he ever knew or heard of, was a single gentlewoman, and for some time carried on the trade of a milliner in Covent Garden. She sent her son, at the age of eight years old, to a charity-school, where he remained till he was of the age of fourteen, without making any great proficiency in learning. Indeed it is not very probable he should; for the master, who, in preference to a very learned and proper man, was chosen by a party into this school, the salary of which was upwards of a hundred pounds a year, had himself never travelled through the Latin Grammar, and was, in truth, a most consummate blockhead.

At the age of fifteen Mr. Trent was put clerk to an attorney, where he remained a very short time before he took leave of his master; rather, indeed, departed without taking leave; and, having broke open his mother's escritore, and carried off with him all the valuable effects he there found, to the amount of about fifty pounds, he marched off to sea, and went on board a merchantman, whence he was afterwards pressed into a man of war.

In this service he continued above three years; during which time he behaved so ill in his moral character that he twice underwent a very severe discipline for thefts in which he was detected; but at the same time, he behaved so well as a sailor in an engagement with some pirates, that he wiped off all former scores, and greatly recommended himself to his captain.

At his return home, he being then about twenty years of age, he found that the attorney had in his absence married his mother, had buried her, and secured all her effects, to the amount, as he was informed, of about fifteen hundred pound. Trent applied to his stepfather, but to no purpose; the attorney utterly disowned him, nor would he suffer him to come a second time within his doors.

It happened that the attorney had, by a former wife, an only daughter, a great favourite, who was about the same age with Trent himself, and had, during his residence at her father's house, taken a very great liking to this young fellow, who was extremely handsome and perfectly well made. This her liking was not, during his absence, so far extinguished but that it immediately revived on his return. Of this she took care to give Mr. Trent proper intimation; for she was not one of those backward and delicate ladies who can die rather than make the first overture. Trent was overjoyed at this, and with reason, for she was a very lovely girl in her person, the only child of a rich father; and the prospect of so complete a revenge on the attorney charmed him above all the rest. To be as short in the matter as the parties, a marriage was soon consummated between them.

The attorney at first raged and was implacable; but at last fondness for his daughter so far overcame resentment that he advanced a sum of money to buy his son-in-law (for now he acknowledged him as such) an ensign's commission in a marching regiment then ordered to Gibraltar; at which place the attorney heartily hoped that Trent might be knocked on the head; for in that case he thought he might marry his daughter more agreeably to his own ambition and to her advantage.

The regiment into which Trent purchased was the same with that in which Booth likewise served; the one being an ensign, and the other a lieutenant, in the two additional companies.

Trent had no blemish in his military capacity. Though he had had but an indifferent education, he was naturally sensible and genteel, and Nature, as we have said had given him a very agreeable person. He was likewise a very bold fellow, and, as he really behaved himself every way well enough while he was at Gibraltar, there was some degree of intimacy between him and Booth.

When the siege was over, and the additional companies were again reduced, Trent returned to his wife, who received him with great joy and affection. Soon after this an accident happened which proved the utter ruin of his father-in-law, and ended in breaking his heart. This was nothing but making a mistake pretty common at this day, of writing another man's name to a deed instead of his own. In truth this matter was no less than what the law calls forgery, and was just then made capital by an act of parliament. From this offence, indeed, the attorney was acquitted, by not admitting the proof of the party, who was to avoid his own deed by his evidence, and therefore no witness, according to those excellent rules called the law of evidence; a law very excellently calculated for the preservation of the lives of his majesty's roguish subjects, and most notably used for that purpose.

But though by common law the attorney was honourably acquitted, yet, as common sense manifested to every one that he was guilty, he unhappily lost his reputation, and of consequence his business; the chagrin of which latter soon put an end to his life.

This prosecution had been attended with a very great expence; for, besides the ordinary cost of avoiding the gallows by the help of the law, there was a very high article, of no less than a thousand pounds, paid down to remove out of the way a witness against whom there was no legal exception. The poor gentleman had besides suffered some losses in business; so that, to the surprise of all his acquaintance, when his debts were paid there remained no more than a small estate of fourscore pounds a year, which he settled upon his daughter, far out of the reach of her husband, and about two hundred pounds in money.

The old gentleman had not long been in his grave before Trent set himself to consider seriously of the state of his affairs. He had lately begun to look on his wife with a much less degree of liking and desire than formerly; for he was one of those who think too much of one thing is good for nothing. Indeed, he had indulged these speculations so far, that I believe his wife, though one of the prettiest women in town, was the last subject that he would have chose for any amorous dalliance.

Many other persons, however, greatly differed from him in his opinion. Amongst the rest was the illustrious peer of amorous memory. This noble peer, having therefore got a view of Mrs. Trent one day in the street, did, by means of an emissary then with him, make himself acquainted with her lodging, to which he immediately laid siege in form, setting himself down in a lodging directly opposite to her, from whence the battery of ogles began to play the very next morning.

This siege had not continued long before the governor of the garrison became sufficiently apprized of all the works which were carrying on, and, having well reconnoitered the enemy, and discovered who he was, notwithstanding a false name and some disguise of his person, he called a council of war within his own breast. In fact, to drop all allegory, he began to consider whether his wife was not really a more valuable possession than he had lately thought her. In short, as he had been disappointed in her fortune, he now conceived some hopes of turning her beauty itself into a fortune.

Without communicating these views to her, he soon scraped an acquaintance with his opposite neighbour by the name which he there usurped, and counterfeited an entire ignorance of his real name and title. On this occasion Trent had his disguise likewise, for he affected the utmost simplicity; of which affectation, as he was a very artful fellow, he was extremely capable.

The peer fell plumb into this snare; and when, by the

simplicity, as he imagined, of the husband, he became acquainted with the wife, he was so extravagantly charmed with her person, that he resolved, whatever was the cost or the consequence, he would possess her.

His lordship, however, preserved some caution in his management of this affair; more, perhaps, than was necessary. As for the husband, none was requisite, for he knew all he could; and, with regard to the wife herself, as she had for some time perceived the decrease of her husband's affection (for few women are, I believe, to be imposed upon in that matter), she was not displeased to find the return of all that complaisance and endearment, of those looks and languishments, from another agreeable person, which she had formerly received from Trent, and which she now found she should receive from him no longer.

My lord, therefore, having been indulged with as much opportunity as he could wish from Trent, and having received rather more encouragement than he could well have hoped from the lady, began to prepare all matters for a storm, when luckily, Mr. Trent declaring he must go out of town for two days, he fixed on the first day of his departure as the time of carrying his design into execution.

And now, after some debate with himself in what manner he should approach his love, he at last determined to do it in his own person; for he conceived, and perhaps very rightly, that the lady, like Semele, was not void of ambition, and would have preferred Jupiter in all his glory to the same deity in the disguise of an humble shepherd. He dressed himself, therefore, in the richest embroidery of which he was master, and appeared before his mistress arrayed in all the brightness of peerage; a sight whose charms she had not the power to resist, and the consequences are only to be imagined. In short, the same scene which Jupiter acted with his above-mentioned mistress of old was more than beginning, when Trent burst from the closet into which he had conveyed himself, and unkindly interrupted the action.

His lordship presently ran to his sword; but Trent, with great calmness, answered, "That, as it was very well known he durst fight, he should not draw his sword on this occasion; for sure," says he, "my lord, it would be the highest imprudence in me to kill a man who is now become so considerably my debtor." At which words he fetched a person from the

closet, who had been confined with him, telling him he had
done his business, and might now, if he pleased, retire.

It would be tedious here to amuse the reader with all
that passed on the present occasion; the rage and confusion
of the wife, or the perplexity in which my lord was involved.
We will omit therefore all such matters, and proceed directly
to business, as Trent and his lordship did soon after. And
in the conclusion my lord stipulated to pay a good round
sum, and to provide Mr. Trent with a good place on the first
opportunity.

On the side of Mr. Trent were stipulated absolute remission
of all past, and full indulgence for the time to come.

Trent now immediately took a house at the polite end of
the town, furnished it elegantly, and set up his equipage,
rigged out both himself and his wife with very handsome
clothes, frequented all public places where he could get
admission, pushed himself into acquaintance, and his wife
soon afterwards began to keep an assembly, or, in the fashion-
able phrase, to be at home once a week; when, by my lord's
assistance, she was presently visited by most men of the
first rank, and by all such women of fashion as are not very
nice in their company.

My lord's amour with this lady lasted not long; for, as
we have before observed, he was the most inconstant of all
the human race. Mrs. Trent's passion was not however of
that kind which leads to any very deep resentment of such
fickleness. Her passion, indeed, was principally founded
upon interest; so that foundation served to support another
superstructure; and she was easily prevailed upon, as well
as her husband, to be useful to my lord in a capacity which,
though very often exerted in the polite world, hath not as
yet, to my great surprise, acquired any polite name, or,
indeed, any which is not too coarse to be admitted in this
history.

After this preface, which we thought necessary to account
for a character of which some of my country and collegiate
readers might possibly doubt the existence, I shall proceed
to what more immediately regards Mrs. Booth. The reader
may be pleased to remember that Mr. Trent was present
at the assembly to which Booth and his wife were carried by
Mrs. James, and where Amelia was met by the noble peer.

His lordship, seeing there that Booth and Trent were old

acquaintance, failed not, to use the language of sportsmen, to put Trent upon the scent of Amelia. For this purpose that gentleman visited Booth the very next day, and had pursued him close ever since. By his means, therefore, my lord learned that Amelia was to be at the masquerade, to which place she was dogged by Trent in a sailor's jacket, who, meeting my lord, according to agreement, at the entrance of the opera-house, like the four-legged gentleman of the same vocation, made a dead point, as it is called, at the game.

My lord was so satisfied and delighted with his conversation at the masquerade with the supposed Amelia, and the encouragement which in reality she had given him, that, when he saw Trent the next morning, he embraced him with great fondness, gave him a bank note of a hundred pound, and promised him both the Indies on his success, of which he began now to have no manner of doubt.

The affair that happened at the gaming-table was likewise a scheme of Trent's, on a hint given by my lord to him to endeavour to lead Booth into some scrape or distress; his lordship promising to pay whatever expense Trent might be led into by such means. Upon his lordship's credit, therefore, the money lent to Booth was really advanced. And hence arose all that seeming generosity and indifference as to the payment; Trent being satisfied with the obligation conferred on Booth, by means of which he hoped to effect his purpose.

But now the scene was totally changed; for Mrs. Atkinson, the morning after the quarrel, beginning seriously to recollect that she had carried the matter rather too far, and might really injure Amelia's reputation, a thought to which the warm pursuit of her own interest had a good deal blinded her at the time, resolved to visit my lord himself, and to let him into the whole story; for, as she had succeeded already in her favourite point, she thought she had no reason to fear any consequence of the discovery. This resolution she immediately executed.

Trent came to attend his lordship, just after Mrs. Atkinson had left him. He found the peer in a very ill humour, and brought no news to comfort or recruit his spirits; for he had himself just received a billet from Booth, with an excuse for himself and his wife from accepting the invitation at Trent's house that evening, where matters had been previously concerted for their entertainment, and when his lordship was by accident to drop into the room where Amelia was, while Booth was to be engaged at play in another.

And now after much debate, and after Trent had acquainted my lord with the wretched situation of Booth's circumstances, it was resolved that Trent should immediately demand his money of Booth, and upon his not paying it, for they both concluded it impossible he should pay it, to put the note which Trent had for the money in suit against him by the genteel means of paying it away to a nominal third person; and this they both conceived must end immediately in the ruin of Booth, and, consequently, in the conquest of Amelia.

In this project, and with this hope, both my lord and his setter, or (if the sportsmen please) setting-dog, both greatly exulted; and it was next morning executed, as we have already seen.

CHAPTER IV

Containing some distress.

TRENT'S letter drove Booth almost to madness. To be indebted to such a fellow at any rate had stuck much in his stomach, and had given him very great uneasiness; but to answer this demand in any other manner than by paying the money was absolutely what he could not bear. Again, to pay this money, he very plainly saw there was but one way, and this was, by stripping his wife, not only of every farthing, but almost of every rag she had in the world; a thought so dreadful that it chilled his very soul with horror: and yet pride, at last, seemed to represent this as the lesser evil of the two.

But how to do this was still a question. It was not sure, at least he feared it was not, that Amelia herself would readily consent to this; and so far from persuading her to such a measure, he could not bear even to propose it. At length his determination was to acquaint his wife with the whole affair, and to ask her consent, by way of asking her advice; for he was well assured she could find no other means of extricating him out of his dilemma. This he accordingly did, representing the affair as bad as he could; though, indeed, it was impossible for him to aggravate the real truth.

Amelia heard him patiently, without once interrupting him. When he had finished, she remained silent some time: indeed, the shock she received from this story almost deprived her of the power of speaking. At last she answered, "Well, my dear, you ask my advice; I certainly can give you no other than that the money must be paid."

"But how must it be paid?" cries he. "O, heavens! thou sweetest creature! what, not once upbraid me for bringing this ruin on thee?"

"Upbraid you, my dear!" says she; "would to heaven I could prevent your upbraiding yourself. But do not despair. I will endeavour by some means or other to get you the money."

"Alas! my dear love," cries Booth, "I know the only way by which you can raise it. How can I consent to that? do you forget the fears you so lately expressed of what would be our wretched condition when our little all was mouldered away? O my Amelia! they cut my very heart-strings when you spoke then; for I had then lost this little all. Indeed, I assure you, I have not played since, nor ever will more."

"Keep that resolution," said she, "my dear, and I hope we shall yet recover the past."—At which words, casting her eyes on the children, the tears burst from her eyes, and she cried—"Heaven will, I hope, provide for us."

A pathetic scene now ensued between the husband and wife, which would not, perhaps, please many readers to see drawn at too full a length. It is sufficient to say that this excellent woman not only used her utmost endeavours to stifle and conceal her own concern, but said and did everything in her power to allay that of her husband.

Booth was, at this time, to meet a person whom we have formerly mentioned in the course of our history. This gentleman had a place in the War Office, and pretended to be a man of great interest and consequence; by which means he did not only receive great respect and court from the inferior officers, but actually bubbled several of their money, by undertaking to do them services which, in reality, were not within his power. In truth, I have known few great men who have not been beset with one or more such fellows as these, through whom the inferior part of mankind are obliged to make their court to the great men themselves; by which means, I believe, principally, persons of real merit have been often deterred from the attempt; for these subaltern coxcombs ever assume an equal state with their masters, and look for an equal degree of respect to be paid to them; to which men of spirit, who are in every light their betters, are not easily brought to submit. These fellows, indeed, themselves have a jealous eye towards all great abilities, and are sure, to the utmost of their power, to keep all who are so endowed from the presence of their masters. They use their masters as bad ministers have sometimes used a prince—they keep all men of merit from his ears, and daily sacrifice his true honour and interest to their own profit and their own vanity.

As soon as Booth was gone to his appointment with this

man, Amelia immediately betook herself to her business with the highest resolution. She packed up, not only her own little trinkets, and those of the children, but the greatest part of her own poor clothes (for she was but barely provided), and then drove in a hackney-coach to the same pawnbroker's who had before been recommended to her by Mrs. Atkinson, who advanced her the money she desired.

Being now provided with her sum, she returned well pleased home, and her husband coming in soon after, she with much cheerfulness delivered him all the money.

Booth was so overjoyed with the prospect of discharging his debt to Trent, that he did not perfectly reflect on the distress to which his family was now reduced. The good humour which appeared in the countenance of Amelia was, perhaps, another help to stifle those reflections; but, above all, were the assurances he had received from the great man, whom he had met at a coffee-house, and who had promised to do him all the service in his power; which several half-pay subaltern officers assured him was very considerable.

With this comfortable news he acquainted his wife, who either was, or seemed to be, extremely well pleased with it. And now he set out with the money in his pocket to pay his friend Trent, who unluckily for him happened not to be at home.

On his return home he met his old friend the lieutenant, who thankfully paid him his crown, and insisted on his going with him and taking part of a bottle. This invitation was so eager and pressing, that poor Booth, who could not resist much importunity, complied.

While they were over this bottle Booth acquainted his friend with the promises he had received that afternoon at the coffee-house, with which the old gentleman was very well pleased: "For I have heard," says he, "that gentleman hath very powerful interest"; but he informed him likewise that he had heard that the great man must be touched, for that he never did anything without touching. Of this, indeed, the great man himself had given some oblique hints, by saying, with great sagacity and slyness, that he knew where fifty pound might be deposited to much advantage.

Booth answered that he would very readily advance a small sum if he had it in his power, but that at present it was not so, for that he had no more in the world than the

sum of fifty pounds, which he owed Trent, and which he,
intended to pay him the next morning.

"It is very right, undoubtedly, to pay your debts," says
the old gentleman; "but sure, on such an occasion, any man
but the rankest usurer would be contented to stay a little
while for his money; and it will be only a little while I am
convinced; for, if you deposit this sum in the great man's
hands, I make no doubt but you will succeed immediately
in getting your commission; and then I will help you to a
method of taking up such a sum as this." The old gentleman persisted in this advice, and backed it with every
argument he could invent, declaring, as was indeed true,
that he gave the same advice which he would pursue was
the case his own.

Booth long rejected the opinion of his friend, till, as they
had not argued with dry lips, he became heated with wine
and then at last the old gentleman succeeded. Indeed, such
was his love, either for Booth or for his own opinion, and
perhaps for both, that he omitted nothing in his power. He
even endeavoured to palliate the character of Trent, and un-
said half what he had before said of that gentleman. In the
end, he undertook to make Trent easy, and to go to him the
very next morning for that purpose.

Poor Booth at last yielded, though with the utmost
difficulty. Indeed, had he known quite as much of Trent as
the reader doth, no motive whatsoever would have prevailed
on him to have taken the old gentleman's advice.

CHAPTER V

Containing more wormwood and other ingredients.

In the morning Booth communicated the matter to Amelia, who told him she would not presume to advise him in an affair of which he was so much the better judge.

While Booth remained in a doubtful state what conduct to pursue Bound came to make him a visit, and informed him that he had been at Trent's house, but found him not at home, adding that he would pay him a second visit that very day, and would not rest till he found him.

Booth was ashamed to confess his wavering resolution in an affair in which he had been so troublesome to his friend; he therefore dressed himself immediately, and together they both went to wait on the little great man, to whom Booth now hoped to pay his court in the most effectual manner.

Bound had been longer acquainted with the modern methods of business than Booth; he advised his friend, therefore, to begin with tipping (as it is called) the great man's servant. He did so, and by that means got speedy access to the master.

The great man received the money, not as a gudgeon doth a bait, but as a pike receives a poor gudgeon into his maw. To say the truth, such fellows as these may well be likened to that voracious fish, who fattens himself by devouring all the little inhabitants of the river. As soon as the great man had pocketed the cash he shook Booth by the hand, and told him he would be sure to slip no opportunity of serving him, and would send him word as soon as any offered.

Here I shall stop one moment, and so, perhaps, will my good-natured reader; for surely it must be a hard heart which is not affected with reflecting on the manner in which this poor little sum was raised, and on the manner in which it was bestowed. A worthy family, the wife and children of a man who had lost his blood abroad in the service of his country, parting with their little all, and exposed to cold and hunger, to pamper such a fellow as this!

And if any such reader as I mention should happen to be in reality a great man, and in power, perhaps the horror of this picture may induce him to put a final end to this abominable practice of touching, as it is called, by which, indeed, a set of leeches are permitted to suck the blood of the brave and the indigent, of the widow and the orphan.

Booth now returned home, where he found his wife with Mrs. James. Amelia had, before the arrival of her husband, absolutely refused Mrs. James's invitation to dinner the next day; but when Booth came in the lady renewed her application, and that in so pressing a manner, that Booth seconded her; for, though he had enough of jealousy in his temper, yet such was his friendship to the colonel, and such his gratitude to the obligations which he had received from him, that his own unwillingness to believe anything of him, cooperating with Amelia's endeavours to put everything in the fairest light, had brought him to acquit his friend of any ill design. To this, perhaps, the late affair concerning my lord had moreover contributed; for it seems to me that the same passion cannot much energize on two different objects at one and the same time: an observation which, I believe, will hold as true with regard to the cruel passions of jealousy and anger as to the gentle passion of love, in which one great and mighty object is sure to engage the whole passion.

When Booth grew importunate, Amelia answered, "My dear, I should not refuse you whatever was in my power; but this is absolutely out of my power; for since I must declare the truth, I cannot dress myself."

"Why so?" said Mrs. James. "I am sure you are in good health."

"Is there no other impediment to dressing but want of health, madam?" answered Amelia.

"Upon my word, none that I know of," replied Mrs. James.

"What do you think of want of clothes, madam?" said Amelia.

"Ridiculous!" cries Mrs. James. "What need have you to dress yourself out? You will see nobody but our own family, and I promise you I don't expect it. A plain nightgown will do very well."

"But if I must be plain with you, madam," said Amelia, "I have no other clothes but what I have now on my back.

I have not even a clean shift in the world; for you must know, my dear," said she to Booth, "that little Betty is walked off this morning, and hath carried all my linen with her."

"How, my dear?" cries Booth; "little Betty robbed you?"

"It is even so," answered Amelia. Indeed, she spoke truth; for little Betty, having perceived the evening before that her mistress was moving her goods, was willing to lend all the assistance in her power, and had accordingly moved off early that morning, taking with her whatever she could lay her hands on.

Booth expressed himself with some passion on the occasion, and swore he would make an example of the girl. "If the little slut be above-ground," cried he, "I will find her out, and bring her to justice."

"I am really sorry for this accident," said Mrs. James, "and (though I know not how to mention it) I beg you'll give me leave to offer you any linen of mine till you can make new of your own."

Amelia thanked Mrs. James, but declined the favour, saying, she should do well enough at home; and that, as she had no servant now to take care of her children, she could not, nor would not, leave them on any account.

"Then bring master and miss with you," said Mrs. James. "You shall positively dine with us to-morrow."

"I beg, madam, you will mention it no more," said Amelia; "for, besides the substantial reasons I have already given, I have some things on my mind at present which make me unfit for company; and I am resolved nothing shall prevail on me to stir from home."

Mrs. James had carried her invitation already to the very utmost limits of good breeding, if not beyond them. She desisted therefore from going any further, and, after some short stay longer, took her leave, with many expressions of concern, which, however, great as it was, left her heart and her mouth together before she was out of the house.

Booth now declared that he would go in pursuit of little Betty, against whom he vowed so much vengeance, that Amelia endeavoured to moderate his anger by representing to him the girl's youth, and that this was the first fault she had ever been guilty of. "Indeed," says she, "I should be very glad to have my things again, and I would have the girl too punished in some degree, which might possibly be for her own good; but I tremble to think of taking away her life"; for Booth in his rage had sworn he would hang her.

"I know the tenderness of your heart, my dear," said Booth, "and I love you for it; but I must beg leave to dissent from your opinion. I do not think the girl in any light an object of mercy. She is not only guilty of dishonesty but of cruelty; for she must know our situation, and the very little we had left. She is besides guilty of ingratitude to you, who have treated her with so much kindness, that you have rather acted the part of a mother than of a mistress. And, so far from thinking her youth an excuse, I think it rather an aggravation. It is true, indeed, there are faults which the youth of the party very strongly recommends to our pardon. Such are all those which proceed from carelessness and want of thought; but crimes of this black dye, which are committed with deliberation, and imply a bad mind, deserve a more severe punishment in a young person than in one of riper years; for what must the mind be in old age which hath acquired such a degree of perfection in villany so very early? Such persons as these it is really a charity to the public to put out of society; and, indeed, a religious man would put them out of the world for the sake of themselves; for whoever understands anything of human nature must know that such people, the longer they live, the more they will accumulate vice and wickedness."

"Well, my dear," cries Amelia, "I cannot argue with you on these subjects. I shall always submit to your superior judgment, and I know you too well to think that you will ever do anything cruel."

Booth then left Amelia to take care of her children, and went in pursuit of the thief.

CHAPTER VI

A scene of the tragic kind.

HE had not been long gone before a thundering knock was heard at the door of the house where Amelia lodged, and presently after a figure all pale, ghastly, and almost breathless, rushed into the room where she then was with her children.

This figure Amelia soon recognized to be Mrs. Atkinson, though indeed she was so disguised that at her first entrance Amelia scarce knew her. Her eyes were sunk in her head, her hair dishevelled, and not only her dress but every feature in her face was in the utmost disorder.

Amelia was greatly shocked at this sight, and the little girl was much frightened; as for the boy, he immediately knew her, and, running to Amelia, he cried, "La! mamma, what is the matter with poor Mrs. Atkinson?"

As soon as Mrs. Atkinson recovered her breath she cried out, "O, Mrs. Booth! I am the most miserable of women— I have lost the best of husbands."

Amelia, looking at her with all the tenderness imaginable, forgetting, I believe, that there had ever been any quarrel between them, said—"Good Heavens, madam, what's the matter?"

"O, Mrs. Booth!" answered she, "I fear I have lost my husband: the doctor says there is but little hope of his life. O, madam! however I have been in the wrong, I am sure you will forgive me and pity me. I am sure I am severely punished; for to that cursed affair I owe all my misery."

"Indeed, madam," cries Amelia, "I am extremely concerned for your misfortune. But pray tell me, hath anything happened to the serjeant?"

"O, madam!" cries she, "I have the greatest reason to fear I shall lose him. The doctor hath almost given him over—he says he hath scarce any hopes. O, madam! that evening that the fatal quarrel happened between us my dear captain took it so to heart that he sat up all night and drank a whole bottle of brandy. Indeed, he said he wished to kill himself; for nothing could have hurt him so much in the world, he said, as to have any quarrel between you and me. His concern, and what he drank together, threw him into a high fever. So that, when I came home from my lord's—(for indeed, madam, I have been, and set all to rights —your reputation is now in no danger)—when I came home, I say, I found the poor man in a raving delirious fit, and in that he hath continued ever since till about an hour ago, when he came perfectly to his senses; but now he says he is sure he shall die, and begs for Heaven's sake to see you first. Would you, madam, would you have the goodness to grant my poor captain's desire? Consider he is a dying man, and neither he nor I shall ever ask you a second favour. He says he hath something to say to you that he can mention to no other person, and that he cannot die in peace unless he sees you."

"Upon my word, madam," cries Amelia, "I am extremely concerned at what you tell me. I knew the poor serjeant from his infancy, and always had an affection for him, as I think him to be one of the best-natured and honestest creatures upon earth. I am sure if I could do him any service—but of what use can my going be?"

"Of the highest in the world," answered Mrs. Atkinson. "If you knew how earnestly he entreated it, how his poor breaking heart begged to see you, you would not refuse."

"Nay, I do not absolutely refuse," cries Amelia. "Something to say to me of consequence, and that he could not die in peace unless he said it! did he say that, Mrs. Atkinson?"

"Upon my honour he did," answered she, "and much more than I have related."

"Well, I will go with you," cries Amelia. "I cannot guess what this should be; but I will go."

Mrs. Atkinson then poured out a thousand blessings and thanksgivings; and, taking hold of Amelia's hand, and eagerly kissing it, cried out, "How could that fury passion drive me to quarrel with such a creature?"

Amelia told her she had forgiven and forgot it; and then, calling up the mistress of the house, and committing to her the care of the children, she cloaked herself up as well as she could and set out with Mrs. Atkinson.

When they arrived at the house, Mrs. Atkinson said she would go first and give the captain some notice; for that, if Amelia entered the room unexpectedly, the surprise might have an ill effect. She left therefore Amelia in the parlour, and proceeded directly upstairs.

Poor Atkinson, weak and bad as was his condition, no sooner heard that Amelia was come than he discovered great joy in his countenance, and presently afterwards she was introduced to him.

Atkinson exerted his utmost strength to thank her for this goodness to a dying man (for so he called himself). He said he should not have presumed to give her this trouble, had he not had something which he thought of consequence to say to her, and which he could not mention to any other person. He then desired his wife to give him a little box, of which he always kept the key himself, and afterwards begged her to leave the room for a few minutes; at which neither she nor Amelia expressed any dissatisfaction.

When he was alone with Amelia, he spoke as follows: "This, madam, is the last time my eyes will ever behold what —do pardon me, madam, I will never offend you more." Here he sunk down in his bed, and the tears gushed from his eyes.

"Why should you fear to offend me, Joe?" said Amelia. "I am sure you never did anything willingly to offend me."

"No, madam," answered he, "I would die a thousand times before I would have ventured it in the smallest matter. But—I cannot speak—and yet I must. You cannot pardon me, and yet, perhaps, as I am a dying man, and never shall see you more—indeed, if I was to live after this discovery, I should never dare to look you in the face again; and yet, madam, to think, I shall never see you more is worse than ten thousand deaths."

"Indeed, Mr. Atkinson," cries Amelia, blushing, and looking down on the floor, "I must not hear you talk in this manner. If you have anything to say, tell it me, and do not be afraid of my anger; for I think I may promise to forgive whatever it was possible you should do."

"Here then, madam," said he, "is your picture; I stole it when I was eighteen years of age, and have kept it ever since. It is set in gold, with three little diamonds; and yet I can truly say it was not the gold nor the diamonds which

I stole—it was that face; which, if I had been the emperor of the world——"

"I must not hear any more of this," said she. "Comfort yourself, Joe, and think no more of this matter. Be assured, I freely and heartily forgive you—But pray compose yourself; come, let me call in your wife."

"First, madam, let me beg one favour," cried he: "consider it is the last, and then I shall die in peace—let me kiss that hand before I die."

"Well, nay," says she, "I don't know what I am doing—well—there." She then carelessly gave him her hand, which he put gently to his lips, and then presently let it drop, and fell back in the bed.

Amelia now summoned Mrs. Atkinson, who was indeed no farther off than just without the door. She then hastened down stairs, and called for a great glass of water, which having drank off, she threw herself into a chair, and the tears ran plentifully from her eyes with compassion for the poor wretch she had just left in his bed.

To say the truth, without any injury to her chastity, that heart, which had stood firm as a rock to all the attacks of title and equipage, of finery and flattery, and which all the treasures of the universe could not have purchased, was yet a little softened by the plain, honest, modest, involuntary, delicate, heroic passion of this poor and humble swain; for whom, in spite of herself, she felt a momentary tenderness and complaisance, at which Booth, if he had known it, would perhaps have been displeased.

Having staid some time in the parlour, and not finding Mrs. Atkinson come down, (for indeed her husband was then so bad she could not quit him,) Amelia left a message with the maid of the house for her mistress, purporting that she should be ready to do anything in her power to serve her, and then left the house with a confusion on her mind that she had never felt before, and which any chastity that is not hewn out of marble must feel on so tender and delicate an occasion.

CHAPTER VII

In which Mr. Booth meets with more than one adventure.

BOOTH, having hunted about for two hours, at last saw a young lady in a tattered silk gown stepping out of a shop in Monmouth Street into a hackney-coach. This lady, notwithstanding the disguise of her dress, he presently discovered to be no other than little Betty.

He instantly gave the alarm of stop thief, stop coach! upon which Mrs. Betty was immediately stopped in her vehicle, and Booth and his myrmidons laid hold of her.

The girl no sooner found that she was seized by her master than the consciousness of her guilt overpowered her; for she was not yet an experienced offender, and she immediately confessed her crime.

She was then carried before a justice of peace, where she was searched, and there was found in her possession four shillings and sixpence in money, besides the silk gown, which was indeed proper furniture for rag-fair, and scarce worth a single farthing, though the honest shopkeeper in Monmouth Street had sold it for a crown to this simple girl.

The girl, being examined by the magistrate, spoke as follows: "Indeed, sir, an't please your worship, I am very sorry for what I have done; and to be sure, an't please your honour, my lord, it must have been the devil that put me upon it; for to be sure, please your majesty, I never thought upon such a thing in my whole life before, any more than I did of my dying-day; but, indeed, sir, an't please your worship——"

She was running on in this manner when the justice interrupted her, and desired her to give an account of what she had taken from her master, and what she had done with it.

"Indeed, an't please your majesty," said she, "I took no more than two shifts of madam's, and I pawned them for five shillings, which I gave for the gown that's upon my back; and as for the money in my pocket, it is every farthing of it my own. I am sure I intended to carry back the shifts too as soon as ever I could get money to take them out."

The girl having told them where the pawnbroker lived, the justice sent to him, to produce the shifts, which he presently did; for he expected that a warrant to search his house would be the consequence of his refusal.

The shifts being produced, on which the honest pawnbroker had lent five shillings, appeared plainly to be worth above thirty; indeed, when new they had cost much more: so that, by their goodness as well as by their size, it was certain they could not have belonged to the girl. Booth grew very warm against the pawnbroker. "I hope, sir," said he to the justice, "there is some punishment for this fellow likewise, who so plainly appears to have known that these goods were stolen. The shops of these fellows may indeed be called the fountains of theft; for it is in reality the encouragement which they meet with from these receivers of their goods that induces men very often to become thieves, so that these deserve equal if not severer punishment than the thieves themselves."

The pawnbroker protested his innocence, and denied the taking in the shifts. Indeed, in this he spoke truth, for he had slipped into an inner room, as was always his custom on these occasions, and left a little boy to do the business; by which means he had carried on the trade of receiving stolen goods for many years with impunity, and had been twice acquitted at the Old Bailey, though the juggle appeared upon the most manifest evidence.

As the justice was going to speak he was interrupted by the girl, who, falling upon her knees to Booth, with many tears begged his forgiveness.

"Indeed, Betty," cries Booth, "you do not deserve forgiveness; for you know very good reasons why you should not have thought of robbing your mistress, particularly at this time. And what further aggravates your crime is, that you robbed the best and kindest mistress in the world. Nay, you are not only guilty of felony, but of a felonious breach of trust, for you know very well everything your mistress had was entrusted to your care."

Now it happened, by very great accident, that the justice before whom the girl was brought understood the law.

Turning therefore to Booth, he said, "Do you say, sir, that this girl was entrusted with the shifts?"

"Yes, sir," said Booth, "she was entrusted with everything."

"And will you swear that the goods stolen," said the justice, "are worth forty shillings?"

"No, indeed, sir," answered Booth, "nor that they are worth thirty either."

"Then, sir," cries the justice, "the girl cannot be guilty of felony."

"How, sir," said Booth; "is it not a breach of trust? and is not a breach of trust felony, and the worst felony too?"

"No, sir," answered the justice; "a breach of trust is no crime in our law, unless it be in a servant; and then the act of parliament requires the goods taken to be of the value of forty shillings."

"So then a servant," cries Booth, "may rob his master of thirty-nine shillings whenever he pleases, and he can't be punished."

"If the goods are under his care, he can't," cries the justice.

"I ask your pardon, sir," says Booth. "I do not doubt what you say; but sure this is a very extraordinary law."

"Perhaps I think so too," said the justice; "but it belongs not to my office to make or to mend laws. My business is only to execute them. If therefore the case be as you say, I must discharge the girl."

"I hope, however, you will punish the pawnbroker," cries Booth.

"If the girl is discharged," cries the justice, "so must be the pawnbroker; for, if the goods are not stolen, he cannot be guilty of receiving them knowing them to be stolen. And, besides, as to his offence, to say the truth, I am almost weary of prosecuting it; for such are the difficulties laid in the way of this prosecution, that it is almost impossible to convict any one on it. And, to speak my opinion plainly, such are the laws, and such the method of proceeding, that one would almost think our laws were rather made for the protection of rogues than for the punishment of them."

Thus ended this examination: the thief and the receiver went about their business, and Booth departed in order to go home to his wife.

In his way home Booth was met by a lady in a chair, who, immediately upon seeing him, stopped her chair, bolted out of it, and, going directly up to him, said, "So, Mr. Booth, you have kept your word with me."

This lady was no other than Miss Matthews, and the speech she meant was of a promise made to her at the masquerade of visiting her within a day or two; which, whether he ever intended to keep I cannot say; but, in truth, the several accidents that had since happened to him had so discomposed his mind that he had absolutely forgotten it.

Booth, however, was too sensible and too well-bred to make the excuse of forgetfulness to a lady; nor could he readily find any other. While he stood therefore hesitating, and looking not over-wise, Miss Matthews said, "Well, sir, since by your confusion I see you have some grace left, I will pardon you on one condition, and that is that you will sup with me this night. But, if you fail me now, expect all the revenge of an injured woman." She then bound herself by a most outrageous oath that she would complain to his wife—"And I am sure," says she, "she is so much a woman of honour as to do me justice. And, though I miscarried in my first attempt, be assured I will take care of my second."

Booth asked what she meant by her first attempt; to which she answered that she had already writ his wife an account of his ill-usage of her, but that she was pleased it had miscarried. She then repeated her asseveration that she would now do it effectually if he disappointed her.

This threat she reckoned would most certainly terrify poor Booth; and, indeed, she was not mistaken; for I believe it would have been impossible, by any other menace or by any other means, to have brought him once even to balance in his mind on this question. But by this threat she prevailed; and Booth promised, upon his word and honour, to come to her at the hour she appointed. After which she took leave of him with a squeeze by the hand, and a smiling countenance, and walked back to her chair.

But, however she might be pleased with having obtained this promise, Booth was far from being delighted with the thoughts of having given it. He looked, indeed, upon the consequences of this meeting with horror; but, as to the consequence which was so apparently intended by the lady, he resolved against it. At length he came to this determination, to go according to his appointment, to argue the matter with the lady, and to convince her, if possible, that, from a regard to his honour only, he must discontinue her acquaintance. If this failed to satisfy her, and she still persisted in her threats to acquaint his wife with the affair, he then resolved, whatever pains it cost him, to communicate the whole truth himself to Amelia, from whose goodness he doubted not but to obtain an absolute remission.

CHAPTER VIII

In which Amelia appears in a light more amiable than gay.

WE will now return to Amelia, whom we left in some perturbation of mind departing from Mrs. Atkinson.

Though she had before walked through the streets in a
very improper dress with Mrs. Atkinson, she was unwilling,
especially as she was alone, to return in the same manner.
Indeed, she was scarce able to walk in her present condition;
for the case of poor Atkinson had much affected her tender
heart, and her eyes had overflown with many tears.

It occurred likewise to her at present that she had not a
single shilling in her pocket or at home to provide food for
herself and her family. In this situation she resolved to go
immediately to the pawnbroker whither she had gone before,
and to deposit her picture for what she could raise upon it. She
then immediately took a chair and put her design in execution.

The intrinsic value of the gold in which this picture was
set, and of the little diamonds which surrounded it, amounted
to nine guineas. This therefore was advanced to her, and
the prettiest face in the world (such is often the fate of
beauty) was deposited, as of no value, into the bargain.

When she came home she found the following letter from
Mrs. Atkinson:—

MY DEAREST MADAM,—As I know your goodness, I could not
delay a moment acquainting you with the happy turn of my
affairs since you went. The doctor, on his return to visit my
husband, has assured me that the captain was on the recovery,
and in very little danger; and I really think he is since mended.
I hope to wait on you soon with better news. Heaven bless you,
dear madam! and believe me to be, with the utmost sincerity

Your most obliged, obedient, humble servant,

ATKINSON.

Amelia was really pleased with this letter; and now, it
being past four o'clock, she despaired of seeing her husband
till the evening. She therefore provided some tarts for her
children, and then, eating nothing but a slice of bread and
butter herself, she began to prepare for the captain's supper.

There were two things of which her husband was particularly fond, which, though it may bring the simplicity of his

taste into great contempt with some of my readers, I will venture to name. These were a fowl and egg sauce and mutton broth; both which Amelia immediately purchased.

As soon as the clock struck seven the good creature went down into the kitchen, and began to exercise her talents in cookery, of which she was a great mistress, as she was of every economical office from the highest to the lowest; and, as no woman could outshine her in a drawing-room, so none could make the drawing-room itself shine brighter than Amelia. And, if I may speak a bold truth, I question whether it be possible to view this fine creature in a more amiable light than while she was dressing her husband's supper, with her little children playing round her.

It was now half an hour past eight, and the meat almost ready, the table likewise neatly spread with materials borrowed from her landlady, and she began to grow a little uneasy at Booth's not returning when a sudden knock at the door roused her spirits, and she cried, "There, my dear, there is your good papa"; at which words she darted swiftly upstairs and opened the door to her husband.

She desired her husband to walk up to the dining-room, and she would come to him in an instant; for she was desirous to increase his pleasure by surprising him with his two favourite dishes. She then went down again to the kitchen, where the maid of the house undertook to send up the supper, and she with her children returned to Booth.

He then told her concisely what had happened with relation to the girl—to which she scarce made any answer, but asked him if he had not dined? He assured her he had not ate a morsel the whole day. "Well," says she, "my dear, I am a fellow-sufferer; but we shall both enjoy our supper the more; for I have made a little provision for you, as I guessed what might be the case. I have got you a bottle of wine too. And here is a clean cloth and a smiling countenance, my dear Will. Indeed, I am in unusual good spirits to-night, and I have made a promise to the children, which you must confirm; I have promised to let them sit up this one night to supper with us.—Nay, don't look so serious: cast off all uneasy thoughts, I have a present for you here —no matter how I came by it."—At which words she put eight guineas into his hand, crying, "Come, my dear Bill, be gay—Fortune will yet be kind to us—at least let us be happy this night. Indeed, the pleasures of many women during their whole lives will not amount to my happiness this night if you will be in good humour."

Booth fetched a deep sigh, and cried, "How unhappy am I, my dear, that I can't sup with you to night!"

As in the delightful month of June, when the sky is all serene, and the whole face of nature looks with a pleasing and smiling aspect, suddenly a dark cloud spreads itself over the hemisphere, the sun vanishes from our sight, and every object is obscured by a dark and horrid gloom; so happened it to Amelia; the joy that had enlightened every feature disappeared in a moment; the lustre forsook her shining eyes, and all the little loves that played and wantoned in her cheeks hung their drooping heads, and with a faint trembling voice she repeated her husband's words, "Not sup with me to-night, my dear!"

"Indeed, my dear," answered he, "I cannot. I need not tell you how uneasy it makes me, or that I am as much disappointed as yourself; but I am engaged to sup abroad. I have absolutely given my honour; and besides, it is on business of importance."

"My dear," said she, "I say no more. I am convinced you would not willingly sup from me. I own it is a very particular disappointment to me to-night, when I had proposed unusual pleasure; but the same reason which is sufficient to you ought to be so to me."

Booth made his wife a compliment on her ready compliance, and then asked her what she intended by giving him that money, or how she came by it?

"I intend, my dear," said she, "to give it you; that is all. As to the manner in which I came by it, you know, Billy, that is not very material. You are well assured I got it by no means which would displease you; and, perhaps, another time I may tell you."

Booth asked no further questions; but he returned her, and insisted on her taking, all but one guinea, saying she was the safest treasurer. He then promised her to make all the haste home in his power, and he hoped, he said to be with her in an hour and half at farthest, and then took his leave.

When he was gone the poor disappointed Amelia sat down to supper with her children, with whose company she was forced to console herself for the absence of her husband.

CHAPTER IX

A very tragic scene.

THE clock had struck eleven, and Amelia was just proceeding
to put her children to bed, when she heard a knock at the
street door; upon which the boy cried out, "There's papa,
mamma; pray let me stay and see him before I go to bed."
This was a favour very easily obtained; for Amelia instantly
ran down-stairs, exulting in the goodness of her husband for
returning so soon, though half an hour was already elapsed
beyond the time in which he promised to return.

Poor Amelia was now again disappointed; for it was not
her husband at the door, but a servant with a letter for him,
which he delivered into her hands.   She immediately returned
up-stairs, and said — "It was not your papa, my dear;
but I hope it is one who hath brought us some good news."
For Booth had told her that he hourly expected to receive
such from the great man, and had desired her to open any
letter which came to him in his absence.

Amelia therefore broke open the letter, and read as follows:

SIR,—After what hath passed between us, I need only tell
you that I know you supped this very night alone with Miss
Matthews: a fact which will upbraid you sufficiently, without
putting me to that trouble, and will very well account for my
desiring the favour of seeing you to-morrow in Hyde-park at
six in the morning.   You will forgive me reminding you once
more how inexcusable this behaviour is in you, who are possessed
in your own wife of the most inestimable jewel.

Yours, etc.

T. JAMES.

I shall bring pistols with me.

It is not easy to describe the agitation of Amelia's mind
when she read this letter.   She threw herself into her chair,
turned as pale as death, began to tremble all over, and had
just power enough left to tap the bottle of wine, which she
had hitherto preserved entire for her husband, and to drink
off a large bumper.

The little boy perceived the strange symptoms which
appeared in his mother; and running to her, he cried,

"What's the matter, my dear mamma? you don't look well!—No harm hath happened to poor papa, I hope— Sure that bad man hath not carried him away again?"

Amelia answered, "No, child, nothing—nothing at all." And then a large shower of tears came to her assistance, which presently after produced the same in the eyes of both the children.

Amelia, after a short silence, looking tenderly at her children, cried out, "It is too much, too much to bear. Why did I bring these little wretches into the world? why were these innocents born to such a fate?" She then threw her arms round them both (for they were before embracing her knees), and cried, "O my children! my children! forgive me, my babes! Forgive me that I have brought you into such a world as this! You are undone—my children are undone!"

The little boy answered with great spirit, "How undone, mammy? my sister and I don't care a farthing for being undone. Don't cry so upon our accounts—we are both very well; indeed we are. But do pray tell us. I am sure some accident hath happened to poor papa."

"Mention him no more," cries Amelia; "your papa is— indeed he is a wicked man—he cares not for any of us. O Heavens! is this the happiness I promised myself this evening?" At which words she fell into an agony, holding both her children in her arms.

The maid of the house now entered the room, with a letter in her hand which she had received from a porter, whose arrival the reader will not wonder to have been unheard by Amelia in her present condition.

The maid, upon her entrance into the room, perceiving the situation of Amelia, cried out, "Good Heavens! madam, what's the matter?" Upon which Amelia, who had a little recovered herself after the last violent vent of her passion, started up and cried, "Nothing, Mrs. Susan—nothing extraordinary. I am subject to these fits sometimes; but I am very well now. Come, my dear children, I am very well again; indeed I am. You must now go to bed; Mrs. Susan will be so good as to put you to bed."

"But why doth not papa love us?" cried the little boy. "I am sure we have none of us done anything to disoblige him."

This innocent question of the child so stung Amelia that she had the utmost difficulty to prevent a relapse. However, she took another dram of wine; for so it might be called to her, who was the most temperate of women, and never exceeded three glasses on any occasion. In this glass she drank her children's health, and soon after so well soothed and composed them that they went quietly away with Mrs. Susan.

The maid, in the shock she had conceived at the melancholy, indeed frightful scene, which had presented itself to her at her first coming into the room, had quite forgot the letter which she held in her hand. However, just at her departure she recollected it, and delivered it to Amelia, who was no sooner alone than she opened it, and read as follows:

My dearest, sweetest Love,—I write this from the bailiff's house where I was formerly, and to which I am again brought at the suit of that villain Trent. I have the misfortune to think I owe this accident (I mean that it happened to-night) to my own folly in endeavouring to keep a secret from you. O my dear! had I had resolution to confess my crime to you, your forgiveness would, I am convinced, have cost me only a few blushes, and I had now been happy in your arms. Fool that I was, to leave you on such an account, and to add to a former transgression a new one!—Yet, by Heavens! I mean not a transgression of the like kind; for of that I am not nor ever will be guilty; and when you know the true reason of my leaving you to-night I think you will pity rather than upbraid me. I am sure you would if you knew the compunction with which I left you to go to the most worthless, the most infamous. Do guess the rest—guess that crime with which I cannot stain my paper—but still believe me no more guilty than I am, or, if it will lessen your vexation at what hath befallen me, believe me as guilty as you please, and think me, for a while at least, as undeserving of you as I think myself. This paper and pen are so bad, I question whether you can read what I write: I almost doubt whether I wish you should. Yet this I will endeavour to make as legible as I can. Be comforted, my dear love, and still keep up your spirits with the hopes of better days. The doctor will be in town to-morrow, and I trust on his goodness for my delivery once more from this place, and that I shall soon be able to repay him. That Heaven may bless and preserve you is the prayer of, my dearest love,

> Your ever fond, affectionate,
> and hereafter faithful husband,
>
> W. Booth.

Amelia pretty well guessed the obscure meaning of this letter, which, though at another time it might have given her unspeakable torment, was at present rather of the medicinal

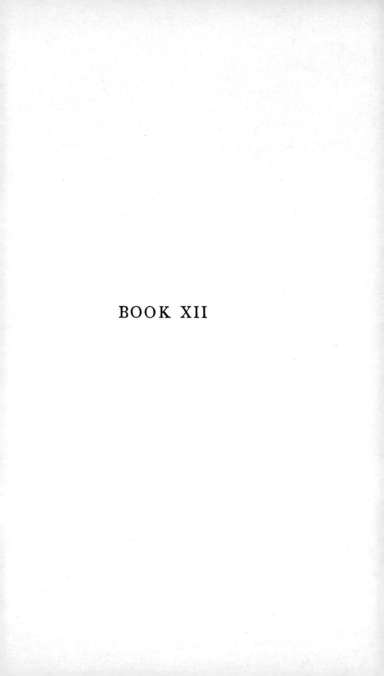
BOOK XII

CHAPTER I

The book begins with polite history.

BEFORE we return to the miserable couple whom we left at the end of the last book we will give our reader the more cheerful view of the gay and happy family of Colonel James.

Mrs. James, when she could not, as we have seen, prevail with Amelia to accept that invitation which, at the desire of the colonel, she had so kindly and obediently carried her, returned to her husband and acquainted him with the ill success of her embassy; at which, to say the truth, she was almost as much disappointed as the colonel himself; for he had not taken a much stronger liking to Amelia than she herself had conceived for Booth. This will account for some passages which may have a little surprised the reader in the former chapters of this history, as we were not then at leisure to communicate to them a hint of this kind; it was, indeed, on Mr. Booth's account that she had been at the trouble of changing her dress at the masquerade.

But her passions of this sort, happily for her, were not extremely strong; she was therefore easily baulked; and, as she met with no encouragement from Booth, she soon gave way to the impetuosity of Miss Matthews, and from that time scarce thought more of the affair till her husband's design against the wife revived her's likewise; insomuch that her passion was at this time certainly strong enough for Booth to produce a good hearty hatred for Amelia, whom she now abused to the colonel in very gross terms, both on the account of her poverty and her insolence, for so she termed the refusal of all her offers.

The colonel, seeing no hopes of soon possessing his new mistress, began, like a prudent and wise man, to turn his thoughts towards the securing his old one. From what his wife had mentioned concerning the behaviour of the shepherdess, and particularly her preference of Booth, he had little doubt but that this was the identical Miss Matthews. He resolved therefore to watch her closely, in hopes of discovering Booth's intrigue with her. In this, besides the remainder of affection which he yet preserved for that lady, he had another view, as it would give him a fair pretence to quarrel with Booth; who, by carrying on this intrigue, would have broke his word and honour given to him. And he began now to hate poor Booth heartily, from the same reason from which Mrs. James had contracted her aversion to Amelia.

The colonel therefore employed an inferior kind of pimp to watch the lodgings of Miss Matthews, and to acquaint him if Booth, whose person was known to the pimp, made any visit there.

The pimp faithfully performed his office, and, having last night made the wished-for discovery, immediately acquainted his master with it.

Upon this news the colonel presently despatched to Booth the short note which we have before seen. He sent it to his own house instead of Miss Matthews's, with hopes of that very accident which actually did happen. Not that he had any ingredient of the bully in him, and desired to be prevented from fighting, but with a prospect of injuring Booth in the affection and esteem of Amelia, and of recommending himself somewhat to her by appearing in the light of her champion; for which purpose he added that compliment to Amelia in his letter. He concluded upon the whole that, if Booth himself opened the letter, he would certainly meet him the next morning; but if his wife should open it before he came home it might have the effects before mentioned; and, for his future expostulation with Booth, it would not be in Amelia's power to prevent it.

Now it happened that this pimp had more masters than one. Amongst these was the worthy Mr. Trent, for whom he had often done business of the pimping vocation. He had been employed indeed in the service of the great peer himself, under the direction of the said Trent, and was the very person who had assisted the said Trent in dogging Booth and his wife to the opera-house on the masquerade night.

This subaltern pimp was with his superior Trent yesterday morning, when he found a bailiff with him in order to receive his instructions for the arresting Booth, when the bailiff said it would be a very difficult matter to take him, for that to his knowledge he was as shy a cock as any in England. The subaltern immediately acquainted Trent with the business in which he was employed by the colonel; upon which Trent enjoined him the moment he had set him to give immediate notice to the bailiff, which he agreed to, and performed accordingly.

The bailiff, on receiving the notice, immediately set out for his stand at an alehouse within three doors of Miss Matthews's lodgings; at which, unfortunately for poor Booth, he arrived a very few minutes before Booth left that lady in order to return to Amelia.

These were several matters of which we thought necessary our reader should be informed; for, besides that it conduces greatly to a perfect understanding of all history, there is no exercise of the mind of a sensible reader more pleasant than the tracing the several small and almost imperceptible links in every chain of events by which all the great actions of the world are produced. We will now in the next chapter proceed with our history.

CHAPTER II

In which Amelia visits her husband.

AMELIA, after much anxious thinking, in which she sometimes flattered herself that her husband was less guilty than
she had at first imagined him, and that he had some good
excuse to make for himself (for, indeed, she was not so able
as willing to make one for him), at length resolved to set out
for the bailiff's castle. Having therefore strictly recommended the care of her children to her good landlady, she
sent for a hackney-coach, and ordered the coachman to
drive to Gray's-inn Lane.

When she came to the house, and asked for the captain,
the bailiff's wife, who came to the door, guessing, by the
greatness of her beauty and the disorder of her dress, that
she was a young lady of pleasure, answered surlily, "Captain! I do not know of any captain that is here, not I!"
For this good woman was, as well as dame Purgante in
Prior, a bitter enemy to all whores, especially to those of the
handsome kind; for some such she suspected to go shares
with her in a certain property to which the law gave her the
sole right.

Amelia replied she was certain that Captain Booth was
there. "Well, if he is so," cries the bailiff's wife, "you may
come into the kitchen if you will, and he shall be called down
to you if you have any business with him." At the same
time she muttered something to herself, and concluded a
little more intelligibly, though still in a muttering voice, that
she kept no such house.

Amelia, whose innocence gave her no suspicion of the true
cause of this good woman's sullenness, was frightened, and
began to fear she knew not what. At last she made a shift
to totter into the kitchen, when the mistress of the house
asked her, "Well, madam, who shall I tell the captain wants
to speak to him?"

"I ask your pardon, madam," cries Amelia; "in my confusion I really forgot you did not know me—tell him, if you
please, that I am his wife."

"And you are indeed his wife, madam?" cries Mrs. Bailiff, a little softened.

"Yes, indeed, and upon my honour," answers Amelia.

"If this be the case," cries the other, "you may walk upstairs, if you please. Heaven forbid I should part man and wife! Indeed, I think they can never be too much together. But I never will suffer any bad doings in my house, nor any of the town ladies to come to gentlemen here."

Amelia answered that she liked her the better: for, indeed, in her present disposition, Amelia was as much exasperated against wicked women as the virtuous mistress of the house, or any other virtuous woman could be.

The bailiff's wife then ushered Amelia up-stairs, and, having unlocked the prisoner's doors, cried, "Captain, here is your lady, sir, come to see you." At which words Booth started up from his chair, and caught Amelia in his arms, embracing her for a considerable time with so much rapture, that the bailiff's wife, who was an eye-witness of this violent fondness, began to suspect whether Amelia had really told her truth. However, she had some little awe of the captain; and for fear of being in the wrong did not interfere, but shut the door and turned the key.

When Booth found himself alone with his wife, and had vented the first violence of his rapture in kisses and embraces, he looked tenderly at her, and cried, "Is it possible, Amelia, is it possible you can have this goodness to follow such a wretch as me to such a place as this—or do you come to upbraid me with my guilt, and to sink me down to that perdition I so justly deserve?"

"Am I so given to upbraiding then?" says she, in a gentle voice; "have I ever given you occasion to think I would sink you to perdition?"

"Far be it from me, my love, to think so," answered he. "And yet you may forgive the utmost fears of an offending, penitent sinner. I know, indeed, the extent of your goodness, and yet I know my guilt so great——"

"Alas! Mr. Booth," said she, "what guilt is this which you mention, and which you writ to me of last night?—Sure, by your mentioning to me so much, you intend to tell me more, —nay, indeed, to tell me all; and not leave my mind open to suspicions perhaps ten times worse than the truth."

"Will you give me a patient hearing?" said he.

"I will indeed," answered she; "nay, I am prepared to hear the worst you can unfold; nay, perhaps, the worst is short of my apprehensions."

Booth then, after a little further apology, began and related to her the whole that had passed between him and Miss Matthews, from their first meeting in the prison to their separation the preceding evening. All which, as the reader knows it already, it would be tedious and unpardonable to transcribe from his mouth. He told her likewise all that he had done and suffered to conceal his transgression from her knowledge. This he assured her was the business of his visit last night, the consequence of which was, he declared in the most solemn manner, no other than an absolute quarrel with Miss Matthews, of whom he had taken a final leave.

When he had ended his narration, Amelia, after a short silence, answered, "Indeed, I firmly believe every word you have said, but I cannot now forgive you the fault you have confessed; and my reason is—because I have forgiven it long ago. Here, my dear," said she, "is an instance that I am likewise capable of keeping a secret."—She then delivered her husband a letter which she had some time ago received from Miss Matthews, and which was the same which that lady mentioned, and supposed, as Booth had never heard of it, that it had miscarried; for she sent it by the penny post. In this letter, which was signed by a feigned name, she had acquainted Amelia with the infidelity of her husband, and had besides very greatly abused him; taxing him with many falsehoods, and, among the rest, with having spoken very slightingly and disrespectfully of his wife.

Amelia never shined forth to Booth in so amiable and great a light; nor did his own unworthiness ever appear to him so mean and contemptible as at this instant. However, when he had read the letter, he uttered many violent protestations to her, that all which related to herself was absolutely false.

"I am convinced it is," said she. "I would not have a suspicion of the contrary for the world. I assure you I had, till last night revived it in my memory, almost forgot the letter; for, as I well knew from whom it came, by her mentioning obligations which she had conferred on you, and which you had more than once spoken to me of, I made large allowances for the situation you was then in; and I was the more satisfied, as the letter itself, as well as many other circumstances, convinced me the affair was at an end."

Booth now uttered the most extravagant expressions of admiration and fondness that his heart could dictate, and accompanied them with the warmest embraces. All which warmth and tenderness she returned; and tears of love and joy gushed from both their eyes. So ravished indeed were their hearts, that for some time they both forgot the dreadful situation of their affairs.

This, however, was but a short reverie. It soon recurred to Amelia, that, though she had the liberty of leaving that house when she pleased, she could not take her beloved husband with her. This thought stung her tender bosom to the quick, and she could not so far command herself as to refrain from many sorrowful exclamations against the hardship of their destiny; but when she saw the effect they had upon Booth she stifled her rising grief, forced a little chearfulness into her countenance, and, exerting all the spirits she could raise within herself, expressed her hopes of seeing a speedy end to their sufferings. She then asked her husband what she should do for him, and to whom she should apply for his deliverance.

"You know, my dear," cries Booth, "that the doctor is to be in town some time to-day. My hopes of immediate redemption are only in him; and, if that can be obtained, I make no doubt of the success of that affair which is in the hands of a gentleman who hath faithfully promised, and in whose power I am so well assured it is to serve me."

Thus did this poor man support his hopes by a dependence on that ticket which he had so dearly purchased of one who pretended to manage the wheels in the great state lottery of preferment. A lottery, indeed, which hath this to recommend it—that many poor wretches feed their imaginations with the prospect of a prize during their whole lives, and never discover they have drawn a blank.

Amelia, who was of a pretty sanguine temper, and was entirely ignorant of these matters, was full as easy to be deceived into hopes as her husband; but in reality at present she turned her eyes to no distant prospect; the desire of regaining her husband's liberty having engrossed her whole mind.

While they were discoursing on these matters they heard a violent noise in the house, and immediately after several persons passed by their door up-stairs to the apartment over their head. This greatly terrified the gentle spirit of Amelia, and she cried—"Good Heavens, my dear, must I leave you in this horrid place? I am terrified with a thousand fears concerning you."

Booth endeavoured to comfort her, saying that he was in no manner of danger, and that he doubted not but that the doctor would soon be with him—"And stay, my dear," cries he; "now I recollect, suppose you should apply to my old friend James; for I believe you are pretty well satisfied that your apprehensions of him were groundless. I have no reason to think but that he would be as ready to serve me as formerly."

Amelia turned pale as ashes at the name of James, and, instead of making a direct answer to her husband, she laid hold of him, and cried, "My dear, I have one favour to beg of you, and I insist on your granting it me."

Booth readily swore he would deny her nothing.

"It is only this, my dear," said she, "that, if that detested colonel comes, you will not see him. Let the people of the house tell him you are not here."

"He knows nothing of my being here," answered Booth; "but why should I refuse to see him if he should be kind enough to come hither to see me? Indeed, my Amelia, you have taken a dislike to that man without sufficient reason."

"I speak not upon that account," cries Amelia; "but I have had dreams last night about you two. Perhaps you will laugh at my folly, but pray indulge it. Nay, I insist on your promise of not denying me."

"Dreams! my dear creature," answered he. "What dream can you have had of us?"

"One too horrible to be mentioned," replied she.—"I cannot think of it without horror; and, unless you will promise me not to see the colonel till I return, I positively will never leave you."

"Indeed, my Amelia," said Booth, "I never knew you unreasonable before. How can a woman of your sense talk of dreams?"

"Suffer me to be once at least unreasonable," said Amelia, "as you are so good-natured to say I am not often so. Consider what I have lately suffered, and how weak my spirits must be at this time."

As Booth was going to speak, the bailiff, without any ceremony, entered the room, and cried, "No offence, I hope, madam; my wife, it seems, did not know you. She thought the captain had a mind for a bit of flesh by the bye. But I have quieted all matters; for I know you very well: I have seen that handsome face many a time when I have been waiting upon the captain formerly. No offence, I hope, madam; but if my wife was as handsome as you are I should not look for worse goods abroad."

Booth conceived some displeasure at this speech, but he did not think proper to express more than a pish; and then asked the bailiff what was the meaning of the noise they heard just now?

"I know of no noise," answered the bailiff. "Some of my men have been carrying a piece of bad luggage up-stairs; a poor rascal that resisted the law and justice; so I gave him a cut or two with a hanger. If they should prove mortal, he must thank himself for it. If a man will not behave like a gentleman to an officer, he must take the consequence; but I must say that for you, captain, you behave yourself like a gentleman, and therefore I shall always use you as such; and I hope you will find bail soon with all my heart. This is but a paltry sum to what the last was; and I do assure you there is nothing else against you in the office."

The latter part of the bailiff's speech somewhat comforted Amelia, who had been a little frightened by the former; and she soon after took leave of her husband to go in quest of the doctor, who, as Amelia had heard that morning, was expected in town that very day, which was somewhat sooner than he had intended at his departure.

Before she went, however, she left a strict charge with the bailiff, who ushered her very civilly down-stairs, that if one Colonel James came there to inquire for her husband he should deny that he was there.

She then departed; and the bailiff immediately gave a very strict charge to his wife, his maid, and his followers, that if one Colonel James, or any one from him, should inquire after the captain, that they should let him know he had the captain above-stairs; for he doubted not but that the colonel was one of Booth's creditors, and he hoped for a second bail-bond by his means.

CHAPTER III

Containing matter pertinent to the history.

AMELIA, in her way to the doctor's, determined just to stop at her own lodgings, which lay a little out of the road, and to pay a momentary visit to her children.

This was fortunate enough; for, had she called at the doctor's house, she would have heard nothing of him, which would have caused in her some alarm and disappointment; for the doctor was set down at Mrs. Atkinson's, where he was directed to Amelia's lodgings, to which he went before he called at his own; and here Amelia now found him playing with her two children.

The doctor had been a little surprised at not finding Amelia at home, or any one that could give an account of her. He was now more surprised to see her come in such a dress, and at the disorder which he very plainly perceived in her pale and melancholy countenance. He addressed her first (for indeed she was in no great haste to speak), and cried, "My dear child, what is the matter? where is your husband? some mischief I am afraid hath happened to him in my absence."

"O my dear doctor!" answered Amelia, "sure some good angel hath sent you hither. My poor Will is arrested again. I left him in the most miserable condition in the very house whence your goodness formerly redeemed him."

"Arrested!" cries the doctor. "Then it must be for some very inconsiderable trifle."

"I wish it was," said Amelia; "but it is for no less than fifty pounds."

"Then," cries the doctor, "he hath been disingenuous with me. He told me he did not owe ten pounds in the world for which he was liable to be sued."

"I know not what to say," cries Amelia. "Indeed, I am afraid to tell you the truth."

"How, child?" said the doctor—"I hope you will never

disguise it to any one, especially to me. Any prevarication, I promise you, will forfeit my friendship for ever."

"I will tell you the whole," cries Amelia, "and rely entirely on your goodness." She then related the gaming story, not forgetting to set in the fullest light, and to lay the strongest emphasis on, his promise never to play again.

The doctor fetched a deep sigh when he had heard Amelia's relation, and cried, "I am sorry, child, for the share you are to partake in your husband's sufferings; but as for him, I really think he deserves no compassion. You say he hath promised never to play again, but I must tell you he hath broke his promise to me already; for I had heard he was formerly addicted to this vice, and I had given him sufficient caution against it. You will consider, child, I am already pretty largely engaged for him, every farthing of which I am sensible I must pay. You know I would go to the utmost verge of prudence to serve you; but I must not exceed my ability, which is not very great; and I have several families on my hands who are by misfortune alone brought to want. I do assure you I cannot at present answer for such a sum as this without distressing my own circumstances."

"Then Heaven have mercy upon us all!" cries Amelia, "for we have no other friend on earth: my husband is undone, and these poor little wretches must be starved."

The doctor cast his eyes on the children, and then cried, "I hope not so. I told you I must distress my circumstances, and I will distress them this once on your account, and on the account of these poor little babes. But things must not go on any longer in this way. You must take an heroic resolution. I will hire a coach for you to-morrow morning which shall carry you all down to my parsonage-house. There you shall have my protection till something can be done for your husband; of which, to be plain with you, I at present see no likelihood."

Amelia fell upon her knees in an ecstasy of thanksgiving to the doctor, who immediately raised her up, and placed her in her chair. She then recollected herself, and said, "O my worthy friend, I have still another matter to mention to you, in which I must have both your advice and assistance. My soul blushes to give you all this trouble; but what other friend have I?—indeed, what other friend could I apply to so properly on such an occasion?"

The doctor, with a very kind voice and countenance, desired her to speak. She then said, "O sir! that wicked colonel whom I have mentioned to you formerly hath picked some quarrel with my husband (for she did not think proper to mention the cause), and hath sent him a challenge. It came to my hand last night after he was arrested: I opened and read it."

"Give it me, child," said the doctor.

She answered she had burnt it, as was indeed true. "But I remember it was an appointment to meet with sword and pistol this morning at Hyde Park."

"Make yourself easy, my dear child," cries the doctor; "I will take care to prevent any mischief."

"But consider, my dear sir," said she, "this is a tender matter. My husband's honour is to be preserved as well as his life."

"And so is his soul, which ought to be the dearest of all things," cries the doctor. "Honour! nonsense! Can honour dictate to him to disobey the express commands of his Maker, in compliance with a custom established by a set of block-heads, founded on false principles of virtue, in direct opposition to the plain and positive precepts of religion, and tending manifestly to give a sanction to ruffians, and to protect them in all the ways of impudence and villany?"

"All this, I believe, is very true," cries Amelia; "but yet you know, doctor, the opinion of the world."

"You talk simply, child," cries the doctor. "What is the opinion of the world opposed to religion and virtue? but you are in the wrong. It is not the opinion of the world; it is the opinion of the idle, ignorant, and profligate. It is impossible it should be the opinion of one man of sense, who is in earnest in his belief of our religion. Chiefly, indeed, it hath been upheld by the nonsense of women, who, either from their extreme cowardice and desire of protection, or, as Mr. Bayle thinks, from their excessive vanity, have been always forward to countenance a set of hectors and bravoes, and to despise all men of modesty and sobriety; though these are often, at the bottom, not only the better but the braver men."

"You know, doctor," cries Amelia, "I have never presumed to argue with you; your opinion is to me always instruction, and your word a law."

"Indeed, child," cries the doctor, "I know you are a good woman; and yet I must observe to you, that this very desire of feeding the passion of female vanity with the heroism of her man, old Homer seems to make the characteristic of a bad and loose woman. He introduces Helen upbraiding her gallant with having quitted the fight, and left the victory to Menelaus, and seeming to be sorry that she had left her husband only because he was the better duellist of the two: but in how different a light doth he represent the tender and chaste love of Andromache to her worthy Hector! she dissuades him from exposing himself to danger, even in a just cause. This is indeed a weakness, but it is an amiable one, and becoming the true feminine character; but a woman who, out of heroic vanity (for so it is), would hazard not only the life but the soul too of her husband in a duel, is a monster, and ought to be painted in no other character but that of a Fury."

"I assure you, doctor," cries Amelia, "I never saw this matter in the odious light in which you have truly represented it, before. I am ashamed to recollect what I have formerly said on this subject. And yet, whilst the opinion of the world is as it is, one would wish to comply as far as possible, especially as my husband is an officer of the army. If it can be done, therefore, with safety to his honour——"

"Again honour!" cries the doctor; "indeed I will not suffer that noble word to be so basely and barbarously prostituted. I have known some of these men of honour, as they call themselves, to be the most arrant rascals in the universe."

"Well, I ask your pardon," said she; "reputation then, if you please, or any other word you like better; you know my meaning very well."

"I do know your meaning," cries the doctor, "and Virgil knew it a great while ago. The next time you see your friend Mrs. Atkinson, ask her what it was made Dido fall in love with Æneas?"

"Nay, dear sir," said Amelia, "do not rally me so unmercifully; think where my poor husband is now."

"He is," answered the doctor, "where I will presently be with him. In the meantime, do you pack up everything in order for your journey to-morrow; for if you are wise, you will not trust your husband a day longer in this town— therefore to packing."

Amelia promised she would, though indeed she wanted not any warning for her journey on this account; for when she packed up herself in the coach, she packed up her all. However, she did not think proper to mention this to the doctor; for, as he was now in pretty good humour, she did not care to venture again discomposing his temper.

The doctor then set out for Gray's-inn Lane, and, as soon as he was gone, Amelia began to consider of her incapacity to take a journey in her present situation without even a clean shift. At last she resolved, as she was possessed of seven guineas and a half, to go to her friend and redeem some of her own and her husband's linen out of captivity; indeed just so much as would render it barely possible for them to go out of town with any kind of decency. And this resolution she immediately executed.

As soon as she had finished her business with the pawn-broker (if a man who lends under thirty *per cent* deserves that name), he said to her, "Pray, madam, did you know that man who was here yesterday when you brought the picture?" Amelia answered in the negative. "Indeed, madam," said the broker, "he knows you, though he did not recollect you while you was here, as your hood was drawn over your face; but the moment you was gone he begged to look at the picture, which I, thinking no harm, permitted. He had scarce looked upon it when he cried out, "By heaven and earth it is her picture!" He then asked me if I knew you. "Indeed," says I, "I never saw the lady before."

In this last particular, however, the pawnbroker a little savoured of his profession, and made a small deviation from the truth, for, when the man had asked him if he knew the lady, he answered she was some poor undone woman who had pawned all her clothes to him the day before; and I suppose, says he, this picture is the last of her goods and chattels. This hint we thought proper to give the reader, as it may chance to be material.

Amelia answered coldly that she had taken so very little notice of the man that she scarce remembered he was there.

"I assure you, madam," says the pawnbroker, "he hath taken very great notice of you; for the man changed counten-ance upon what I said, and presently after begged me to give him a dram. Oho! thinks I to myself, are you thereabouts? I would not be so much in love with some folks as some

people are for more interest than I shall ever make of a
thousand pounds."

Amelia blushed, and said, with some peevishness, "That
she knew nothing of the man, but supposed he was some
impertinent fellow or other."

"Nay, madam," answered the pawnbroker, "I assure you
he is not worthy your regard. He is a poor wretch, and I
believe I am possessed of most of his movables. However,
I hope you are not offended, for indeed he said no harm;
but he was very strangely disordered, that is the truth of it."

Amelia was very desirous of putting an end to this conversation, and altogether as eager to return to her children;
she therefore bundled up her things as fast as she could, and
calling for a hackney-coach, directed the coachman to her
lodgings, and bid him drive her home with all the haste
he could.

CHAPTER IV

In which Dr. Harrison visits Colonel James.

THE doctor, when he left Amelia, intended to go directly to Booth, but he presently changed his mind, and determined first to call on the colonel, as he thought it was proper to put an end to that matter before he gave Booth his liberty.

The doctor found the two colonels, James and Bath, together. They both received him very civilly, for James was a very well-bred man, and Bath always showed a particular respect to the clergy, he being indeed a perfect good Christian, except in the articles of fighting and swearing.

Our divine sat some time without mentioning the subject of his errand, in hopes that Bath would go away, but when he found no likelihood of that (for indeed Bath was of the two much the most pleased with his company), he told James that he had something to say to him relating to Mr. Booth, which he believed he might speak before his brother.

"Undoubtedly, sir," said James; "for there can be no secrets between us which my brother may not hear."

"I come then to you, sir," said the doctor, "from the most unhappy woman in the world, to whose afflictions you have very greatly and very cruelly added by sending a challenge to her husband, which hath very luckily fallen into her hands; for, had the man for whom you designed it received it, I am afraid you would not have seen me upon this occasion."

"If I writ such a letter to Mr. Booth, sir," said James, "you may be assured I did not expect this visit in answer to it."

"I do not think you did," cries the doctor; "but you have great reason to thank Heaven for ordering this matter contrary to your expectations. I know not what trifle may have drawn this challenge from you, but, after what I have some reason to know of you, sir, I must plainly tell you that, if you had added to your guilt already committed against this man that of having his blood upon your hands, your soul would have become as black as hell itself."

"Give me leave to say," cries the colonel, "this is language

which I am not used to hear; and if your cloth was not
your protection you should not give it me with impunity.
After what you know of me, sir! What do you presume to
know of me to my disadvantage?"

"You say my cloth is my protection, colonel," answered the
doctor; "therefore pray lay aside your anger: I do not come
with any design of affronting or offending you."

"Very well," cries Bath; "that declaration is sufficient from
a clergyman, let him say what he pleases."

"Indeed, sir," says the doctor very mildly, "I consult
equally the good of you both, and, in a spiritual sense, more
especially yours; for you know you have injured this poor
man."

"So far on the contrary," cries James, "that I have been
his greatest benefactor. I scorn to upbraid him, but you
force me to it. Nor have I ever done him the least injury."

"Perhaps not," said the doctor; "I will alter what I have
said. But for this I apply to your honour—Have you not
intended him an injury, the very intention of which cancels
every obligation?"

"How, sir?" answered the colonel; "what do you mean?"

"My meaning," replied the doctor, "is almost too tender to
mention. Come, colonel, examine your own heart, and then
answer me, on your honour, if you have not intended to do
him the highest wrong which one man can do another?"

"I do not know what you mean by the question," answered
the colonel.

"D—n me, the question is very transparent!" cries Bath.
"From any other man it would be an affront with the
strongest emphasis, but from one of the doctor's cloth it
demands a categorical answer."

"I am not a papist, sir," answered Colonel James, "nor am
I obliged to confess to my priest. But if you have anything
to say speak openly, for I do not understand your meaning."

"I have explained my meaning to you already," said the
doctor, "in a letter I wrote to you on the subject—a subject
which I am sorry I should have any occasion to write upon
to a Christian."

"I do remember now," cries the colonel, "that I received a
very impertinent letter, something like a sermon, against
adultery; but I did not expect to hear the author own it to
my face."

"That brave man, then sir," answered the doctor, "stands before you who dares own he wrote that letter, and dares affirm too that it was writ on a just and strong foundation. But if the hardness of your heart could prevail on you to treat my good intention with contempt and scorn, what, pray, could induce you to show it, nay, to give it Mr. Booth? What motive could you have for that, unless you meant to insult him, and provoke your rival to give you that opportunity of putting him out of the world which you have since wickedly sought by your challenge?"

"I give him the letter!" said the colonel.

"Yes, sir," answered the doctor, "he showed me the letter, and affirmed that you gave it him at the masquerade."

"He is a lying rascal, then!" said the colonel very passionately. "I scarce took the trouble of reading the letter, and lost it out of my pocket."

Here Bath interfered, and explained this affair in the manner in which it happened, and with which the reader is already acquainted. He concluded by great eulogiums on the performance, and declared it was one of the most enthusiastic (meaning, perhaps, ecclesiastic) letters that ever was written. "And d—n me," says he, "if I do not respect the author with the utmost emphasis of thinking."

The doctor now recollected what had passed with Booth, and perceived he had made a mistake of one colonel for another. This he presently acknowledged to Colonel James, and said that the mistake had been his, and not Booth's.

Bath now collected all his gravity and dignity, as he called it, into his countenance, and, addressing himself to James, said, "And was that letter writ to you, brother?—I hope you never deserved any suspicion of this kind."

"Brother," cries James, "I am accountable to myself for my actions, and shall not render an account either to you or to that gentleman."

"As to me, brother," answered Bath, "you say right; but I think this gentleman may call you to an account; nay, I think it is his duty so to do. And let me tell you, brother, there is one much greater than he to whom you must give an account. Mrs. Booth is really a fine woman, a lady of most imperious and majestic presence. I have heard you often say that you liked her; and, if you have quarrelled with her husband upon this account, by all the dignity of man I think you ought to ask his pardon."

"Indeed, brother," cries James, "I can bear this no longer —you will make me angry presently."

"Angry! brother James," cries Bath; "angry!—I love you, brother, and have obligations to you. I will say no more; but I hope you know I do not fear making any man angry."

James answered he knew it well; and then the doctor, apprehending that while he was stopping up one breach he should make another, presently interfered, and turned the discourse back to Booth. "You tell me, sir," said he to James, "that my gown is my protection; let it then at least protect me where I have had no design in offending—where I have consulted your highest welfare, as in truth I did in writing this letter. And if you did not in the least deserve any such suspicion, still you have no cause for resentment. Caution against sin, even to the innocent, can never be unwholesome. But this I assure you, whatever anger you have to me, you can have none to poor Booth, who was entirely ignorant of my writing to you, and who, I am certain, never entertained the least suspicion of you; on the contrary, reveres you with the highest esteem, and love, and gratitude. Let me therefore reconcile all matters between you, and bring you together before he hath even heard of this challenge."

"Brother," cries Bath, "I hope I shall not make you angry —I lie when I say so; for I am indifferent to any man's anger. Let me be an accessory to what the doctor hath said. I think I may be trusted with matters of this nature, and it is a little unkind that, if you intended to send a challenge, you did not make me the bearer. But, indeed, as to what appears to me, this matter may be very well made up; and, as Mr. Booth doth not know of the challenge, I don't see why he ever should, any more than your giving him the lie just now; but that he shall never have from me, nor, I believe, from this gentleman; for, indeed, if he should, it would be incumbent upon him to cut your throat."

"Lookee, doctor," said James, "I do not deserve the unkind suspicion you just now threw out against me. I never thirsted after any man's blood; and, as for what hath passed since this discovery hath happened, I may, perhaps, not think it worth my while to trouble myself any more about it."

The doctor was not contented with perhaps, he insisted on

a firm promise, to be bound with the colonel's honour. This at length he obtained, and then departed well satisfied.

In fact, the colonel was ashamed to avow the real cause of the quarrel to this good man, or indeed, to his brother Bath, who would not only have condemned him equally with the doctor, but would possibly have quarrelled with him on his sister's account, whom, as the reader must have observed, he loved above all things; and, in plain truth, though the colonel was a brave man, and dared to fight, yet he was altogether as willing to let it alone; and this made him now and then give a little way to the wrongheadedness of Colonel Bath, who, with all the other principles of honour and humanity, made no more of cutting the throat of a man upon any of his punctilios than a butcher doth of killing sheep.

CHAPTER V

What passed at the bailiff's house.

THE doctor now set forwards to his friend Booth, and, as he passed by the door of his attorney in the way, he called upon him and took him with him.

The meeting between him and Booth need not be expatiated on. The doctor was really angry, and, though he deferred his lecture to a more proper opportunity, yet, as he was no dissembler (indeed, he was incapable of any disguise), he could not put on a show of that heartiness with which he had formerly used to receive his friend.

Booth at last began himself in the following manner: "Doctor, I am really ashamed to see you; and, if you knew the confusion of my soul on this occasion, I am sure you would pity rather than upbraid me; and yet I can say with great sincerity I rejoice in this last instance of my shame, since I am like to reap the most solid advantage from it." The doctor stared at this, and Booth thus proceeded: "Since I have been in this wretched place I have employed my time almost entirely in reading over a series of sermons which are contained in that book (meaning Dr. Barrow's works, which then lay on the table before him) in proof of the Christian religion; and so good an effect have they had upon me, that I shall, I believe, be the better man for them as long as I live. I have not a doubt (for I own I have had such) which remains now unsatisfied. If ever an angel might be thought to guide the pen of a writer, surely the pen of that great and good man had such an assistant." The doctor readily concurred in the praises of Dr. Barrow, and added, "You say you have had your doubts, young gentleman; indeed, I did not know that—and, pray, what were your doubts?" "Whatever they were, sir," said Booth, "they are now satisfied, as I believe those of every impartial and sensible reader will be if he will, with due attention, read over these excellent sermons." "Very well," answered the doctor, "though I have conversed, I find, with a false brother hitherto, I am glad you are reconciled to truth at last, and I hope your future faith will have some influence on your future life." "I need not tell you, sir," replied Booth, "that will always be the case where faith is sincere, as I

assure you mine is. Indeed, I never was a rash disbeliever;
my chief doubt was founded on this—that, as men appeared
to me to act entirely from their passions, their actions could
have neither merit nor demerit." "A very worthy conclusion
truly!" cries the doctor; "but if men act, as I believe they
do, from their passions, it would be fair to conclude that
religion to be true which applies immediately to the strongest
of these passions, hope and fear; choosing rather to rely on
its rewards and punishments than on that native beauty of
virtue which some of the ancient philosophers thought proper
to recommend to their disciples. But we will defer this
discourse till another opportunity; at present, as the devil
hath thought proper to set you free, I will try if I can prevail
on the bailiff to do the same."

The doctor had really not so much money in town as
Booth's debt amounted to, and therefore, though he would
otherwise very willingly have paid it, he was forced to give
bail to the action. For which purpose, as the bailiff was a
man of great form, he was obliged to get another person to be
bound with him. This person, however, the attorney undertook to procure, and immediately set out in quest of him.

During his absence the bailiff came into the room, and,
addressing himself to the doctor, said, "I think, sir, your
name is Doctor Harrison?" The doctor immediately
acknowledged his name. Indeed, the bailiff had seen it to
a bail-bond before. "Why then, sir," said the bailiff, "there
is a man above in a dying condition that desires the favour
of speaking to you; I believe he wants you to pray by him."

The bailiff himself was not more ready to execute his office on
all occasions for his fee than the doctor was to execute his for
nothing. Without making any further inquiry therefore into
the condition of the man, he immediately went up-stairs.

As soon as the bailiff returned down-stairs, which was
immediately after he had lodged the doctor in the room,
Booth had the curiosity to ask him who this man was.
"Why, I don't know much of him," said the bailiff; "I had
him once in custody before now; I remember it was when
your honour was here last; and now I remember, too, he
said that he knew your honour very well. Indeed, I had
some opinion of him at that time for he spent his money
very much like a gentleman; but I have discovered since
that he is a poor fellow, and worth nothing. He is a mere

shy cock; I have had the stuff about me this week, and could never get at him till this morning; nay, I don't believe we should ever have found out his lodgings had it not been for the attorney that was here just now, who gave us information. And so we took him this morning by a comical way enough; for we dressed up one of my men in women's clothes, who told the people of the house that he was his sister, just come to town—for we were told by the attorney that he had such a sister, upon which he was let up-stairs—and so kept the door ajar till I and another rushed in. Let me tell you, captain, there are as good stratagems made use of in our business as any in the army."

"But pray, sir," said Booth, "did not you tell me this morning that the poor fellow was desperately wounded; nay, I think you told the doctor that he was a dying man?"

"I had like to have forgot that," cries the bailiff. "Nothing would serve the gentleman but that he must make resistance, and he gave my man a blow with a stick; but I soon quieted him by giving him a wipe or two with a hanger. Not that, I believe, I have done his business neither; but the fellow is faint-hearted, and the surgeon, I fancy, frightens him more than he need. But, however, let the worst come to the worst, the law is all on my side, and it is only *se fendendo.* The attorney that was here just now told me so, and bid me fear nothing; for that he would stand my friend, and undertake the cause; and he is a devilish good one at a defence at the Old Bailey, I promise you. I have known him bring off several that everybody thought would have been hanged."

"But suppose you should be acquitted," said Booth, "would not the blood of this poor wretch lie a little heavy at your heart?"

"Why should it, captain?" said the bailiff. "Is not all done in a lawful way? Why will people resist the law when they know the consequence? To be sure, if a man was to kill another in an unlawful manner as it were, and what the law calls murder, that is quite and clear another thing. I should not care to be convicted of murder any more than another man. Why now, captain, you have been abroad in the wars they tell me, and to be sure must have killed men in your time. Pray, was you ever afraid afterwards of seeing their ghosts?"

"That is a different affair," cries Booth; "but I would not kill a man in cold blood for all the world."

*K 853

"There is no difference at all, as I can see," cries the bailiff. "One is as much in the way of business as the other. When gentlemen behave themselves like unto gentlemen, I know how to treat them as such, as well as any officer the king hath; and when they do not, why they must take what follows, and the law doth not call it murder."

Booth very plainly saw that the bailiff had squared his conscience exactly according to law, and that he could not easily subvert his way of thinking. He therefore gave up the cause, and desired the bailiff to expedite the bonds, which he promised to do; saying, he hoped he had used him with proper civility this time, if he had not the last, and that he should be remembered for it.

But before we close this chapter we shall endeavour to satisfy an inquiry, which may arise in our most favourite readers (for so are the most curious), how it came to pass that such a person as was Doctor Harrison should employ such a fellow as this Murphy?

The case then was thus: this Murphy had been clerk to an attorney in the very same town in which the doctor lived, and, when he was out of his time, had set up with a character fair enough, and had married a maid-servant of Mrs. Harris, by which means he had all the business to which that lady and her friends, in which number was the doctor, could recommend him.

Murphy went on with his business, and thrived very well, till he happened to make an unfortunate slip, in which he was detected by a brother of the same calling. But, though we call this by the gentle name of a slip, in respect to its being so extremely common, it was a matter in which the law, if it had ever come to its ears, would have passed a very severe censure, being, indeed, no less than perjury and subornation of perjury.

This brother attorney, being a very good-natured man, and unwilling to bespatter his own profession, and considering, perhaps, that the consequence did in no wise affect the public, who had no manner of interest in the alternative whether A., in whom the right was, or B., to whom Mr. Murphy, by the means aforesaid, had transferred it, succeeded in an action; we mention this particular, because, as this brother attorney was a very violent party man, and a professed stickler for the public, to suffer any injury to have been done to that, would have been highly inconsistent with his principles.

This gentleman, therefore, came to Mr. Murphy, and, after showing him that he had it in his power to convict him of the aforesaid crime, very generously told him that he had not the least delight in bringing any man to destruction, nor the least animosity against him. All that he insisted upon was, that he would not live in the same town or county with one who had been guilty of such an action. He then told Mr. Murphy that he would keep the secret on two conditions; the one was, that he immediately quitted that county; the other was, that he should convince him he deserved this kindness by his gratitude, and that Murphy should transfer to the other all the business which he then had in those parts, and to which he could possibly recommend him.

It is the observation of a very wise man, that it is a very common exercise of wisdom in this world, of two evils to choose the least. The reader, therefore, cannot doubt but Mr. Murphy complied with the alternative proposed by his kind brother, and accepted the terms on which secrecy was to be obtained.

This happened while the doctor was abroad, and with all this, except the departure of Murphy, not only the doctor, but the whole town (save his aforesaid brother alone), were to this day unacquainted.

The doctor, at his return, hearing that Mr. Murphy was gone, applied to the other attorney in his affairs, who still employed this Murphy as his agent in town, partly, perhaps, out of good will to him, and partly from the recommendation of Miss Harris; for, as he had married a servant of the family, and a particular favourite of hers, there can be no wonder that she, who was entirely ignorant of the affair above related, as well as of his conduct in town, should continue her favour to him. It will appear, therefore, I apprehend, no longer strange that the doctor, who had seen this man but three times since his removal to town, and then conversed with him only on business, should remain as ignorant of his life and character, as a man generally is of the character of the hackney-coachman who drives him. Nor doth it reflect more on the honour or understanding of the doctor, under these circumstances, to employ Murphy, than it would if he had been driven about the town by a thief or a murderer.

CHAPTER VI

What passed between the doctor and the sick man.

WE left the doctor in the last chapter with the wounded man, to whom the doctor, in a very gentle voice, spoke as follows:

"I am sorry, friend, to see you in this situation, and am very ready to give you any comfort or assistance within my power."

"I thank you kindly, doctor," said the man. "Indeed I should not have presumed to have sent to you had I not known your character; for, though I believe I am not at all known to you, I have lived many years in that town where you yourself had a house; my name is Robinson. I used to write for the attorneys in those parts, and I have been employed on your business in my time."

"I do not recollect you nor your name," said the doctor; "but consider, friend, your moments are precious, and your business, as I am informed, is to offer up your prayers to that great Being before whom you are shortly to appear. But first let me exhort you earnestly to a most serious repentance of all your sins."

"O doctor!" said the man; "pray, what is your opinion of a death-bed repentance."

"If repentance is sincere," cries the doctor, "I hope, through the mercies and merits of our most powerful and benign Intercessor, it will never come too late."

"But do not you think, sir," cries the man, "that, in order to obtain forgiveness of any great sin we have committed, by an injury done to our neighbours, it is necessary, as far as in us lies, to make all the amends we can to the party injured, and to undo, if possible, the injury we have done?"

"Most undoubtedly," cries the doctor; "our pretence to repentance would otherwise be gross hypocrisy, and an impudent attempt to deceive and impose upon our Creator himself."

"Indeed, I am of the same opinion," cries the penitent;

"and I think further, that this is thrown in my way, and hinted to me by that great Being; for an accident happened to me yesterday, by which, as things have fallen out since, I think I plainly discern the hand of Providence. I went yesterday, sir, you must know, to a pawnbroker's, to pawn the last movable, which, except the poor clothes you see on my back, I am worth in the world. While I was there a young lady came in to pawn her picture. She had disguised herself so much, and pulled her hood so over her face, that I did not know her while she stayed, which was scarce three minutes. As soon as she was gone the pawnbroker, taking the picture in his hand, cried out, *Upon my word, this is the handsomest face I ever saw in my life!* I desired him to let me look on the picture, which he readily did—and I no sooner cast my eyes upon it, than the strong resemblance struck me, and I knew it to be Mrs. Booth."

"Mrs. Booth! what Mrs. Booth?" cries the doctor.

"Captain Booth's lady, the captain who is now below," said the other.

"How?" cries the doctor with great impetuosity.

"Have patience," said the man, "and you shall hear all. I expressed some surprise to the pawnbroker, and asked the lady's name. He answered, that he knew not her name; but that she was some undone wretch, who had the day before left all her clothes with him in pawn. My guilt immediately flew in my face, and told me I had been accessory to this lady's undoing. The sudden shock so affected me, that, had it not been for a dram which the pawnbroker gave me, I believe I should have sunk on the spot."

"Accessory to her undoing! how accessory?" said the doctor. "Pray tell me, for I am impatient to hear."

"I will tell you all as fast as I can," cries the sick man. "You know, good doctor, that Mrs. Harris of our town had two daughters, this Mrs. Booth and another. Now, sir, it seems the other daughter had, some way or other, disobliged her mother a little before the old lady died; therefore she made a will, and left all her fortune, except one thousand pounds, to Mrs. Booth; to which will Mr. Murphy, myself, and another who is now dead, were the witnesses. Mrs. Harris afterwards died suddenly; upon which it was contrived by her other daughter and Mr. Murphy to make a new will, in which Mrs. Booth had a legacy of ten pounds, and all the rest was given to the other. To this will, Murphy, myself, and the same third person, again set our hands."

"Good Heaven! how wonderful is thy providence!" cries the doctor—"Murphy, say you?"

"He himself, sir," answered Robinson; "Murphy, who is the greatest rogue, I believe, now in the world."

"Pray, sir, proceed," cries the doctor.

"For this service, sir," said Robinson, "myself and the third person, one Carter, received two hundred pounds each. What reward Murphy himself had I know not. Carter died soon afterwards; and from that time, at several payments, I have by threats extorted above a hundred pounds more. And this, sir, is the whole truth, which I am ready to testify if it would please Heaven to prolong my life."

"I hope it will," cries the doctor; "but something must be done for fear of accidents. I will send to counsel immediately to know how to secure your testimony.—Whom can I get to send?—Stay, ay—he will do—but I know not where his house or his chambers are. I will go myself—but I may be wanted here."

While the doctor was in this violent agitation the surgeon made his appearance. The doctor stood still in a meditating posture, while the surgeon examined his patient. After which the doctor begged him to declare his opinion, and whether he thought the wounded man in any immediate danger of death. "I do not know," answered the surgeon, "what you call immediate. He may live several days—nay, he may recover. It is impossible to give any certain opinion in these cases." He then launched forth into a set of terms which the doctor, with all his scholarship, could not understand. To say the truth, many of them were not to be found in any dictionary or lexicon.

One discovery, however, the doctor made, and that was, that the surgeon was a very ignorant, conceited fellow, and knew nothing of his profession. He resolved, therefore, to get better advice for the sick; but this he postponed at present, and, applying himself to the surgeon, said, "He should be very much obliged to him, if he knew where to find such a counsellor, and would fetch him thither. I should not ask such a favour of you, sir," says the doctor, "if it was not on business of the last importance, or if I could find any other messenger."

"I fetch, sir!" said the surgeon very angrily. "Do you take me for a footman or a porter? I don't know who you are; but I believe you are full as proper to go on such an errand as I am." (For as the doctor, who was just come off his journey, was very roughly dressed, the surgeon held him in no great respect.) The surgeon then called aloud from the top of the stairs, "Let my coachman draw up," and strutted off without any ceremony, telling his patient he would call again the next day.

At this very instant arrived Murphy with the other bail, and, finding Booth alone, he asked the bailiff at the door what was become of the doctor? "Why the doctor," answered he, "is above-stairs, praying with ——." "How!" cries Murphy. "How came you not to carry him directly to Newgate, as you promised me?" "Why, because he was wounded," cries the bailiff. "I thought it was charity to take care of him; and, besides, why should one make more noise about the matter than is necessary?" "And Doctor Harrison with him?" said Murphy. "Yes, he is," said the bailiff; "he desired to speak with the doctor very much, and they have been praying together almost this hour." "All is up and undone!" cries Murphy. "Let me come by, I have thought of something which I must do immediately."

Now, as by means of the surgeon's leaving the door open the doctor heard Murphy's voice naming Robinson peevishly, he drew softly to the top of the stairs, where he heard the foregoing dialogue; and as soon as Murphy had uttered his last words, and was moving downwards, the doctor immediately sallied from his post, running as fast as he could, and crying, "Stop the villain! stop the thief!"

The attorney wanted no better hint to accelerate his pace; and, having the start of the doctor, got downstairs, and out into the street; but the doctor was so close at his heels, and being in foot the nimbler of the two, he soon overtook him, and laid hold of him, as he would have done on either Broughton or Slack in the same cause.

This action in the street, accompanied with the frequent cry of "Stop thief!" by the doctor during the chase, presently drew together a large mob, who began, as is usual, to enter immediately upon business, and to make strict inquiry into the matter, in order to proceed to do justice in their summary way.

Murphy, who knew well the temper of the mob, cried out, "If you are a bailiff, show me your writ. Gentlemen, he pretends to arrest me here without a writ."

Upon this one of the sturdiest and forwardest of the mob, and who by a superior strength of body and of lungs presided in this assembly, declared he would suffer no such thing. "D—n me," says he, "away to the pump with the catchpole directly—show me your writ, or let the gentleman go—you shall not arrest a man contrary to law."

He then laid his hands on the doctor, who, still fast griping the attorney, cried out, "He is a villain—I am no bailiff, but a clergyman, and this lawyer is guilty of forgery, and hath ruined a poor family."

"How!" cries the spokesman—"a lawyer!—that alters the case."

"Yes, faith," cries another of the mob, "it is lawyer Murphy. I know him very well."

"And hath he ruined a poor family?—like enough, faith, if he's a lawyer. Away with him to the justice immediately."

The bailiff now came up, desiring to know what was the matter; to whom Dr. Harrison answered that he had arrested that villain for a forgery. "How can you arrest him?" cries the bailiff; "you are no officer, nor have any warrant. Mr. Murphy is a gentleman, and he shall be used as such."

"Nay, to be sure," cries the spokesman, "there ought to be a warrant; that's the truth on't."

"There needs no warrant," cries the doctor. "I accuse him of felony; and I know so much of the law of England, that any man may arrest a felon without any warrant whatever. This villain hath undone a poor family; and I will die on the spot before I part with him."

"If the law be so," cries the orator, "that is another matter. And to be sure, to ruin a poor man is the greatest of sins. And being a lawyer too makes it so much the worse. He shall go before the justice, d—n me if he shan't go before the justice! I says the word, he shall."

"I say he is a gentleman, and shall be used according to law," cries the bailiff; "and, though you are a clergyman," said he to Harrison, "you don't show yourself as one by your actions."

"That's a bailiff," cries one of the mob: "one lawyer will always stand by another; but I think the clergyman is a very good man, and acts becoming a clergyman, to stand by the poor."

At which words the mob all gave a great shout, and several cried out, "Bring him along, away with him to the justice!"

And now a constable appeared, and with an authoritative voice declared what he was, produced his staff, and demanded the peace.

The doctor then delivered his prisoner over to the officer, and charged him with felony; the constable received him, the attorney submitted, the bailiff was hushed, and the waves of the mob immediately subsided.

The doctor now balanced with himself how he should proceed: at last he determined to leave Booth a little longer in captivity, and not to quit sight of Murphy before he had lodged him safe with a magistrate. They then all moved forwards to the justice; the constable and his prisoner marching first, the doctor and the bailiff following next, and about five thousand mob (for no less number were assembled in a very few minutes) following in the procession.

They found the magistrate just sitting down to his dinner; however, when he was acquainted with the doctor's profession, he immediately admitted him, and heard his business; which he no sooner perfectly understood, with all its circumstances, than he resolved, though it was then very late, and he had been fatigued all the morning with public business, to postpone all refreshment till he had discharged his duty. He accordingly adjourned the prisoner and his cause to the bailiff's house, whither he himself, with the doctor, immediately repaired, and whither the attorney was followed by a much larger number of attendants than he had been honoured with before.

CHAPTER VII

In which the history draws towards a conclusion.

NOTHING could exceed the astonishment of Booth at the behaviour of the doctor at the time when he sallied forth in pursuit of the attorney; for which it was so impossible for him to account in any manner whatever. He remained a long time in the utmost torture of mind, till at last the bailiff's wife came to him, and asked him if the doctor was not a madman? and, in truth, he could hardly defend him from that imputation.

While he was in this perplexity the maid of the house brought him a message from Robinson, desiring the favour of seeing him above-stairs. With this he immediately complied.

When these two were alone together, and the key turned on them (for the bailiff's wife was a most careful person, and never omitted that ceremony in the absence of her husband, having always at her tongue's end that excellent proverb of "Safe bind, safe find"), Robinson, looking stedfastly upon Booth, said, "I believe, sir, you scarce remember me."

Booth answered that he thought he had seen his face somewhere before, but could not then recollect when or where.

"Indeed, sir," answered the man, "it was a place which no man can remember with pleasure. But do you not remember, a few weeks ago, that you had the misfortune to be in a certain prison in this town, where you lost a trifling sum at cards to a fellow-prisoner?"

This hint sufficiently awakened Booth's memory, and he now recollected the features of his old friend Robinson. He answered him a little surlily, "I know you now very well, but I did not imagine you would ever have reminded me of that transaction."

"Alas, sir!" answered Robinson, "whatever happened then was very trifling compared to the injuries I have done you; but if my life be spared long enough I will now undo it all:

and, as I have been one of your worst enemies, I will now be one of your best friends."

He was just entering upon his story when a noise was heard below which might be almost compared to what have been heard in Holland when the dykes have given way, and the ocean in an inundation breaks in upon the land. It seemed, indeed, as if the whole world was bursting into the house at once.

Booth was a man of great firmness of mind, and he had need of it all at this instant. As for poor Robinson, the usual concomitants of guilt attended him, and he began to tremble in a violent manner.

The first person who ascended the stairs was the doctor, who no sooner saw Booth than he ran to him and embraced him, crying, "My child, I wish you joy with all my heart. Your sufferings are all at an end, and Providence hath done you the justice at last which it will, one day or other, render to all men. You will hear all presently; but I can now only tell you that your sister is discovered and the estate is your own."

Booth was in such confusion that he scarce made any answer, and now appeared the justice and his clerk, and immediately afterwards the constable with his prisoner, the bailiff, and as many more as could possibly crowd up-stairs.

The doctor now addressed himself to the sick man, and desired him to repeat the same information before the justice which he had made already; to which Robinson readily consented.

While the clerk was taking down the information the attorney expressed a very impatient desire to send instantly for his clerk, and expressed so much uneasiness at the confusion in which he had left his papers at home, that a thought suggested itself to the doctor that, if his house was searched some lights and evidence relating to this affair would certainly be found; he therefore desired the justice to grant a search-warrant immediately to search his house.

The justice answered that he had no such power; that, if there was any suspicion of stolen goods, he could grant a warrant to search for them.

"How, sir!" said the doctor, "can you grant a warrant to search a man's house for a silver tea-spoon, and not in a case like this, where a man is robbed of his whole estate."

"Hold, sir," says the sick man; "I believe I can answer that point; for I can swear he hath several title-deeds of the estate now in his possession, which I am sure were stolen from the right owner."

The justice still hesitated. He said title-deeds savoured of the Realty, and it was not felony to steal them. If, indeed, they were taken away in a box, then it would be felony to steal the box.

"Savour of the Realty! Savour of the f—talty," said the doctor. "I never heard such incomprehensible nonsense. This is impudent, as well as childish trifling with the lives and properties of men."

"Well, sir," said Robinson, "I now am sure I can do his business; for I know he hath a silver cup in his possession which is the property of this gentleman (meaning Booth), and how he got it but by stealth let him account if he can."

"That will do," cries the justice, with great pleasure. "That will do; and if you will charge him on oath with that, I will instantly grant my warrant to search his house for it." "And I will go and see it executed," cries the doctor; for it was a maxim of his that no man could descend below himself in doing any act which may contribute to protect an innocent person or to bring a rogue to the gallows.

The oath was instantly taken, the warrant signed, and the doctor attended the constable in the execution of it.

The clerk then proceeded in taking the information of Robinson, and had just finished it, when the doctor returned with the utmost joy in his countenance, and declared that he had sufficient evidence of the fact in his possession. He had, indeed, two or three letters from Miss Harris in answer to the attorney's frequent demands of money for secrecy, that fully explained the whole villany.

The justice now asked the prisoner what he had to say for himself, or whether he chose to say anything in his own defence.

"Sir," said the attorney, with great confidence, "I am not to defend myself here. It will be of no service to me; for I know you neither can nor will discharge me. But I am extremely innocent of all this matter, as I doubt not but to make appear to the satisfaction of a court of justice."

The legal previous ceremonies were then gone through of binding over the prosecutor, etc., and then the attorney was committed to Newgate, whither he was escorted amidst the acclamations of the populace.

When Murphy was departed, and a little calm restored in the house, the justice made his compliments of congratulation to Booth, who, as well as he could in his present tumult of joy, returned his thanks to both the magistrate and the doctor. They were now all preparing to depart, when Mr. Bondum stepped up to Booth, and said, "Hold, sir, you have forgot one thing—you have not given bail yet."

This occasioned some distress at this time, for the attorney's friend was departed; but when the justice heard this, he immediately offered himself as the other bondsman, and thus ended the affair.

It was now past six o'clock, and none of the gentlemen had yet dined. They very readily, therefore, accepted the magistrate's invitation, and went all together to his house.

And now the very first thing that was done, even before they sat down to dinner, was to despatch a messenger to one of the best surgeons in town to take care of Robinson, and another messenger to Booth's lodgings to prevent Amelia's concern at his staying so long.

The latter, however, was to little purpose; for Amelia's patience had been worn out before, and she had taken a hackney-coach and driven to the bailiff's, where she arrived a little after the departure of her husband, and was thence directed to the justice's.

Though there was no kind of reason for Amelia's fright at hearing that her husband and Doctor Harrison were gone before the justice, and though she indeed imagined that they were there in the light of complainants, not of offenders, yet so tender were her fears for her husband, and so much had her gentle spirits been lately agitated, that she had a thousand apprehensions of she knew not what. When she arrived, therefore, at the house, she ran directly into the room where all the company were at dinner, scarce knowing what she did or whither she was going.

She found her husband in such a situation, and discovered such chearfulness in his countenance, that so violent a turn was given to her spirits that she was just able, with the assistance of a glass of water, to support herself. She soon, however, recovered her calmness, and in a little time began to eat what might indeed be almost called her breakfast.

The justice now wished her joy of what had happened that day, for which she kindly thanked him, apprehending he meant the liberty of her husband. His worship might perhaps have explained himself more largely had not the doctor given him a timely wink; for this wise and good man was fearful of making such a discovery all at once to Amelia, lest it should overpower her, and luckily the justice's wife was not well enough acquainted with the matter to say anything more on it than barely to assure the lady that she joined in her husband's congratulation.

Amelia was then in a clean white gown, which she had that day redeemed, and was, indeed, dressed all over with great neatness and exactness; with the glow therefore which arose in her features from finding her husband released from his captivity, she made so charming a figure, that she attracted the eyes of the magistrate and of his wife, and they both agreed when they were alone that they had never seen so charming a creature; nay, Booth himself afterwards told her that he scarce ever remembered her to look so extremely beautiful as she did that evening.

Whether Amelia's beauty, or the reflection on the remarkable act of justice he had performed, or whatever motive filled the magistrate with extraordinary good humour, and opened his heart and cellars, I will not determine; but he gave them so hearty a welcome, and they were all so pleased with each other, that Amelia, for that one night, trusted the care of her children to the woman where they lodged, nor did the company rise from table till the clock struck eleven.

They then separated. Amelia and Booth, having been set down at their lodgings, retired into each other's arms; nor did Booth that evening, by the doctor's advice, mention one word of the grand affair to his wife.

CHAPTER VIII

Thus this history draws nearer to a conclusion.

IN the morning early Amelia received the following letter from Mrs. Atkinson:

The surgeon of the regiment, to which the captain my husband lately belonged, and who came this evening to see the captain, hath almost frightened me out of my wits by a strange story of your husband being committed to prison by a justice of peace for forgery. For Heaven's sake send me the truth. If my husband can be of any service, weak as he is, he will be carried on a chair to serve a brother officer for whom he hath a regard, which I need not mention. Or if the sum of twenty pounds will be of any service to you, I will wait upon you with it the moment I can get my clothes on, the morning you receive this; for it is too late to send to-night. The captain begs his hearty service and respects, and believe me,

Dear Madam,

Your ever affectionate friend,

and humble servant,

F. ATKINSON.

When Amelia read this letter to Booth they were both equally surprised, she at the commitment for forgery, and he at seeing such a letter from Mrs. Atkinson; for he was a stranger yet to the reconciliation that had happened.

Booth's doubts were first satisfied by Amelia, from which he received great pleasure; for he really had a very great affection and fondness for Mr. Atkinson, who, indeed, so well deserved it. "Well, my dear," said he to Amelia, smiling, "shall we accept this generous offer?"

"Oh, fie! no, certainly," answered she.

"Why not?" cries Booth; "it is but a trifle; and yet it will be of great service to us."

"But consider, my dear," said she, "how ill these poor people can spare it."

"They can spare it for a little while," said Booth, "and we shall soon pay it them again."

"When, my dear?" said Amelia. "Do, my dear Will,

consider our wretched circumstances. I beg you let us go
into the country immediately, and live upon bread and
water till Fortune pleases to smile upon us."

"I am convinced that day is not far off," said Booth.
"However, give me leave to send an answer to Mrs. Atkinson, that we shall be glad of her company immediately to
breakfast."

"You know I never contradict you," said she, "but I assure
you it is contrary to my inclinations to take this money."

"Well, suffer me," cries he, "to act this once contrary to
your inclinations." He then writ a short note to Mrs.
Atkinson, and despatched it away immediately; which when
he had done, Amelia said, "I shall be glad of Mrs. Atkinson's
company to breakfast; but yet I wish you would oblige me
in refusing this money. Take five guineas only. That is
indeed such a sum as, if we should never pay it, would sit
light on my mind. The last persons in the world from whom I
would receive favours of that sort are the poor and generous.

"You can receive favours only from the generous," cries
Booth; "and, to be plain with you, there are very few who
are generous that are not poor."

"What think you," said she, "of Doctor Harrison?"

"I do assure you," said Booth, "he is far from being rich.
The doctor hath an income of little more than six hundred
pounds a year, and I am convinced he gives away four of it.
Indeed, he is one of the best economists in the world: but
yet I am positive he never was at any time possessed of five
hundred pounds, since he hath been a man. Consider, dear
Emily, the late obligations we have to this gentleman; it
would be unreasonable to expect more, at least at present;
my half-pay is mortgaged for a year to come. How then
shall we live?"

"By our labour," answered she; "I am able to labour, and
I am sure I am not ashamed of it."

"And do you really think you can support such a life?"

"I am sure I could be happy in it," answered Amelia.
"And why not I as well as a thousand others, who have not
the happiness of such a husband to make life delicious? why
should I complain of my hard fate while so many who are
much poorer than I enjoy theirs? Am I of a superior rank
of being to the wife of the honest labourer? am I not partaker
of one common nature with her?"

"My angel," cries Booth, "it delights me to hear you talk thus, and for a reason you little guess; for I am assured that one who can so heroically endure adversity, will bear prosperity with equal greatness of soul; for the mind that cannot be dejected by the former, is not likely to be transported with the latter."

"If it had pleased Heaven," cried she, "to have tried me, I think, at least I hope, I should have preserved my humility."

"Then, my dear," said he, "I will relate you a dream I had last night. You know you lately mentioned a dream of yours."

"Do so," said she; "I am attentive."

"I dreamt," said he, "this night, that we were in the most miserable situation imaginable; indeed, in the situation we were yesterday morning, or rather worse; that I was laid in a prison for debt, and that you wanted a morsel of bread to feed the mouths of your hungry children. At length (for nothing you know is quicker than the transition in dreams) Doctor Harrison methought came to me, with cheerfulness and joy in his countenance. The prison-doors immediately flew open, and Doctor Harrison introduced you, gaily though not richly dressed. That you gently chid me for staying so long. All on a sudden appeared a coach with four horses to it, in which was a maid-servant with our two children. We both immediately went into the coach, and, taking our leave of the doctor, set out towards your country-house; for yours I dreamt it was. I only ask you now, if this was real, and the transition almost as sudden, could you support it?"

Amelia was going to answer, when Mrs. Atkinson came into the room, and after very little previous ceremony, presented Booth with a bank-note, which he received of her, saying he would very soon repay it; a promise that a little offended Amelia, as she thought he had no chance of keeping it.

The doctor presently arrived, and the company sat down to breakfast, during which Mrs. Atkinson entertained them with the history of the doctors that had attended her husband, by whose advice Atkinson was recovered from everything but the weakness which his distemper had occasioned.

When the tea-table was removed Booth told the doctor that he had acquainted his wife with a dream he had last night. "I dreamt, doctor," said he, "that she was restored to her estate."

"Very well," said the doctor; "and if I am to be the Oneiropolis, I believe the dream will come to pass. To say the truth, I have rather a better opinion of dreams than Horace had. Old Homer says they come from Jupiter; and as to your dream, I have often had it in my waking thoughts, that some time or other that roguery (for so I was always convinced it was) would be brought to light; for the same Homer says, as you, madam (meaning Mrs. Atkinson), very well know,

Εἴπερ γάρ τε καὶ αὐτίκ᾽ Ὀλύμπιος οὐκ ἐτέλεσσεν,
Ἐκ τε καὶ ὀψὲ τελεῖ· σύν τε μεγάλῳ ἀπέτισαν
Σὺν σφῆσιν κεφαλῇσι, γυναιξί τε καὶ τεκέεσσιν.[1]

I have no Greek ears, sir," said Mrs. Atkinson. "I believe I could understand it in the Delphin Homer."

"I wish," cries he, "my dear child (to Amelia), you would read a little in the Delphin Aristotle, or else in some Christian divine, to learn a doctrine which you will one day have a use for. I mean to bear the hardest of all human conflicts, and support with an even temper, and without any violent transports of mind, a sudden gust of prosperity."

"Indeed," cries Amelia, "I should almost think my husband and you, doctor, had some very good news to tell me, by your using, both of you, the same introduction. As far as I know myself, I think I can answer I can support any degree of prosperity, and I think I yesterday showed I could: for I do assure you it is not in the power of fortune to try me with such another transition from grief to joy as I conceived from seeing my husband in prison and at liberty."

"Well, you are a good girl," cries the doctor, "and after I have put on my spectacles I will try you."

The doctor then took out a newspaper and read as follows:

"Yesterday one Murphy, an eminent attorney-at-law, was committed to Newgate for the forgery of a will under which an estate hath been for many years detained from the right owner."

"Now in this paragraph there is something very remark-

[1] If Jupiter doth not immediately execute his vengeance, he will however execute it at last; and their transgression shall fall heavily on their own heads, and on their wives and children.

AMELIA

able, and that is—that it is true: but *opus est explanatu.*
In the Delphin edition of this newspaper there is the following note upon the words right owner: "The right owner
of this estate is a young lady of the highest merit, whose
maiden name was Harris, and who some time since was
married to an idle fellow, one Lieutenant Booth. And the
best historians assure us that letters from the elder sister of
this lady, which manifestly prove the forgery and clear up
the whole affair, are in the hands of an old parson called
Doctor Harrison."

"And is this really true?" cries Amelia.

"Yes, really and sincerely," cries the doctor. "The whole
estate; for your mother left it you all, and is as surely yours
as if you was already in possession."

"Gracious Heaven!" cries she, falling on her knees, "I
thank you!" And then starting up, she ran to her husband,
and, embracing him, cried, "My dear love, I wish you joy;
and I ought in gratitude to wish it you; for you are the
cause of mine. It is upon yours and my children's account
that I principally rejoice."

Mrs. Atkinson rose from her chair, and jumped about the
room for joy, repeating,

> *Turne, quod optanti divûm promittere nemo*
> *Auderet, volvenda dies, en, attulit ultro.*[1]

Amelia now threw herself into a chair, complained she was
a little faint, and begged a glass of water. The doctor
advised her to be blooded; but she refused, saying she required
a vent of another kind. She then desired her children to be
brought to her, whom she immediately caught in her arms,
and, having profusely cried over them for several minutes,
declared she was easy. After which she soon regained her
usual temper and complexion.

That day they dined together, and in the afternoon they
all, except the doctor, visited Captain Atkinson; he repaired
to the bailiff's house to visit the sick man, whom he found
very chearful, the surgeon having assured him that he was
in no danger.

The doctor had a long spiritual discourse with Robinson,
who assured him that he sincerely repented of his past life,

[1] What none of all the Gods could grant thy vows,
That, Turnus, this auspicious day bestows.

that he was resolved to lead his future days in a different manner, and to make what amends he could for his sins to the society, by bringing one of the greatest rogues in it to justice. There was a circumstance which much pleased the doctor, and made him conclude that, however Robinson had been corrupted by his old master, he had naturally a good disposition. This was, that Robinson declared he was chiefly induced to the discovery by what had happened at the pawnbroker's, and by the miseries which he there perceived he had been instrumental in bringing on Booth and his family.

The next day Booth and his wife, at the doctor's instance, dined with Colonel James and his lady, where they were received with great civility, and all matters were accommodated without Booth ever knowing a syllable of the challenge even to this day.

The doctor insisted very strongly on having Miss Harris taken into custody, and said, if she was his sister, he would deliver her to justice. He added besides, that it was impossible to screen her and carry on the prosecution, or, indeed, recover the estate. Amelia at last begged the delay of one day only, in which time she wrote a letter to her sister, informing her of the discovery, and the danger in which she stood, and begged her earnestly to make her escape, with many assurances that she would never suffer her to know any distress. This letter she sent away express, and it had the desired effect; for Miss Harris, having received sufficient information from the attorney to the same purpose, immediately set out for Poole, and from thence to France, carrying with her all her money, most of her clothes, and some few jewels. She had, indeed, packed up plate and jewels to the value of two thousand pounds and upwards. But Booth, to whom Amelia communicated the letter, prevented her by ordering the man that went with the express (who had been a serjeant of the foot-guards recommended to him by Atkinson) to suffer the lady to go whither she pleased, but not to take anything with her except her clothes, which he was carefully to search. These orders were obeyed punctually, and with these she was obliged to comply.

Two days after the bird was flown a warrant from the lord chief justice arrived to take her up, the messenger of which returned with the news of her flight, highly to the satisfaction of Amelia, and consequently of Booth, and, indeed, not greatly to the grief of the doctor.

About a week afterwards Booth and Amelia, with their children, and Captain Atkinson and his lady, all set forward together for Amelia's house, where they arrived amidst the acclamations of all the neighbours and every public demonstration of joy.

They found the house ready prepared to receive them by Atkinson's friend the old serjeant, and a good dinner prepared for them by Amelia's old nurse, who was addressed with the utmost duty by her son and daughter, most affectionately caressed by Booth and his wife, and by Amelia's absolute command seated next to herself at the table. At which, perhaps, were assembled some of the best and happiest people then in the world.

CHAPTER IX

In which the history is concluded.

HAVING brought our history to a conclusion, as to those points in which we presume our reader was chiefly interested, in the foregoing chapter, we shall in this, by way of epilogue, endeavour to satisfy his curiosity as to what hath since happened to the principal personages of whom we have treated in the foregoing pages.

Colonel James and his lady, after living in a polite manner for many years together, at last agreed to live in as polite a manner asunder. The colonel hath kept Miss Matthews ever since, and is at length grown to doat on her (though now very disagreeable in her person, and immensely fat) to such a degree, that she submits to be treated by her in the most tyrannical manner.

He allowed his lady eight hundred pounds a year, with which she divides her time between Tunbridge, Bath, and London, and passes about nine hours in the twenty-four at cards. Her income is lately increased by three thousand pounds left her by her brother Colonel Bath, who was killed in a duel about six years ago by a gentleman who told the colonel he differed from him in opinion.

The noble peer and Mrs. Ellison have been both dead several years, and both of the consequences of their favourite vices; Mrs. Ellison having fallen a martyr to her liquor, and the other to his amours, by which he was at last become so rotten that he stunk above-ground.

The attorney, Murphy, was brought to his trial at the Old Bailey, where, after much quibbling about the meaning of a very plain act of parliament, he was at length convicted of forgery, and was soon afterwards hanged at Tyburn.

The witness for some time seemed to reform his life, and received a small pension from Booth; after which he returned to vicious courses, took a purse on the highway, was detected and taken, and followed the last steps of his old master. So apt are men whose manners have been once thoroughly corrupted, to return, from any dawn of an amendment, into the dark paths of vice.

As to Miss Harris, she lived three years with a broken heart at Boulogne, where she received annually fifty pounds from her sister, who was hardly prevailed on by Doctor Harrison not to send her a hundred, and then died in a most miserable manner.

Mr. Atkinson upon the whole hath led a very happy life with his wife, though he hath been sometimes obliged to pay proper homage to her superior understanding and knowledge. This, however, he chearfully submits to, and she makes him proper returns of fondness. They have two fine boys, of whom they are equally fond. He is lately advanced to the rank of captain, and last summer both he and his wife paid a visit of three months to Booth and his wife.

Doctor Harrison is grown old in years and in honour, beloved and respected by all his parishioners and by all his neighbours. He divides his time between his parish, his old town, and Booth's—at which last place he had, two years ago, a gentle fit of the gout, being the first attack of that distemper. During this fit Amelia was his nurse, and her two eldest daughters sat up alternately with him for a whole week. The eldest of those girls, whose name is Amelia, is his favourite; she is the picture of her mother, and it is thought the doctor hath distinguished her in his will, for he hath declared that he will leave his whole fortune, except some few charities, among Amelia's children.

As to Booth and Amelia, Fortune seems to have made them large amends for the tricks she had played them in their youth. They have, ever since the above period of this history, enjoyed an uninterrupted course of health and happiness. In about six weeks after Booth's first coming into the country he went to London and paid all his debts of honour; after which, and a stay of two days only, he returned into the country, and hath never since been thirty miles from home. He hath two boys and four girls; the eldest of the boys, he who hath made his appearance in this history, is just come from the university, and is one of the finest gentlemen and best scholars of his age. The second is just going from school, and is intended for the Church, that being his own choice. His eldest daughter is a woman grown, but we must not mention her age. A marriage was proposed to her the other day with a young fellow of a good estate, but she never would see him more than once: "For Doctor Harrison," says she, "told me he was illiterate, and I am sure he is ill-natured." The second girl is three years younger than her sister, and the others are yet children.

Amelia is still the finest woman in England of her age. Booth himself often avers she is as handsome as ever. Nothing can equal the serenity of their lives. Amelia declared to me the other day, that she did not remember to have seen her husband out of humour these ten years; and, upon my insinuating to her that he had the best of wives, she answered with a smile that she ought to be so, for that he had made her the happiest of women.

THE END